THE KING'S MAN

ALISON STUART

Continuing the GUARDIANS OF THE CROWN series with a story of spies and traitors and a time when the price of betrayal is death...

London 1654: As England languishes in the grip of the reign of Oliver Cromwell, there are those who plot to restore the King.

Fleeing her old life, Thamsine Granville has nothing left to lose, not even her life. Alone and friendless the desperate act of throwing a brick at the coach of Oliver Cromwell could well mean her death. Only the act of a stranger saves her.

Kit Lovell is one of the King's men, a disillusioned Royalist who passes his time cheating at cards, living off his wealthy and attractive mistress, and plotting the death of Oliver Cromwell.

Far from the bored, benevolent rescuer that he seems, Kit plunges Thamsine into his world of espionage and betrayal – a world that has no room for falling in love.

Torn between Thamsine and loyalty to his master and King, Kit's carefully constructed web of lies begins to unravel and to save Thamsine he must make one last desperate gamble – the cost of which might be his life.

THE KING'S MAN

GUARDIANS OF THE CROWN BOOK 3

ALISON STUART

The King's Man

Copyright © 2007 by Alison Stuart

ISBN (paperback): 9780645237863

4th edition: Oportet Publishing 2022

Cover Design: Fiona Jayde

Discover other titles by Alison Stuart at

Author website: http://www.alisonstuart.com

ABOUT THE AUTHOR

Alison Stuart writes historical romances and short stories set in England and Australia and across different periods of history. She is best known for her English Civil War stories and also THE POSTMISTRESS and THE GOLDMINER'S SISTER, stories set in the Victorian goldfields in the 1870s.

She also writes historical mysteries as A.M. Stuart and her popular Harriet Gordon mystery series is set in Singapore in 1910.

She lives in Melbourne, Australia with her husband and a geriatric cat. In a past life Alison worked as a lawyer across a variety of disciplines including the military and emergency services. She has lived in Africa and Singapore and, when circumstances permit, travels extensively - all for research of course!

To discover more about Alison Stuart visit her website or follow her on her social media accounts.

www.alisonstuart.com

BOOKS BY ALISON STUART

Australian Historical Romance

THE POSTMISTRESS (also in audio)

THE GOLDMINER'S SISTER (also in audio)

THE HOMECOMING (also in audio)

The Guardians of the Crown Series

BY THE SWORD

THE KING'S MAN

EXILE'S RETURN

GUARDIANS OF THE CROWN (BOX SET)

The Feathers in the Wind Collection

AND THEN MINE ENEMY

HER REBEL HEART

SECRETS IN TIME (also in audio)

FEATHERS IN THE WIND (BOX SET)

Regency/World War One

GATHER THE BONES (also in audio)

LORD SOMERTON'S HEIR

A CHRISTMAS LOVE REDEEMED (Novella)

(Writing as A.M. Stuart)

The Harriet Gordon Mysteries

SINGAPORE SAPPHIRE (Book 1)

REVENGE IN RUBIES (Book 2)

EVIL IN EMERALD (Book 3)

TERROR IN TOPAZ (Book 4)

DEDICATION

This book is dedicated to the memory of my father, Arthur,
who taught me a love of history.

THE KING'S MAN

GUARDIANS OF THE CROWN
BOOK TWO

ALISON STUART

OPORTET PUBLISHING

CHAPTER 1

LONDON FEBRUARY 1654

Thamsine Granville had not begun the day with the intention of killing Oliver Cromwell.

Around her a jovial crowd pressed against the barricades, determined to enjoy the spectacle of the Lord Protector's ride in state to dine with the Lord Mayor of London. The bells of London, silenced for so many years, rang out, and above her, the flags of the City Guilds flapped in the chill wind.

But from across the road, she had been seen and recognised. A triumphant smile crossed her nemesis's handsome face and he raised his hand to his hat, doffing it as he bowed. He mouthed her name and started to push his way towards the barricade.

Thamsine swallowed, her mouth dry with fear. She only had a few moments to make good her escape, but the press of people to her rear hemmed her in, pushing her towards the barriers.

A roar went up from the crowd as the coach bearing Cromwell approached. As it drew closer, the Lord Protector, clad in a reddish-coloured suit embroidered with gold, inclined his head to acknowledge the cheers of the crowd with all the aplomb of a man born to such a station. She could see no trace of the simple farmer he had once professed to be.

Thamsine's heart beat a rapid tattoo as she stooped and gathered up the broken piece of brick at her feet. Oliver Cromwell, Lord Protector, the false King, was about to become Thamsine Granville's unwitting protector.

Oblivious to his fate, Cromwell smiled, his right hand raised in a parody of benediction as if forgiving them their sins. At the sight of his face, solid and pudding-like, framed by the open window of the carriage, she raised her arm and threw with all the strength that she could muster.

The brickbat hit the body of the coach barely inches from the open window. She got a brief impression of surprise on her intended victim's face. The coach stopped, the horses rising in their traces, whinnying in alarm. The crowd, stunned into silence, held its collective breath, every eye fixed on the ugly graze on the coach's paintwork where the brickbat had struck.

A roar of approbation went up, but Thamsine Granville had disappeared. In the instant her fingers uncurled from the missile, someone had grabbed her from behind. Strong fingers dug into her arm and drove her with force through the crowd that parted before them like the Red Sea.

The world roared in Thamsine's ears. She was only dimly aware of a commotion in the press around her. Soldiers yelled and a woman screamed but all she felt was utter despair. Despite her reckless act, somehow *he* had reached her.

Her captor thrust her down a dark, noisome alley. It was all going to end here, she thought.

Her knees buckled and she could feel herself slipping into unconsciousness, only to be drawn back by a sharp, agonising tug on her arm as it was cruelly and expertly bent behind her.

'Don't faint. Don't you dare faint. Now, unless you want to end your life on a gibbet on Tower Hill, you will co-operate fully in what we are about to do,' he said.

She didn't recognise the voice, and her senses sprang back. She nearly screamed with relief. It wasn't *him* but her relief was short-lived as he turned her to face him, pushing her back against the wall and pinioning her arms at her side.

She closed her eyes as his body pressed against her and she braced herself for the blow or whatever punishment or unspeakable act was coming her way.

She did not expect to be kissed, firmly and expertly.

Her instinctive reaction was to resist, but with her arms and her head immobilised she was reduced to trying to kick her assailant. He responded by placing a booted foot on her instep. She gave a muffled yelp of pain.

'Who's down there, then?'

A voice from the entrance to the alleyway caused her assailant to break off, allowing Thamsine the luxury of taking a deep breath. The fingers holding her arm tightened, digging into her flesh. It was a warning not to move, not to make another sound.

The soldier gave a ribald whistle. 'Got yourself a tasty piece, then?'

In the shadows, she saw her assailant turn his head towards the soldier. 'Now then, sergeant. Can't a man get a bit of privacy around here?' he said in a low and well-modulated voice, with an unusual undertone to the accent that she could not place.

'What's her charge?' The soldier said.

Thamsine shifted, determined to protest the insinuation, but the firm and painful pressure on her upper left arm deepened and she kept her peace.

'My dear sir, there are some pleasures beyond price.'

'We're looking for a woman.' The soldier's voice became

clipped and businesslike. 'Just tried to kill the Lord Protector. Has she come this way?'

'I doubt I would have noticed. I have been otherwise occupied these minutes past.'

Thamsine squirmed in the tight grasp. The easy, lascivious intonation of his voice made her want to slap him. He may well have saved her life but his intentions seemed far from honourable.

'Good day to you, sir. I wish you the joy of it.'

'He's gone.' Her rescuer removed his boot from her foot and stepped back, although he maintained his hold on her arm.

Thamsine found her voice. 'Let me go. You're hurting me.'

'Hurting you? Is that gratitude for saving you from the gibbet?'

He released her and she straightened, rubbing at the place where his fingers had pressed. In the gloom of the alley, it was hard to make out his appearance, and he wore a wide-brimmed hat that hid his face, but she could see that he was clean-shaven, his hair, dark and rough-cut, skimming an immaculate, white collar.

'Maybe I didn't want saving.'

He waved at the entrance to the alleyway. 'Very well. No doubt you can catch up with the good sergeant if that's what you wish.'

To her embarrassment, she started to tremble with cold, fright, and with delayed shock, as the audacity and foolishness of what she had done began to sink in.

She had tried to kill the Lord Protector. Men had hanged for less.

In her desperate bid to escape the greater threat, she had given no thought to what penalty she may have had to pay had she been apprehended.

She looked up at her rescuer. She owed this man thanks for her deliverance, but the words stuck in her throat.

'You do realise what you just did?' he asked.

She nodded.

'May I ask why?'

'Because I wanted him dead,' she said, without much conviction in her voice. It was not the Lord Protector she had wanted dead.

'Well, I'm sure there are plenty who would share the sentiment, but hurling brickbats at a coach is hardly the best way to accomplish that end.'

She drew herself up to her full height. 'And what do you care?'

'I don't,' he answered. 'I have enough problems of my own without rescuing dim-witted whores who choose to hurl objects at the Lord Protector.'

'I'm not a whore.'

He touched his mouth. 'Well, you certainly kiss like one.'

She raised her hand to give the impudent cad a good slap, but he caught her wrist. 'Now, now, mistress. I apologise for calling you a whore. Perhaps you prefer 'failed assassin'?'

He let her wrist go and her arm fell to her side.

'I have nothing more to say to you, sir,' she said, gathering what remained of her pride. 'Thank you for saving my neck from the gibbet. I bid you good day.'

He did not attempt to stop her, standing aside to let her pass. As she did so, he bowed. 'Good fortune to you, mistress.'

She gave him what she hoped was a withering glance and stepped back onto the street. It seemed unnatural that the crowd had resumed its normal bustle. Soldiers mingled with the passers-by, occasionally stopping a person to question them.

Thamsine, in her threadbare cloak and patched and faded dress, attracted no attention. With dragging footsteps, she traced the familiar way to the dreary, rodent-infested hovel on the outskirts of Blackfriars where she had lodged for the last few months.

The smell of cooking coming from the shops and homes she passed made her stomach growl in protest. She had not eaten since the previous day, and even that had been no more than a morsel of stale bread and a thin broth bought with her last coin.

If she wanted to eat, if she wanted to keep a roof over her head, she had only one choice.

The man who had rescued her had called her a whore and she, with her last shred of dignity, had denied it. She could never deny it again. She had sold everything worth selling and now she had only one thing left.

A couple of streets away from her lodging, she stopped in a boarded-up doorway. She loosed her hair and shook it out. With shaking fingers she unlaced her bodice a little way, displaying a hint of her almost-flat chest. She hitched one side of her skirt to show what she hoped was a tantalising glimpse of ankle above the cracked shoes. It was not, she thought, a very alluring picture, but it would have to do.

She took a deep breath and stepped back into the street, tossing her cloak back over her shoulders and adopting the hip-swinging saunter she had observed others of her newly adopted profession use.

Prospective customers should be in no doubt as to what trade she was plying. They would not see how her heart hammered against her ribs and her stomach had become a hard ball of fear and self-loathing. The part of her that still remembered who she was and where she had come from hoped and prayed that the men who frequented the dismal streets of Blackfriars would pass her by without a second glance.

A hand grabbed her shoulder and she gave a small yelp of alarm as she turned to face the man who had accosted her. A bearded face scrutinised her closely, his fingers digging painfully into her wrist.

'What's yer charge?' His breath smelt as if it came directly from the pits of a Hell charged with rotten teeth, onion and stale wine.

Her eyes widened. 'Charge?'

'For your body.' One hand slid down her bodice and the other caught her arm with such ferocity that she cried out in pain and pulled back.

His fingers tightened, drawing her towards him.

'Half a crown,' she said. Her attempt at bravado sounded pathetic even to her ears.

He gave a guffaw of laughter. 'Half a crown for a tight, skinny little arse like yours? Sixpence is all you'll get and count yourself lucky!'

Sixpence would buy a wedge of stale bread and thin broth.

Thamsine nodded.

'Got somewhere to go?'

The thought of plying her trade in the pathetic room that had been her lodgings for the past month horrified her more than the thought of what she was about to do. She shook her head.

'Never mind. Down 'ere will do as good as any.'

Propelling Thamsine by the arm, he thrust her down a filthy alley. A small part of Thamsine's brain registered the irony that it was the second time in one day a man had dragged her down just such a laneway. This time the intention was real and there would be no escaping the consequences.

He pushed her up against the slimy wall and his mouth clamped onto hers, his beard rasping her skin. His tongue, hard and insistent, penetrated her mouth, thrusting inside her while his spare hand grappled with her skirts.

She felt his hand on her thigh. His vile, stinking breath, the taste of him, the insistent probing of his tongue began to suffocate her. Nausea rose in her throat and she tried to twist away but he held her too close. Her struggles were as useless as a reed against the wind.

He leered at her. 'You're a tight little bitch. I reckon you need a bit of softening up.'

The blow came with such ferocity that she fell sideways, her head ringing, her world exploding into a thousand different-coloured lights. Hard fingers closed on her arm, hauling her to her feet.

'Don't hit me. I'll do whatever you want.'

Her plea went unregarded and she sensed rather than saw the shadow of his hand ready to strike. She closed her eyes and with the last of her strength, she braced herself.

The blow did not come.

Instead, the man gave a strangled cry and released her arm, causing her to fall to her knees in the stinking mire. She cowered away, covering her face with her hands as her client said 'Oi! What's yer game! There'll be plenty left for you,'

'Leave the lady be.'

At the sound of the familiar voice, Thamsine felt tears prick the back of her eyes. For the second time in the day, the stranger had come to her rescue, completing her humiliation.

'Lady … ?'

The sound of a fist on bone cut short the scoffing voice. A heavy body fell to the ground beside her. Through her fingers, she saw the man rise and heard the sound of feet scuffling and the grunts of a struggle in progress. Someone spat at the ground by her feet.

'Take her! She's yours if you want her that bad, but you'll get no joy from her. Not worth a farthing.'

'Get out of here!' The words were followed by the rattle of a sword loosened in the scabbard followed by the clatter of running feet and then silence.

A hand touched her shoulder. 'Let's see the damage.'

'I can't,' she mumbled into her hands.

'Come on, lass, he fetched you a mighty wallop. You weren't much to look at before. I doubt your appearance has been much improved by his handiwork.'

She screwed her eyes tightly shut as he pried her hands away from her face and gave a low whistle. With surprising gentleness, his fingers probed along her right cheekbone. She flinched.

'You've the makings of a truly spectacular black eye but I don't think anything's broken. Now, open your eyes and look at me! I'm not going to hurt you.'

With a supreme effort, she obeyed. Her saviour had crouched in front of her and surveyed her with his grey-green eyes. Nice eyes, she thought, with the lines of humour crinkling at the corners. But she saw no humour in them now, only pity, and pity was the last thing on Earth she wanted.

The shame overwhelmed her and the last of her rigid self-control evaporated. She lowered her head to her knees and began to weep, slow, silent sobs that wracked her thin body.

He made no move towards her; just let her cry until there was no more misery to expend. With a supreme effort, she choked back her misery, wiping her eyes on the sleeve of her dress and forcing herself to look at the man who still crouched before her.

He had a sharp, clever face dominated by a nose that was slightly too long and a mouth that curled as if about to break into a smile.

His hat had fallen to the ground during the scuffle with the bearded man and a cowlick of dark hair fell over his eyes. He pushed it back and reached out a finger, curling a lock of her hair in a gesture that was more paternal than sexual.

He shook his head. 'You'll be dead by week's end if you persist in this chosen vocation,' he said. 'Whoever you are, you're no whore by nature or, I warrant, necessity.'

'You're wrong. I've no choice,' she mumbled.

She wiped the back of her hand across lips that felt bruised and swollen. The vile taste of the man who had violated her rose in her mouth. She leaned away and retched onto the revolting cobbles.

Her rescuer picked up his hat and stood up, fastidiously brushing the mud from the brim. She expected to see him walk away but he remained standing, looking down at her.

'Go away,' she said.

She lowered her head, her hands hanging limply between her knees. She could debase herself no further.

'When did you last eat?'

She looked up at him. 'Yesterday.'

'Come.' He held out a hand to her. 'At least permit me to buy you a decent meal. Take a moment to tidy yourself.'

With an effort she pulled herself to her feet, declining his proffered hand. He strolled to the end of the lane and stood with his back turned as she re-laced her bodice and straightened her skirt, grateful for the time to collect her scattered thoughts. Her head still rang from the blow and she put her fingers to her face, tentatively exploring the bruising.

Taking a deep breath, she addressed his back in a stiff, formal voice. 'I thank you for your assistance, sir, but I beg you, leave me. I'm not fit company for you.'

He turned to face her. 'I'll be the judge of that.' A slow, sardonic smile crossed his face. 'It may be that I'm not fit company for you.'

She regarded him through narrowed eyes. 'Who are you? How

do you come to be here? Were you following me?' The questions rushed out.

'As to the first, my name is Christopher Lovell, although my friends call me Kit.' He swept her a bow. 'Your servant, ma'am. As to the second and third questions … yes, I admit I was following you.'

'Why?'

'I was concerned for you.'

'Concerned for me?'

He cocked his head to one side. 'Are you so far lost that you don't recognise genuine concern when you see it?'

It had been so long since anyone showed her any kindness that she viewed it with suspicion.

'You don't know me, sir. You know nothing about me.' She brought her chin up and met his gaze.

'True, but I've seen your like before. Unless I'm gravely mistaken, you are like me, the flotsam of war, one of the survivors. We're what is left when our friends and our family have nobly sacrificed their fortunes and their lives for a lost cause. I am right, am I not, Mistress … ?'

'Granville,' Thamsine said, too tired to lie. 'Thamsine Granville.'

Her teeth began to chatter and she drew her inadequate cloak tightly around her. It afforded little protection from the biting cold.

His fingers tugged at the cords of his cloak and he swung it around her shoulders. It settled on her thin frame, still warm from his body and Thamsine pulled it close around her.

He hunched his shoulders against the sudden chill and gave a deep, indrawn breath. 'Mistress Granville, it's cold and we've both had a trying day. I meant what I said about a meal.'

She looked down at the toe of her scuffed and leaking shoe.

There seemed little point in any more displays of stubborn pride. For the first time in weeks, she had the prospect of warmth and food. Only a fool would decline, and God alone knew she had already played the fool enough times in one day. There may be a price to pay but at least this Kit Lovell presented a more attractive prospect than her previous 'client'.

She raised her face and met his eyes. She inclined her head as if accepting an invitation to dance and he smiled and crooked his arm.

'Mistress Granville?'

She accepted his arm and he drew her close, shielding her from the icy wind that blew down the narrow streets. Through the sturdy cloth of his jacket, his muscles tensed at her touch and he placed a gloved hand over her cold, dirty fingers. The simple gesture permeated her icy bones, thawing the cold places of her soul.

CHAPTER 2

*K*it threw open the door to the busy taproom of
The Ship Inn. Beside him, Thamsine pulled his
cloak tightly across her thin body as she surveyed the crowd. He
put an arm around her and began to guide her towards his usual
table. The woman within the circle of his arm had no more
substance to her slender frame than a sparrow and she trembled
like a trapped bird as he led her to a secluded corner of the
taproom.

She subsided onto a stool with her back to the wall, her eyes
darting around the room. The sister of the publican, a young
woman with a riot of blonde curls falling from beneath a disreputable cap bounded forward, hooking her arm into his and
beaming up at him.

'Cap'n Lovell! We didn't expect to see you out so soon!' May's
gaze switched to Thamsine and the smile disappeared. 'Got
company I see.'

Kit suppressed a smile at the jealous suspicion in her voice.

'A friend of mine, May,' he replied. 'Now, a slice of pie and a jug of ale would be appreciated.'

May sniffed and disappeared into the kitchens.

'What did she mean when she said she didn't expect to see you "out so soon"?' Thamsine asked.

Kit smiled. 'I have spent the last couple of months in the Clink. A small misunderstanding concerning a horse. Now happily resolved,' he added

Thamsine's eyes widened. 'You've been in prison?'

He shrugged. 'I'm often in prison. It's an occupational hazard. Ah, here come the girls with our food.'

May was accompanied by her twin. May and Nan were identical in nearly all respects, although Nan was slightly taller with a warier, more knowing expression on her face and a sharper tongue in her head.

The girls slapped the food and drink down in front of Thamsine. May gave her one last, baleful glance before tending to the demands of another customer. Nan stood behind Kit running her fingers through his hair and, he had no doubt, casting Thamsine a proprietorial and suspicious look as she did so, before returning to the kitchen.

'They seem to regard you as their private property,' Thamsine observed. 'Is this pie safe to eat?'

Kit laughed. 'Those two girls have the biggest hearts in London.'

'And the widest legs, I wouldn't mind betting,' she observed, her eyes on May, who flirted outrageously with a bearded man by the fireplace.

'You are hardly in a position to cast stones on that count, Mistress Granville,' Kit reminded her. 'Now eat before it goes cold. I'll warrant it's the best pie you'll have tasted for some little while.'

Kit picked up the pot of ale and took a deep draught as he regarded the woman who sat opposite him, demolishing the pie with all the grace and elegance of the roughest soldier he had ever known.

Thamsine Granville, if that was her real name, appeared to be an educated and intelligent woman. Even if properly nourished she would still have been considered too thin for beauty. However, beneath the grime, she had an arresting face with high cheekbones and large brown eyes. Her mouth was wide and mobile. Her long nose curved slightly upwards. A strong nose on an interesting face. In the right circumstances, he thought, Thamsine Granville would not go unnoticed.

He finished his ale and poured himself another one. His reasons for going to her aid, not once but twice, went beyond altruism. True, her haunted eyes had touched something within him. He, more than anyone, knew what it was to be balanced on the edge, as this woman seemed to be. However, he also recognised that she could be useful; a card to be played when the time was right.

In the meantime, it seemed he was stuck with her.

He pushed his platter, with his serving of pie, across to her. She looked up at him and he inclined his head. After a momentary hesitation, she polished it off, wiping the last of the gravy up with a piece of bread. When she had done, she set aside the shining platters, taking a deep draught of ale from her tankard.

'You have some colour in your cheeks again. Do you feel better?' Kit remarked, refilling her cup.

She nodded. 'Better than I have for months. Thank you, Master Lovell, or is that Captain Lovell?'

He waved his hand. 'Kit. I think after what you and I have been through today, we can dispense with formalities. May I call you Thamsine? That is your name?'

She hesitated for a moment and nodded. 'It is.'

He leaned forward. 'Well, Thamsine Granville, as I have saved your life twice today, I think it is time to claim some form of reward.'

Her eyes widened and her cheeks coloured. Her lips parted slightly and she swallowed. 'Do you have a room we could go to? I have no wish to try another alley and no coin to pay you.'

Kit stared at her. Did she think that after everything she had been through that day, he wanted her body? The idea was preposterous. Anyway, why would he want this scrawny, dirty scrap of womanhood when Lucy waited for him in her warm, comfortable house in Holborn?

Without thinking, he laughed out loud. 'My dear Thamsine, did you think I meant that sort of payment?'

The colour in her cheeks darkened and she looked away. 'I have nothing else.'

His smile faded at the misery on her face. 'I'm sorry. I shouldn't have laughed. I'm not so mean-minded as to demand such a recompense.' The smile crept back onto his face. 'Anyway, I prefer my women with a bit more meat on them. No, Mistress Granville, all I request by way of reward is your story.'

She looked at him, her eyes widening. 'My story?'

He nodded. 'I would like to know how the gently born Thamsine Granville came to be trying her hand at whoring in the streets of London. Oh yes – with a bit of attempted assassination on the side.'

'How do you know I was gently born?'

Your voice, your demeanour, everything about you.

'A guess, nothing more. Let us start with a simple question. Where are you from?'

She took a deep breath, her gaze flitting to a space above his head. 'You've been very good to me, Master Lovell, but you owe me no more kindness. You must have a wife and a home to go to.'

'Neither. I told you I am like you, flotsam adrift on the streets of London. I have all night to hear your tale if that's what it takes.'

He refilled both their cups and sat back, crossing his arms and stretching out his legs as if in anticipation of the tale that would follow.

Thamsine's eyes darted around the crowded taproom. Was she seeking inspiration or an escape route?

Kit tried again. 'All I wish to know, Thamsine Granville, is what has brought you to this impasse?'

'Captain Lovell.' She returned her gaze to him. This time her eyes were steady. 'What has brought me to my present position is of no interest or concern to you. I have no wish to confide my story in anyone, whatever the debt I owe them. Suffice to say that I have lost everything in the world I hold dear and what little I brought with me to London has been either stolen or sold. I have nothing of interest or value.'

'So you're reduced to selling yourself?'

The blunt words caused a flush to rise again to her pale cheeks. She looked away, resting her chin on her hand and he thought he could detect the glint of tears on her eyelashes.

He tried again. 'What did you hope to achieve by killing the Lord Protector?'

This time what little colour she had drained from her cheeks as she stared at him. 'Kill the Lord Protector? I didn't mean ... I would never ...'

She recollected herself and looked down at her cup and this time a tear dropped from her lashes into the dregs of the ale.

Kit leaned forward. 'Whatever your intention, you only missed him by inches. You could hang if they caught you. If you are intent on assassinating Cromwell, you won't kill him with brickbats, Mistress Granville.' He lowered his voice, 'There are better ways to kill a king.'

She looked up. 'Is that what brings you to London?'

He laughed and sat back, taking a draught of ale. 'Me? No, Thamsine. All that brings me to London is the pretty face of my mistress and the promise of some lucrative games of cards. I'm done with soldiering and conspiracies. As far as I'm concerned Cromwell is welcome to England.' He spread his hands in a gesture of hopelessness. 'Like you, I've lost everything. Some would say that the only thing I have left is my honour and, believe me, even that is a poor commodity.'

She tilted her head, her gaze scrutinising his face. 'And Where are you from, Captain Lovell?'

He raised a finger. 'Ah, now, the arrangement was that you told me your story, not that I tell you mine.'

'There is something in the way you speak. Your accent ...'

'My accent?'

'It's not quite ... English.'

Kit raised his ale in a mock salute. 'How very perceptive of you, Mistress Granville. You're quite right. My mother was French and by dint of my parents' unhappy marital arrangements, I didn't learn a word of English until I was eight. The accent has never quite left me. My friends tell me it only becomes noticeable when I'm in my cups.' Kit looked into the depths of his tankard. 'Obviously I've reached that point. Now you've elicited far more information from me than I have from you so, in fairness, I must insist that I hold your answers in credit for another time.'

She rose to her feet. 'Thank you for your kindness. Now I must leave you to return to the arms of your pretty mistress, who is, no doubt, wondering where you are.'

He regarded her for a moment. 'And where would you be going?'

She glanced at the window, where snow now tumbled softly against the heavy glass, and before she could answer he raised a hand. 'I've not gone to all the trouble of pulling you out of the gutter just to send you back out there on a cold, February night. The landlord of this establishment, Jem Marsh, is a friend of mine. He'll give you lodging.'

She frowned. 'As we may have already established, I've no means of paying for this meal let alone lodging.'

'Can you cook?'

'No.'

'Wash dishes?'

She paused. 'I suppose so.'

'Make beds?'

A smile lifted the corners of her mouth. 'As long as I'm not expected to lie in them.'

Kit stood up and beckoned May. She sauntered over to the table and he put an arm around her waist, drawing her in towards him. 'May, my dear. Can you fetch your brother for me?'

May's mouth drooped. 'That all?'

'That's all.' He released her and gave her a playful slap on the rump. The girl squealed and with a coquettish glance over her shoulder to him disappeared into the kitchen.

Wiping his hands on a grubby apron, Jem Marsh appeared in the kitchen door and lumbered over to the table. The badly tied patch over his left eye didn't quite disguise the ugly scar that ran from his temple to his cheekbone. Out of the corner of his eye, Kit saw Thamsine recoil as he loomed over them. What Jem Marsh lacked in looks he made up for in his good nature.

'Well, Cap'n Lovell. The girls said you was out of the Clink. You must have the luck of the Devil. I thought you was locked away for a goodly time.'

'Mercifully, Jem, that little misunderstanding was resolved.

Now, old friend, I have a favour to ask of you.'

'Anything, as long as 'tis legal.' The big man laughed.

Kit indicated Thamsine. 'This is my friend, Thamsine Granville. Mistress Granville is a lady, who through the vicissitudes of fortune with which we are all familiar, finds herself in somewhat dire circumstances. Thamsine this is my old sergeant, Jem Marsh.'

Jem looks Thamsine up and down. 'She doesn't look much like a lady.'

'Well she is, and she needs some work, Jem, to pay for lodgings and food.'

'What's she good at?'

Kit gave Thamsine a quick, appraising look and said, 'Not much that is useful, but I'll warrant she's a quick learner.'

Doubt creased Jem's brow and he cast a glance at Thamsine.

'You wouldn't want to work here, love.'

'I have little choice, Master Marsh.' Thamsine looked up at him.

'Jem to me friends, miss.' He scratched his head. 'Well if you've a mind to it and can manage a few rough sorts, I'll take you on Capn' Lovell's recommendation.' He tapped his patch and in a lowered voice, added, 'If you've a mind to making a few shillings on the side, I'm willing to turn a blind eye, lady or no.'

'No,' Thamsine said, the colour staining her cheeks as she caught his meaning. 'I've no need of those sorts of shillings. I am happy to serve drinks, sweep floors, wash dishes, anything, Master Marsh.'

Jem shrugged. 'You can doss in with the girls. You met my sisters, Nan and May? Nan's got a bit of a tongue in her head but she don't mean much by it. You won't mind, will you, girls?' he bellowed across the room.

Nan and May poked their heads out of the kitchen. 'Mind

what?' Nan asked.

'This here's Cap'n Lovell's friend, Thamsine. She's coming to work for us. You don't mind her dossing down with you?'

The ensuing pause indicated that neither girl thought this arrangement particularly satisfactory.

'Just as long as she's the open-minded sort,' May said at last.

'Good. That's settled.' Kit drained his cup and rose to his feet. 'Now, if you'll excuse me, Thamsine, I have an appointment to be kept.'

'Will I see you again?' Thamsine clutched his sleeve.

He looked down at the small, cold, chapped hand and put his hand over it, squeezing the fingers. 'My friends and I meet here regularly for a drink and a game of cards. You will probably see me tomorrow night.'

She released her grip on his arm and straightened. A small smile caught at the corners of her mouth. 'Good night, Captain Lovell, and thank you.'

He inclined his head. 'Until next time, Thamsine. Keep her away from brickbats, Jem.'

The big man frowned. 'Brickbats?'

Thamsine stared at Kit, the alarm shining in her eyes.

'Doesn't matter,' Kit said and winked at her. 'Until tomorrow.'

'Private parlour?' Jem asked.

Kit nodded, shrugging his cloak across his shoulders. As he opened the door on a flurry of snow, he turned to look back.

Thamsine had turned to face the Marsh twins, who regarded her with such intensity that she looked like a moth trapped in a flame, her wings singeing under their gaze.

'So, m'lady, fancy yourself as a taproom wench, do you?' Nan flung a grimy apron at Thamsine. 'Well, you can start with washing the platters.'

Kit smiled and shut the door.

~

K IT WALKED through the snow-driven streets to High Holborn where Lucy Talbot, the widow of the late Martin Talbot, wine merchant, had a small, comfortable dwelling above what used to be the wine shop.

'Kit!'

He barely had time to shut the door against the snow as Lucy hurled herself down the stairs and into his arms, covering his face with kisses.

'Where have you been?' she cried, repeating the phrase between kisses.

He disengaged her, allowing himself the luxury of one last, lingering kiss. 'Lucy, dearest, I'm cold and wet and longing for the warmth of your fire.'

She fumbled at the sodden knot on his cloak, pulling the wet garment from his shoulders and abandoning it in a soggy pile on the floor. Kit retrieved it and, carrying it before him, followed Lucy upstairs into the warmth of her parlour. He flung the cloak over the back of a chair to dry, together with his hat and gloves. He gave the dispirited feather in his new hat a regretful glance, setting it down to take the glass of wine that Lucy offered him.

He held up the fine glass, his fingers ridiculously large for the slender, twisted stem, and swirled the ruby contents, watching the play of light from the candles through the liquid before taking a deep draught of the excellent vintage. He silently thanked the good fortune that had thrown him in the path of a wealthy wine merchant's widow.

Lucy traced a finger across his brow and down his nose. Her touch sent lightning bolts of desire shooting through his body.

'You haven't answered my question,' Lucy pouted. 'Where have you been these last weeks?'

'Ah!' Kit set the glass down and took a seat by the fire, stretching out his long legs to dry the damp boots. He took Lucy's small hand and drew her down onto his lap. 'I have a confession, Mistress Mouse.'

'What confession?' she asked.

'I've been in the Clink.'

'Again!' Lucy squeaked with indignation and thumped him firmly in the chest. 'What over this time?'

'The small matter of a horse.'

'A horse is not a small matter!'

'Well, no, it was quite a large horse.'

'And who paid your debts this time?' Her lip curled in derision.

'The matter was settled amicably.'

'Cards, I wager!' she spat at him. ', Kit Lovell, you are incorrigible.'

'But you must admit you missed me,' he wheedled, curling his mistress's blonde locks around his finger.

'Not for a moment!' she protested without conviction, her head tilting backward as his fingers strayed to the soft part of her throat, tracing a line down to the top of the bodice.

He replaced his finger with his mouth, blowing soft butterfly kisses on her clean, soft, white skin, while his fingers grappled with the knot on her bodice laces. She moaned as his kisses dropped lower and his hand fought with the layers of skirts and petticoats, finding its way up past the wool of her stockings to the smooth skin of her upper thigh and heaven where he could lose himself.

As he fumbled with his belt, Lucy took advantage of the distraction and with a shriek of laughter, gathered up her skirts and ran from the room. He caught her on the staircase and together they slithered and tripped up the stairs to the warmth and comfort of Lucy's large tester bed.

CHAPTER 3

*T*hamsine wiped her hands on a dirty rag and surveyed the pile of dishes stacked on the kitchen table. She looked down at her fingers and sniffed them, wrinkling her nose. The tips were shrivelled like dried sweetmeats and smelt of grease.

Her father would turn in his grave if he could see her now, but when she considered the alternative, she gave a silent prayer of thanks. The Ship Inn offered her a respite, time to consider what path to take. For now, the mindless repetition of physical tasks was a balm to her weary soul and she turned to the basket of carrots that Nan had set her to peel.

She sat down on a rickety stool, picked up the first carrot and regarded it from all angles. Her life, until recently, had never required the skill of peeling carrots. She picked up the knife and, flinching from its sharp blade, she attacked the vegetable.

'You don't hold the knife like that.'

Thamsine looked up to see Kit Lovell standing over her, his

well-shaped lips curved in amusement. Flustered, Thamsine nicked her finger. With a yelp of pain, she dropped both carrot and knife.

'Didn't your mother teach you anything?' he asked.

'My mother? No, she didn't.' Thamsine retorted, removing her cut finger from her mouth and picking up another carrot from the pile. 'She died when I was nine after a long illness that kept her from teaching me any form of useful domestic skill and nowhere did my books include a lesson on how to peel carrots..'

Kit pulled up a stool. 'Look, I'll demonstrate.' He picked up a carrot and a knife from the table and with remarkable dexterity peeled four carrots in the time it had taken Thamsine to produce one badly mutilated vegetable.

'Well, well, look who's here?' Nan swaggered in carrying a tray of empty platters. She set them down and put her arms around Kit's neck, pressing her ample bosom to his back and blowing in his ear. 'Where've you been, lover?' She sniffed. 'You smell nice. Been off visiting your lady friend?'

Kit looked up at her and winked.

Nan straightened and cuffed his ear. 'Ah, you're no fun these days, Cap'n Lovell.' She shook her head and sauntered out of the kitchen.

Thamsine stifled her laughter as Kit turned to regard her through narrowed eyes.

'What are you smiling at?'

'Is there a woman in London you don't share a bed with?'

Kit returned his attention to the carrot. 'That is a harsh remark, given I barely know you, Mistress Granville and, indeed, the circumstances of our meeting.'

Thamsine gave the carrot in her hands a couple of vicious swipes.

'The idea is to remove the skin, not the entire carrot,' Kit remarked. 'And I apologise. I didn't mean to remind you of events you'd rather forget.'

Thamsine sighed and looked up at Kit Lovell. She could see the attraction that seemed to set half the women in London falling at this man's feet. The dark hair and the grey-green eyes were an irresistible combination.

Even in London, in February, his skin held a tanned glow, but the lines of a hard soldier's life were etched around his nose and in the shadows of his eyes. She felt a prickle at the back of her neck. She did not doubt that the echoes of laughter in the corners of his mouth could disappear in an instant should he be crossed.

A lock of dark brown hair fell into his eyes and he flicked it back, drawing attention to a thin, pale line of a scar that ran from above his right eye to his temple, transecting his eyebrow.

Thamsine reached out a finger, stopping just short of tracing the line of the scar.

'You were lucky not to lose your eye. Did you get that scar at Worcester?' she said aloud.

Kit looked up at her and frowned, puzzled by her question. 'Oh, this,' he said, his fingers going to the scar. 'No. It was a running skirmish in '43. Looks worse than it was.'

'You were there from the beginning?'

'Stormed down a hill at Edgehill and just kept going until the bitter end in '46. I returned in '48 and '51 but I don't need to tell you what disastrous campaigns those were,' Kit said. 'I joined the court in exile, fought a few foreign wars I cared nothing for. Saw things no man should ever see ... '

He lapsed into a silence that spoke more eloquently than words and for a long moment, the only sound in the kitchen was the soft rasp of the knife on a carrot.

'And then?' Thamsine prompted.

He shrugged his shoulders. 'I abhorred exile so I swallowed my pride, apologised for my past misdeeds and came back to England.' He looked up at her and smiled. 'That, Mistress Granville, is my life.'

'And do you truly earn a living playing cards?'

'And dice and whatever else I can find.' He smiled. 'I'm very good at what I do.'

Thamsine sniffed. 'I do not doubt that you are.'

His clothes were not ostentatious, but they were well cut and made from good fabric. Instead of the old-fashioned collar favoured by her father, he wore the more fashionable falling bands. If she passed Kit Lovell in the street, she would probably think him a conservative man of business.

'Is this how you plan to spend the rest of your life?' she asked.

'No,' he snapped, with a hard edge to the single word.

The easy camaraderie on his face had been replaced by a sharp, appraising look. She shrank back on her stool, conscious she had overstepped the unseen line in their relationship.

'What of you, Thamsine Granville? I still hold your mark. When are you going to tell me what has brought you to the kitchen of the Ship Inn?'

When she didn't answer he smiled and shrugged. 'I see. If that is how it is to be, Thamsine, let us agree that I will ask you no more questions about your past if you ask none of mine.'

May poked her head around the door. 'There you are, Cap'n Lovell!' she said. 'Your friends have been waiting on you this half-hour since.'

She walked over and picked up one of Thamsine's efforts. ''Ere, what did this carrot ever do to you?' she asked.

Kit stood up. 'A little patience, May, she's never done this before.'

'Aye well, I need them carrots, so you take your hide out of here where you don't belong, Cap'n. I'll bring some rabbit pie in for you.'

'God bless you, May.' Kit put an arm around the girl's shoulders and kissed her forehead.

She coloured and pushed him away. 'Get away before I start remembering as how you never come visiting no more.'

May watched as the kitchen door closed behind him and sighed with a shake of her head. 'He's a one.'

'What do you mean?' Thamsine looked up from murdering another vegetable.

May sat down on the stool vacated by Kit and picked up the knife he had been using. 'Charm the birds out of the trees, he can, but cross him and he'll show no quarter.'

'How do you know?'

'Jem was his sergeant in the war. Said the men would have followed him into the depths of Hell if he'd just say the word.'

Thamsine glanced at the door through which Kit had left. She could well imagine he would have been an inspiring but ruthless leader.

As KIT OPENED the door to the private parlour, the thick fug of tobacco mingled with smoke from the fire made his eyes begin to water and he coughed. The half-dozen men taking their ease around the table looked up.

'Lovell! As I live and breathe!' Dutton jumped to his feet, slapping Kit on the shoulder with such force that Kit had to take a step to steady himself. 'I'd not expected to see you again so soon!'

'Thank you for your warm welcome.' Kit bowed to the assembly. 'You would think I had been gone years instead of a mere two months.'

'More to the point, how in God's name did you get out this time? The amount you owed, I thought you would never see the light of day! I told you that horse was a bad buy,' Colonel Whitely, a hard-bitten veteran with a cynical sense of humour, remarked, tapping out his pipe on his boot heel.

'Lovell has acquired a most valuable asset.' Fitzjames moved into the circle. 'A wealthy mistress.'

'Lucky dog!' Dutton said.

Kit smiled. 'Indeed, my dearest Lucy could not bear to be without me. Her bed grew uncommon cold in the winter air.'

As the paths of Lucy and these men were never likely to cross, the lie came easily.

Dutton scoffed. 'God rot you, Lovell. Why can't I find some pretty little widow to keep me?'

'One look at your face in the mirror should give you the answer to that question,' Kit rejoined.

'You know everyone here?' Dutton ran an expansive hand around the circle.

Kit recognised the faces of his old companions in arms: his friend Fitzjames, Colonel Whitely, Roger Cotes, Richard Willys and a couple of other familiar faces. The last man was a stranger.

Whitely pulled the young man forward. 'Jack Gerard, meet our friend and fellow sufferer, Captain Christopher Lovell. Jack is the nephew of Lord Gerard, who is with the King in Paris,' Whitely said.

'Welcome to this den of lost causes, Master Gerard,' Kit said.

Gerard smiled. 'No cause is a lost cause, Captain Lovell. Not while we still have breath in our bodies and a King denied his rightful throne.'

Kit regarded the youngster. Jack Gerard was younger than the others, too young to have fought in the wars, Kit observed cynically. That made him a young, dangerous idealist.

'Those indeed are sentiments we all hold dear to our hearts,' Kit said before his hesitation could be mistaken for something else. 'Come, gentlemen, a toast to our King.'

Wine sloshed into the glasses and the brimming cups were held aloft.

'To the King.'

But the words were said in an undertone so as not to carry to the taproom beyond.

Kit set his glass down and settled himself in a chair beside the fire. 'So, what is the news about London? One hears nothing behind the solid walls of the Clink except what your purse can tell you, and mine was sadly empty.'

'I heard that some woman took a pot-shot at the Lord Protector the other day,' Fitzjames said.

'Quite true,' Dutton said. 'I was there. Saw it myself. Hurled a brickbat at him during the parade. Only missed him by a few inches.'

'Women never could throw,' Cotes put in with a snort. 'Did they catch her?'

'Vanished,' Dutton said. 'Disappeared like smoke. Some say it was witchcraft.'

'They'd say that about anybody. Fact is they were too incompetent to catch her,' Whitely said. 'Well good luck to her, wherever she is. Pity is, she missed.'

'Cromwell conducts himself more and more as if he were King, not the usurping yeoman that he is,' Gerard spat.

Kit laughed. 'My young friend, like it or not, he is our head of state. I for one would not have the task!'

'Pssh!' Whitely snorted. 'Gone soft in gaol, Lovell.'

Kit sighed. 'Getting old, Whitely. So what brings this sorry band together?'

The men looked at each other.

Gerard leaned across the table to address Whitely. 'Is he to be trusted?'

Whitely gave the young man a hard look. 'Of course, he's to be trusted. Lovell's a King's man to the bone. He stood behind the King's colours at Edgehill and Worcester.'

Fitzjames placed a hand on Kit's shoulder. 'He's one of us, Gerard.'

The others nodded in agreement.

'So, Dutton,' Fitz said. 'What's the news?'

The gaze of every man in the room turned to Richard Dutton. The man raised his wineglass, took a quaff, wiped his mouth on his sleeve and set the glass down with a dramatic flourish.

'There is a plan,' he announced.

Kit's heart sank. There was always a plan, and if Dutton had anything to do with it, it was unlikely to be a very good plan.

Dutton leaned forward, his voice lowered. 'As we discussed in Lovell's absence, it's early days yet but steps have advanced.'

'And?' Whitely tapped his foot with obvious impatience.

Dutton shook his head. 'I am loath to say much more for the present. However, if we meet back here in a week, I will then have something to report.'

Hiding his frustration with a shrug, Kit produced a battered pack of cards. 'Well, until next week, then. In the meantime, I for one would welcome a diversion, not to mention a small boost to the purse. Anyone willing to take me on?'

After several rounds of cards, Dutton rose unsteadily to his feet.

'Go to go,' he slurred. 'Busy day tomorrow.'

Kit shot to his feet. 'I'll see you to your lodgings,' he said.

The two men lurched into the cold street. Snowflakes fell on their hats and shoulders but melted before reaching the slushy filth of the ground.

'Your damned luck hasn't changed,' Dutton remarked, swaying to one side of the road.

Kit took his arm and propelled him back in a straight line. Dutton was a heavyset man some years older than he was. As with the rest of the company at The Ship Inn, the recent conflicts had dealt ill with him. He had lost his home and family, and the war had left him embittered and penniless, with a fondness for wine that loosened his tongue and made him dangerous.

'Plenty of time in the Clink to hone my skills. You should try it sometime,' Kit said.

'I did.' Dutton spat into the gutter. 'Remember those stinking cells after Worcester?'

Kit suppressed a shudder. There were some memories he preferred not to recall. 'Tomorrow night, Dutton? You and me, a couple of comely wenches ... ?'

Dutton stopped in the middle of the street, swaying slightly. 'Tomorrow ... No, tomorrow I must go away.'

Kit caught the man as he staggered forward. 'So where are you off to, Dutton?'

Dutton tapped the side of his nose and gave Kit a heavy, conspiratorial wink. 'Secret.'

'Good God man, we don't have secrets from each other. Look at all we've been through. Remember Naseby? You saved my life that day.'

This was so far from the truth as to be almost the opposite, but Dutton's wine-soaked mind would remember what he wanted.

'Oh yes, my friend, I remember Naseby and Worcester. Can't forget Worcester.'

'That's right. God's death, Dutton, we've been through a lot together.'

They had reached the man's squalid lodgings. Kit helped him up the stairs and set him down on the bed, pulling off the scuffed and shabby boots. The stench of Dutton's feet made his lip curl.

'So where did you say you were going tomorrow?' he asked.

Dutton lay back on the bed and closed his eyes. He patted his jacket. 'All over. Letters to deliver. Tell you next meeting.'

'Let's get that jacket off you, then.'

Kit hauled Dutton's bulk up and undid the jacket. Dutton let himself be ministered to and when Kit had pulled his arms from the jacket he fell back on his bed, snoring stentoriously.

Kit jerked the covers over the man and pulled the letters from the jacket. Dutton was known to be a fool, and only other fools would entrust him with such a mission.

His unfortunate sojourn in the Clink meant he had some catching up to do and he worked quickly and methodically. There were twelve letters sealed with a plain seal and addressed to well-known royalists in the neighbouring counties. Kit looked at the names and shook his head in disbelief. If these men had any sense they would give Dutton short shrift.

He heated his knife over the candle and slid it under the seal of one of the letters. The signature was that of a Robert West. Not a name known to Kit but he doubted it was real. The message read simply that their uncle was anxious for news, and hoped that the recipient would be able to join him soon as the time was almost upon them.

Really, Kit thought, they made a poor fist of using code. The meaning was plain to even the most untrained observer. The word 'uncle' was a thinly veiled reference to the King, although Kit doubted Charles knew anything about this latest scheme.

He scoured Dutton's room and found a pen and some paper and carefully copied the message and the names of the recipients. When he was done, he resealed and replaced the letter with its companions and blew out the candle. Pausing only to cast poor, stupid Dutton a regretful glance, he slipped from the room.

CHAPTER 4

*E*very time the door to the taproom opened, Thamsine looked around. It had been a week since she had last seen Kit Lovell, and as the other men slipped into the private parlour, she knew tonight he would come. Her heart skipped a beat with the anticipation of being in his company again.

Nan passed her carrying two full jacks of ale.

'You're like a she-cat on heat,' she remarked. 'He'll be here soon enough. In the meantime, go and make yourself useful. There's tables to be wiped and those 'prentices over yon could do with some female company.'

Thamsine cast a glance at the table of rowdy 'prentices and shuddered. If they required female company, they could look elsewhere. Instead, she tightened her apron strings, pulled the grimy rag from the pocket and began the task of wiping down the nearest long oak table.

'Well, well, I hardly recognised you.'

At the sound of Kit's voice, she looked up, unable to stop the smile that crept to her lips.

He stood back and examined her with a critical eye. 'The black eye is now a fetching shade of yellow. As for the clothes, the bodice is perhaps a little immodest and the petticoats a little short, but you pass.'

Thamsine looked down at the clean, serviceable, but faded cloth of the petticoats and tugged at the gaping bodice.

'The twins found them for me. The previous owner was a little shorter and rather fuller of figure,' she said.

Jem Marsh sauntered over and placed a hand on Thamsine's shoulder. 'Quite a little find you dropped on my doorstep, Lovell. Broken just about every dish in my kitchen and dropped more jacks of ale than I can count, but she has one redeeming feature.'

Kit raised an eyebrow. 'And that is?'

'Voice of an angel.' Jem waved a hand around the crowded taproom. 'See this crowd? All thanks to her.'

Thamsine felt the heat rise to her cheeks. 'All those years of music lessons have finally been put to good use,' she said, 'although I am not sure that Signor Capelli had tavern songs in mind when he was teaching me.'

'You're taking a risk, Jem. Public performances of song are frowned upon, you know.' Kit raised a quizzical eyebrow at his friend.

Jem made a contemptuous gesture with his hand. 'Let 'em try and close me down. As long as your girl here fills my taproom, I'm willing to take the risk.' He thrust a jack of ale at Thamsine. 'Here, I don't pay you to stand around gossiping with the customers, go and give this to Abel and tell 'im to get his fiddle out.'

Thamsine took the ale and turned without looking, colliding with a man who had just entered. Ale slopped from the pot over his jacket.

'You stupid girl,' the man roared.

'Why doncha watch where ye're going?' Thamsine snapped

back, employing her best cockney accent.

'Now then, Dutton, it was an accident,' Kit said as Thamsine set the jack down and grabbed the cloth from the table where she had left it and began dabbing ineffectually at the man's damp coat.

'Don't I know you?' Dutton demanded, peering at Thamsine's face.

Thamsine straightened and looked him in the face. The man, middle-aged with fair, greying hair and a moustache and beard of a style fashionable ten years previously, was a stranger to her.

'I don't think so, sir,' she said.

'Damn it, I never forget a face,' Dutton persisted.

'Too many taverns, Dutton,' Kit said. He clapped a hand on the man's shoulder and turned him toward the private parlour. 'Forget about this wench. The others are waiting.'

Dutton cast Thamsine one long, last furious look as Kit propelled him away from her.

Jem clapped a hand on Thamsine's shoulder. 'Don't take Cap'n Dutton to heart, lass. He's a sad excuse for a man. Reckon he's already had a skinful tonight.' He jerked his head in the direction of the fireplace. 'Go on, give us a song. Abel's waiting.'

In the corner by the fireplace, an elderly man had produced a fiddle and struck up a tune. Thamsine set the remains of the jack of ale down beside him and climbed up onto an empty stool.

'Come cease your songs of cuckold's row,
For now 'tis something stale,
And let us sing of beggars now,
For that's in general,
In city and in country,
Men from high to low,
In each degree of quality,
Are beggars all a row.'

The taproom fell silent, the audience listening in rapt attention and occasionally adding an intercession in agreement with the sentiments of the words.

At the door to the private parlour, Kit Lovell leaned against the doorframe, a jack of ale in his hand, to listen. Even with the light behind him and his face in the darkness, she felt his eyes on her face and she felt as if she sang just for him.

> *'I saw a handsome proper youth,*
> *And he was wondrous fine,*
> *But when I understood the truth,*
> *His case was worse than mine,*
> *On wine and drabs, he did all spend,*
> *Which wrought his overthrow,*
> *So fortune plac'd him in the end,*
> *With beggars all a row.'*

Kit's shoulders shook with laughter and he raised his jack to her. A taller, fair-haired man appeared behind Kit and whispered something in his ear. Kit nodded and the door closed behind them.

~

'WHO'S THE SINGER?' Fitzjames asked.

Kit shook his head. 'Some new girl of Marsh's.'

'She's got a good voice,' Fitz commented. 'Good to hear music again.'

'Little bitch is a better singer than she is a skivvy. Spilt half a jack of ale over me,' Dutton growled. 'Sure I've seen her before somewhere. Damn me if I can think where.'

Kit viewed the drunken sot with distaste. Dutton's face was

flushed with drink, dark circles under his eyes. 'Forget her, Dutton. Are you going to tell us your plan?'

Dutton unrolled a map on the table. The men leaned over it, their faces taut with expectation.

'I believe that we can raise six hundred men,' Dutton said. 'With six hundred men we can seize Whitehall, St. James', the Tower and the Guards.' His stubby finger stabbed at the map.

Kit choked on his ale. 'We can do what?' he spluttered.

Six faces turned to look at him. 'Lovell, you have something to say?' Colonel Whitely asked, a cold edge to his voice.

Kit stared at them. 'You make that sound so simple! Just walk in and seize Whitehall? And what happens when we have accomplished this amazing act of daring?'

'The King will be waiting in a ship offshore. We send a signal to the ship and he lands in triumph,' Dutton concluded.

'And we are certain of the support of six hundred men?' Kit failed to hide the incredulity in his voice.

'I have promises of that many.' Dutton's tone was a little less sure, but he hid his uncertainty with bluster.

'And the King knows of this?' Kit said.

'Not at the moment. That is our next task. We must send someone to meet with the King and advise him of our plan.' Dutton looked around the circle of faces. 'Whitely, I for one think that you should go.'

'Of course, I would be honoured, Dutton, but there is the small matter of financing my trip to Paris. I haven't two farthings to rub together, let alone a boat fare to France, hire of horses, accommodation ... '

Dutton started to roll up the map. 'Well I've no money,' he said. 'Cotes? Willys? Fitzjames?'

He was met with downcast eyes and a concerted shaking of heads. 'Lovell?'

Kit raised his hands. 'Don't look to me, Dutton, I'm only just out of debtors' prison.'

Dutton sank onto a chair, his face heavy with gloom. 'We can't act without the King's connivance. The money must be raised for Whitley's passage. Gentlemen, I suggest we adjourn and meet back here the day after tomorrow. In the meantime, see what can be done about raising funds.'

Kit shook his head. 'Dutton, if we've not the funds to send Whitely to France, how do you plan to finance six hundred men? What happened to the loyal subjects you visited over the last week?'

Dutton's mouth took on a stubborn cast that Kit recognised all too well. His requests had, no doubt, met with the refusal they deserved.

'Once we have seized Whitehall and the Tower we will have access to as much money as we like.' Dutton's eyes narrowed. 'I sense doubt, Lovell. Those not with us … '

Kit held up his hands. 'I know, Dutton. Of course, I'm with you.'

He held his tongue and surveyed his companions. *What a miserable band of conspirators we are,* he thought. *Let them dream.* It was not his task to play Devil's advocate.

The party dispersed, leaving Kit alone in the parlour with Fitzjames and Willys. Fitzjames lit a pipe and propped his feet on an abandoned stool and watched the smoke curl up into the beams of the parlour.

Richard Willys toyed with his empty pot before slamming it on the table. 'This is a bad business, Lovell.'

'What is?'

'This mad plot of Dutton's. It'll ruin everything.' Willys' fingers drummed on the rim of his empty pot.

Kit raised an eyebrow. 'What will it ruin?'

Willys looked around the parlour. 'It has no chance of success. You both know that. I saw it in your faces.'

'I agree, but I do not see that it can be prevented,' Fitz said, removing the pipe from his mouth.

Willys looked away. 'No. It has gone too far already.'

'What other plans is it going to ruin?' Kit asked again.

Willys gave him a considered glance. 'You're a good man, Lovell. I've no reason to doubt your loyalty to the King.' He lowered his voice. 'There's a committee with the King's Commission set up to organise an insurrection.'

Kit set his tankard down and leaned forward. '*With* the King's Commission?'

Willys nodded.

'Who's on it?'

'That doesn't matter. What matters is that part of the commission is to prevent such madness as this.'

Kit sat back and shook his head. 'Willys, you, they, whoever this committee is, can't stop it. While the King sits in France and Cromwell in Whitehall there are always going to be hotheads like Dutton who will be plotting in their cups.'

Willys stroked his moustache. 'I know. All I can do is suggest that you disassociate yourself from this plan and try and persuade as many of your comrades as you can. Maybe it will die its natural death.'

Kit sat back, his fingers playing thoughtfully around his tankard. 'They meet tomorrow night. Will you be there?'

Willys shook his head. 'No. I will have no further truck with them.'

'So what does this committee of yours plan?'

Willys shook his head. 'I haven't said I was on the committee, Lovell, but if they should have need of you, can we ... they rely on you?'

'If your enterprise has the King's Commission, then you have my sword.'

'Fitzjames?'

'I'm with you both.'

'Good man.' Willys stood up. 'I wish you luck, Lovell. If they can be dissuaded, you're the man to do it. Dutton trusts you.'

Kit watched Willys as he left the room, shutting the door behind him. In the taproom, Thamsine was singing a sad, mournful ballad. *Beggars all in a row*, Kit thought and stared gloomily at his cup.

'Aren't you tired of this, Fitz?' he asked.

Fitzjames shrugged. 'Of course I am, but I'm tired of this hand-to-mouth existence, Lovell. I want the King back on his rightful throne. If there is a chance that this Committee of Willys' can organise something then yes, I will be there. What will you do?'

'Dutton meets tomorrow night,' Kit said. 'I shall hear what he has to say and try to turn his mind to joining his enterprise with this committee.'

Fitz leaned forward. 'The Sealed Knot,' he said with a wry grin. 'They call themselves the Sealed Knot.'

'What sort of fanciful name is that?'

Fitz shrugged and drained his cup. 'I for one will not attend tomorrow night. I'm with Willys. I want no further part of this plot.'

'Sensible man,' Kit agreed.

'It's getting late.' Fitz rose to his feet.

'I'll walk with you,' Kit said. 'I need some fresh air after that vile tobacco you smoke.'

Fitz smiled and clapped his friend on the shoulder. 'We all have our vices, lad. Yours are women and cards. Mine are tobacco and wine.'

'And execrable poetry,' Kit added. 'Don't forget your talents as a poet, my friend!'

In the taproom, Thamsine turned and he raised a hand in farewell. She smiled in response. He felt a pang of regret. It would have been pleasant to have passed the rest of the evening sparring with Mistress Granville.

Outside the cold air hit them like a belt of sobering water.

'I've no mind for my bed, yet a while,' Fitz said. 'I hear there is a card game at the Saracen's Head. Fancy a chance to improve your purse?'

They lurched down the Strand towards 'the Head'. *Another dingy, smoke-filled tavern*, Kit thought gloomily as Fitz wove his way between the tables to the private parlour.

Through the haze of tobacco smoke, he could make out a table of card players with about a dozen men standing around watching the game.

They waited until the hand had finished and took the seats of the losers.

'Well, well.' The man shuffling the cards set them down. 'Fitz-james, unless I'm mistaken.'

Fitz's face flashed with recognition. 'My God. Ambrose Morton. I haven't seen you since ... must be '47. I heard you were in The Hague. What brings you to London?'

'Personal business,' the man replied, moving his gaze to Kit. Kit met the cold eyes in the dark, handsome face of a man some years older than him.

'Do you know Lovell?' Fitz enquired.

'No, but I have heard the name.' Morton held out his hand. 'Colonel Ambrose Morton.'

'Captain Christopher Lovell,' Kit replied.

Morton spread his hands in an encompassing gesture. 'Shall I deal?'

With practised ease, the cards flew from his hand. Kit took the first hand and Morton dealt the cards again.

'Lovell?' Morton mused, his eyes on his cards. 'Ah yes. Kit Lovell. I have heard of you. Your reputation precedes you. Few can beat you at cards, as I hear tell.'

'I have some poor talent at cards,' Kit replied without looking up.

'There are many ways of winning at cards, is there not, Captain Lovell?'

Kit felt the hackles on the back of his neck rise and he glanced up to see Morton's narrowed eyes fixed on him. 'Are you implying something, Morton?'

Morton raised a placating hand. 'Not at all, Captain Lovell.'

Kit pushed back his chair and rose to his feet. 'I have never met you before tonight, Morton, but I will not sit here and have my honour so impugned. Come, Fitz.'

Fitz rose to his unsteady feet. 'But I've got a good hand, Lovell.'

Kit turned his cards over. 'I would have did not need tricks to win this hand, Morton, but I've lost my taste for cards.'

For a moment the two men's eyes locked. Morton inclined his head. 'I meant no insult, Captain Lovell. Perhaps some other time?'

'Perhaps,' Kit said.

Outside in the cold air, he pulled his cloak around him.

'Not like you to take on so,' Fitz grumbled.

'I have no time for that sort of man,' Kit said striding ahead of Fitz.

'What sort of man?' Fitz asked, puffing to keep pace with his friend.

Kit slowed his pace to allow Fitz a chance to catch up. 'You know the type, Fitz. Cold and vicious bastards.'

'Well, you're probably right.' Fitz clapped an arm around Kit's shoulder and they wove an unsteady path towards Holborn. 'He ran with Goring's crew during the war. You'll have heard the stories...'

George, Lord Goring, had command of the King's Army in the west, and the actions of his unruly rabble had done more to damage the King's cause than the whole of the New Model Army.

'There was a particularly nasty rumour,' Fitz began, then waved a hand. 'Doesn't matter... I don't like to spread gossip.'

'What?' Kit persisted.

Fitz sighed. 'There was a murder. A woman and her daughter. Nasty thing – rape, mutilation. Renegades were blamed, but odd thing was that Morton and his men were the only troops in the area.'

Kit shrugged. 'Proves nothing. Just because he was in the area, doesn't implicate him.'

'No, no, you're quite right,' Fitz slurred drunkenly.

Kit shivered. As he had looked into Morton's cold eyes, he could well imagine the man capable of such an atrocity.

'Where are you going now?' he changed the subject. 'Your lodgings are not in this direction.'

Fitz smiled. 'A beautiful nymph awaits me...'

'I hope she gives you a discount for persistence,' Kit said with a laugh.

'Not that sort of nymph!' Fitz protested. 'You don't think me sufficiently desperate that I must pay for my pleasure!'

'Not at all,' Kit smiled.

'Well, this is me. See that light in the window? My darling awaits. Good night to you, Lovell.'

Kit watched Fitz weave across to the door and open it. He smiled and shook his head before turning his heels towards Lucy, waiting for him on Holborn Hill.

CHAPTER 5

*K*it returned to The Ship Inn the following night with a heavy heart. It had snowed earlier in the day but the snow had already turned to slush in the mire, soiling Kit's boots and the gloomy weather reflected his mood.

The inn spilled warm, golden light and drunken 'prentices into the cold London street. He pulled his cloak around him and looked on with distaste as one of the 'prentices vomited loudly and messily against the wall of the inn. His fellows gathered him up and they pushed past Kit, singing discordantly.

Kit opened the door and caught Jem's eye.

'Busy tonight,' he commented.

'Aye. It's that lass of yours, Thamsine. Word's got out, quite an attraction she is.' Jem looked pleased.

The fiddler struck up a tune and Thamsine was hoisted onto a table. Kit smiled. In her tattered gown with her hand on her hip, any semblance between the gentlewoman and this taproom songstress had long since dissipated.

Of all the brave birds that ever I see,
The owl is the fairest in her degree.
For all day long she sits in a tree,
And when the night comes away flies she.
This song is well sung, I make you a vow,
And he is a knave that drinketh now ...

Kit winked at Thamsine who smiled in return as he joined in the rousing chorus of the familiar soldier's drinking song.

... Nose, nose, nose, nose,
And who gave thee that jolly red nose?
Cinnamon and ginger, nutmeg and cloves,
That's what gave me this jolly red nose.

When the song was done, Thamsine shoved a man whose hand strayed to her backside. He fell back among his companions, laughing as Thamsine jumped off the table and pushed her way through the crowd towards Kit.

He inclined his head. 'Mistress Granville. You have a fine repertoire of songs guaranteed to make your late father turn in his grave.'

She smiled. He liked the way her smile lit up her face.

'My poor father. If he could only see me now. He loved madrigals and sad ballads. My brother and I would sing to entertain his friends. Now ... ' She waved a hand at the crowded taproom. 'I sing bawdy songs in a tavern and consider myself fortunate.' The smile fell away and she looked into his face, earnestly seeking his eyes. 'I do consider myself fortunate, Captain Lovell. If I haven't thanked you properly ... '

An unfamiliar heat rose to Kit's face and he waved a deprecating hand. 'I am glad it has worked out for you,' he said. 'Now if you would excuse me, my friends are awaiting me.'

Thamsine nodded. 'They're in the parlour.'

May tugged at Thamsine's arm. 'Thamsine, another song …'

With the opening stanza of a ballad of love lost filling the taproom behind him, Kit knocked on the door to the private parlour. Cotes let him in and he looked around the crowded, smoke-filled room.

It seemed an unusually good turnout. Despite the absence of Willys, Fitzjames and young Gerard, Dutton had assembled eleven in all, mostly familiar faces. Spirits seemed high.

Men without hope suddenly had a cause they could turn to.

Kit bent over the map of London unfurled on the table, feigning an enthusiasm he did not feel. Even with the six hundred mythical men, the task seemed hopeless. Seize Whitehall? Kidnap Cromwell? Take the Tower for God's sake! Oh well, let them dream. Dreams hurt no one, he thought

'I've come up with a few pounds,' Dutton said. 'Enough for the fare.' He pushed the purse across to Whitely.

Whitely gathered the purse, weighing it in his hand. 'What did you sell?'

'My pistols,' Dutton replied, with a downcast mouth.

'You don't think you might have needed those?' Kit asked, the sarcasm heavy in his voice.

'Lovell, if you have no wish to be a part of this, then go now,' Whitely said.

Kit pulled out his purse. 'Apologies. There is my contribution.'

Others added coins to the pile and Whitely nodded. 'Good, that should be enough.'

Cotes opened the door to a gentle knock. Thamsine stood there with two jugs of ale.

'Come in, lass,' Cotes said. 'We've thirsty work ahead of us.'

'You've a good voice,' Whitely said. 'Should be on the stage.'

'Thank 'ee, sir,' Thamsine said. 'But there's no theatres and nowhere else for the likes of I.'

Kit hid a smile in his tankard. She did a good cockney accent. He would have sworn she'd been born and brought up within the sound of Bow Bells.

'Perhaps you can give us a song – ' one of the others began, only to stop abruptly at the sound of a crash and loud raised voices from the taproom. 'What was that?'

Cotes opened the door to the parlour a crack. He turned back to face the room, the colour draining from his face. 'Soldiers. Dutton, you fool, get that map onto the fire.'

Even as Dutton hurled the paper onto the flames, the door crashed open and an officer stepped into the room, to be met with the hiss and rattle of swords being eased from scabbards.

The man put his hands on his hips and surveyed the pathetic band of conspirators.

The officer smiled. 'Gentlemen, good evening. What do we have here? A pretty bunch of conspirators, so I hear tell. Put those weapons down. I have men in the taproom and behind that window.'

Whitely stood up. 'I must protest. We are old comrades doing no more than enjoying a quiet ale and a pipe.'

The officer strolled over to the fireplace and retrieved the singed map. He blew out the glowing embers, scrutinised the remains of the parchment, and then looked around at the faces in the room. 'You can tell that to the Council of State. In the meantime, the Lieutenant of the Tower has some pleasant accommodation planned for you.'

He looked around the room and his gaze looked on Thamsine. A slow smile spread across his face.

'Well, well, 'tis my lucky night,' he said.

His hand closed over Thamsine's arm and he drew her towards him. He took her chin in his fingers and turned her head to the light.

'A red-headed woman with a black eye,' he said. 'I hear tell you tried to kill our Lord Protector.'

'Tweren't me, sir,' Thamsine said. 'I must be getting back to my work.'

The man pulled her closer.

'What's your name, girl?'

Thamsine said nothing. Her eyes, in her thin face, had become huge with fear. Kit's fingers clenched and unclenched in impotent fury.

'I asked your name.' The officer's voice had become low and menacing.

'Thamsine Granville,' she stuttered.

'There must be some mistake,' Kit said.

'Oh, there's no mistake. Seen here and identified, she was.'

'I knew I'd seen her before!' Dutton almost screamed. 'I can confirm, Captain, that this is indeed the woman that threw the rock at the Lord Protector's coach. Saw her with my own eyes.'

The officer turned to look at Dutton.

'Are you sure?'

'I never forget a face. Now, Captain, I have confirmed you have a dangerous assassin in your custody. Perhaps you will let me go.'

The officer laughed. 'I think not. You've enough troubles of your own without minding others. It's not up to me to say if she did or she didn't do what was alleged. She can come with us.' He released Thamsine with such force she staggered and would have fallen if Kit hadn't caught her. 'Now let's get this lot out of here.'

He gave a nod and two of his soldiers grabbed Thamsine's arms. Thamsine cast Kit a brief, despairing look as the manacles were fastened around her slender wrists.

As the captives were pushed into the taproom, a murmur of outrage began to grow.

'What you got our girl for? You leave her be, yer girt thug!' One of the customers rose to his feet to be joined by the others. The level of anger rose, and chunks of bread and pint pots began to fly at the heads of the soldiers.

The soldiers ducked. Shielding Thamsine with their bulk, they dragged her out onto the street and flung her against the tray of one of two carts that stood waiting.

'Kit!'

Kit heard her despairing cry and shook off his captor's hand. 'Let me go with her.'

'Friend of yours, is she?' The officer pushed Kit towards her. 'Well, you both keep bad company.'

Kit fell against Thamsine and they lost their footing on the icy mire, falling to their knees in the filthy street.

'Get up.' A muddy boot swung in Thamsine's direction. Kit flung out his arm, catching the full brunt of the boot on his elbow. He subsided, cursing in French. A soldier seized Thamsine's arm and hauled her roughly to her feet.

Kit managed to pick himself up, shaking his arm and flexing his numbed fingers. They were both thrown bodily onto the back of the second cart. The first cart, bearing Dutton and the other conspirators, already lurched down the street ahead of them.

Thamsine began to shiver. She lacked a cloak and the night air was perishing. Kit moved closer to her, his fingers closing over her icy hand.

'I'm sorry, Thamsine.' He spoke in French.

'It wasn't your doing,' she replied in the same language. 'That awful man Dutton. He's signed my death warrant, hasn't he?' She leaned her head against his arm. 'What will they do to me?' Her voice quavered.

He shook his head. 'I don't know.' He gripped her hand. 'Thamsine, whatever happens, remember who you are. Don't be bullied or intimidated.'

'I wasn't trying to kill him. I wasn't.' She choked back a sob. 'What about you? Why were you arrested? What were you doing in the parlour?'

He gave a hollow laugh. 'Conspiring to overthrow Cromwell.'

'Were you? I thought you just played cards.'

Kit lowered his voice. 'Every drunken Royalist conspires to overthrow Cromwell.'

Silent tears ran unchecked down her face. Kit stroked the back of her hand with his thumb. He bent his head, so it rested on hers. Her hair smelt of rosemary and chamomile.

'Thamsine,' he whispered, 'I wish I could say it will all be right.'

'I'm so scared,' was her small, tight reply.

'Take heart. You have great strength. I think you will find the courage to get through the next few weeks,' he said.

She leaned her head against his shoulder. 'You make that sound so easy!' she said in English.

CHAPTER 6

*A*s the cart crossed the stinking moat and passed through the gates of the Tower, tales of misery, despair and the deaths of Queens dragged screaming to the block crowded Thamsine's mind. Those long-forgotten history lessons did not relate tales of those who walked free through its gates.

Kit's fingers tightened on hers and she closed her eyes against the fear that rose like gall in her throat. The cart rumbled into a cobbled courtyard and drew to a halt. The soldiers pulled Thamsine from the cart and she fell to her knees on the stones. As she struggled to rise, Kit jumped down beside her, putting his body between the soldiers and her.

'Quite the gentleman, aren't you?' the sergeant sneered. 'Out of the way, Lovell!'

Kit stood his ground. The sergeant gave an exasperated grunt and swung his fist. Thamsine flinched at the resounding crunch of fist on bone, and Kit reeled back against the cart, sliding to the ground beside her in an ungainly heap. Thamsine had no time to see to him. A soldier pulled her to her feet and, barely allowing her time for a backward glance, thrust her towards a door.

Despite the almost cloying warmth of the room in which she found herself, she shivered, clasped her manacled hands tightly together and stared fixedly at the ground.

'Is this the woman?'

Thamsine raised her eyes to look at the speaker. A well-dressed, heavyset man rose from behind the table and circled her as if she were an animal in the market square.

'It is. Denies it of course but the description fits.' The sergeant who had brought her in pushed her forward into the light.

'You had to drag her through the mud to get her here?'

The man resumed his seat, put his forearms on the table, clasped his hands and leaned forward.

'What's your name, woman?'

Thamsine didn't answer.

'Tell me your name or the sergeant here will add another black eye to the one you already have.'

Thamsine swallowed, and remembering Kit's words about finding the strength within her, she looked up, meeting the man's eyes. 'Thamsine Granville.'

'Granville, is it? Well, my name is Barkstead, Colonel Barkstead, and I am the Lieutenant of the Tower.'

She straightened. 'Colonel Barkstead, I must protest at my treatment.' She summoned her last shreds of dignity. 'Whatever it is I am accused of, I am completely innocent.'

He looked her up and down, his eyes taking in the old, broken shoes, the torn and mended petticoats and stained bodice.

'Well, well, that is the voice of a gently born woman, I warrant. Makes no difference. I have a Tower full of innocent babes just like you, m'lady.' The last word was uttered in a tone heavy with contempt.

He rose to his feet and gave her a mocking bow. 'Now if you have a mind to it, allow me to show you to your accommodation. Sergeant!'

The promised accommodation proved somewhat better than she could have hoped for; a grey stone cell, barely large enough to contain a low cot, a small table and a stool. A narrow window high up on the wall admitted light and air and a tiny, but empty, fireplace had been built into the corner. It could have been much, much worse. She doubted Kit and his fellows enjoyed such luxuries.

The turnkey undid the manacles, and as the door slammed behind Colonel Barkstead, she lay down on the bed and covered her eyes with her left arm. She needed to think clearly.

She wondered if she would be tortured. She'd heard such dreadful stories, and doubted that she had the fortitude to withstand such pressure should it be brought to bear. Would it be best to co-operate? Maybe present herself as she had to Kit Lovell, a gentlewoman reduced in circumstances and driven to desperation? That at least was the truth.

The thought of Kit caused her to stumble in her resolve. She remembered his hand closing on hers and the strength he had conveyed in that simple gesture. A choking sob rose to her throat. She wanted him here beside her, not incarcerated somewhere else behind these unforgiving walls.

The moment of despair had to be overcome. She swallowed back the tears and sat up. With cold, desperate fingers she tugged at the stitches that held her pathetically small collection of coins, earned from her singing and secured from the twins' acquisitive fingers in the inside of her petticoat. It would be enough to ameliorate her condition for a little while, and she stood a better chance if she met her inquisitors at least clean and strong within herself.

She stood up and crossed to the door. In response to her knock, the pockmarked face of the turnkey appeared at the grate.

'I want a bowl of water.'

'Oh yes?' he sneered.

She held up a coin and his attitude changed markedly. He gave her a leering smile. 'Anything else, yer ladyship?'

'A comb.'

'At your service!' he snarled and stumped away.

He returned with the bowl of water and a revolting comb that was missing half its teeth. She tossed him the coin.

He jerked his head at her. 'How much more you got there? Y'know, I charge for services like emptying your bucket.' He indicated the slops bucket in the corner. 'And if y'want a candle and some decent food, it's all extra. Mind you … ' He licked his lips. ' … I'd do it for a taste of what's under yer skirts.'

Thamsine straightened, looking down on him. Her height often proved to be a blessing when it came to intimidating stupid people.

'Get out of here.'

He gave her a contemptuous look. 'In a few weeks, ye'll be begging for it!'

'Not unless Hell freezes over.'

'We'll see, yer ladyship, we'll see.'

The man slammed the door behind him.

Her few coins would not last out the week at the rate he charged, and she wondered how long she could maintain her defiance. In a few weeks or a month, would she be reduced to letting him grope under her skirts for the sake of a decent meal?

Putting that thought to one side, Thamsine washed her face and hands, cleaned the comb, and pulled it through her hair. She then tried to rinse the worst of the mud and filth from her gown.

The result was rudimentary, but if nothing else it made her feel better.

She looked around the cell, shivered, wrapped herself in the one blanket, and lay down on the hard cot. Exhausted by the shock of her sudden arrest, sleep came with surprising ease and she woke, cold and stiff, to bright sunlight streaming in through the high window.

She tore at the hunk of stale bread that had been provided to break the fast, washed, tidied her hair, and settled herself to wait.

The hours passed with nothing to relieve them except the noises from the world beyond the walls. Soldiers paraded in the courtyard, doors slammed, keys rattled and, incongruously, she could hear the laughter of children playing nearby. The waiting proved to be worse than any interrogation could be, and she wondered if it was a deliberate ploy to unsettle her. If so, then it proved very effective.

It had gone dark when the key rattled in the lock and the turnkey flung the door open with a thud. He held up a lantern.

'You've been sent for.'

'By whom?'

'By whom?' he scoffed. 'You'll see soon enough. Up.' She rose stiffly to her feet.

He held up a set of manacles. 'Hold out your hands.'

She recoiled. She had not expected irons. 'I don't need those! I'm not going to escape.'

'Orders is orders.' He grabbed her arm and jerked her hand out. 'Such pretty hands too.'

The hard metal felt cold on her skin and the unfamiliar weight dragged her spirits down with it. For a moment she panicked, her firm assurance of the morning evaporating. She closed her eyes and took a deep breath, remembering who she was. With her back straight and her head held high she marched out of her cell.

Her courage failed her again as the door to the room where her inquisitor waited opened. She held back, her breath coming in short, frantic bursts, her hands sweating.

The turnkey put a hand on her back and pushed her forward. She stumbled across the threshold, the door slamming shut behind her. She stood for a moment, gathering herself, staring at the well-polished floorboards. Then slowly she raised her eyes, taking in the pleasant, wood-panelled room with its low, plaster ceiling. Two wax candles stood on the table and a cheerful fire burned in the grate. It gave the room a homely feel she found more disquieting than the cold cell.

A man in the sombre clothes of a clerk sat to one side of a large table, paper and pen in hand. He gave her a cursory glance and returned to sharpening his pen. A second, dark-haired man stood by the window, his back to her and his hands loosely clasped behind his back. He did not turn around as she entered.

'A pleasant outlook, Mistress Granville. Come and join me.'

Her knees shook and her stomach roiled as she walked across the expanse of floor that stood between them. At every step, the rattle of the chains filled the quiet room. She stopped beside him, her hands resting on the windowsill. Below her, the lights of the wherries on the river danced and swayed.

'Do you know Queen Elizabeth herself once looked out of these very windows? She was a prisoner too. She must have thought, as you are now, *Out there is freedom. In here is only death and despair.*' He turned to face her. 'Mistress Granville, I trust they are treating you well?'

'Well enough.'

He inclined his head. 'I am glad to hear it. Do you know who I am?'

She shook her head.

'My name is John Thurloe, and I am the Secretary to the

Council of State. Now tell me, Mistress Granville, is that your name?'

'Of course it is my name.'

'Who is your father? Where are you from?'

She met his eyes – dark, hooded eyes that froze her blood – and found herself unable to speak.

He sighed and asked again, his tone slow and heavy with threat. 'Mistress Granville, do not trifle with me. When I ask you a question, I require you to answer me.'

'I am from Hampshire,' she said. 'My family home is … was Hartley Court. My father, William Granville, is dead.' She squared her shoulders. 'I mean to protest my innocence.'

'Your innocence of what? Do you know why you are being held?'

'Some foolish allegation that I hurled a brickbat at the Lord Protector?'

He raised an eyebrow. 'A foolish allegation, is it?' He paused, studying her face, 'Among my many duties, I have the pleasure of weeding out enemies of the Lord Protector.'

'That must be an interesting task. I am sure the Lord Protector has many enemies.'

'He does and you, Mistress Granville, can count yourself among them.'

His eyes narrowed and his face hardened. This was a man not to be crossed. Thamsine felt her knees go weak and she swallowed.

'Sit down.' He turned and indicated a chair that stood by itself in the middle of the room. Thamsine complied, sitting rigid, her hands clasped in her lap.

Thurloe gave a barely perceptible nod to the clerk, who began writing.

'Mistress Granville, do you deny that you threw a brickbat at the carriage of the Lord Protector on the eighth day of February?'

'I do.'

Thurloe sighed. 'I see. Do you know what the punishment is for the attempted assassination of the Lord Protector?'

Thamsine stared at him.

'Hanging, drawing and quartering. Have you ever seen a man hanged, drawn and quartered?'

She shook her head.

'First, they will take you to the gibbet and hang you until you are not quite dead. Then you will be cut down and you will be disembowelled, your head and limbs cut from the body and dispersed about the kingdom as a warning to others.' He watched her face from beneath his hooded eyes. 'It is an unpleasant way to die.'

'For a woman?' Thamsine's voice shook.

He shrugged.

'What proof do you have that I committed this deed?' Her voice wavered.

'I am afraid, my dear Mistress Granville, I have a witness who has identified you as the perpetrator of this heinous act.'

'Who is this eye-witness?'

'Someone who saw you hurl the brickbat and then saw you again singing I believe, another violation of the law by the way, in a tavern. There is no mistake.'

She took a deep, shuddering breath and looked down at her manacled hands. 'If, just if, I were to admit to such an offence would it ... ? Would it make it easier?'

Thurloe moved from his place by the window to the fire. He prodded the logs for a moment or two, watching the sparks flying up the chimney, as if deep in thought.

'It may depend on the reason why such an act was committed,' he said at last. He turned to face her, crossing his arms, his dark eyes skewering her to her chair like a moth trapped in the light. 'Do you admit you threw the brickbat?'

She nodded.

'Did you act alone or in concert with others?'

She looked up at him. 'Quite alone.'

'The State has many enemies, Mistress Granville. Some would use any means to see the death of the Lord Protector. You have never had any business with such malignants, who might have ordered you to take this step?'

She shook her head. 'Master Thurloe, I assure you I acted quite alone.'

'What of those who were also taken at The Ship Inn? What dealings have you had with them?'

'None,' Thamsine protested. "I have recently secured employment at the inn. That is all."

'You have never attended any of their meetings? Been privy to their plotting?'

'No.' Thamsine's voice rose. 'I knew none of them, except ... ' She bit off the last name.

'Except?'

'Except Captain Lovell.'

'And how do you know him?'

'He ... he was a friend of my brother.' The lie came easily.

'How do you come to be working in a tavern known to be haunted by Lovell and his friends?'

Thamsine swallowed. Her mouth was dry. 'He helped me gain employment there.'

Thurloe did not respond, watching her face from under his hooded eyes. 'You are evidently well-born. What about your family, Mistress Granville? How do you come to be singing tavern ditties and serving ale in a common inn?'

'I have told you the truth, Master Thurloe. I have no family. They are all dead.' Her voice began to waver. 'I had been forced to vacate my home and had been living on the streets of London for nearly six months. That day, the day... I threw the brick at the coach, I reached a point of despair. There was no premeditation. It was an impulsive act of desperation, nothing more sinister than that.'

Thurloe regarded her thoughtfully for a long moment. 'I am inclined to believe you, Mistress Granville,' he said at last. 'The question is, did you intend by your actions to kill the Lord Protector?' As he spoke, he crossed to the table and sat down on the far side of it.

Thamsine managed a wan smile, spreading her hands in a dissembling motion. 'My Lord, I'm a woman. Do you truly believe that I have the strength or capability to hurl such an awkward missile with an intent to kill?'

'For a frail woman, you made quite a dent in the carriage, Mistress Granville.' He sat back considering her, one finger laid against his mouth. Thamsine shifted in her chair. His silences were disconcerting.

'Will I die?' Thamsine looked down at her manacled hands, twisted together so tightly that the knuckles showed white.

'I shall make a report to Council and they shall decide your fate, Mistress.'

Thamsine's hand instinctively went to her throat and for the first time, Thurloe smiled, a cold, unpleasant smile that did not touch his eyes.

'The Council of State is not likely to look kindly on a murderess, however pitiful her tale.'

'I haven't murdered anyone. All I have done is dent a coach.' She could hear the desperation rising in her voice.

Thurloe did not respond. He rang a small bell on the table and the turnkey appeared at the door with the sort of speed that indicated he had been listening at the keyhole.

'See Mistress Granville back to her cell.'

CHAPTER 7

$\mathcal{K}$it pressed his hands against the damp, unyielding brick wall of the prison. If he closed his eyes, he could almost feel the centuries of misery ingrained in the stones. He squinted up at the small aperture that admitted a pitiful degree of light and air. The Tower offered no chance of escape. It had been built for just this purpose and it served it well. He turned around and leaned his back against the wall, his ankles crossed, and surveyed his silent companions.

His gaze fell on Dutton, who sat on the filthy straw, his head in his hands, his shoulders heaving.

'We're dead,' Dutton groaned. 'We're all dead.'

'Keep your peace, Dutton,' Whitely said with a voice of authority. 'They have no evidence against us, just a map of London.'

'And the word of an informer,' Cotes said, his narrow eyes darting from man to man.

Dutton raised his head. 'What do you mean?'

'Someone told them we were meeting and why.'

'You're surely not suggesting one of us turned cloak?' Whitely said.

'I'm not suggesting anything,' Cotes said. 'I'm telling you.'

'And who more likely than you?' Kit said.

Cotes paled. 'Me?'

'The mouse that squeals loudest is the one with the cheese, as my old nurse used to say,' Thomas Smith muttered darkly.

'It wasn't me!' Cotes protested, his voice rising an octave in alarm.

'Throwing allegations isn't going to help. Look at who wasn't there.' Whitely's sensible voice stilled the anxiety. 'Young Gerard, Willys or Fitzjames. It is more likely one of them.'

'Not Fitzjames,' Kit said, with a pang of guilt.

'What about Willys?' Smith said. 'It's my betting that this is the work of the Sealed Knot. They want us out of the way.'

There was silence.

'What did you say?' Whitely said at last.

''Tis well known in Paris that there is a committee holding the King's Commission with orders to undermine any other plans. They call themselves the Sealed Knot. My bet is that this is their work,' Smith said.

'What committee? Who's on it?' Dutton asked. From his face, it was evident that the existence of the Sealed Knot was news to him.

Smith shrugged. 'No one knows, but there is word that Willys is one of them.'

'They hold the King's Commission you say?' Dutton was incredulous. 'If Willys is one of them, then why not confide in us? Together we could have raised an army.'

'An army? For Christ's sake Dutton, we couldn't organise a small riot!' Kit said. 'You didn't really believe we could muster six hundred men?'

'With the King's Commission, we could have done.'

'Enough!' Whitely rose to his feet. 'In case you gentlemen haven't noticed, we are in the Tower of London and these walls have ears. Not another word.'

'What about the girl?' Smith broke the ensuing silence. 'Is it true she threw a brickbat at Cromwell a week or so back?'

'I saw her!' Dutton looked up. 'Dammit, I knew her face was familiar. A bit thinner and a bit grubbier but it was her right enough. I saw her throw the brickbat. Only missed by a couple of inches.'

'Well, you can just keep quiet about it,' Kit said sharply. 'No point sending the girl to the gallows for nearly succeeding at something we have come nowhere close to doing!'

'You're quick to defend her,' Dutton sneered. 'Got a hand under her skirts, have you?'

Kit cast Dutton a filthy look that was lost in the dark. He slid down the wall and sat with his hands hanging loosely over his knees. He closed his eyes and wondered how Thamsine fared, locked within these same forsaken walls.

A FITFUL RAY of sunlight struggled through the foetid London air, penetrating the warm, panelled room and briefly illuminating the large, oaken table behind which John Thurloe, Secretary to the Council of State, sat waiting for his visitor. As Kit strolled into the room, Thurloe looked up from perusing the scattered papers before him. He set down his pen and, leaning his elbows on the table, placed the tips of his fingers together and said in a low, purring voice, 'Captain Lovell. I trust you are well?'

Kit gave the Secretary of State the benefit of a flourishing bow, which lost something when executed wearing manacles. Without waiting for an invitation, he seated himself in one of the solid oak chairs facing the table.

'Tolerably well, Master Thurloe. The hostelry is overrun with bed bugs and lice, the rats are a truly incredible size and the food is execrable, but my day is much improved for seeing you of course.'

Thurloe sighed. 'Spare me the charm, Lovell. You know it's wasted on me.'

Kit casually flicked at a piece of imaginary lint on his sleeve, causing the chains on his wrists to rattle. The gesture was purely an affectation. The sleeve of his jacket, like the rest of his attire and indeed himself, after a week's incarceration, was very much the worse for wear. Unshaven, soiled, stained and carrying the unmistakable stench of prison, Kit was far from his sartorial best. Thurloe's long nose wrinkled in distaste.

Kit caught the gesture. 'I pray your pardon for my appearance, Thurloe, but as you are well aware the accommodation has afforded me few luxuries.'

'Indeed, but then it was not intended to,' agreed Thurloe.

Kit raised a hand to a livid bruise on his right cheekbone. 'Was this strictly necessary?'

Thurloe shrugged. 'Adds a degree of authenticity. I trust Sergeant Harris was not too rough on you?'

Kit glared at the Secretary of State. 'I am lucky he did not break a bone.'

'How are your fellow captives?'

Kit shrugged. 'Surprised that their idiotic plan was discovered.'

'And who do they suspect of betraying them?'

Kit shook his head. 'The suspects abound. Roger Cotes now seems to be the principal object of their blame. Never one to be trusted was Roger. Shifty eyes.'

Thurloe smiled. 'Not you?'

'Never me, Thurloe.' Kit's finger traced the carving on the arm of the chair. He looked up and met Thurloe's eye. 'What do you intend to do with them?'

Thurloe's long fingers drummed the table. 'They're a sorry enough crew. Very quick to talk and there are titbits of information I find quite intriguing. As for the plot itself?' He shrugged. 'Pathetic, laughable in fact.' He shook his head. 'When all is considered, there is precious little evidence to hold them on. To be honest I doubt that they will see a trial. We'll hold them long enough to make them think twice about entering into conspiracies and then let them go again.'

'Good of you. What about me?'

'Well, I can hardly let you go without attracting some sort of suspicion.'

Kit narrowed his eyes. 'You enjoy this, don't you? You're like a cat playing with a mouse. You allow me so much freedom and then haul me back in. Is that why you've waited so long to see me?'

'I wouldn't want you to be in any doubt about your position, Captain Lovell. If you don't care for the life I allow you, there is always an alternative!' Thurloe leaned forward. 'Now pay your dues! What do you know about a committee sanctioned by Charles Stuart?'

Long practice prevented Kit's face from betraying his surprise. His eyes widened. 'Another committee?'

Thurloe sat back in his chair. 'Don't play the innocent with me, Lovell. Do I need to remind you of the reason you work for me?'

Kit's mouth tightened and he leaned forward. 'Thurloe, our arrangement is at an end. I gave you the girl. I have given you Dutton and the others. You cannot ask any more of me.'

'An overwrought woman and a pack of fools? Hardly the stuff

to unsettle the Commonwealth,' Thurloe sneered. 'And in the meantime, you have been more than a drain on the purse, Captain Lovell. May I remind you how much it cost to settle your debts and get you out of the Clink over that matter of the horse?'

'A gentleman must maintain his standards, Thurloe.' A sardonic smile lifted the corners of Kit's mouth.

'A gentleman of no means must learn to lower his standards,' Thurloe rejoined. 'Now tell me what you know.'

Kit looked down at his right hand. He had gripped the arm of the chair so hard the knuckles showed white. 'All I know is that there is a new committee that holds a commission from the King to organise a general insurrection.'

'The Sealed Knot?'

Kit blinked in surprise. 'You know about them?'

'I know they call themselves the Sealed Knot. Now tell me something I don't know.'

Sudden anger flared in Kit's eyes. 'If you already know about it, then why ask me?'

Thurloe held up his hand. 'I know what it is. What I need to know is who is involved and what they plan. I want names.'

Kit took a breath. 'I don't have names. There are too few of them and they are playing it close.'

'You're lying.'

Kit spread his hands, the chains rattling. 'God's death! I can't tell you what I don't know! What are you going to do – employ some other means of persuasion on me?'

Thurloe sat back in his chair, his gaze on Kit's face.

'I don't need to, Lovell. If you don't know any more than you're telling, the effort will be wasted, and I know you have good enough reason not to withhold information. I'm sure you'll tell me as soon as you have anything useful.' He paused, his eyes narrowing, 'And as for our arrangement, Captain Lovell, I assure you I intend to keep my word when I am satisfied that you have outlived your use to me.'

'Your use of words is hardly subtle, Thurloe.' Kit smiled bitterly.

'It's not intended to be,' Thurloe snapped. 'If not for me you would have swung on a gibbet long before this or died, forgotten, in some prison. If you don't like "outlive", well then, maybe when I am satisfied that there is no more to be usefully gained by your employment. Now think again. Names, Lovell.'

'Maybe Richard Willys,' Kit said in a low, sullen voice.

Thurloe picked up his pen and began smoothing the feathers. 'Willys? Yes, that would make sense, but there must be others, bigger fish than Willys.' He broke off from his musings and looked at Kit. 'What about Fitzjames?'

Kit's lips tightened and his guts clenched. 'If Fitzjames is involved with the Sealed Knot, it is only on the edge,' he said. 'Willys is your man.'

Thurloe's eyes narrowed. 'Then work on Fitzjames, use your friendship with him. I don't have to tell you how to do your job, Lovell.'

Kit felt the bile rise to his throat. 'No,' he replied shortly. 'You don't have to tell me.'

'We have dealt neatly with this one pathetic plot, but I believe that this Sealed Knot poses a much bigger threat. As you surmise, there is an element of organisation to it I have not seen since Charles Stuart attempted to reclaim his throne in '51. If indeed they carry his commission then that is a matter of grave concern. I need to know who is involved and what they plan. I also want to know if the French are involved.'

'The French?' Kit raised an eyebrow.

'You're probably aware that England stands in a precarious position with the French and the Spanish. I would not be surprised if the French use a little civil unrest here in England to sway Spain's sympathies. We have a new envoy from Mazarin here in London. The Baron de Baas.' Thurloe paused, raising his eyebrows in uncharacteristic distaste at the mention of the name. 'De Baas has a very high opinion of himself and he is not a man I trust. The French Ambassador, Bordeaux, seems unhappy at Baas' presence but appears powerless to do anything about it, which is what makes me think de Baas has a specific commission from Mazarin.'

'I have had no dealings with this man nor heard the name mentioned,' Kit responded. 'What do you expect me to do?'

Thurloe paused and leaned forward on his elbows, his interlaced fingers supporting his chin. 'Exactly what you do so well, Captain Lovell. Play dice and cards and get your friends appallingly drunk.'

Kit looked affronted. 'Thurloe, I thought you had a better opinion of me than that.'

'Let me remind you, my friend, that I have a full accounting of your debts, so I know exactly what it is that you do. Now, are we clear, Lovell? I want to know who and what your friends in the Sealed Knot are up to and I want to know what game the Baron de Baas is playing.'

Kit raised his eyes to the ceiling for a moment, bringing his gaze back to meet the eyes of the Secretary of State. 'If this plot is serious, I could be a dead man, Thurloe.'

'You're a survivor, Lovell, and you and I both know that you have a good reason to ensure that you stay healthy.'

'God damn you to Hell, Thurloe.' Kit couldn't hide the bitterness in his voice.

'I shall be in good company. You may go, Captain Lovell.'

Kit stood and turned for the door. As an afterthought, he stopped and looked back. 'The girl … '

Thurloe blinked. 'What girl?'

'Thamsine Granville.'

'What about her?'

'What do you know about her?'

Thurloe shrugged.

'She says she's from Hampshire – Hartley Court. Father dead, dispossessed and reduced to penury on the streets of London. Why? What interest do you have in her?'

None, Kit told himself. However, he needed to assuage his guilt. He had been the one to send her to the Tower. She had been a useful pawn in this ongoing game of chess with John Thurloe.

Kit shook his head. 'What are you going to do with her?'

'What would you like me to do with her?'

'Let her go, Thurloe,' Kit said.

'Now, why should I do that? She has admitted her guilt.'

'Are you going to try her?'

'Not my decision.' Thurloe shrugged.

'I'm not a fool, Thurloe. The Council will make whatever decision you recommend.'

'The Lord Protector is ill-disposed to women who throw brickbats at his coach.'

'She's not a conspirator, Thurloe, just a woman at the end of her means. Let her go.' He paused, casting around for reasons to undo the damage he had done. 'She's an intelligent woman and she could be useful.'

'To you or to me?'

Kit shrugged. 'Let her go, Thurloe, and we'll see.'

Thurloe considered him for a moment. 'I agree, she is an intelligent woman, Lovell. Does she have any particular skills that may be of use?'

Kit frowned. 'She speaks fluent French and appears to be a relatively accomplished musician.'

Thurloe straightened. 'She speaks French?'

'As well as I do.'

'And a musician as well. A good one?'

Kit shrugged. 'She has had the benefit of a good education, and she sings well.'

'Ah yes, I've heard about her talents in the taproom. Perhaps we could reconsider Mistress Granville's fate.' Thurloe's lips twitched into what may have been considered by some a smile. 'In fact, now I think on it, I have a task ideally suited to a woman of her talents.'

Kit stared at his master. 'She doesn't know that I ... '

'Betrayed her? No. I'm sure she still thinks of you as her saviour and friend.'

'Then shall we leave it that way?'

Thurloe shrugged. 'She is bound to find out one day,' he said.

'Can I see her?' Kit asked.

'Dear me, Captain Lovell, if I'm not mistaken I detect a soft spot for Mistress Granville. A dangerous weakness in the game you play.'

Kit narrowed his eyes. 'I assure you I have no weakness as regards Mistress Granville. I think she can be useful, that's all. It is surely in both our interests for her to continue to trust me.'

'If you say so.' Thurloe waved a hand. 'Oh, very well, you can go and play comforter to her if you wish.'

'An accidental meeting, Thurloe?'

Thurloe nodded. 'It can be arranged.'

]

CHAPTER 8

*N*othing could have prepared Thamsine for the insufferable boredom of imprisonment. She had counted every stone in the walls of her cell and spent the long hours lying on her cot composing melodies in her head. Her dwindling supply of coins did not run to the luxury of pen and paper.

She was deeply absorbed in a reworking of a familiar piece for the lute when her door opened with a thud.

'You've visitors,' the turnkey said with a suitable amount of surprise in his voice.

Thamsine rose to her feet and smoothed her rumpled skirts. She could think of no one who would be visiting her other than that awful man, Thurloe, and she had no wish to see him again.

'Well, well, Lady Muck, this is quite a comedown, ain't it?'

The shock of seeing Nan Marsh caused Thamsine to take two steps backward. She tripped over the stool and fell back onto the narrow, flea-infested cot.

Nan stood at the door, looking around her with a faintly

bemused air. 'So this is the Tower of London? I thought they'd throw you in a dungeon. You did all right for yourself.'

Thamsine buried her head in her hands. 'Nan, what are you doing here?'

'I thought a pleasant stroll in the Tower of London – what a stupid question!'

'Hello, Thamsine.' May's head appeared around the door.

Thamsine stared at them both in disbelief, as Nan set a basket down on the table with a thump and began unpacking it.

'May and I reckons you might need a few things: clean linen, stockings, cloak, petticoat and bodice. Comb. Candle, tinder, a flagon of wine and one of me pies, some bread and cheese and most importantly … ' There was a jangle of coins as a purse landed on the bed beside Thamsine. 'That's your earnings from t'other night. Jem was right peeved when those soldiers took you away. Thought you was a nice little earner.'

Thamsine stared at the girls. Nothing in their short acquaintance had given any indication of friendship.

'You didn't have to do this,' she said.

Nan's lip curled. 'Nah, ye're right. No one made us do it but after all the bother you caused us, we had a bit of an investment in you.'

'Did you really hurl a brickbat at the Lord Protector?' May asked

Thamsine nodded.

'Why d'ya go and do a stupid thing like that?' Nan demanded.

Thamsine looked from one twin to the other.

'I needed a diversion,' she said. 'I didn't stop to think what I was doing.'

'A diversion? What from?' Nan looked incredulous. 'Come on, Thamsine. I reckons you owe us your story.'

Thamsine shrugged. There seemed little point in keeping her silence.

'I ran away from a man,' she said. 'A man who wanted to marry me.'

'Well that's not such a bad thing, in't it? I wish there was someone who wanted to marry me,' May said.

'Not like this man. He is violent and vicious and his motives for wanting to marry me have nothing to do with love and everything to do with money.'

'Oh, so you have money then?' Nan's eyes narrowed. 'Could've fooled me.'

Thamsine gave a bitter laugh. 'Yes, but when I marry it goes to my husband and until I marry it is controlled by my guardian, who is the same man who thinks he has a right to marry me.'

'Same man?'

Thamsine nodded.

May shook her head. 'Sometimes I reckon it's best to be poor, then if a man marries you, you can think it's coz he likes you ... ' she sighed, '... or coz he got you in the family way.'

'So what happened?' Nan put in over her sister's musings.

'He ... treated me badly.'

May's eyes widened. 'He didn't ...?'

Thamsine grimaced as she took the girl's meaning. Of course, he had tried. It had only been the chance intervention of another that had prevented it.

'He is capable of that and worse. He thought he could force me into marriage with him,' she said

'How d'ya get away?'

Thamsine swallowed, the memory of that terrible night as vivid as if it had only just occurred. 'I shot him. I thought I'd killed him. I ran away to London to hide.'

'You didn't kill 'im?'

Thamsine shook her head. 'No. I know I didn't kill him and he's here in London looking for me.'

'How'd you know that?'

'I saw him in the crowd that day. That's why I threw the brickbat. If I hadn't, he would have caught me and then ... and then ... ' An unimaginable fate, far worse than her present predicament, loomed before her. At least he couldn't find her while she was incarcerated in the Tower.

May put an arm around her shoulders and hugged her.

'Well I reckon you had as good a reason as any for throwing brickbats at Cromwell,' she said. 'Have you told 'em why you did it?'

Thamsine shook her head. 'I can't,' she said. 'I would rather hang than go back to that man.'

'Are they going to hang you?' Nan asked.

'I don't know. I had a meeting with an awful man called John Thurloe. I think whatever happens to me will be his decision.' She sighed and changed the subject. 'Is there any news of Kit Lovell and the others?'

Nan shook her head. 'Nah. I feel quite sorry for poor old Noll Cromwell. Everyone seems to be trying to do him in. I tell you having half your patrons hauled away by the poll heads is not good for business. Jem's threatening death if he finds who squealed on 'em.'

'Where's your brother's loyalties?' Thamsine asked.

Nan was silent for a moment. 'D'ya mean was it Jem what squealed on yer all? You can put that thought away. Jem is dead loyal to the King. Always has been, always will be. Mind you, another week like this and my betting is they'll find some way to shut him down. He don't need Cromwell's soldiers tramping around arresting his customers. Now you need to eat that pie before it goes stone cold.'

Thamsine sat down on the stool and attacked the pie with relish. A week of the cold, gelatinous gruel the turnkey dished up was enough to have reduced her to a state of semi-starvation again. Nan wandered around the cell, perusing it as if it were a possible apartment to purchase.

May sat on the cot. 'One blanket? Cold enough in 'ere to freeze your tits off. If we can get in again, we'll bring yer another blanket.'

'So how'd you come to know Kit Lovell?' Nan asked. 'I never believed the "old friend of me brother" story you both span.'

Thamsine looked up from the pie. 'The truth is he pulled me out of the crowd that day I threw the brickbat.'

'You never knew 'im before?'

Thamsine shook her head.

The sisters exchanged glances.

'We thought you was sweet on him or summat,' May said

Thamsine forced a laugh. 'Me? Sweet on Kit Lovell? What about you?'

To her surprise, Nan flushed. 'Hard not to be a little sweet on him, I admit it, but he's well set with that widow up in Holborn!' She shrugged. 'Anyway, he's not for the likes of May or I.'

There was the sound of heavy footsteps in the corridor outside. The turnkey appeared in the doorway like an avenging angel.

'Time's up. Out!' He jerked a thumb at Nan.

Thamsine rose to her feet and embraced both the girls.

'Thank you for coming. You're better friends than I deserve.'

Nan patted her shoulder and broke the embrace.

'That's enough of that. Don't need you getting all sentimental on me. I just does me bit, that's all.'

At the door, she stopped. 'It'll all be right in the end, Thamsine.

You see if it isn't and if they lets you out, there's a place for you at the Ship.'

Thamsine forced a smile. 'I wish I had your optimism, Nan.'

Nan shook her head. 'You be sure to guard that purse well. Turnkeys like this bastard are just as likely to sneak in while you are asleep and steal it.' She gave the turnkey a foul look.

The door closed heavily behind the girls and an overwhelming sense of loneliness washed over Thamsine. She carefully packed away the provender that Nan had brought and counted the coins. Not enough to sustain her for more than a few more days. She sighed and lay down on the cot with her arms behind her head, forcing her mind to return to the lute melody.

'COLONEL BARKSTEAD SAYS, seeing as it's a fine day, you can take a turn on the walls,' the turnkey said, holding the door open for Thamsine.

Since the twins' visit, the walls of her cell had closed in around her, and the chance to walk on the walls and stretch her legs and her lungs was one she seized with alacrity.

Thamsine wrapped her cloak tighter around her as the cold wind blew in a gust off the river and turned her face to it, taking a deep, thankful breath. From her narrow walkway, she could see down into the inner and outer courtyards of the Tower.

In the outer courtyards, children played while women stood and gossiped, babies or baskets of washing on their hips. Watching them gave her a feeling of normality. No one paid any heed to the prisoner on the wall above them.

A cheerful whistling diverted her attention to the inner court-yard. A prisoner, accompanied by a solitary guard, came through the gate. Despite being hampered by the wrist and leg irons, he still managed a familiar swagger.

'Lovell!' She had yelled his name before she knew what she was saying.

He stopped whistling and looked up.

'Thamsine Granville, as I live and breathe! "Ill met by moonlight, proud Titania".' He managed a clumsy bow, cut short as his escort hauled at his chains.

Kit lowered his head to speak to the man. The soldier shrugged and stepped back. Kit walked over to the wall and looked up at Thamsine. She crouched, looking down into his dirty, bruised, unshaven face.

Despite the ten yards of wall that lay between them, he grinned and spread his hands as wide as the manacles would let him.

'Here we are, Thamsine. Still alive. Are they treating you well?'

She shrugged. 'I suppose as well as could be expected in the circumstances.' She managed a small smile. 'But Nan Marsh has looked after me.'

'Nan?' Kit's eyebrows rose in surprise.

'Yes, she and May brought me a basket of food and some clean clothes.'

'I told you she had a big heart.'

'And I take back my comment about the widest legs. What about you?'

Kit shook his head and shrugged. 'They'll play with us for a while. Maybe put a couple on trial but who knows … ?' He shrugged. 'I have learned to have no expectations.'

The soldier put his hand on Kit's shoulders. 'Time's up! Don't want you getting too friendly, unless you're willin' to pay for the privilege. No? Then say your farewells.'

Kit stayed put, his eyes resting on Thamsine's face.

'Take care, Thamsine.'

He smiled at her as the soldier's grip tightened and he turned Kit, propelling him in the direction of one of the round towers.

'Kit?' she called after him.

He stopped and turned back.

She spoke in French, not wishing the guard to understand her. 'What will become of us?'

His eyes held hers, his face unreadable, and he replied in French, 'Take each day as it comes, Thamsine, and if you believe in God, pray for us both.'

The soldier gave him a shove and Kit stumbled, hampered by the chains. He exchanged some sharp words with his escort that Thamsine could not quite make out. She watched until he had been swallowed up by the dark mouth of the Tower, then sank onto the damp stones with her back to the wall, hugging her knees to her chest. She lowered her head and for the first time in her weeks of incarceration, she wept.

'Dry your tears, Mistress Granville.' The hard voice of Barkstead made her look up. He stood looking down at her, his hands on his hips. 'Master Thurloe wishes to speak with you.'

The room overlooking the Thames was just as she remembered it and would remember it until her dying day. This time John Thurloe was alone and she was not manacled. She dropped a respectful curtsey, which he acknowledged with an inclination of his head.

'Imprisonment has taught you some manners, Mistress Granville. Take a seat.' He gestured at the same oak chair she had sat in last time. As she settled herself, he sat back in his chair and considered her. 'You will be relieved to know that the Lord Protector has reviewed your case and has decided that no further action is to be taken against you. You will be released at the conclusion of this interview.'

Thamsine raised her eyes and looked up at the Secretary of State. She could feel the relief flooding her body.

'Oh thank you!'

'Don't thank me, Mistress Granville. There are conditions attached.'

'Anything.' Anything would be better than another day, another hour in the Tower of London.

'You must repay the damage to the coach.'

Panic arose like a gorge in her throat as the walls closed in on her once more.

'I have no money. I have nothing.'

'I am aware of your circumstances, Mistress Granville.' He pressed his fingers together. 'The debt can be repaid through means other than money.'

She paled, her mind turning over the possibilities, none of them good. 'What do you mean?'

Thurloe regarded her with hooded eyes. 'I mean, Mistress Granville, that you are now indebted to the Commonwealth and that debt may be called in at any time.' He paused, his lips twitching in a smile. Thamsine sensed that he took some pleasure from her paling face. 'However,' he continued, 'I think I may have a solution to this dilemma. A means by which the debt can be repaid that I am sure you will find acceptable.'

'What do you want me to do?'

Thurloe pressed his fingertips together. 'I believe you have some talent with music, Mistress Granville.'

'Some,' conceded Thamsine. 'Although lately it has been confined to singing bawdy songs in an inn.'

'Do you play the lute?'

She nodded. 'And the virginals.'

'Excellent.' Thurloe smiled. 'In fact, it couldn't be better.'

Thamsine shifted in her chair. Thurloe's smile was unsettling.

'You will be happy to know I have some useful employment for you.'

'Doing what?'

'Doing what you do best. Teaching music, Mistress Granville. Would that present a problem?'

Thamsine shook her head in amazement at this extraordinary turn in her fortunes. She had expected a pronouncement of death, not the offer of freedom and useful employment.

'Who?' She could barely aspirate the word.

'The French Ambassador, Baron Bordeaux, has a pretty English mistress, Mary Skippon. He is anxious for Mistress Skippon to improve her accomplishments and has been looking for a suitable music teacher. He will pay handsomely, I do not doubt.'

Thamsine frowned. 'And you wish me to teach this woman music?'

'Singing, lute and virginals. Three mornings a week.'

'And my remuneration will go to the repair of the coach?'

'Oh no. What you do with your coin is your concern. I imagine food and lodging would be something of a priority.' Thurloe leaned forward. 'No, all I ask of you, Mistress Granville, is to keep your ears and eyes open. You speak French?'

Thamsine nodded.

'You speak it well?'

'Very well.'

'Then you are to act as if you don't. If they believe you do not understand what is being said, things may be said in your presence that would normally be kept behind closed doors.'

Thamsine's eyes widened as the implications of what he was saying dawned on her. 'You want me to be a spy for you?'

He flinched. 'I prefer the word *agent*.'

'What do you want to know?'

Thurloe shrugged. 'Anything that you think may be of interest. Any mention of Charles Stuart, for example. I am particularly interested in a man called Baron de Baas. Indeed, if an opportunity arises, it would be helpful if you were to befriend the good Baron.'

'You expect a lot of me.'

'The Baron likes a pretty face, and … ' Thurloe regarded her with his head cocked on one side ' … clean and in a decent gown I am sure you would be quite presentable.'

'Thank you,' Thamsine replied in a voice heavy with sarcasm. 'How friendly am I expected to be?'

If Thurloe detected the edge of sarcasm in her voice, he chose to ignore it. 'That is entirely up to you, Mistress Granville. Now, do I have your agreement to this proposal?'

'Do I have a choice?'

Thurloe's hooded eyes considered her from over the top of his steepled fingers. 'You always have choices, Mistress Granville. The alternative is to spend the next few years in the Tower. Now, do I have your agreement? Your debt to the Commonwealth stands, and my next offer may not be quite so agreeable.'

Thamsine looked up at the intricate knots in the plasterwork on the ceiling. He had her trapped and he knew it. She gave a small shrug of her right shoulder.

'Very well. When do I start?'

'Baron Bordeaux will expect you the day after tomorrow at ten in the morning at his residence. You have been recommended to him by my wife, Dame Elizabeth Thurloe, should the question arise. You have been instructing her in music for the last six months.'

Thamsine blinked. 'I have?'

'And she is most satisfied.'

'I am pleased to hear it.'

'Of course, I would only employ the best tutor for my wife, and she has written you a letter of recommendation. Now one last thing.' Thurloe pushed a small purse across the table. 'That should be sufficient to purchase some respectable clothes more suitable to your genteel station in life, Mistress Granville.'

Thamsine's fingers closed over the purse, feeling the hard edges of the coin through the soft leather.

'There is also the question of your lodging,' Thurloe continued. 'I would advise you not to return to the Ship Inn. Apart from the fact that singing bawdy songs in a tavern is hardly suitable employment for a lady, the inn is a den of known malignants and is not, I suggest, a sensible place for you to be. Seek respectable lodgings, Mistress Granville.' Thurloe pushed a paper over to her. 'Now sign this acknowledgement and you're free.'

Thamsine picked up the pen he proffered and stared at the paper, a short, concise acknowledgement of debt, omitting any reference as to how the debt was to be repaid. She signed her name. She was now in the employment of the man she had tried to kill. The world turned in a strange manner.

'How do I inform you of any information I acquire?'

'I will provide you with a contact. He will make himself known to you soon enough. You and I should have no reason to meet again. I will expect at least a weekly report, even if there is nothing of apparent interest.'

Thamsine looked down at the purse in her hand. 'And this money?'

'Repayable in six months. An interest-free loan.' Thurloe was no longer looking at her, his face hidden behind a large paper. 'Now, good day to you, Mistress Granville.'

Thamsine rose and turned to leave. She had almost reached the door when she hesitated, swivelling to look back at John Thurloe.

'Master Thurloe, what is to become of Captain Lovell?'

He set down the paper and stared at her, unblinking.

'Captain Lovell's fate is no concern of yours. Now go, before you try my patience.'

The last few steps to the door were accomplished in quick time. She shut the door behind her and found the Lieutenant of the Tower waiting for her. He thrust a bundle at her.

'Your belongings, Mistress. The Lord Protector must be feeling in a particularly generous mood today. Follow me.'

Clutching her bundle to her chest, she followed the Lieutenant through the gates, taking in all the details that had been lost on her when she had arrived.

It had been snowing and the snow lay in drifts against the grey walls. Thamsine shivered as the cold wind off the river bit through her inadequate clothes as she waited for the heavy gate to be opened. Barkstead took her by the arm and thrust her out onto the bridge across the foetid moat.

'If you've any sense in your head, young woman, you won't be back again,' he said.

As the gates closed behind her, Thamsine set down her bundle and stretched out her arms, taking a deep breath. Much as she had hated it, freedom was now as precious to her as her own life had been. As she began to walk through the narrow streets, she contemplated the strange twist of fate.

I am merely a music teacher, she told herself, *with a penchant for gossip. That's all I am. Not a spy, not an agent.* She felt the comforting weight of the coins in her purse and smiled. Maybe there were worse things in life to be than an agent for John Thurloe, at least for the moment.

CHAPTER 9

$\mathcal{N}$othing could have prepared Thamsine for the insufferable boredom of imprisonment. She had counted every stone in the walls of her cell and spent the long hours lying on her cot composing melodies in her head. Her dwindling supply of coin did not run to the luxury of pen and paper.

She was deeply absorbed in a reworking of a familiar piece for the lute when her door opened with a thud.

'You've visitors,' the turnkey said with a suitable amount of surprise in his voice.

Thamsine rose to her feet and smoothed her rumpled skirts. She could think of no one who would be visiting her other than that awful man, Thurloe, and she had no wish to see him again.

'Well, well, Lady Muck, this is quite a comedown, ain't it?'

The shock of seeing Nan Marsh caused Thamsine to take two steps backward. She tripped over the stool and fell back onto the narrow, flea-infested cot.

Nan stood at the door, looking around her with a faintly

bemused air. 'So this is the Tower of London? I thought they'd throw you in a dungeon. You done all right for yourself.'

Thamsine buried her head in her hands. 'Nan, what are you doing here?'

'I thought a pleasant stroll in the Tower of London – what a stupid question!'

'Hello, Thamsine.' May's head appeared around the door.

Thamsine stared at them both in disbelief, as Nan set a basket down on the table with a thump and began unpacking it.

'May and I reckons you might need a few things: clean linen, stockings, cloak, petticoat and bodice. Comb. Candle, tinder, flagon of wine and one of me pies, some bread and cheese and most importantly … ' There was a jangle of coins as a purse landed on the bed beside Thamsine. 'That's your earnings from t'other night. Jem was right peeved when those soldiers took you away. Thought you was a nice little earner.'

Thamsine stared at the girls. Nothing in their short acquaintance had given any indication of friendship.

'You didn't have to do this,' she said.

Nan's lip curled. 'Nah, ye're right. No one made us do it but after all the bother you caused us, we had a bit of an investment in you.'

'Did you really hurl a brickbat at the Lord Protector?' May asked

Thamsine nodded.

'Why d'ya go and do a stupid thing like that?' Nan demanded.

Thamsine looked from one twin to the other.

'I needed a diversion,' she said. 'I didn't stop to think what I was really doing.'

'A diversion? What from?' Nan looked incredulous. 'Come on, Thamsine. I reckons you owe us your story.'

Thamsine shrugged. There seemed little point in keeping her silence.

'I ran away from a man,' she said. 'A man who wanted to marry me.'

'Well that's not such a bad thing, in't it? I wish there was someone who wanted to marry me,' May said.

'Not like this man. He is violent and vicious and his motives for wanting to marry me have nothing to do with love and everything to do with money.'

'Oh, so you have money then?' Nan's eyes narrowed. 'Could've fooled me.'

Thamsine gave a bitter laugh. 'Yes, but when I marry it goes to my husband and until I marry it is controlled by my guardian, who is the same man who thinks he has a right to marry me.'

'Same man?'

Thamsine nodded.

May shook her head. 'Sometimes I reckon it's best to be poor, then if a man marries you, you can think it's coz he likes you ... ' she sighed, ' ... or coz he got you in the family way.'

'So what happened?' Nan put in over her sister's musings.

'He ... treated me badly.'

May's eyes widened. 'He didn't ... ?'

Thamsine grimaced as she took the girl's meaning. Of course he had tried. It had only been the chance intervention of another that had prevented it.

'He is capable of that and worse. He thought he could force me into marriage with him,' she said

'How d'ya get away?'

Thamsine swallowed, the memory of that terrible night as vivid as if it had only just occurred. 'I shot him. I thought I'd killed him. I ran away to London to hide.'

'You didn't kill 'im?'

Thamsine shook her head. 'No. I know I didn't kill him and he's here in London looking for me.'

'How'd you know that?'

'I saw him in the crowd that day. That's why I threw the brick-bat. If I hadn't, he would have caught me and then … and then … ' An unimaginable fate, far worse than her present predicament, loomed before her. At least he couldn't find her while she was incarcerated in the Tower.

May put an arm around her shoulders and hugged her.

'Well I reckon you had as good a reason as any for throwing brickbats at Cromwell,' she said. 'Have you told 'em why you did it?'

Thamsine shook her head. 'I can't,' she said. 'I would rather hang than go back to that man.'

'Are they going to hang you?' Nan asked.

'I don't know. I had a meeting with a really frightening man called John Thurloe. I think whatever happens to me will be his decision.' She sighed, and changed the subject. 'Is there any news of Kit Lovell and the others?'

Nan shook her head. 'Nah. I feel quite sorry for poor old Noll Cromwell. Everyone seems to be trying to do him in. I tell you having half your patrons hauled away by the poll heads is not good for business. Jem's threatening death if he finds who squealed on 'em.'

'Where's your brother's loyalties?' Thamsine asked.

Nan was silent for a moment. 'D'ya mean was it Jem what squealed on yer all? You can put that thought away. Jem is dead loyal to the King. Always has been, always will be. Mind you, another week like this and my betting is they'll find some way to shut him down. He don't need Cromwell's soldiers tramping around arresting his customers. Now you need to eat that pie before it goes stone cold.'

Thamsine sat down on the stool and attacked the pie with relish. A week of the cold, gelatinous gruel the turnkey dished up was enough to have reduced her to a state of semi-starvation again. Nan wandered around the cell, perusing it as if it were a possible apartment to purchase.

May sat on the cot. 'One blanket? Cold enough in 'ere to freeze your tits off. If we can get in again, we'll bring yer another blanket.'

'So how'd you come to know Kit Lovell?' Nan asked. 'I never bought the "old friend of me brother" story.'

Thamsine looked up from the pie. 'The truth is he pulled me out of the crowd that day I threw the brickbat.'

'You never knew 'im before?'

Thamsine shook her head.

The sisters exchanged glances.

'We thought you was sweet on him or summat,' May said

Thamsine forced a laugh. 'Me? Sweet on Kit Lovell? What about you?'

To her surprise, Nan flushed. 'Hard not to be a little sweet on him, I admit it, but he's well set with that widow up in Holborn!' She shrugged. 'Anyway, he's not for the likes of May or I.'

There was the sound of heavy footsteps in the corridor outside. The turnkey appeared in the doorway like an avenging angel.

'Time's up. Out!' He jerked a thumb at Nan.

Thamsine rose to her feet and embraced both the girls.

'Thank you for coming. You're better friends than I deserve.'

Nan patted her shoulder and broke the embrace.

'That's enough of that. Don't need you getting all sentimental on me. I just does me bit that's all.'

At the door she stopped. 'It'll all be right in the end, Thamsine.

You see if it isn't and if they lets you out, there's a place for you at the Ship.'

Thamsine forced a smile. 'I wish I had your optimism, Nan.'

Nan shook her head. 'You be sure to guard that purse well. Turnkeys like this bastard are just as likely to sneak in while you are asleep and steal it.' She gave the turnkey a foul look.

The door closed heavily behind the girls and an overwhelming sense of loneliness washed over Thamsine. She carefully packed away the provender that Nan had brought and counted the coins. Only enough to sustain her for a few more days.

She sighed and lay down on the cot with her arms behind her head, forcing her mind to return to the lute melody.

∿

'COLONEL BARKSTEAD SAYS, seeing as it's a fine day, you can take a turn on the walls,' the turnkey said, holding the door open for Thamsine.

Since the twins' visit, the walls of her cell had closed in around her, and the chance to walk on the walls and stretch her legs and her lungs was one she seized with alacrity.

Thamsine wrapped her cloak tighter around her as the cold wind blew in a gust off the river and turned her face to it, taking a deep, thankful breath. From her narrow walkway she could see down into the inner and outer courtyards of the Tower.

In the outer courtyards, children played while women stood and gossiped, babies or baskets of washing on their hips. Watching them gave her a feeling of normality. No one paid any heed to the prisoner on the wall above them.

A cheerful whistling diverted her attention to the inner courtyard. A prisoner, accompanied by a solitary guard, came through the gate. Despite being hampered by wrist and leg irons, he still managed a familiar swagger.

'Lovell!' She had yelled his name before she knew what she was saying.

He stopped whistling and looked up.

'Thamsine Granville, as I live and breathe! "Ill met by moonlight, proud Titania".' He managed a clumsy bow, cut short as his escort hauled at his chains.

Kit lowered his head to speak to the man. The soldier shrugged and stepped back. Kit walked over to the wall and looked up at Thamsine. She crouched, looking down into his dirty, bruised, unshaven face.

Despite the ten yards of wall that lay between them, he grinned and spread his hands as wide as the manacles would let him.

'Here we are, Thamsine. Still alive. Are they treating you well?'

She shrugged. 'I suppose as well as could be expected in the circumstances.' She managed a small smile. 'But Nan Marsh has looked after me.'

'Nan?' Kit's eyebrows rose in surprise.

'Yes, she and May brought me a basket of food and some clean clothes.'

'I told you she had a big heart.'

'And I take back my comment about the widest legs. What about you?'

Kit shook his head and shrugged. 'They'll play with us for a while. Maybe put a couple on trial but who knows … ?' He shrugged. 'I have learned to have no expectations.'

The soldier put his hand on Kit's shoulders. 'Time's up! Don't want you getting too friendly, unless you're willin' to pay for the privilege. No? Then say your farewells.'

Kit stayed put, his eyes resting on Thamsine's face.

'Take care, Thamsine.'

He smiled at her as the soldier's grip tightened and he turned Kit, propelling him in the direction of one of the round towers.

'Kit?' she called after him.

He stopped and turned back.

She spoke in French, not wishing the guard to understand her. 'What will become of us?'

His eyes held hers, his face unreadable, and he replied in French, 'Take each day as it comes, Thamsine, and if you believe in God, pray for us both.'

The soldier gave him a shove and Kit stumbled, hampered by the chains. He exchanged some sharp words with his escort that Thamsine could not quite make out. She watched until he had been swallowed up by the dark mouth of the Tower, then sank down on the damp stones with her back to the wall, hugging her knees to her chest. She lowered her head and for the first time in her weeks of incarceration, she wept.

'Dry your tears, Mistress Granville.' The hard voice of Barkstead made her look up. He stood looking down at her, his hands on his hips. 'Master Thurloe wishes to speak with you.'

The room overlooking the Thames was just as she remembered it and would remember it until her dying day. This time John Thurloe was alone and she was not manacled. She dropped a respectful curtsey, which he acknowledged with an inclination of his head.

'Imprisonment has taught you some manners, Mistress Granville. Take a seat.' He gestured at the same oak chair she had sat in last time. As she settled herself, he sat back in his chair and considered her. 'You will be relieved to know that the Lord Protector has reviewed your case and has decided that no further action is to be taken against you. You will be released at the conclusion of this interview.'

Thamsine raised her eyes and looked up at the Secretary of State. She could feel the relief flooding her body.

'Oh thank you!'

'Don't thank me, Mistress Granville. There are conditions attached.'

'Anything.' Anything would be better than another day, another hour in the Tower of London.

'You must repay the damage to the coach.'

Panic arose like a gorge in her throat as the walls closed in on her once more.

'I have no money. I have nothing.'

'I am aware of your circumstances, Mistress Granville.' He pressed his fingers together. 'The debt is one that can be repaid through means other than money.'

She paled, her mind turning over the possibilities, none of them good. 'What do you mean?'

Thurloe regarded her with hooded eyes. 'I mean, Mistress Granville, that you are now indebted to the Commonwealth and that debt may be called in at any time.' He paused, his lips twitching in a smile. Thamsine sensed that he took some pleasure from her paling face. 'However,' he continued, 'I think I may have a solution to this dilemma. A means by which the debt can be repaid that I am sure you will find acceptable.'

'What do you want me to do?'

Thurloe pressed his fingertips together. 'I believe you have some talent with music.'

'Some,' conceded Thamsine. 'Although lately it has been confined to singing bawdy songs in an inn.'

'Do you play the lute?'

She nodded. 'And the virginals.'

'Excellent.' Thurloe smiled. 'In fact, it couldn't be better.'

Thamsine shifted in her chair. Thurloe's smile was unsettling.

'You will be happy to know I have some useful employment for you.'

'Doing what?'

'Doing what you do best. Teaching music, Mistress Granville. Would that present a problem?'

Thamsine shook her head in amazement at this extraordinary turn in her fortunes. She had expected a pronouncement of death, not the offer of freedom and useful employment.

'Who?' She could barely aspirate the word.

'The French Ambassador, Baron Bordeaux, has a pretty English mistress, Mary Skippon. He is anxious for Mistress Skippon to improve her accomplishments and has been looking for a suitable music teacher. He will pay handsomely, I do not doubt.'

Thamsine frowned. 'And you wish me to teach this woman music?'

'Singing, lute and virginals. Three mornings a week.'

'And my remuneration will go to the repair of the coach?'

'Oh no. What you do with your coin is your concern. I imagine food and lodging would be something of a priority.' Thurloe leaned forward. 'No, all I ask of you, Mistress Granville, is to keep your ears and eyes open. You speak French?'

Thamsine nodded.

'You speak it well?'

'Very well.'

'Then you are to act as if you don't. If they believe you do not understand what is being said, things may be said in your presence that would normally be kept behind closed doors.'

Thamsine's eyes widened as the implications of what he was saying dawned on her. 'You want me to be a spy for you?'

He flinched. 'I prefer the word *agent*.'

'What do you want to know?'

Thurloe shrugged. 'Anything that you think may be of interest. Any mention of Charles Stuart, for example. I am particularly interested in a man called Baron de Baas. Indeed, if an opportunity arises, it would be helpful if you were to befriend the good Baron.'

'You expect a lot of me.'

'The Baron likes a pretty face, and ... ' Thurloe regarded her with his head cocked on one side ' ... clean and in a decent gown I am sure you would be quite presentable.'

'Thank you,' Thamsine replied in a voice heavy with sarcasm. 'How friendly am I expected to be?'

If Thurloe detected the edge of sarcasm in her voice, he chose to ignore it. 'That is entirely up to you, Mistress Granville. Now, do I have your agreement to this proposal?'

'Do I have a choice?'

Thurloe's hooded eyes considered her from over the top of his steepled fingers. 'You always have choices, Mistress Granville. The obvious alternative is to spend the next few years in the Tower. Now, do I have your agreement? Your debt to the Commonwealth stands, and my next offer may not be quite so agreeable.'

Thamsine looked up at the intricate knots in the plasterwork on the ceiling. He had her trapped and he knew it. She gave a small shrug of her right shoulder.

'Very well. When do I start?'

'Baron Bordeaux will expect you the day after tomorrow at ten in the morning at his residence. You have been recommended to him by my wife, Dame Elizabeth Thurloe, should the question arise. You have been instructing her in music for the last six months.'

Thamsine blinked. 'I have?'

'And she is most satisfied.'

'I am pleased to hear it.'

'Of course I would only employ the best tutor for my wife, and she has written you a letter of recommendation. Now one last thing.' Thurloe pushed a small purse across the table. 'That should be sufficient to purchase some respectable clothes more suitable to your genteel station in life, Mistress Granville.'

Thamsine's fingers closed over the purse, feeling the hard edges of the coin through the soft leather.

'There is also the question of your lodging,' Thurloe continued. 'I would advise you not to return to the Ship Inn. Apart from the fact that singing of bawdy songs in a tavern is hardly suitable employment for a lady, the inn is a den of known malignants and is not, I suggest, a sensible place for you to be. Seek respectable lodgings, Mistress Granville.' Thurloe pushed a paper over to her. 'Now sign this acknowledgement and you're free.'

Thamsine picked up the pen he proffered and stared at the paper, a short, concise acknowledgement of debt, omitting any reference as to how the debt was to be repaid. She signed her name.

She was now in the employment of the man she had tried to kill. The world turned in a strange manner.

'How do I inform you of any information I acquire?'

'I will provide you with a contact. He will make himself known to you soon enough. You and I should have no reason to meet again. I will expect at least a weekly report, even if there is nothing of apparent interest.'

Thamsine looked down at the purse in her hand. 'And this money?'

'Repayable in six months. An interest-free loan.' Thurloe was no longer looking at her, his face hidden behind a large paper. 'Now, good day to you, Mistress Granville.'

Thamsine rose and turned to leave. She had almost reached

the door when she hesitated, swivelling to look back at John Thurloe.

'Master Thurloe, what is to become of Captain Lovell?'

He set down the paper and stared at her, unblinking.

'Captain Lovell's fate is no concern of yours. Now go, before you try my patience.'

The last few steps to the door were accomplished in quick time. She shut the door behind her and found the Lieutenant of the Tower waiting for her. He thrust a bundle at her.

'Your belongings, Mistress. The Lord Protector must be feeling in a particularly generous mood today. Follow me.'

Clutching her bundle to her chest, she followed the Lieutenant through the gates, taking in all the details that had been lost on her when she had arrived.

It had been snowing and the snow lay in drifts against the grey walls. Thamsine shivered as the cold wind off the river bit through her inadequate clothes as she waited for the heavy gate to be opened. Barkstead took her by the arm and thrust her out onto the bridge across the foetid moat.

'If you've any sense in your head, young woman, you won't be back again,' he said.

As the gates closed behind her, Thamsine set down her bundle and stretched out her arms, taking a deep breath. Much as she had hated it, freedom was now as precious to her as her own life had been. As she began to walk through the narrow streets, she contemplated the strange twist of fate.

I am merely a music teacher, she told herself, *with a penchant for gossip. That's all I am. Not a spy, not an agent.*

She felt the comforting weight of the coins in her purse and smiled. Maybe there were worse things in life to be than an agent for John Thurloe, at least for the moment.

CHAPTER 10

*D*espite Thurloe's advice, Thamsine returned to The Ship Inn. At the end of the day she had nowhere else to go, and no one who could offer her friendship as the Marshes had done.

She pushed open the door of the quiet taproom. Jem looked up from polishing the pewter mugs and smiled.

'Well, well, let you go, did they?'

She nodded. 'It was a misunderstanding.'

'Of course,' Jem agreed with a knowing wink. 'Looking for your old job, are you?'

Thamsine shook her head and straightened. 'No, I am seeking proper lodgings.'

Jem squinted at her with his one good eye. 'Come into some money, have you?'

Thamsine produced the purse. 'I have secured respectable employment. Now, Master Marsh, a plain, comfortable room is all I need.'

A shriek from the doorway announced May Marsh. 'You're back! Nan, she's back.'

Clasped to May's ample bosom, Thamsine looked over her head at May's twin who gave a cursory nod and a half smile of welcome.

'She's here for lodging. Got herself a proper job, she has. Show Mistress Granville to the small bedchamber,' Jem said, with a low bow.

'Oh!' May released Thamsine and looked up at her. 'Watcha going to be doing?'

'A music tutor in the household of the French Ambassador.'

'Go on!' Nan's voice was disbelieving. 'You get carted off to the Tower, on charges of attempting to do in Old Ironsides no less, and a few weeks later you're released with a job at the Frog Ambassador's?'

Thamsine shrugged. 'That's how it happened. Now I am filthy and stinking and would like a bath. Is such a thing possible?'

The twins looked at each other. 'A bath?' they chorused, as if such an idea had never entered their heads.

'A bath to begin with,' Thamsine said. 'And if I can borrow some respectable petticoats from someone, I must go shopping for new clothes.

THAMSINE SMOOTHED the petticoats of her new green wool gown. A spotless collar and cuffs edged with lace, new shoes that pinched her feet, and a hat and sturdy cloak completed the ensemble. She had tamed her hair within the confines of a neat white cap, and she hoped that she presented a picture of genteel modesty.

Clutching the folio containing some sheet music that she had also purchased the previous day, she knocked on the door of the French Ambassador's house.

Baron Bordeaux greeted her in the parlour.

'Mademoiselle Granville, I am so glad you could come,' he enthused, as if she were an honoured guest, not a prospective employee. 'The Lord Protector spoke most highly of you.'

Thamsine's eyes widened. 'The Lord Protector?'

'Indeed, he said that you had made quite an impression on him at your last meeting.'

Thamsine swallowed. 'Well, I hope that I can live up to the Lord Protector's opinion of me,' she said.

'Now, tell me, do you speak French?'

'I am afraid not,' Thamsine replied.

'It must be something of a problem for you in the rendering of French lyrics, mam'selle,' he observed.

Thamsine flushed. 'I read the words but I am afraid I do not understand the meaning.'

'Well, perhaps we can help with that. A little, how would you say ... "quid pro quo"? As it is, your pupil is English so language will not be a problem. Marie, *ma cherie?*'

He only raised his voice slightly, and a side door opened to admit a slight woman with protruding teeth and freckles. Bordeaux's mistress was not what Thamsine had expected. Thurloe's idea of the "pretty English mistress" was not hers.

Even in a poor light, Mary Skippon would only be described as passably plain. However, Thamsine considered uncharitably, she must be possessed of hidden talents that brought her to the bed of one of the most powerful men in the country.

'Mistress Skippon is most anxious to improve her skills in the lute and the virginals.' Bordeaux indicated a table in the corner of the room where a closed, painted box sat beside a lute. 'Would you be so kind as to give us an example of your work, mademoiselle?'

Thamsine selected a piece of music from her folio and opened the box. A pretty piece, she thought, running an appreciative hand over the bucolic scenes of shepherds and shepherdesses cavorting across the inside of the lid. She spared a thought for her own plain and unadorned virginals, sitting disused at Hartley Court.

It had been a long time since she had played, but her fingers caressed the keys with practised familiarity. She had selected a simple English country air and she sang as she played. Mary Skippon applauded as the last note died away.

'Oh, that was lovely. Do you think I shall play like that, Baron?' She looked up at her lover and he smiled and patted her hand.

'I am sure Mistress Granville will do her very best for you, my dear. We are agreed, Mistress Granville, that you will come on Tuesday, Wednesday and Thursday at ten in the morning and spend two hours in the instruction of Mistress Skippon.'

He named, as Thurloe had said he would, a comfortable fee.

'If Mistress Skippon wishes, we could start instruction immediately,' Thamsine said.

'*Excellente!*' Bordeaux smiled. He had a charming smile beneath the moustache. He picked up Mary Skippon's hand and kissed it. 'Until this evening, *cherie.*'

She giggled and watched as the door closed behind him. 'You are not shocked, Mistress Granville?'

'Why should I be shocked? You are fortunate to have so attentive a man.'

'His wife does not agree,' Mary said with a smile. 'She will be even less than enamoured when she discovers that I am with child.'

As she spoke she placed a hand protectively on her still-flat stomach, her lips curling in a small, tight smile of triumph. An ugly look on the plain face, Thamsine thought.

Thamsine retrieved a piece of music from her folio. 'Now, Mistress Skippon, shall we commence with the lute?'

Mary Skippon had no ear for music. After half an hour, Thamsine tried not to grimace as the girl hit yet another wrong note in the simple air that she was attempting. She wondered, as she gazed out of the window at the wintry sunshine, whether she should have accepted Thurloe's offer with quite such alacrity.

Both women looked up as the door opened to admit a man dressed in what Thamsine could only hazard was the most outrageous of Paris fashion, a red velvet suit covered in silver lace and bows. He gave them both a deep, florid, all-encompassing bow.

'Pardonez-moi,' he said, as he straightened. 'I heard the voice of an angel and just had to see for myself. Mademoiselle Skippon ... '

He crossed to the virginals, where Mary had risen to her feet, her plain face colouring as he took her hand and kissed it.

'Oh, Baron,' she giggled.

'And who is this exquisite creature?' The Baron spoke in English as he turned to Thamsine.

No one had ever described Thamsine as an "exquisite creature" before. She bit her lip and lowered her head as she curtsied to hide the smile.

'Mistress Granville is my new music teacher, Baron,' Mary Skippon said.

The Baron minced towards Thamsine and took her hand, pressing it to his lips.

'Baron de Baas, my dear lady. Why have I not seen you before?' This time he spoke in French.

Thamsine looked blankly at him.

'Mistress Granville does not speak French, Baron,' Mary Skippon explained, speaking French with an appalling accent. She addressed Thamsine in English. 'He asked why he has not seen you before.'

'I am sorry Baron, but I have been in London but a short time,' Thamsine responded in English.

'Ah, an English country rose ... perhaps you will allow me to sing a little duet with dear Mistress Skippon here.' De Baas returned to his heavily accented English.

'Please.' Thamsine held herself in rigid control, resisting the urge to laugh at this absurd creature. What was it about him that so intrigued John Thurloe?

'When did you arrive back in London, Baron?' Mary asked in French.

'Yesterday evening,' he replied, also in French.

Thamsine had to school her face not to display any interest in the conversation. This, she supposed, was the sort of intelligence that Thurloe wanted.

'How was Paris?' Mary continued, ignoring Thamsine.

The Baron rolled his eyes. 'An oasis of civilization compared to this dank country. How I suffer!' He pressed a kerchief to his lips as he raised his eyes heavenwards.

Mary Skippon's lips tightened. 'England is not that bad, surely?' she continued in her atrocious French.

'No, no, of course,' the Baron replied, 'but your English politics are causing much concern at court in Paris.'

'How is that, Baron?'

'The presence of Charles Stuart is an embarrassment. A king with no throne and no money! It is only the generosity of his cousin that keeps him in Paris. God willing, this is a situation that will not continue long.'

'Why do you say that, Baron?' Mary asked ingenuously.

'There are ways of returning your King to his rightful throne.' The Baron smiled. 'But come, Mademoiselle Skippon, we are being impolite to your teacher, who is waiting patiently for us.'

The Baron smiled at Thamsine. 'My apologies, Mademoiselle Granville,' he said in English. 'We have been rude. I see the music you have selected. Perhaps you will allow me to take the lute part?'

De Baas picked up a lute and began to strum with some talent, Thamsine conceded, and indeed he had quite a fine tenor voice.

At the conclusion of the lesson, the Baron lingered as Thamsine collected her music and put away the instruments. As he nattered on about the latest French fashions, Thamsine nodded and made the appropriate noises. As she walked to the door, he intercepted her, seizing her hand and placing it to his lips.

'You are a very talented musician, mademoiselle.'

'You are too kind, Baron.' Thamsine tugged at her hand. 'You are a fine musician yourself.'

He inclined his head. '*Merci*, mademoiselle.'

Thamsine freed her hand. 'Good day to you, Baron.'

He opened the door for her. 'Until next time, *chere* Mademoiselle Granville.'

CHAPTER 11

'No!' Kit brought his manacled hand crashing down on the table.

The pen stand jumped out of its neat alignment with the inkpot. Thurloe calmly restored it to its rightful place.

'You have no choice, Lovell. The girl trusts you.'

'Trusts me? Thurloe, she's no fool. As soon as I reveal my colours, she will work out who put her in the Tower in the first place. What trust will she have in me then?'

'It doesn't matter what she feels about you,' Thurloe replied, the hooded eyes cold. 'She has no more choice in this matter than you.'

Kit ran his hands through his hair, causing the chains to clank. 'Thurloe, she's a friend.'

Thurloe's eyes flashed. 'They're all friends, Lovell, and yet you have no compunction about turning them in. I've told you before, you cannot afford to allow friendships to stand in the way of this business.'

Kit stared at the man, hating him with every fibre of his being. Thurloe rendered him as helpless as a fly struggling in a spider's web. The harder the small creature struggled, the stronger the bonds around it became. It seemed every time he met with John Thurloe another part of his soul became ensnared by the man. He wondered how long it would be before Thurloe's web bound him forever.

Kit's fingers closed over the bag of coins Thurloe pushed across the table, and he strode from the room without another word.

THE FOLLOWING MORNING, Kit lay in Lucy's commodious bed, reflecting that life did have its compensations. With the exception of Dutton and Whitely, who remained incarcerated, the conspirators had been cast out into the dank streets. It would not be long before they reassembled for cards and a continuation of the endless game of trying to restore the King. Kit would go on encouraging them and turning them in.

Thinking of that miserable band of plotters, he sighed. He despised himself, but Thurloe had left him with little option.

Lucy sat at her dressing table, twisting her hair into the complex pattern of ringlets that suited her so well.

'I think we shall go shopping this morning,' she said, 'if you have nothing else to do.'

Kit went through a mental list of things that required doing and found none that were sufficiently pressing as to delay a shopping trip. His wardrobe had been sadly depleted by his recent incarcerations and he had no desire to seek out Thamsine Granville and impart his nasty little secret.

He could already see the hurt and betrayal in her eyes as she realised that the man who had professed to be her friend had only been waiting for the opportunity to turn her over. She would hate him, but nowhere near as much as he hated himself. She could wait.

He rolled over to watch Lucy finish her toilette. He liked the way her small hands tweaked and tugged at her hair, forcing it to her will. Thamsine could learn a trick or two from Mistress Mouse, but then, he reflected, he doubted Lucy's curls would suit Thamsine. The untamed chestnut locks would look ridiculous.

As they stepped out into the cold, damp streets, Kit knew that if he played his cards right and endured Lucy's vacillations, he might end up with some new bit of frippery. While he did not consider himself a fop, he did like to dress well, and with the current state of his purse and his wardrobe, any contributions were gratefully accepted.

He endured Lucy's indecision over a dozen pairs of embroidered gloves and a length of Belgian lace, and a long discussion on the merits of apricot satin over green velvet. She rewarded him for his patience and well-chosen comments with a fine pair of embroidered kid gloves.

As they walked back to High Holborn, Lucy tucked her arm into his. 'It's so nice to have you all to myself for a little while,' she said.

He drew her little hand closer. 'I count myself a very lucky man,' he said, 'to have such an undemanding woman on my arm.'

Lucy gave him a coquettish smile. 'Undemanding, am I? Just wait till we get home, Captain Lovell, and then you will see just how undemanding I can be!'

Kit laughed. The prospect of an afternoon in bed with Lucy stretched ahead of him. Life could be worse.

'Captain Lovell, is it not?' A tall, dark-haired man stepped into their path and bowed, sweeping his hat from his head.

Kit acknowledged the bow. 'Colonel Morton.'

Morton straightened, allowing Kit the first real look at the man's face in daylight. Long, thick, coal-black hair, peppered lightly with grey at the temples, curled to his shoulders, framing an oval face. Kit saw the arrogance in the man's light grey eyes and the twist of his full lips, and felt the hairs on the back of his neck rise. Even if he had not been apprised of Morton's reputation, he knew his type and instinctively disliked it.

Beside him, Lucy stirred as Morton's eyes turned to her.

'Mistress Talbot, Colonel Ambrose Morton.' Kit made the introduction with some reluctance. He did not like the way Morton's gaze slithered over Lucy's small but perfect body, lingering on her heart-shaped face.

'Mistress Talbot, your servant.' Morton lifted Lucy's gloved hand to his lips.

Kit felt a shiver run through Lucy's body, and he put a hand possessively over the small hand that clasped his arm.

'A pleasure, Colonel Morton. Are you and Kit old friends?'

Morton's eyes flicked onto Kit's face. 'Not so much friends perhaps as casual acquaintances, Mistress Talbot. We share the unhappy circumstance of having wasted our youth in pursuit of a losing cause.'

'I am not sure I quite share that sentiment,' Kit demurred.

'Oh come, Lovell, you must admit that it is time to make a fresh start in life. Or do you still hanker after what cannot be?'

Kit stared at the man's handsome, smiling face, unsure of how to answer the question.

Lucy interposed before he could reply. 'Are you staying in London, Colonel?'

He shook his head. 'At the moment I lodge with friends at Turnham Green, Mistress Talbot.'

'Oh, a pretty village,' Lucy exclaimed. 'I know of someone who lives there. Who is your friend?'

'Master Roger Knott. He is a lawyer of some repute. Are you acquainted with him?'

Lucy's face lit up and she withdrew her hand from Kit's arm.

'Oh, I know him well. My late husband used his services as a lawyer, and he has been a great support to me since Martin's death.'

Ambrose raised an eyebrow. 'Ah, so you are Martin Talbot's widow?'

Lucy's head bobbed, the feather in her hat rising and falling. 'Indeed. Did you know my husband?'

Ambrose shook his head. 'No, but I have heard Knott speak of him ... and you.'

Kit shifted his feet. 'Lucy, it's getting late and it's cold ... '

Lucy looked up at him and smiled. 'Of course.' She held out her hand to Morton, curtseying as he bowed over it. 'I bid you a good day, Colonel.'

'And I you, Mistress Talbot.' Morton inclined his head to Kit. 'Lovell.'

Putting his hand under Lucy's elbow, Kit propelled her forward. Only when they were well past Ambrose Morton did he slacken his pace, allowing them both to fall back to an amble. Lucy tucked her hand into the crook of Kit's arm again.

'What a charming man,' she mused.

Kit grunted.

Lucy continued, 'And so handsome.'

'What makes a man handsome in your eyes?' Kit struggled to keep the irritation from his voice.

Lucy flicked her hand at his upper arm. 'You wouldn't under-stand,' she said. Kit gave a snort of disgust.

Lucy sighed and leaned her head against his arm. 'Do I detect a hint of jealousy, Captain Lovell?'

'Don't be ridiculous,' Kit scoffed. 'There is just something about the man I neither like nor trust. It has nothing to do with his handsome face or his charming manners.'

'If you say so,' Lucy said, and smiled.

CHAPTER 12

it's brief respite from the troubles of the world in the arms of Lucy had to come to an end. He rose early on Monday morning to go in search of Fitzjames and the others. He knew better than to look for them at The Ship Inn, but there were a number of other inns where they could be found.

He came across Fitzjames drinking with Jack Gerard at the Saracen's Head in Carter Lane. As Kit sat down Fitz raised his cup and sent for a jug of ale.

'I heard they'd let you go,' Fitz said.

'Those of us they felt they couldn't hold. Only Dutton and Whitely are being held.'

'Poor old Dutton. Will they hang him?' Gerard asked.

Kit shook his head. 'I doubt it. There is very little evidence against him.' He sighed and stretched his right leg. After the cold and the damp of the Tower, the wound he had sustained at Worcester was playing merry Hell with him. 'I am getting too old to play amateur games such as that Dutton had in mind,' he grumbled.

'Then you were lucky to slip through the net.'

'Damned lucky,' Kit agreed. 'You and Willys were wise to stay away.'

'No doubt they suspect one of us of informing on them?' Fitz asked.

Kit shrugged. 'What do you expect?'

Fitz's face tightened. 'Well, I can assure you I had no part in it. Whatever my feelings about the stupidity of the plan, I would not have turned them in. I have no time for turncoats.' He leaned forward. 'Nor do we have time for amateurs. As I intimated at our last meeting, there are plans in the wind that Dutton and his cronies nearly put paid to.'

Gerard took a thoughtful sip of his ale. 'Are we wise to involve another, Fitzjames?'

Fitz cast Gerard a hard look. 'Lovell could be useful. He speaks fluent French, among his many talents. His name was mentioned before as being a possibility.'

A possible what? Kit wondered.

'I've had my fill of plots and plans, Fitz. Two weeks in the Tower saw to that. My leg hurts damnably, and all I want is a few quiet evenings of cards to restore my fortunes.'

'Don't be ridiculous, Lovell,' Fitz smiled. 'I know you. You'll be bored within two days. You see those gentlemen who have just entered?'

Kit turned to look at the two plainly dressed men who stood at the entrance looking around the gloomy taproom.

'Do you know them?' Fitz enquired.

Kit nodded. 'The shorter one is Henshaw. I presume the other to be his brother, Wiseman. Not men I would want dealings with.'

It struck him as ironic that he would trust neither of them as far as he could throw them. Thurloe's web stretched wide, and he was almost certain these two were in Thurloe's pay.

'At least listen to what they have to say,' Fitz whispered.

Fitz caught the eye of the taller man. They removed their hats and cloaks and sauntered over to the table with a look of studied casualness as if such a meeting was pure coincidence. The introductions to Gerard were made quickly.

'Lovell,' Henshaw said as he sat down, 'I heard tales that you were one of The Ship Inn Plotters.'

'So they have a name now, do they?' Kit shrugged. 'I was in the wrong place at the wrong time.'

'Lovell was against the plan,' Fitzjames said. 'It was unfortunate that he was rounded up with the rest of them.'

'So, Lovell,' Gerard leaned forward. 'Are you interested in a more serious game?'

'A more serious game?'

'To kill Cromwell,' Wiseman said in a low voice.

Kit swallowed. This was not what he expected. He doubted very much that these two were agents of the Sealed Knot, which meant they, like Dutton, were off on a dangerous frolic of their own.

'What will that achieve?' he asked carefully.

'Without Cromwell, this Commonwealth is nothing. There is no one to succeed him, they will be begging the King to return,' Wiseman said.

'What about Ireton?'

Henshaw's mouth twisted into a grim smile. 'We kill him too.'

'You make that sound easy! What of the other generals? Knock off one head and another will replace it,' Kit scoffed. 'Does the King know of this plan?'

Gerard spoke up. 'Not yet. Henshaw and Wiseman are leaving for France tonight. My uncle has arranged an introduction to Prince Rupert. With that, they hope to see Charles.'

'And if he won't see you?' Kit gave both men a hard look.

Henshaw shrugged. 'We'll cross that bridge when we come to it.'

'So why include me? Surely The Ship Inn debacle should teach you that the fewer who know the better.'

'Because you're a good man, Lovell. We can trust you, and let's face it, you speak French,' Fitz said.

At the word "trust", a shiver ran down Kit's spine.

'All of you speak French. So why does being fluent in French make me useful?'

'You don't just speak French, you *are* French, Lovell,' Fitzjames said and caught his friend's eyes. 'Well, half-French. There is someone we must meet with and we don't want any French tricks. If he knows we have one of our number who can't be fooled, he's less likely to try to outsmart us.'

Kit's ears pricked. 'Why would the French get involved in such a plan?'

'Cromwell is treating with the French King over the Huguenot business. Not all the French agree with what is being discussed,' Henshaw said.

'They would like to continue massacring innocent women and children just because they are Protestant?' Kit curled his lip in distaste.

Fitzjames laughed. 'You're a damned cynic, Lovell. Yes, let them do it if it keeps Charles in Paris and the French on his side.'

Kit kept his peace. This was not the time or the place to discuss the politics of the French or to mention that his mother's family were Protestants. 'Who is this Frenchman you are meeting with?' he asked.

'It doesn't matter for now,' Henshaw replied.

Kit looked around the circle of faces with a heavy heart. *Another tavern, another plot.*

'If you need me, my sword is yours,' he said, trying to keep the tone of dull resignation from his voice.

'Good man.' Fitzjames nodded approval and turned to Henshaw and Wiseman. 'God speed you both on your journey.'

They clasped hands across the table. 'We will get word to you as soon as we can.' Henshaw said with a smile

After Henshaw and Wiseman left, Kit turned to Gerard and Fitzjames.

'You trust them?'

Fitzjames shrugged. 'We have to. There are so few left, Lovell.'

'Charles won't see them, Fitz. Their reputations stink as high as a week-old corpse. Do you know their history? They're deserters and opportunists.'

'Rumours, Lovell, just rumours.'

What truth there was to those rumours, Kit had no idea. Thurloe was not in the habit of disclosing who else was in his pay. He could just as easily have Fitzjames as Henshaw in his pocket, and there would be no way of knowing. At the end of the day, no one could truly be trusted.

'What of the Sealed Knot?' he ventured.

Fitz looked at him. 'What about it?'

'Are they involved in this or is it another frolic?'

Gerard narrowed his eyes. 'Fitzjames is right. I detect a tone of cynicism, Lovell.'

'I've just spent three long weeks in the Tower of London, Gerard, so forgive me if I sound cynical,' Kit snapped.

Fitz placed a restraining hand on his arm. 'To answer your question, Lovell, no, the Knot is not involved, but with the influence of Lord Gerard in Paris, the King's consent to this venture can be obtained and with it the co-operation of the Sealed Knot.'

Kit ran a hand through his hair. 'I wish I had your confidence, Fitz.'

Fitz shrugged. 'Confidence or foolhardiness, Lovell?'

Kit shook his head. 'Whatever it is, shall we leave all talk of it for now? Are either of you game for cards?'

CHAPTER 13

Thamsine chewed the end of her pen and scratched a few more notes of her small composition onto the paper. She felt it would suit Mary Skippon's limited musical abilities and give the girl some confidence. Fortunately, the taproom was quiet and the fire burned brightly, making it a more congenial place to work than her room.

'Am I disturbing you?'

Thamsine looked up. Kit Lovell stood watching her, his hat in his hand. Her heart gave a skip at the sight of his smile.

'Lovell! You're free.'

He inclined his head. 'The same could be said for you, Mistress Granville.' He tilted his head to one side and looked her up and down. 'Might I say you look remarkably respectable for someone who has just spent the better part of a month in the Tower of London.'

Thamsine felt the heat rise to her cheeks. 'My fortunes are somewhat changed since last we met. I have employment.'

Kit raised an eyebrow. 'Indeed?'

'I am tutoring a member of the French Ambassador's household in music.'

Kit raised his eyebrows. 'You surprise me! How did you stumble on this good fortune?'

Thamsine looked down at the paper she had been working on. 'Through a friend,' she mumbled and hoped Kit would ask no more questions.

Unbidden, Kit sat down opposite her. 'Is it going well?' he asked.

Thamsine looked up and gave a wry smile. 'The girl has no ear for music. Hence ... ' She waved a hand at her simple composition.

Kit turned it towards him and frowned in concentration.

'A pretty piece,' he commented. 'Your work?'

She nodded. 'You read music?'

He shrugged. 'I had a well-rounded gentleman's education. Can't sing a note to save my life, but I can find a tune on a guitar or the lute. My brother had a marvellous voice when he was younger ... ' He broke off abruptly. 'Anyway, among my many talents, music sadly is not one I have had much time to pursue in recent years.'

'I suppose not.' Thamsine smiled. 'And you, Lovell? You're free to roam the streets of London again?'

'They had no evidence to hold us, so we were released a few days ago. Dutton and Whitely are still languishing in the confines of the Tower.'

A few days ago? Thamsine felt a knot of disappointment settle in her stomach. He had been free and not sought her out until now?

He looked around the quiet taproom. 'Why did you come back here?'

She shrugged. 'I feel safe here and I had nowhere else to go. What about you?'

He hesitated a moment before answering. 'My mistress has, as always, proved remarkably good about taking me back in.'

'I see.'

A heavy feeling settled in the pit of her stomach as she imagined Lovell with another woman.

'You don't seem the domestic type, Lovell.'

'My arrangement with Lucy is just temporary. Lucy's not the domestic type either, Thamsine. She's a wealthy widow who likes her independence.'

'Lucky woman,' Thamsine replied with feeling.

'Not always so lucky. She did have to endure ten years of marriage to a man thirty years her senior.'

Thamsine shrugged. 'At least your Lucy is now free. For those of us who are forced into marriage against our wills, it is a frightening prospect.'

His eyes narrowed and the sharp, evaluating look he gave her surprised her.

'Is that what you are running from?'

She hesitated, her usual denial on her lips, but his unexpected honesty with her invited a return of confidence.

'Yes,' she said. 'I am running from a marriage that is far from my choice or desire, and which would be contracted for no other reason than the benefit of the man involved.'

'And your father sanctioned it?'

She gave a hollow laugh. 'My father thought he was looking after my best interests. Before he died he not only contracted the marriage but made the man my guardian until such a marriage took place.'

'Is that why you ran?'

She met his eyes. *Time for the truth.* 'I ran because I thought I had killed the man.'

Kit's eyebrows shot up. 'You killed a man? Mistress Granville!'

She shook her head. 'No, he is alive and well and stalking the streets of London looking for me. I know because I saw him in the crowd that day I met you. That's why I threw the brick. I needed a distraction.'

'Ah.' Kit sat back and regarded her for a long moment. 'You must have been desperate to go to such lengths. Is there no one you can turn to?'

She shook her head. 'My one hope proved to be as duplicitous as my suitor. Now, can we talk of more pleasant topics?'

Kit looked out of the smoky window. 'Would you care for a walk? It is a surprisingly fine day. One could almost think spring was imminent.'

Thamsine considered for a moment. He might be living with his mistress, but an hour or so of his company would be preferable to her present occupation. She nodded.

Kit looked her up and down as she returned with her cloak and hat. 'Might I say your new gown becomes you well?'

She could not resist a small smile of pleasure at the compliment and dipped a curtsey. 'Why thank you, kind sir. 'Tis a long time since someone paid me such a compliment and it's good to be clean, well-fed and have some coin in my pocket, all for doing what I do best.'

'Amen to that sentiment,' he said, returning the curtsey with a studied, courtly bow. He raised an eyebrow and crooked his arm. Thamsine tucked her hand into his elbow. They ambled at a gentle pace, in perfect step with each other.

'Do you intend to stay at the Ship?' Kit asked.

'It suits me. I have nowhere else to stay. Where are we going?' Thamsine asked.

'I thought we might stroll to the New Exchange,' Kit said. 'I heard that a coffee house has opened there. Have you ever sampled coffee?'

'No. What is it?'

'It is a brew made from a bean they discovered in the New World. It is becoming quite fashionable, particularly among those who abhor strong drink.'

'What does it taste like?'

Kit shrugged. 'I've no idea. I've not sampled it myself. Does a bit of adventure suit you?'

'It sounds a mild adventure compared to my recent experience.'

Kit grimaced and stopped, rubbing his right leg.

'Are you all right?' Thamsine asked.

'An old wound that did not take kindly to the conditions in the Tower. Pay me no heed.'

He took her hand in his arm and they started walking again, but Kit's limp had become noticeably more pronounced than she remembered it being before.

'Does it bother you much?' she asked needlessly.

'Only when it gets cold and damp, or I ride for too long. In other words, most of the winter,' Kit grumbled. 'But I've learned to live with it.'

'How did you get it?'

'Worcester,' he said shortly.

'My brother died at Worcester,' Thamsine said. 'He wanted his chance of glory.'

The muscles beneath her hand tensed and his lips tightened. Without looking at her he said, 'He was not the only hot-headed young fool who thought to avenge his family's honour.'

She bit back the questions that rose to her mind but decided instead to change the subject. 'So, Kit Lovell, are you done with conspiracies?'

He looked down at her, and the twinkle of humour returned to his eyes. 'I can make no promises. Don't look like that, Mistress Granville. It's hard to break the habits of a lifetime.'

'Why not give it all away and settle for a quiet life?'

'What's a quiet life?'

'Have you no home at all here in England?'

His face shadowed. 'There is the pathetic remnant of the family estates in Cheshire, but my welcome there would hardly be warm. Anyway, even if I wished to settle to what you call a quiet life, it wouldn't be in England.'

'Then where?'

He shrugged. 'There is France, but in truth, it is the lure of the New World that attracts me.'

'I have estates in Virginia,' Thamsine said.

He looked down at her. 'You are a surprising woman,' he said.

'My grandfather and my father made their fortunes trading in tobacco and other commodities from the New World.'

'Kit!' A woman's voice came from behind them.

At the sound of his name, Kit froze, dropping Thamsine's hand from his arm. They both turned to face a small, fair-haired woman who stood no more than five paces behind them, her arms full of parcels.

'Lucy, what are you doing here?'

Thamsine had to bite her lip to stop from laughing. The woman he had called Lucy looked Thamsine up and down, a quizzical look on her face. From her proprietorial air and hard eyes, Thamsine did not doubt that they had encountered Kit's long-suffering mistress.

She had not thought that Kit Lovell was the sort of man to become discomposed, but he looked distinctly flustered.

'Well, aren't you going to introduce us?' Lucy's frosty smile fixed on Thamsine.

Kit made the formal introductions and Thamsine, biting her lip to stop from smiling, curtsied. Lucy returned the compliment, made awkward by her parcels.

'My brother served with Captain Lovell in the late wars,' Thamsine said in an attempt to provide Kit with a reason for being caught in the company of another woman.

'By happy chance, I encountered Mistress Granville this morning,' Kit added.

Thamsine smiled sweetly. 'Just pure coincidence. We were just going to the new coffee house. Would you care to join us, Mistress Talbot?'

'I don't care for coffee.' Lucy's blue eyes bored into Thamsine's tall, slender frame. 'What brings you to London, Mistress Granville?'

'I have a position as a music tutor, Mistress Talbot.'

Lucy's eyes widened. 'Really? I have been meaning to engage the services of a music tutor. Would you be willing to take me on, Mistress Granville?'

'Mouse, I don't think you need to trouble Mistress Granville,' Kit spluttered.

Lucy looked up at him. 'On the contrary, Kit. It is something I have been meaning to do for some time. Will you be able to come to my house on Friday, Mistress Granville?'

Thamsine looked at Kit, delighted to see him flushed scarlet with embarrassment. Kit always seemed so much in control of his life and everything in it that she saw no harm in causing him some discomfiture. Besides, the thought of spending some time with his mistress intrigued her.

'I would be delighted,' Thamsine said.

Lucy smiled and held out her hand to Thamsine. 'Shall we say two in the afternoon? Talbot's Wine Merchants in High Holborn; you can't miss it. Now, I have an appointment with my tailor. If you will excuse me, Mistress Granville.'

The women curtsied with punctilious politeness.

'Kit, I shall see you this evening.' Lucy smiled and held out her hand. Kit bent low and kissed it.

Lucy gave Thamsine a last, triumphant look before pushing her way through the crowd, her high pattens clattering on the cobbles. 'So that is your Lucy,' Thamsine said.

Kit looked defensive. 'She is not *my* Lucy, any more than I am hers. I assure you, our relationship is one of pure mutual convenience, not ownership.'

'I am not sure that she shares that sentiment,' Thamsine observed.

'What do you mean?'

Thamsine shrugged. 'I'm a woman, Captain Lovell. I know these things.'

'Then you are mistaken,' he replied, 'and as for this ridiculous notion of music lessons, I am asking you, as a friend, not to do it, Thamsine.'

She gave him a quick sideways glance. His mouth had set in a thin, hard line, the brows creased.

'I am hardly in a position to refuse work when it is offered, Captain Lovell.'

'Well, you will refuse this!'

She brought her chin up and looked him squarely in the eye. 'I'm sorry, Captain Lovell. This is a private matter between Mistress Talbot and me, and if it causes you awkwardness then I make no apology.'

'Causes me awkwardness?' Kit's eyes widened. 'I try very hard to keep my private life just that, private!'

'And your private life is entirely your concern, just as my right to accept a commission is my concern!' Thamsine said. 'Do you still wish to partake in coffee?'

Kit brought his attention back to her. 'Yes. That was the purpose of this excursion.'

They walked in silence. Kit glowered and limped beside her, his hands behind his back. Thamsine, unrepentant, straightened her back and ignored her surly companion.

The smell emanating from the coffee house hit them even before the door opened. Thamsine stood still, breathing in the heady aroma. 'Oh, I have never smelt anything like that. Do you suppose it tastes as good?'

Kit's face lightened and he closed his eyes. 'It does have a pleasant smell. After you, Thamsine.'

They secured a small table, in a dark corner away from the crowd, and a servant brought them two small cups filled to the brim with the dark, steaming brew. Thamsine sniffed it suspiciously and took a tentative sip. The smell belied the bitter taste. She wrinkled her nose and set the cup down.

Kit watched her. 'Is it bad?'

'It's an acquired taste!' she said, watching as Kit took a sip.

He frowned. 'I must agree with you. I can't see it replacing a good ale.'

'So, tell me how you met Lucy Talbot,' Thamsine asked.

He gave a heavy sigh. 'Am I to get no peace on this subject? Very well! I bumped into her, or should I say, she bumped into me. She was not watching her step owing to the number of parcels she carried. Lucy and the parcels went flying. What more could a gentleman do than assist her?' He set the cup down and looked at her. 'Now, tell me how things are with the French Ambassador.'

She shrugged. 'There is nothing to tell. His mistress is pleasant but rather dull. Bordeaux himself is charming, and then there is this odious little man called Baron de Baas … ' She broke off as Kit looked up. 'Do you know him?'

'I … ' Kit grimaced and looked out of the window for a moment before turning his attention back to her. He sighed. 'I think it is time for honesty with each other.'

'What do you mean?'

'Thamsine, when you were in the Tower, I believe you met with a man called John Thurloe.'

Thamsine felt her heart skip a beat. Did he suspect her of being a spy? She bit her lip and replied slowly. 'I was questioned by a man of that name. What of him?'

'I know why you're working for Bordeaux. Thurloe put you there.'

'What do you mean?' Her heart skipped a beat. She must be bad at this game if he had already guessed. *Best to try and brazen it out*, she thought.

Kit's shoulders hunched and he looked away. 'Thamsine, this isn't easy for me.' He took a deep breath. 'We are in the pay of the same employer. Thurloe told you he would provide you with a contact. I … I am to be your contact.'

'What!'

'Keep your voice down. You heard what I said.'

'You mean you are in his pay?'

He looked over her shoulder and swallowed. 'Yes.'

She stared at him as the implications of his words sank in. 'You're a turncoat?'

He flinched. 'Keep your voice down, woman! I take no pride in it, but it pays well and I do it.'

Thamsine stared at him in disbelief. 'All your professions of loyalty to the King's cause and all the time you take Cromwell's shilling?'

He returned her gaze, his green eyes flashing. 'Before you start throwing stones, Thamsine Granville, may I remind you that you have sold your soul to the same Devil?'

'I ... ' she began but realised she couldn't deny it. 'I had no choice.'

'Well, neither did I!'

'Why? What does Thurloe hold over you, Lovell? What possible reason could you have other than the money? Tired of scraping a living in exile so you returned to trade your friends' confidences for Cromwell's shilling?'

She had hurt him. She could see the pain in his eyes. 'My reasons are my own,' he said in a low, flat tone.

'I suppose it was you who betrayed The Ship Inn Plotters?'

He swallowed. 'Yes.'

Her eyes widened as a thought occurred to her. 'And me? You betrayed me?'

His momentary silence was all she needed. She rose to her feet and struck him across the face with all the force she could muster.

'*Tais-toi!*' Kit grasped her wrist and pulled her downwards. 'Sit down and stop making a spectacle of yourself,' he continued in French. 'You have to trust me. You have no choice.'

She recognised the tone of command in his voice and sank to her seat, glowering at him. The man she had thought had saved her had thrown her into the Tower of London for his own reasons, and now he wanted her to trust him?

'You hypocrite. All those solicitations, all that concern for my wellbeing. I was just a prize to be handed over to Thurloe when the time was right,' she said in a low, angry voice.

Kit rubbed his stinging face, his eyes flashing. 'I am not going to deny it. Now,' he said, his mouth a thin, angry line, 'put the slanging to one side, Thamsine. We have work to do.'

She glared at him. 'What work?'

'I am your contact. Is there anything I need to know?'

She looked away, fighting back the stinging tears that gathered in the corners of her eyes. The first rush of anger slipped away, to be replaced by hurt and betrayal.

'I thought you were my friend,' Thamsine said in a low, uneven voice. She looked up at him, searching for the man she thought she knew, the man she had thought of every day since they had met.

'I don't have friends,' he said.

She looked into the face of a man who had commanded men, men who would have followed him to Hell if he had asked. They were both bound for Hell, and she had no choice but to follow him.

'How do I know you're telling me the truth?' she asked, summoning the last edge of defiance.

He shook his head. 'You have no reason to trust me, but ask yourself – how would I know that you are in Thurloe's employ unless he had told me?'

She lowered her head. 'I am repaying a debt.' She looked up at him. 'But you were always a King's man. What has Thurloe got over you?'

A muscle in Kit's cheek twitched as his mouth tightened. After a long moment, he said, 'I owe you the truth. I've already told you I was wounded and taken prisoner after Worcester. The choice Thurloe offered me was simple – take his coin or I died in a stinking hellhole.' He looked away and she sensed that she had not heard the whole story, but before she could question him further, he brought his hands down on the table. 'Enough idle chatter, Mistress Granville. It is of no matter to me whether you hate me or not. The fact remains we must work together on this. Thurloe has placed you inside Bordeaux's house for a reason.'

'He wants to know about the man de Baas.'

Kit nodded. 'And what can you tell me about him?'

'Nothing!' She looked up at him, hoping he could see the hurt in her eyes. 'I have met him once and all I can tell you is that he has just returned from France, a fact your Master Thurloe is probably well aware of.'

There was a moment of profound silence, while Kit took a sip from the cup. He set it down and looked at her, a humourless smile on his lips. 'That wasn't so very hard, was it, Mistress Granville?'

She looked down at her cup. 'He talked of steps being taken to restore Charles Stuart.'

'Names? Dates? Plans?'

She shook her head.

'Never mind. Next time you will have something tangible for me.'

'I like your confidence,' she scoffed.

He leaned across the table and lowered his voice. 'You *will* have something for me.'

Her eyes widened at the order. 'I can only do my best. I have limited access.'

'It is de Baas I am interested in. I am sure you can find a way to … ingratiate yourself with him.'

She stared at him. His meaning was plain and she loathed him for it with every fibre of her being. She rose to her feet and looked at him contemptuously. 'I hate you.'

'Fine.' Kit stood up and tied his cloak. 'You can hate me. Now, do you wish to be escorted back to the Ship?'

She shook her head. 'No. I can find my own way, Captain Lovell.'

A flicker of a smile twitched at Kit's lips. 'Very well, Mistress Granville. I will bid you good day until we meet again, which will be soon.'

Thamsine gathered herself together and walked away from

him with every shred of dignity and outrage that she could muster, but as her steps took her further from him, her show of bravado began to ebb away from her.

She stopped and leaned against a mounting block outside an inn, her breath coming in short gasps as the extent of his duplicity sank in. The man she had considered her friend, had maybe considered to be slightly *more* than her friend, had betrayed her. He had taken her off the street for one reason only, and that was to use her as a card in his own private game with John Thurloe.

Thurloe had outplayed him. He had turned the game on Kit Lovell, making him her contact. If he had not done so, would she ever have known? Would Kit have gone on using her, lulling her with false blandishments?

She drew a heavy, uneven breath and walked on. She despised him for his deceit. The hurt he had caused her would probably never heal. She wanted to hate him, but as she turned her face to the leaden sky glimpsed between the crooked buildings and felt the rain on her face, she knew that what she felt for Kit Lovell was not hate. She had hated a man enough to kill him, and somewhere in these dark, narrow streets Ambrose Morton still stalked her.

CHAPTER 14

*K*it stood at the door of the coffee house watching until Thamsine's tall, slim figure had been swallowed up by the crowd. He turned and stormed up the Strand in a filthy temper. He didn't know quite what put him in a rage – John Thurloe, Thamsine's hurt and the truth of her allegations, or the thought that she would be teaching music to Lucy.

It hurt too much to consider the first two options, so he turned his mind to Lucy. If Lucy wanted music lessons it was hardly his concern. Thamsine would be a good teacher and she needed the money. Where was the problem?

The problem was that Thamsine Granville spent far more time in his thoughts than he felt she deserved, and he did not like the thought of her closeted with his mistress for any length of time. Women gossiped.

He had arranged to meet Fitzjames at the Saracen's Head. He was coming to hate the secret assignations in corners of stinking alehouses. The smell of smoke, ale and unwashed bodies seemed to cling to him, tainting him in much the same way as his growing distaste for what he was doing. He pulled off his hat and stepped around the crowded tables. It was not a good time to be developing a conscience.

It did not improve his temper to find his friend in the company of Ambrose Morton. The sight of the arrogant, handsome face turned his stomach. He flung himself down on the stool opposite Fitz and acknowledged Morton with a grunt.

Fitz regarded him calmly. 'Lucy do something to annoy you?'

Kit summoned the potboy and took out his cards, shuffling them to calm his nerves.

'Lucy ... women,' he grumbled. 'Damned if I'll ever understand them. What about you, Morton? Is there a woman to plague your life?'

Morton's lip curled into a vicious sneer. 'Don't talk to me of the perfidy of women,' he said. 'That is what brings me to London.'

'Really?' Kit dealt the cards.

'My betrothed has run off.'

Fitz gave a snort of laughter. 'With another man?'

Morton shrugged. 'I can only presume so. Bloody woman was worth a fortune too, a fortune I need.'

'I see.' Kit picked up his hand and noted that the cards were not with him either. 'Not a love match, then?'

'Hardly. Her father promised her to me some ten years ago. Returned from the Continent to find the old fool had allowed her too much freedom and she had become headstrong and obdurate. Not what I look for in a woman, but she could be curbed. Women are like horses, Lovell. They can be broken to the saddle. When I find the bitch I will soon teach her compliance and duty.'

Kit looked up at the handsome face and felt his flesh creep. He did not doubt that Morton's means of ensuring compliance and duty would not be pleasant. He had some sympathy for the runaway bride.

'And if I find the man who stole her away, I will kill him,' Morton said in a calm voice. 'I need her money to make good my estate again.'

'We all need that sort of money, Morton,' Kit scoffed.

'Well, you won't earn it playing cards, Lovell.' Morton set down his hand.

Kit groaned and tossed his hand in.

'It's not my day today. As for our lost fortunes, the King himself is living on the charity of his cousin.'

'At least you still have your estate, Lovell,' Fitz said.

'Half of it's been sold off to pay the fines. The other half barely supports my family,' Kit said.

'Where is your estate, Lovell?' Morton did not look at him as he dealt the cards.

'Cheshire.'

'Whereabouts?' Morton persisted.

'It's at Midhurst,' Fitz said before Kit had a chance to answer.

Kit glared at his friend. He'd had no intention of being that specific. Fitz's tongue had been loosened by drink.

'Who did you serve with during the war?' Morton enquired, picking up his hand of cards, his face betraying nothing.

'My father raised a regiment of foot.'

Morton's eyes met Kit's over the cards. 'I would have thought you a cavalry man.'

Kit met the cold eyes. 'I was loyal to my father.'

'Did he survive the war?'

'No,' Kit said shortly. He could have added *he died in my arms on the front steps of our family home with a musket ball in the chest.* Even after all these years, the memory of his father's death brought a knot of pain to his heart.

'Well, I enjoyed the war,' Morton said. 'I miss those heady days.'

Fitz and Kit stared at him.

'Enjoyed it?' Kit said.

Morton did not raise his eyes from his cards. 'We had some high times.'

'You were with Goring,' Kit replied, the distaste evident in his voice. 'Looting, raping and destruction were your orders for the day.'

Morton looked up sharply. 'And you were a saint?'

'I'm not saying I was a saint,' Kit replied. 'And I'm not saying there weren't times that I will remember with a degree of affection, but at no time will I ever forget that we fought a civil war and that the enemy were my own countrymen.'

Morton shrugged. 'Own countrymen or not, if they were trying to kill me, far better I kill them first. Anyway, that is in the past. My concern now is to rebuild my future.'

'And find your heiress?'

Morton shrugged. 'I will find her. I know she's in London. I've seen the little bitch. She can't hide forever.'

God help her when you do find her, Kit thought. His sympathies were with the girl. Marriage to Ambrose Morton did not seem an agreeable prospect for any woman, let alone a woman of substance.

Something in that thought recalled his conversation with Thamsine: "I am running from a marriage that is far from my choice or desire, and which would be contracted for no other reason than the benefit of the man involved."

He looked up at Morton and felt his blood run cold.

They finished the game in silence. Morton cleared the table of the coins and stood up.

'If you will excuse me, gentleman, I have an assignation.'

'Pretty?' Fitz enquired.

'Charming as a picture,' Morton said. 'She is waiting for me. Good day to you.' He inclined his head and left, pushing past Gerard who had just entered.

Gerard removed his hat and took Morton's seat. 'Who was that?'

'Ambrose Morton,' Kit said with disgust. 'A disgrace to the King's colours if ever there was one.'

'I've heard of Morton,' Gerard said. 'One of Goring's crew, and from the way my uncle tells it, not one of the better ones.'

Fitz straightened. He seemed to have sobered up a little. Maybe the loss of his purse to Morton had helped slow the intake of wine. 'Forget him. What's the news?' he asked.

'Not good,' said Gerard. 'Charles has refused to see Henshaw.'

'I told you he would,' Kit said. 'His reputation preceded him.' He sighed and ran his fingers through his hair. 'Who would be Charles? Who can he trust?'

'Well, you and I to begin with,' Fitz replied, throwing an arm around his friend's shoulders in drunken bonhomie.

'But the news is not all bad,' Gerard said. 'The King has summoned us. He wants to talk directly with us.'

'Who's "us"?' Kit enquired.

'Fitzjames and I and you, of course. We'll sail on Friday.'

'Sail?' Kit's nose pinched at the thought of tossing around on the English Channel for twenty-four hours. 'Why me? What can I accomplish?'

'You speak French a damned sight better than we do and the King knows you. He trusts you. Between us, we can persuade him.'

Kit leaned forward. 'What about Willys and his committee?'

Fitz narrowed his eyes. 'What about Willys?'

'I only know that whatever committee he is involved with

already holds the King's Commission. Are we not better advised to pool our resources? Lend our support to their venture?'

Fitz gave a deprecatory snort. 'From what I know of them, Willys' committee is a pack of old fools. There is not one person of worth willing to lend his name to it. All they do is talk. With the King's blessing, I believe we can achieve something.'

'My uncle has the King's ear,' Gerard put in. 'All it needs is for us to convince him that our plan is feasible.'

'And is it?' Kit bit down on his irritation. *More foolish plots.*

'If we can take Cromwell the rest will fall into place,' Gerard continued.

'But there is the fundamental error,' Kit said. 'It's not just Cromwell. There is Ireton, Thurloe – do you want me to go on listing names?'

He was wasting his breath. The two obdurate faces looking at him told him that their minds were settled.

'Anyway, we have help,' Fitz said. 'Mazarin will supply us with whatever we need to accomplish the task.'

Cardinal Mazarin, was the real power behind the French throne. Kit's heart skipped a beat. Was this the connection with the French court that Thurloe was looking for?

'What do you mean?' he asked.

'The French want Charles out of Paris and they want him back on the throne of England, all without being seen to assist.'

'Such as the necessary military force?' Kit asked.

'Exactly. We have a contact here in London, sent here by Mazarin,' Gerard said.

De Baas? Kit held his breath.

Fitzjames continued. 'Gerard and I have met with him and it is clear that they have the means to help us in an assassination attempt.'

Kit ran his hand through his hair. 'Assassination is not the answer. This is madness, Fitz!'

'It will work, Lovell.' Fitz's eyes blazed with a new passion. 'Don't you see? With Cromwell and Ireton dead, the army and government will be in disarray and begging for the King to return.'

'And if it doesn't?' Kit asked.

'They have a French assassin who knows nothing.'

Kit rolled his eyes. 'Who is Mazarin's contact here?'

Fitz and Gerard looked at each other. 'The Baron de Baas,' Fitz said in a low voice. 'Do you know him?' Fitz asked.

'No,' Kit said.

'He is a confidante of Cardinal Mazarin,' Fitz said.

The pieces had begun to fall into place. Mazarin had sent De Baas to London to assist with the assassination of Cromwell, although for what purpose Kit still didn't know. Was it just to put Charles back on the throne, or did it carry deeper into France's war with Spain?

Gerard drained his glass. 'Until we have spoken to the King, there is nothing we can do at present except waiting.' He stood up. 'We will meet in Paris, gentlemen.'

Kit watched the young man's confident swagger as he pushed his way out of the crowded inn, and wished he still felt that sense of immortality. Every day, he felt Death's hot breath on his neck. He played a dangerous game and he had begun to wonder if he was losing his nerve.

'Deep in thought?' Fitz raised an eyebrow at Kit and lifted his cup. Kit nodded and Fitz summoned the potboy for a jug of wine.

'Am I getting old, Fitz?'

'I don't know. You turned thirty yet?'

Kit nodded. 'Just before Christmas. Do you think that's why I am losing my taste for excitement and starting to think of hearth and home?'

'God forbid!' Fitz filled their cups again. 'Lovell, I despair of you. Your Lucy will have you before a priest before you can say "praise the Lord".'

'Lucy? No, Lucy's not the sort I see myself settling with.'

'What became of that girl in the Ship?' Fitz asked. 'Now, she had something about her. Where'd you meet her?'

'I knew her brother. He died at Worcester,' Kit said, grateful for Thamsine's confidence that lessened the lie. He *could* have known her brother. 'Anyway, what about you, Fitz, still pining for the lovely Althea?'

'I wrote another poem. Want to hear it?'

'No,' said Kit shortly. He had heard too many of Fitz's sentimental poems dedicated to that particular lovely, but unattainable, young woman.

'Oh, very well,' Kit conceded as his friend affected a downcast look. 'Let us hear of nymphs, shepherds, and the lovely Althea. It makes a pleasant change from talk of assassination.'

CHAPTER 15

'**M**ademoiselle Granville!'

Thamsine heard the Baron's affected voice and stopped in her tracks. She turned to face him, a smile fixed on her face.

'Baron De Baas.' She curtsied.

'Mademoiselle, might I say how radiant you are looking this morning?'

De Baas grasped her fingers and held them to his lips in a lingering kiss, his beard and moustache rasping her skin. Thamsine extricated her hand and surreptitiously wiped it on her skirts.

'You are too kind, Baron,' she responded.

'Mistress Skippon's music lessons are progressing?'

'Very well.'

'Good, good.' De Baas looked distracted.

'You wanted something, Baron?'

The Baron took a step towards her and clasped her hand again.

'My dear Mademoiselle, I should be most obliged if you could attend my apartment for a little supper tonight. I require assistance with some music I wish to perform at the next *soiree*.'

A shudder ran down Thamsine's spine. Everything in her screamed out to refuse, but then she remembered who she was and why she was there. *Use your charms*, Kit had told her.

She gave a nervous laugh. 'My dear Baron, I'm not sure ... '

He raised a hand, a look of pain crossing his face. 'Please do not be alarmed, mademoiselle, it will be quite ... *innocente*. I wish merely to share some music with you and perhaps some talk. I have been rather ... ' He frowned as if searching for the word. 'Rather lonely since I have been in England.'

Thamsine bit her tongue and replied sweetly. 'I'm so sorry to hear that, Baron. Very well, what time?'

An eager light sprang into his eyes. 'Shall we say seven in the evening?'

Thamsine nodded. 'Until tonight, Baron.'

A door was flung open with a crash and Bordeaux stood brandishing a piece of paper.

'De Baas, you fool!' he exclaimed in French. 'What game are you playing?'

'My dear Bordeaux, what do you mean?' De Baas replied, also in French.

'You have been sending correspondence directly to Mazarin without my consent.'

'I do not need your consent.'

'You do when the matter affects the relationship with this country.'

Thamsine affected a bemused stare, looking from one to the other.

'My dear Ambassador,' de Baas remembered Thamsine's presence and gave her a reassuring smile, continuing in French. 'I think this conversation is one best conducted in private.'

'Then in here, now!' Bordeaux stood aside to let De Baas pass into the room beyond.

De Baas bowed to Thamsine. 'Until tonight, mademoiselle,' he said in English.

Thamsine waited until the door closed behind them, and was on the verge of pressing her ear to the door when a servant entered, carrying her cloak and hat.

She walked slowly back to the Ship, lost in thoughts of how best to avoid the Baron's roving hands while extricating useful information from him.

'Thamsine!' She jumped at the sound of her name.

Kit stood on the corner of the street, hunched into his cloak. He had a pinched look, as if he had been waiting a while in the cold. She hadn't seen him since their vitriolic conversation of the previous day.

'What are you doing here?' she enquired with a frosty edge to her voice.

'Waiting for you.'

'Why?'

'Because ... ' Kit grimaced. 'I have to. Now we can stand here getting cold or you can tell me if you have anything to report.'

She began to walk away from him. 'You can stand here and freeze by all means, Captain Lovell. I am going home.'

Kit caught her by the arm. 'Enough. Tell me what I need to know.'

She glared at him. 'Bordeaux is displeased with De Baas. He accused him of communicating directly with Mazarin.'

'And?'

'De Baas didn't deny it.' She recounted the brief conversation she had been privy to that morning. 'That's all, except ... ' She paused, frowning. 'De Baas has invited me for supper tonight in his apartment.'

Kit's eyes widened. 'Excellent.'

She stared at him. 'Have you met the man? He says he is lonely, and I can only hazard a guess that it is not my musical talents he has in mind for company.'

Kit smiled. 'I am sure you will find some excuse to avoid any unnecessary advances, and if nothing else it will provide an ideal opportunity to search his apartment.'

She looked at him with distaste. 'You have no idea what you are asking me to do, Lovell ... '

'I am not asking you to prostitute yourself, Thamsine.' All humour had gone from Kit's face. 'Do what you think is necessary but extricate yourself before things become uncomfortable for you.'

Her eyes narrowed. 'And how do you suppose I do that? You're a man ... you have no idea ... ' She shrugged. 'Do not concern yourself on my account, Captain Lovell. I shall advise you if I find anything useful. As that is all I have to tell you, I bid you good day.'

She began to walk again, and to her annoyance, he broke into stride beside her.

'Thamsine, I'm not good at apologies ... '

She turned on him, her eyes blazing.

'You betrayed me, Kit Lovell. Not only did you betray me to the authorities, but you also betrayed my trust in you. Now I am tied to you by a bargain made with the Devil. I hate it and I despise you!'

He took her gloved hand in his. 'Thamsine, I am sorry, but I can't afford to have regrets, not in this business. At least you're under no illusions about me now. Please, let us call it a truce.'

She withdrew her hand from his, and without a word walked away from him.

A SERVANT ADMITTED Thamsine to the well-lit parlour of the Baron's apartment. The gaudy red and gold-painted furniture and drapery provided a stark contrast to the familiar dark English oak of her world. She set her music portfolio down beside the elaborately painted virginals, which stood open on a small table, letting her fingers trail over the notes. The sweet tone tempted her to sit and play, but conscious of the real reason for her presence, she looked around the room.

She had never seen a room so stuffed with furniture – chairs and tables of all descriptions and in the corner a small writing desk covered in papers. An ornately carved table, set for two, dominated the centre of the room.

She crossed to the window, where the heavy red velvet curtains remained open, and looked down into the quiet street below. A light fog played around the lanterns hung by the front door, giving the streetscape a sinister appearance. She shivered and turned as the door opened with a quiet click. Baron de Baas, casually dressed in a long gown over breeches and unlaced shirt, stood in the doorway.

'My dear Mademoiselle Granville,' he said while advancing on her, 'you look charming this evening.'

Thamsine had gone to little trouble with her appearance, so the blatant exaggeration struck her as amusing.

'Baron.' She extricated her fingers as they were pressed against his lips. 'It is very kind of you to invite me. Do you wish to practice your music first?'

'*Non.* I think we should eat and then practice. What is it your William Shakespeare says, 'If music be the food of love … '?'

De Baas rang a bell and the manservant appeared. Without bidding he filled two glasses of wine, presenting them to Thamsine and De Baas on a silver tray. Thamsine took a careful sip. Tempting though it was to steel her resolve with wine, it would not help her wits to become the slightest bit inebriated.

'This is a lovely piece,' she said, seating herself at the virginals.

De Baas stood behind her. 'I had it brought from France. I cannot abide the solid, boring English furniture.'

She looked up at him. 'There seems little about England you like.'

He shuddered and threw his hands in the air. 'Where do I begin? The food, the wine, the weather … and, *mon Dieu*, the so-called English court!'

'What of it?'

'Where is the grandeur, where is the formality? A farmer who calls himself King?' The Baron's lip curled in a sneer. 'I would not lower myself to remove my hat in his presence.'

Thamsine bit her lip to stop herself from smiling. Farmer or not, Cromwell was the head of state, and by refusing to remove his hat in his presence the Baron had probably committed a grave breach of protocol.

As she began to play, De Baas stood over her, so close she could feel his breath on the back of her neck. She shrugged her shoulders but he failed to take the hint.

'You play well, mademoiselle,' he purred in her ear as he traced the line of her spine from her collar to the hairline with his forefinger. The unwelcome touch made her feel physically nauseous.

'Thank you, Baron,' she said and began another piece of music, anything to distract herself. As she felt his lips brush her hair, she stood with an abruptness that threw him off balance. 'Did you say we were to eat?' she demanded.

The Baron recovered himself. 'Of course.'

He clapped his hands and the manservant appeared at the door. 'Joachim, food ... '

'Sir, there are two men outside who wish to speak with you.' The servant spoke in French.

De Baas waved a hand. 'Not now,' he replied in the same language.

'Sir, they are most insistent.'

'Who are they?'

'Messieurs Gerard and Fitzjames.'

At the names, De Baas went silent. 'Very well, show them in.' He turned to Thamsine and addressed her in English. 'My dear, I have some tedious business to discuss. Perhaps you would be so good as to wait next door?' He indicated the door through which he had entered. 'I shall not be long.'

The room beyond the door proved to be De Baas' bedchamber. Thamsine shuddered. The light of a dozen candles filled the chamber and the massive bed had been turned down, no doubt in expectation of her agreeing to a night between the fine linen sheets. If those were his intentions, he would be sorely disappointed.

She had left the door open a barest crack and she knelt on the floor to see who entered. Her eyes widened as she recognised both men from The Ship Inn: the tall, fair-haired man was Kit Lovell's friend, Fitzjames; the younger one must be Gerard.

Kit's friend? Her jaw tightened. Kit did not have friends. Did Fitzjames know his friend was a turncoat, hanging on his every word, ready to betray him when the time was right?

The men spoke in low voices that made it hard to understand what was being said. De Baas glanced at the door and suggested they speak in French. Secure in the mistaken belief that they were not being overheard, their voices raised to a level that Thamsine could understand.

Fitzjames gestured at the table. 'We have interrupted you, Baron.'

De Baas waved a hand. 'I just request that you are brief.'

'It is on the matter of the Lord Protector ... '

'Your Lord Protector ... ' De Baas wrinkled his nose as if he had detected a bad smell. ' ... is an incompetent nobody. A farmer, playing at being a statesman. He knows nothing of international diplomacy.'

'What about Bordeaux?' Gerard asked.

De Baas dismissed the French Ambassador with a wave of his hand. 'Bordeaux is also incompetent. My God, he has even taken an Englishwoman as a mistress.' De Baas leaned closer to Fitzjames. 'Your Cromwell is playing a dangerous game. He can lie down with the bear or the wolf, but not with both.'

'What do you mean?' Gerard asked.

'Spain or France, the choice is simple.' De Baas illustrated his point by turning first his left hand palm-up and then the right. 'This regime of Cromwell's is ready to be overthrown. I have seen the soldiers. They are feeble and dissipated.'

'What makes you say that?' Fitz asked.

De Baas sat bolt upright and threw his hands in the air. '*Mon Dieu*, they wear nightcaps under their hats!'

'Pardon?' Gerard asked.

'I have seen them in Whitehall standing sentinel with these absurd nightcaps under their hats. No real soldier would condescend to wear such foolish clothing.'

The two Englishmen stared at him. 'It probably keeps their heads warm,' Fitz commented, his brow creased in perplexity.

'So what do you propose you can do for us, De Baas?' Gerard changed the subject.

'I can assist with the overthrow of this Lord Protector.'

'How?'

'You need a skilled assassin to kill Cromwell. I know of just such a man.'

A thrill of excitement ran down Thamsine's spine. *This* was what Thurloe wanted to hear.

'What makes you think we are not capable of doing the job?' Fitzjames asked, his tone defensive.

De Baas scoffed, dabbing the corners of his mouth with his kerchief. 'Cromwell is guarded well. He knows he is not immortal. You may have been fine soldiers, my friends, but this is a task for a specialist.'

'And what is the price of this specialist service?' Fitzjames asked.

De Baas shrugged. 'Call it mutual benefit. You will get your King back and France will be free of interference from England. That is the offer, my friends.'

'And Cardinal Mazarin, does he know of this proposal?'

De Baas sniffed, holding the lace-edged kerchief to his nose. 'He may or then again, he may not.'

'Baron de Baas. You must understand that this is not a matter we can decide on now. It has to be discussed with and approved by the King before we can act,' Fitzjames said.

De Baas spread his hands. 'Of course, I understand. There is no hurry. I suggest you speak with your superiors in Paris, convince your King of this matter, and we can talk again in a few weeks. Now, gentlemen, if you will excuse me ... ' he looked towards the bedroom door but by the time he reached it, Thamsine had gone, slipping through the servant's door and down the back stairs into the cold night air.

~

'Well?'

Thamsine flushed at Kit's peremptory greeting. She set her hat and cloak down on an empty stool and sat down at the table. She looked around but the taproom of the Ship was quiet.

'The man is insufferable,' she said in a low voice. 'His bedchamber resembled a brothel.'

'And how would you know what a brothel looks like?' Kit raised an eyebrow. 'Did he ... '

'No,' Thamsine snapped. 'It was fortunate for me that our little tryst was interrupted by two of your friends.'

'My friends?'

Thamsine nodded. 'I've seen them here. The tall, fair-haired man and the young man. Fitzjames and Gerard, I think he called them.'

'Hmm,' Kit said, more to himself than to her. 'Could you hear what was said?'

Thamsine related the gist of the conversation and Kit's eyes gleamed in the gloom.

He tapped his fingers on the side of his mug. 'So they are set on this course. Fools! If they think the King will ever agree to assassination ... '

Thamsine rose to her feet. 'If that is all, Captain Lovell. It has been a long day and I have an appointment with your lovely mistress tomorrow.'

A muscle twitched in Kit's cheek. 'Sit down!'

She lowered herself back onto the seat.

He closed his eyes. 'Sorry, Thamsine. I didn't mean that to sound like an order. I meant only to thank you for your work tonight.'

'I do what I'm required to do.'

'No, tonight you were prepared to go a little further and for that I thank you.' He ran a hand across his eyes. 'I am tired and short of temper. I didn't mean to snap at you.'

She shrugged. 'You're playing a dangerous game, Captain Lovell. I hope the stakes are worth it.'

'I play for a life, Thamsine. The stakes cannot be raised any higher.'

'Whose life? Yours?'

He shook his head. 'Not me. My life doesn't matter.'

She watched him in silence. He looked tired. The shadows around his eyes seemed to have sunk deeper and the lilt of laughter had gone from his mouth.

'Lucy will be waiting for you,' she said, her tone softening.

'Lucy can wait. I am not her lapdog, to come and go at her bidding. The reason I lodge with her is one of convenience,' he snapped.

Thamsine shrugged. 'You could find lodging elsewhere.'

'You're right, I could, but Lucy is an escape from this mess ... ' He ran his hand through his hair, a gesture she'd noticed before when he felt under any pressure. 'Do you hate me, Thamsine?'

She shook her head. 'No, but I won't forget what you did to me.'

'If I had let you be caught on the day you tried to kill our beloved Lord Protector, what do you think would have happened to you? Newgate or the Fleet, the gallows even. You wouldn't have stood a chance.'

'You didn't have to turn me in.'

'And if I hadn't, would you be sitting there in a new gown, considering retiring to a comfortable bed upstairs? We're all governed by fate, Thamsine.'

'Do you believe we have no say in how our lives go, Lovell? Is life pre-ordained by God?'

'God and I have not been on speaking terms for some years now, Thamsine, so don't talk to me of God.'

'What did God do to you?'

'Wasn't there when I needed him … ' He looked up at her and smiled. 'Go to your bed, Thamsine. You look tired.'

She rose to her feet. 'Good night, Kit.'

It was the first time she had called him by his first name in a long time. He looked up at her and smiled. 'Good night, Thamsine.'

As he turned to go, he said, 'Thamsine?'

She turned back towards him. He frowned, and his lips parted as if he intended to ask her a difficult question. Then he shook his head. 'Nothing.'

CHAPTER 16

On Friday, promptly at two in the afternoon, Thamsine presented herself at the door to Lucy Talbot's home in High Holborn. A large woman with a sour expression on her face showed Thamsine to a bright, airy parlour on the first floor of the prosperous house. If the late Martin Talbot had shown any interest in the interior decoration of his house, it was not in evidence. A woman's hand had decorated this room. The walls were hung with brightly painted hangings depicting a biblical scene and the solid oak furnishings were alleviated with bright cushions and carpets from the East.

A lute sat on the well-polished table and Thamsine picked it up, allowing herself the luxury of playing a favourite air for the pure pleasure of it. She closed her eyes and let the music fill her soul.

When she opened her eyes again, she saw Kit lounging in the doorway. He had the look of someone who had just risen from his bed, his hair tousled and his chin unshaven. He leaned one arm against the doorframe and his shirt fell away from his left shoulder, revealing a puckered and fading scar.

Thamsine felt something tighten inside her. He had fought for the King and he had been hurt. Not once, but several times, it would seem. No one could doubt his loyalty. Whatever had driven him to Thurloe's service must have been compelling.

'You play well,' he said.

'It has been well-tuned,' she commented. 'I thought Mistress Talbot didn't play?'

He shrugged his shirt back into place and walked into the room. 'I had it out the other night.'

'Well then, you have a good ear.'

'Just don't ask me to sing,' he said, taking the lute from her, testing the notes. 'Thurloe is pleased with your work,' he said in a lowered voice.

'Pleased enough to let me go?' she ventured.

Kit shook his head. 'No. He'll release you when he is ready, not before. While he thinks you can still be of use he'll hold the reins in tight.'

She heard the bitterness in his voice. 'Is that how he controls you?' she demanded.

'Yes,' he answered, abruptly thrusting the lute back at her. 'You should probably know. I am leaving London tonight.'

'Where are you going?'

'Paris.'

'Why?'

He sighed and she answered for him. 'This is to do with De Baas?'

'Partly,' he conceded.

She looked away, her lips tightening. 'You're playing with death here, Captain Lovell.'

He lowered his head. 'I know. I don't need you to tell me.'

'Do you have to go?'

'Yes.' It was a bald word, spoken flatly and intended to convey that it was something he had no say in at all.

'Well, I wish you a good voyage.'

He gave a wry smile. 'I will tell you something about myself, Thamsine. I suffer seasickness in a wherry on the river. I detest boats of any description.'

'So you are not perfect after all?' She allowed herself the flicker of a smile. She would probably never forgive him, but in his company, she found it easy to forget.

He sighed. 'Far from it.'

'When will you be back?'

'As soon as I can, but I could be kicking my heels in Paris for weeks.' He ran a hand through his hair, making the dark, uncombed locks stand up on end like a coxcomb.

'So, what do you tell Lucy?'

'Lucy thinks I am going to visit my Aunt Margaret in Norfolk,' he said.

'You have an Aunt Margaret in Norfolk?'

The corner of his lip twitched. 'Maybe.'

'Who do I contact if I have anything to report?'

'A note to Thurloe. Sign yourself John Grey.' He looked at her. 'Thamsine, will you be all right?'

'What do you mean?'

'By yourself?'

'I have been by myself before. I can manage perfectly well without your help.'

His eyes narrowed. 'Yes, I remember!' he commented with an ironic tone. He laid a hand on her arm. 'If there is any trouble, Jem – '

'I'm so sorry … ' Lucy's breathless voice came from the doorway.

Kit abruptly removed his hand as Lucy set her armful of parcels down on the table and selected one, which she held out to Kit.

'For you,'

Kit flushed. 'Lucy, I – '

'It's nothing exciting, just a new shirt. I am sure your aunt would not wish to see you in such a disreputable state.'

Kit looked at the frayed cuffs of his shirt and took the parcel.

'You're too kind, Lucy.' He bowed. 'Now if you will excuse me, ladies, I have some matters to attend to.' He planted a kiss on Lucy's forehead. 'Now, Mouse, I shall see you this evening before I leave.'

Both women watched as the door closed behind him. Shortly afterwards, they heard Kit's boots on the stairs and the front door slam. Lucy crossed to the window. Her blue satin dress shimmered in the light, setting off the fair ringlets and neat figure to perfection. Thamsine, in her gown of dark green wool, felt like a dour crow beside a brightly plumaged bird. Little wonder Kit had taken her for a mistress. She would have proved quite irresistible.

'Well, there he goes! Forsaking me for some tedious old aunt in Norfolk.' Lucy sighed melodramatically and turned to face Thamsine, a bright smile on her face. 'Mistress Granville, I am so delighted you could come. This is something I have been meaning to do for so long.'

Thamsine curtsied. 'I have no other appointments at this time. This is a lovely room,' she blurted out.

Lucy looked pleased. 'Oh, do you like it? I couldn't abide all that dark wood, so after Martin died I had these hangings made in Antwerp. It's the biblical story of Rachel. Martin traded extensively in his line of business, so the carpets I've had some time. You've found the lute, I see.'

Thamsine picked up the fine, inlaid instrument from where

Kit had set it down and handed it to Lucy, who held it awkwardly, like a man with a baby. 'Martin gave me this but I've never really mastered it. What is your charge?' Lucy said.

Thamsine named the sum Bordeaux paid and saw Lucy's eyebrow lift slightly, but she shrugged.

'Very well,' she said. 'Can we start with the lute?'

'Captain Lovell saw to the tuning,' Thamsine said.

'Oh yes, he was playing it the other night. A man of many hidden talents is my Kit.'

Thamsine heard the possessive "my" and wondered if Kit understood this woman at all.

'Shall we begin?' Thamsine suggested, changing the subject.

But Lucy seemed in no hurry to commence instruction. She summoned Mag for refreshment. The disagreeable servant Thamsine had met at the front door appeared with small ale and sweetmeats.

Lucy nibbled daintily with fine, even, white teeth. Thamsine declined when Lucy offered her the tray.

'Will you miss him while he's gone?' Thamsine enquired.

'Kit?' Lucy shrugged and reached for another sweetmeat. 'I have other visitors. They will see I'm not left bereft for long.' She laughed. 'I've shocked you, Mistress Granville?'

'I am not easily shocked,' Thamsine said. 'I'm here to teach you music, not pass judgment on you. Although I'm curious how you manage such arrangements in the current political climate.'

Lucy shrugged. 'I pay no heed to politics. Let people judge me as they will. I try to be discreet.'

There was nothing discreet about Lucy. From the top of her carefully curled blonde head to the tip of her embroidered slipper, she would turn the head of the most ardent Puritan. In the short time Thamsine had spent with her, she had come to the rapid conclusion that Lucy was one of those fortunate women who lived for the moment, with sufficient income to ensure that she hadn't a care in the world. If Lucy was prepared to pay Thamsine to listen to her prattle, then Thamsine would oblige.

'Your husband was older than you?' she asked.

Lucy pulled a face. 'Oh yes, more than thirty years. Martin was a colleague of my father's – a most suitable business transaction. No one thought to consult me on my feelings. I was only fifteen! Imagine! My only consolation was that he was old and one day I would be a very wealthy widow.' She smiled. 'Which of course, I now am!'

Thamsine regarded the woman for a moment. Her age was indeterminate. She had been blessed with a heart-shaped face and clear skin that could have placed her anywhere between sixteen and thirty. If she was somewhere in her mid-to-late twenties, it would have meant a wait of some years to pass into the blessed state of widowhood she now enjoyed. 'When did your husband die?'

'Just over a year ago. He went to dine with a friend and when he returned he had dreadful stomach pains.' Lucy shuddered. 'It was quite awful, such a relief when death took him.' She tightened her lips. 'I find I miss him sometimes. I was quite fond of him. He had a wonderful sense of humour – but then he must have done to marry me! He was always kind to me and never grudged me a new petticoat or a pair of gloves. But – ' the bow-shaped lips parted in a smile again, '– I am fonder still of my handsome jointure and the freedom to pick and choose my companions.'

Thamsine picked up the lute and idly picked at the strings in the pretence of fine-tuning the instrument. 'And what of Kit Lovell?' she asked casually. 'How did you meet him?' She was interested to hear Lucy's version of the meeting.

Lucy wandered over to the table and began sorting through her packages. 'Oh, Kit … ' She looked up and coloured. 'Well, it's all rather embarrassing. I was shopping and some ill-mannered oaf ran into me, knocking me to the ground. Kit helped me up, retrieved my parcels, and –' she laughed, 'took me to bed!'

It was Thamsine's turn to colour. The story tallied with Kit's in all except the last detail, which she could have done without.

Lucy smiled. 'My dear Thamsine. Please be under no illusions about my relationship with Kit Lovell. Kit is an extremely attractive man. How could I resist? But I am quite well aware that he is also a scapegrace and a scoundrel. We have fun together, that is all.'

'Do you love him?'

'Love him?' Lucy frowned. 'Love has nothing to do with it. We enjoy each other's company and … ' She leaned forward ' … we enjoy each other, but it has nothing to do with love. Have you never taken a man to bed for the sheer pleasure of it?'

Thamsine stiffened. 'No!'

'Then that is your loss. How old are you?'

'Twenty-six.'

'And there has never been any man in your life?'

'I didn't say that. There was someone I thought I loved, a long time ago but … ' She waved a hand. 'Now, my circumstances … '

'Oh, the war!' Lucy must have assumed, wrongly, that Thamsine's sweetheart had died in the war. 'You poor thing. Twenty-six and never had a man?'

Thamsine felt the heat in her cheeks. She looked out of the window where a cold, wintry rain beat at the panes.

'Do you never worry about conceiving?' she asked, turning back to look at Lucy.

Lucy's face became serious. 'I can't bear children, Thamsine. My husband had a son by his first marriage, a sickly boy who died not long after we were married. In ten years of marriage, I never conceived a child. The doctors concluded I was barren.'

'I'm sorry, Lucy.'

'Well, it is something of a blessing, is it not?' Lucy's laugh chimed around the room. 'I'm sure I would have made an appalling mother.' But in the silence that followed Thamsine saw the shadows of sadness in her eyes.

Lucy reclined in the nearest chair and looked up at the ceiling, her eyes narrowed. 'I'm very fond of Kit,' she continued, 'but you see his like in any tavern in London. Good-looking men without hope or purpose.'

'The flotsam of the war?'

Lucy nodded. 'Oh yes, well put. That's exactly what they are.' She spread her hands. 'So there you are, Thamsine. I leave Kit to lead his own life, and if he condescends to spend some time with me then that is always pleasant, but I ask no more. It's an arrangement that suits us both. But of course, as you probably know, he never talks about himself.' Lucy leaned back in her chair, one hand draped elegantly at her shoulder. 'Mind you, I am beginning to become quite used to him being around ... ' She trailed off, thoughtfully biting her lip.

'Will you marry again?' Thamsine asked.

Lucy shrugged. 'Only for money, or a title. Preferably both. I would dearly like to have a title, wouldn't you?'

'Not particularly,' Thamsine said. 'I would only marry for love.'

Lucy waved a hand. 'Love is highly overrated, my dear Thamsine. Marry for practicality but not for love. Tell me, where are you from?'

'My family home was in Hampshire,' Thamsine replied.

'Your family?'

'All gone,' Thamsine said in an abrupt tone that a more astute person than Lucy Talbot would have interpreted as a request to enquire no further.

As Lucy opened her mouth to speak again, Thamsine handed her the lute.

'Now, Mistress Talbot, enough chatter. It's time to work.'

Lucy took the instrument and, grimacing, worked her fingers over the strings. At least, Thamsine conceded, she showed slightly more musical ability than Mary Skippon.

CHAPTER 17

*C*ourts in exile were no different from courts anywhere, Kit thought. The King had kept them waiting nearly two hours while pompous men in shabby suits bustled around them.

A King without a throne, and a court without a purpose.

Kit knew only too well that these bored exiles amused themselves with gossip and rumour in a manner quite unsurpassed by that of any well-established court.

He looked at the self-important faces and wondered how many of them were also taking silver from Thurloe's hand. Nothing the young King said or did went unnoticed or unremarked in London. He had to admire Thurloe for the thoroughness with which he conducted his activities. A court full of spies surrounded Charles, and in the years after Worcester, he had been one of them. All he had to do was pass on the latest court gossip. Life as Thurloe's agent had not been unpleasant in those days. Until Thurloe had summoned him back to London.

Fitz leaned against the wall and stared at the ceiling, while Kit watched young Gerard deep in conversation with his uncle. Lord

Gerard, he remembered now, had been a friend of his father's, a well-intentioned and earnest little man.

The conversation had concluded. Lord Gerard nodded and parted from his nephew. Jack sauntered back to join them.

'Well?' Fitz enquired. 'What's happening? I thought the King was anxious to see us.'

'He is but he has other business to attend to.'

'God, I hate waiting,' muttered Kit. 'What other business can he have, for God's sake?'

'Patience, Lovell!' Fitz counselled.

'I don't have any. I hate Paris and I hate France. I don't know why I even came.'

'Because you were commanded to?' Fitz suggested. 'Anyway, why do you hate France? I thought you were half-French.'

Kit shrugged. 'I would rather be in England.'

Where I have some control over my life, Kit thought. Back in England, where I wouldn't spend every moment worrying about Thamsine Granville.

'You've not met my mother's relatives,' he continued. 'Fortunately, they live well out of the way of Paris and I don't have to trouble myself with them.'

This was rather unjust. His living relatives consisted of a couple of extremely pleasant aunts and some rather distant and dim cousins who lived in the crumbling chateau near Agens, where he had spent the first eight years of his life.

'And now the French are conspiring with bloody Cromwell to have the King evicted from France,' Kit went on, giving vent to his frustrations. 'At least that is one thing the King and I have in common. He's half-French too.' Kit snorted. 'A plague on our poxy French relatives!'

Lord Gerard appeared at the door. 'Gentlemen, the King will see you now.'

There were the usual formalities to be observed and the three men bowed low as they entered the room. Charles sat at a table, his advisors behind him. He had changed immeasurably in the eighteen months since Kit had last seen him. He saw no trace of the eager youngster who had urged them into battle at Worcester. His hopes, his dreams and his innocence had died on that day. For a young man of barely twenty-four, he looked ten years older.

'Your Majesty!' Kit said, marvelling at how odd the words sounded after all this time.

'Lovell, Fitzjames, it is good to see you both again.' Charles inclined his head to acknowledge them.

'My nephew Jack, Your Majesty,' Lord Gerard added.

'I do not intend to waste time with pleasantries,' the King said. 'Word of what you plan has already reached me.'

'Your Majesty, if you would but listen to Major Henshaw ... '

'I will have no truck with Henshaw. He is a murderer and a man not to be trusted.' Charles' gaze ran around the circle of men. 'As indeed are any of you. God's blood, gentlemen, I am surrounded by plots and plans. My mother exhorts me one way, my cousin another. Which way am I to turn?'

'Your Majesty, we want nothing more than your restoration to your rightful throne,' Lord Gerard began.

'Then if that is all you desire, your understanding of my predicament is naïve, Gerard.' Charles closed his eyes and waved a hand. 'Very well, tell me your plan.'

Gerard turned to Fitzjames, who cleared his throat. 'Sire, we have a contact here in the French court who is desirous of assisting us.'

Charles gave a derisive snort of laughter. 'For what purpose?'

'To be blunt,' Lord Gerard said, 'if you were to return to the throne of England, well disposed to the French court, then France will be highly relieved. There is considerable resentment about

Cromwell's high-handed support of the Huguenot cause and the way he is playing the Dutch against the Spanish.'

'And why would I be any different? I cannot countenance the wholesale slaughter of innocents on account of their religion.'

'Your Majesty, we are straying from the point. Our plan is quite simple, to destabilize the army by removing Cromwell.'

Charles' eyes took on a hooded, thoughtful look. 'What do you mean by "remove"?'

Fitz spoke. 'We plan to assassinate him, and while the army is in uproar there will be a rising in London. With less than a thousand men, we could take and hold Whitehall, the Tower and other key positions.'

'And with you waiting in the Thames Estuary to land, England will fall,' Lord Gerard concluded.

'And what help will the French provide?'

'The means to remove Cromwell,' Fitzjames said quietly.

Charles closed his eyes; when he opened them they were fixed on Kit. 'Lovell, you're silent. What are your thoughts on this plan?'

A cold shiver ran down Kit's spine. 'I think we need some guarantee of general support before we embark on it. Without a firm commitment of men and money, we are talking about a dream, Your Majesty.'

'I agree,' Charles said. 'Gentlemen, it is, I believe, now generally well known, that there is a committee in England that holds my commission for a general uprising should the circumstances prevail. I do not believe that the death of Cromwell alone will achieve anything in itself but ... ' he raised a finger, ' ... should such an event occur as a prelude to an uprising sanctioned by the Sealed Knot, then it may be a worthwhile venture.'

'But Your Majesty, we do not know who comprises the Sealed Knot. How can we discuss such matters with them?' Fitz posed the question that had been on the tip of Kit's tongue. He gave his friend a sharp glance, relieved that Fitz seemed ignorant of the composition of the Sealed Knot.

'Who comprises the Sealed Knot is no concern of yours,' the King said. 'Gentlemen, officially I will not countenance an act of aggression against the person of Cromwell unless it is done in conjunction with an organised general insurrection.'

'Your Majesty ... ' Lord Gerard began in a pleading tone.

Charles raised a hand. 'That is my decision, Lord Gerard. Return to England but do nothing until agents of the Sealed Knot contact you. Is that clear?'

The men nodded.

'Good day to you, gentlemen.' The King gestured at the door.

The group walked out of the audience chamber. Heads turned and bent to whisper to companions as they passed by. It was only when they had secured the privacy of their lodgings and adjourned to a private parlour that Lord Gerard gave vent to his frustration by hurling his hat onto the table.

'What is it going to take to convince him?' he snorted.

'I think the memory of Worcester is close to his heart,' Kit said. 'Who can blame him?'

'Worcester was three years ago,' Fitz said. 'Lovell, pour the wine. I feel like getting drunk!'

'Well, that will be a real contribution to the cause,' Kit said. 'Let's all get drunk!'

He looked up as the door opened, without a knock, to admit a tall, dark man. They all jumped to their feet.

'Your Highness!' Lord Gerard said, bowing.

Prince Rupert of the Rhine poured himself a glass of wine and, looking around the assembled company, took a seat.

'I hear your meeting with my cousin was not satisfactory,' he said.

'Not the conclusion we should have wished,' Lord Gerard said glumly.

'Charles has lost his courage,' Rupert remarked.

'He has lost heart,' Kit said.

Rupert looked at him. The sharp eyes, Kit remembered so well, burning into his soul.

'That too.' Rupert took a sip of wine. 'It happens that the Queen does not agree with her son. She believes firmly that the King's fortunes will prosper in more ... ' He frowned, looking for the words, ' ... active hands.'

'I have heard the Duke of York,' Lord Gerard said, referring to Charles' younger brother James, 'would not hesitate.'

'I agree,' Rupert said quietly. 'I would lead an army into England to return the throne to the rightful King.'

'You, Your Highness?' Lord Gerard said.

Rupert's eyes flashed. 'I am hardly in my dotage yet, Gerard.'

'I did not mean it that way, Your Highness. I meant merely to imply that you at the head of an army would have a greater chance of success than any other I could name.'

'But there is one stumbling block.' Rupert leaned forward. 'Cromwell. He is not just the Lord Protector, he is the head of the army and a man to be feared. God knows we all know his power of leadership.'

Kit drained his cup, remembering Cromwell's unprecedented tactics that had won the battle at Worcester.

'Are you saying you agree with us, Your Highness?' Fitz asked carefully.

'Remove Cromwell and the army will be like a chicken without its head.' Rupert swirled the contents of his glass, staring at it thoughtfully.

'What of the Sealed Knot?' Kit asked.

Rupert waved a long, slender hand. 'Politicians. Old men with no wish except to die in their beds.'

'Do you know who they are?' Kit asked.

Rupert shook his head. 'No. That is one of the few closely guarded secrets in this court.'

Kit bit back his frustration. Did no one know who these men were?

'We cannot discount them. They hold the King's Commission,' Lord Gerard said.

'That is just a piece of paper.' Rupert drained his glass and rose to his feet. 'We will talk again tomorrow, Gerard, you and I.'

They bowed as the formidable soldier left the room. Kit watched the door close behind the man he once would have followed to his death. The rumours were true. The court was divided, with the Queen and Rupert firmly in one camp, advocating action, while the King counselled caution. Who, if anyone, was right?

CHAPTER 18

*L*ucy stood by the window, glancing up and down the street.

'Are you waiting for someone?' Thamsine enquired, her patience wearing thin. Lucy had been up and down all through the lesson.

'Just a friend. He said he would call this morning to hear me play.'

A male friend, Thamsine thought. She didn't think Lucy had made quite such good progress as to warrant public performance.

'Is there a particular piece you would like to play for him?' she asked.

Lucy sat down again and made a pretence of studying the music. 'This one, I think.' She picked up the sheet of paper and handed it to Thamsine. 'I told him I had been having lessons and he said he was most anxious to hear me.'

'A good friend?' Thamsine said.

'I'm keen to impress him.' Lucy looked up with a small, smug smile on her lips.

'What about Lovell?'

Lucy gave a careless shrug, dismissing her lover.

'He's been away for two weeks without a word. A woman can get lonely in that time.' She looked at Thamsine through narrowed eyes. 'Why? Do you miss him?'

'Why would I miss him?' Thamsine replied with studied carelessness.

Every Friday she dispatched a note, dutifully signed "John Grey", and waited for Kit Lovell to walk through the door of The Ship Inn. Without him, she felt adrift. His absence from London and from her life left a void that the cheerful company at The Ship Inn failed to fill.

The music lessons at the French Ambassador's continued in Kit's absence. Mary Skippon's little talent had improved, to the evident delight of her lover. Thamsine had not seen De Baas since the night of his planned seduction, and she had little to report to John Thurloe.

She sighed and forced her attention back to her present pupil. Unlike poor Mary Skippon, Lucy Talbot had some natural talent and was a fast learner. However, she was easily distracted and this afternoon seemed worse than usual.

Lucy returned to her seat and picked up the lute. She bent her head to the task, awkwardly feeling for the notes of the simple melody Thamsine had found for her.

A firm knock at the front door made them both start. Lucy jumped to her feet, the neck of the lute clasped firmly in her hands. Thamsine had never seen her so on edge.

She heard footsteps on the stairs and the ill-tempered maid, Mag, flung the door open to admit Lucy's visitor. The blood in Thamsine's veins froze as a tall, dark-haired man stepped into the room.

Ambrose Morton stood framed by the door, savouring the

silence.

'Thamsine,' he said, a slow smile spreading across his face. 'You have led me a pretty dance.'

'Ambrose,' she breathed his name in one long aspiration.

'Is this the girl?' Lucy said. 'Was I right?'

Ambrose crossed the floor to where Thamsine stood rooted to the spot. He put a finger under her chin and lifted her face to look up into his eyes.

'Oh yes, Lucy my dear, this is the girl. My betrothed. Do you know she tried to kill me?' Ambrose curled a lock of her hair around his finger. As he did so he touched his head, just above the right ear. 'You did no more than knock me out. Unfortunately, by the time I had regained my senses you were long gone.'

Thamsine struck his hand away and backed away, her eyes searching for a way out, but Ambrose stood between her and the door. The windows were at least twelve feet from the ground and firmly fastened against the cold, damp spring day.

Ambrose smiled. 'It's pointless looking for an escape, Thamsine. You don't think for a moment I'm letting you go after I have spent months combing the streets of London for you. You've been most elusive, my dear. I thought I had you cornered that day at the Lord Protector's parade. I really must commend you on your ability to disappear.'

'Lucy!' Thamsine turned in appeal to the woman who had betrayed her. 'How do you know this man?'

Lucy smiled a cold, hard smile and moved beside Ambrose, tucking her arm into his.

'Kit Lovell introduced us.' She looked up at Ambrose Morton's handsome face. 'How could I resist? Ambrose had told me all about you, long before I met you. Of course, as soon as I saw you, I knew who you were. Ambrose was so pleased when I told him that you were Kit's little pet.'

Ambrose Morton patted Lucy's dainty little hand.

'Your friend, Lovell, seems curiously protective of you, so we have bided our time until he was out of the way, in Norfolk or wherever he is in reality. Does he know the truth about you, Thamsine?'

Thamsine said nothing.

'He doesn't! You haven't told him,' Lucy declared.

Thamsine turned to Lucy. 'Lucy! You have no idea what this man has done. What he is capable of!'

Lucy shook her head. 'You are legally betrothed to him — '

'A betrothal I broke off ten years ago.'

Ambrose smiled and waved a hand. 'Idle promises made in our youth. What matters is that your father formally contracted our betrothal before his death, Thamsine.'

'My father was not in his right mind. He was ailing ... your mother forced him into it ... ' Thamsine broke off and looked away, the memory of that betrayal still raw.

Lucy studied Thamsine with a humourless smile on her lips. 'I can't think what he saw in you. You're hardly his type.'

'Why are you doing this, Lucy? What do you get from this alliance with the Devil?'

Lucy's lips tightened. 'I am rather possessive about my men, Mistress Granville, and I don't need you to distract my dear Kit any longer. I have my own plans for him.'

Thamsine searched the woman's hard face, looking for a shred of human decency that would respond to an appeal. All she saw was a spoiled woman who let nothing stand in the way of what she wanted – and what she wanted was Kit Lovell. She wondered why. Was it possible, for all her protestations, that Lucy had been betrayed by her own emotions? Had she fallen in love with Kit Lovell?

'If you think Kit Lovell will come to your rescue, forget it,'

Morton said. 'By the time he returns from wherever he is, you will be married and beyond his reach.'

Lucy turned to Ambrose. 'Well, are you taking her? This interview is getting a little tiresome.'

Thamsine made a dive for the windows. Far better to break a leg, or her neck, in a bid for freedom than submit to this man. Ambrose caught her by the waist, lifting her from the ground as if she were a doll. He clapped his hand over her mouth, and numbed shock gave way to desperation. Thamsine kicked and clawed and struggled but Ambrose was a powerful man, and apart from a satisfying scratch on his cheek, her efforts were in vain.

He held her firm as they heard footsteps on the stairs. Mag threw open the door to admit a man of middle age, thin and slightly stooped with lank hair and a long, sad face. Ambrose dropped his hand, and Thamsine felt the breath catch in her throat as she recognised the visitor.

Her sister's husband, the lawyer Roger Knott.

'Roger. Help me, please.'

But her vain hope that Roger had come to rescue her faded as Roger Knott bowed to Lucy, and then turned to where Thamsine stood immobile in Ambrose's grip.

'Thamsine. I am pleased to see you are well,' he said. 'We have been most concerned for your welfare. It pleases me to see you reunited with your betrothed.'

'How nice,' Lucy said. 'A family reunion. You would not know, I suppose, that dear Roger has been a loyal friend of my family for, oh, more years than I can remember!'

Thamsine glared at her brother-in-law. War had torn her family apart, with Roger taking up a sword for Parliament, while her father espoused the King's cause. She had not seen her sister, Jane, or her husband until she had fled to their quiet house in

Turnham Green six months previously. He had betrayed her then, and now it seemed he would betray her again.

'The coach is by the door, Morton,' Roger said, standing aside as Ambrose lifted Thamsine from her feet and carried her down the stairs. He thrust her into a coach, one hand holding her firmly, the other dabbing at his cheek where she had scratched him. Roger Knott climbed into the carriage after them, shrinking into the seat, his pale face shining in the gloom of the carriage.

As the carriage lurched forward she found her voice.

'Where are you taking me?'

'I'm taking you to your sister in Turnham Green,' Ambrose said.

'You can't force me to marry you, Ambrose,' she said with more bravado than she felt.

'Be assured, Thamsine, our marriage will be contracted legally and with your consent. I have no wish for anyone to question its validity at a later date.'

'I will burn in Hell first.'

'You may well do that, Thamsine, but not until I'm ready to let you,' Ambrose replied.

Thamsine spat at him.

'Tut, Mistress Granville. You have been too much in rough company and forgotten your manners,' Ambrose said as he wiped his face. 'You will be pleased to know that your brother-in-law has some scruples and is most insistent that you shall stay at Turnham Green until you are of a more amenable state of mind. Of course, it is not my preferred course, but I am prepared to defer to him in this matter. I want a willing wife to come to my bed.'

Not while I have breath in my body, Thamsine thought as she subsided against the cracked leather of the seat, beyond misery.

She had been delivered up to the enemy, sold on the marriage market by an old, sick man who could not resist his wife's harassment any longer, and then betrayed by her sister's husband, the only other person who had been trusted to see to her welfare.

The house in Turnham Green stood set back from the London road, a pretty red brick building surrounded by a rambling garden that was the delight of her sister, Jane.

Thamsine's heart sank as the coach stopped in the courtyard. Ambrose dragged her from the coach, nearly knocking over the maid who opened the front door to them. As Thamsine stumbled across the doorstep she collided with her sister.

'Jane!' She flung herself at her sister, feeling Jane's arm around her, drawing her close.

'You found her!' Jane spoke over her sister's head, no doubt addressing her husband. 'Oh, my dear, you've no idea how worried I've been.'

Thamsine was wrested away from Jane's reassuring arm by Ambrose. He held her by the shoulder, his fingers digging painfully into her flesh.

Jane looked at her husband. 'Roger, I don't understand.'

Roger swallowed. 'There is nothing to understand. Thamsine is to be confined to the small bedchamber until I am satisfied that she is contrite for her high-handed behaviour towards Colonel Morton.'

'Thamsine?' Jane looked at her sister.

'Jane, I—'

Thamsine opened her mouth to speak, but Ambrose had shifted his grip on her arm. With Roger following, he half-dragged, half-carried her up the stairs and thrust her inside the smallest bedchamber.

Thamsine stumbled against the bed, falling onto it. Ambrose stood over her, his handsome face completely devoid of expression.

'What are you going to do with me?' Her voice quavered. She knew only too well what he was capable of doing.

'Nothing,' he said, straightening. 'I intend to do nothing for the moment. Your brother-in-law seems to think he can persuade you to see sense.'

He took a step back, allowing her to sit up. Roger stood in the doorway. She remembered him as a serious young man with good prospects in the law. Now in early middle age, his narrow face was lined, and the blue eyes faded and sunken. His thinning, fair hair hung lankly to his collar and he looked like a man twice his age.

When he stepped into the room and stood beside Morton. He barely reached Morton's shoulder in height. A little man with big ambitions.

'What do you have to say for yourself?' he asked, employing the tone he would use for one of his daughters.

'Roger,' Thamsine sat up, straightening her collar. 'You know this is wrong. My father was coerced into signing that paper. The Mortons want control of the estate.'

'It's all quite legal, Thamsine. Your father signed the contract before his death and Morton is entirely in the right. But I have told him you must go to the altar willingly. I am hoping that after a day or so you will see sense,' he said, but his eyes avoided hers, giving her the answer she sought.

She took a step back. 'What does he have over you, Roger? How can he bend you to his will?'

Ambrose smirked. 'Your morally upright brother has been a little indiscreet, my dear. There are certain letters in existence which I am sure he would not wish the world to know about, least of all his wife.'

Ambrose cast Roger a sidelong glance that left Thamsine in no doubt as to the nature of the indiscretion.

'I don't believe you. Roger loves my sister – he would never...'

Ambrose cocked his head to one side. 'How little you know of men, my dear. He proved such a comfort to poor Mistress Talbot in her widowhood.'

Thamsine cast her brother-in-law a look of disgust. Bile rose in her throat. This odious man had betrayed her sister with Lucy Talbot.

He looked away, unable to meet her angry gaze.

'You mealy-mouthed hypocrite,' Thamsine spat, 'canting Bible verses while all the time you were swiving that whore!'

'My, my,' Ambrose remarked blandly. 'Six months on the streets of London has taught you some colourful language, my dear Thamsine. That will have to change.'

Roger had gone chalk white, and she closed in on his weakness.

'What is to stop me telling Jane?' Thamsine spat.

'You'll not tell Jane because you love her too much. She's not strong, she couldn't bear it.' Roger's voice lacked conviction.

'You should have thought about that before leaping into bed with Lucy Talbot.'

Roger frowned and she knew she had gone too far. Anger replaced hurt and he crossed to her, striking her across the face. She had not been expecting the blow and the force knocked her back across the bed.

Holding a hand to her face, she sat up, all the fight knocked out of her.

Without looking at Ambrose, Roger said, 'Leave us, Morton!'

Ambrose did not move. 'We are agreed, Knott? If you waver on me, I'll deal with her in my way.'

Roger looked up at the taller man. 'Leave her to me, Morton. She'll marry you willingly, I promise. She just needs to be made to see sense.'

'I'll return in a week, Knott, and I expect her to be agreeable. If she has gone or if she still refuses me, you know the consequences.'

Thamsine saw her brother-in-law swallow. She wondered what had become of the serious young lawyer who had courted her sister. She did not know this man.

Morton left the room, closing the door behind him. Thamsine rose to her feet. Without Ambrose present, Roger did not scare her.

'Roger, how have you let this happen? How could you be such a fool?'

His shoulders hunched. 'Martin Talbot was a friend as well as a client. After he died, his widow looked to me for assistance. I never intended anything to happen.' There were tears in his eyes. 'Jane was at my mother's house. You've met Lucy Talbot. You know what she's like. She flattered me. She captivated me. I was beset by the Devil. The Devil made me write letters I shouldn't have, and neglect my responsibilities. I was led into temptation by a witch and now I must pay the price.'

'You're a fool!' Thamsine looked at him with contempt. 'Now you have fallen into Ambrose Morton's hands. I came to you because I trusted you. What tale did Ambrose spin for you to so turn against me?'

Roger passed his tongue over his dry lips and did not reply.

'You sent for him. It was you who told him I had come to you and Jane for refuge,' she said. 'If I hadn't seen him arrive, you would have handed me over to him, like a prize.'

'Thamsine, I'm a lawyer. All I knew then was that you had a legal arrangement with Colonel Morton. I did what I thought was right. I didn't know him,' he added with bitterness in his voice. 'I thought you were being obdurate. Are you going to tell me now why you won't marry him? Why you tried to kill him?'

'I shot him in self-defence, Roger. He tried to ... ' She struggled with the ugly word that rose to her lips. '...take me without my consent.' She tried to read Roger's face, but it was a mask of lawyerly inscrutability. 'Did you hear what I said, Roger? He tried to rape me and you want me to marry him.'

Roger's pale face remained still. 'Legally, you are contracted to marry him. Your father ... '

Thamsine looked up at the ceiling in despair. 'My father? Oh, Roger, if you could have seen him in those last few months. Isabelle Morton was at him night and day. He needed a male heir. Edward was dead. He couldn't leave the estate in the hands of a mere woman. Who better than her son? Every moment until he could bear it no longer and he signed my life away and even then Ambrose couldn't wait – he is a rapist and probably worse! Roger, I cannot marry him.'

Knott shifted uneasily. His tongue ran around his dry lips. 'Be thankful, Thamsine, that I persuaded him to let you stay here with me.'

'Why? Why not just let him have me?'

'Because none of us wants a scandal, Thamsine. Far better you go to the altar willingly than suffer a repeat of what occurred before.'

'I wish to God I had killed him!' Thamsine sank onto the bed. She looked up at Roger, her mouth twisted in anguish. 'I came here to you for help and you betrayed me. With Ambrose in London, I have had no choice but to hide and while he controls the estate, I have no access to money. I've been living ... *surviving* these past months on nothing.'

Roger looked away, his face unhappy. 'Thamsine, I know you must think I have failed you, but you must see that my future and that of my family are my priority. I suggest you pray for guidance from God. I find him great comfort in such times of adversity. I have left a Bible for you to contemplate.'

He turned on his heel and left the room, locking the door behind him.

A long time later, she lay curled up on the bed, looking at a cold, clear moon rising over the trees through the square of the window. She had no more tears to cry. The nightmare had begun again. Nothing she had endured in London before her path had crossed that of Kit Lovell compared with the horror of finding herself back in the power of Ambrose Morton.

She put her hand on the cold leather of the binding of the Bible Roger had left for her. She had prayed before, prayed many times, but God never listened to her prayers. Was she so insignificant in the great scheme of things? Had she asked too much? She picked up the book and hurled it at the wall.

Hot tears welled again in her eyes and she gave a wail of despair. It seemed everyone she had ever trusted had betrayed her. Even Kit Lovell had betrayed her, but his motives were different and, it was possible, she thought, that he might care for her a little. Lucy had thought that. Lucy had removed her so she could have Kit to herself.

Kit, she thought, screwing her eyes tight shut, please, if you can hear me, come back. I need you.

She shook her head. She could not expect Kit to come to her rescue again. She turned her face to the bolster, her tears soaking the pillow.

When Kit returned from Paris and found her gone, he would make a number of assumptions and they'd all be wrong. His life would continue without her. She had nothing but her own resources, and as parlous as her situation seemed to be, at least she was alive, and while she lived there remained the faintest hope for her to cling to.

CHAPTER 19

Thamsine lay on the narrow bed and looked up at the ceiling. She had been incarcerated for five long days with only the Bible and her thoughts for company, and in many ways, this small, bare room was worse than the cell that she had endured in the Tower of London.

At least since the first day, Roger hadn't raised a hand to her, but he seemed to think nothing of starving her into submission. He brought her just enough bread and water to keep her alive. She felt her physical and mental reserves of strength ebbing.

The sound of the key in the door made her flinch and she rose slowly to her feet, her head spinning. When she saw it was not Roger she fell back on the edge of the bed.

'Oh, Jane!' Tears of relief filled her eyes at the sight of her sister. Despite her requests to see her sister, she had seen only Roger Knott in her whole incarceration.

'Sister,' Jane set the tray of food she carried on the table. 'I have brought you some sustenance.'

Thamsine pulled herself up from the bed and sat on the stool at the table.

'Does Roger know you are here?' Thamsine lifted the cloth covering the tray. A simple meal of soup and bread but to Thamsine it looked like a King's feast.

'Roger has business in London. He will be gone all of the day.'

Thamsine looked up at her half-sister. After Thamsine's mother had died, Jane had provided the much-needed love and affection the small child had sought. Jane's marriage to Roger Knott had separated the sisters, but the war had torn them apart.

Until the night she had turned up on Jane's doorstep, hysterical because she thought she had killed a man, Thamsine had not seen her sister for more than ten years. Now, it seemed to her that the months since she had last seen her had wrought even greater changes in her sister. She looked thin and pale and there were dark shadows under her eyes.

'Ambrose?' Thamsine could hardly bring herself to say his name.

'I haven't seen him since the day he brought you here. It's just you and I.' Jane clasped her hands in front of her apron and frowned unhappily. 'I don't understand any of this, Thamsine. I remember before the war, you were so much in love with Ambrose Morton. You begged Father for the betrothal.'

'That was before I knew what he was.' Thamsine could not hide the bitterness in her voice.

'Are you going to tell me?'

Ambrose Morton brought a miasma of evil with him wherever he went. Jane deserved the truth about him.

Thamsine began, 'You were right, Jane. In those months before the war, he flattered me and courted me. Stupid girl that I was, I fell for his charms and, as you say, I begged Father for the betrothal. All through the war, he wrote to me. Wonderful letters, full of professions of love. On the few occasions he could be spared he came to visit with presents and blandishments. I adored him.' She took a breath, fighting back the memory of that childish infatuation. 'All through those long years, I would visit his mother and sister, Annie at Beverstock Hall. Do you remember Annie?'

'Oh yes, the poor idiot child,' Jane said.

Thamsine felt the heat rise to her cheeks. 'Annie may be a simpleton,' she said, 'but unlike her odious mother and vile brother, she has a pure and loving heart.'

Jane lowered her eyes. 'Of course. I'm sorry, Thamsine. Go on.'

'Early in '46, one of the servants told me that Ambrose had returned to Beverstock, so I decided to ride over to see him and surprise him. All I could think about was that he was home, he had survived, and now we could get married. I didn't wait to be announced. I walked into the parlour and I found him ... ' she swallowed ' ... in congress with one of the maids.'

Jane's eyes widened. 'Oh! That must have been a shock, Thamsine, but these things happen. It was surely not sufficient ... '

'You don't understand, Jane.' Thamsine felt the old anger well in her. 'It was not consensual. She was not some buxom servant girl having a roll with the squire, it was... ' she took a shuddering breath and looked away. 'I will spare you the details but more than her tears, it was the look on his face, Jane. Such unmerciful cruelty. I fled home and told Father the betrothal was over. I didn't tell him why. I thought I need never see Ambrose Morton again. The war was over and he went into exile. Then Father married Isabelle Morton.' Thamsine gave a bitter sigh. 'That was the blackest day of my life. Isabelle Morton wanted only one thing and that was Hartley Court, but she could never have it while Edward lived. I tried to make Edward stay, Jane, I pleaded with him not to go on the fool's errand to the King's cause, but his blood was up and he went and he died. I will never forgive him for that.'

Jane laid a hand on her sister's arm. 'Edward is dead, Thamsine, you must forgive him. He was young and idealistic. He did not die simply to spite you.'

'I know,' Thamsine said unhappily, 'but he left me the heiress to the Granville fortune and the Hartley estate. It was hardly a surprise when Ambrose returned to England and re-established himself at Beverstock Hall. Isabelle began on our father, a ministering angel in his last days. Roger came, the paper was signed, the will was amended, and I was bound to Ambrose Morton again.'

'But Thamsine,' Jane frowned. 'I know enough of the law to know he cannot marry you without your consent.'

'After Father died in May last year, I tried to postpone the marriage. I claimed mourning as my excuse. For six months I managed to find some excuse or another until Ambrose finally lost patience.'

She took a deep breath. 'He'd been drinking. He produced a pistol and I saw the look in his eye. I'd seen it before. That day I came upon him with his maid.' Thamsine felt her voice constrict as the memory of the fear he had instilled in her came back. 'We struggled – I knew what he was going to do, Jane, and I was powerless to prevent it. But he made one mistake. To subdue me, he set the pistol down on the table while he wrestled with me. Annie walked in on us and in that instant, I was able to break free of him. Annie picked up the pistol and gave it to me. Poor, trusting Annie. When Ambrose came for me again, I fired. There was so much blood. I thought for certes he was dead. I took what few possessions I could carry and fled to you and the rest you know.'

'Why didn't you tell us any of this when you came to us?' Jane stared at her sister with wide, horrified eyes.

'Would it have made any difference?' Thamsine said. 'I was frightened – I had shot a man. I thought I'd killed him. I lived in dread of every knock on the door. Little did I know that the knock on the door would come from the man I thought I had killed. Roger had sent for him. It was just by pure chance that I saw him and was able to make my escape.'

Jane shook her head in disbelief. 'If only I had known!'

'What could you have done? Besides, you were not well and you had the girls to consider. I couldn't bring myself to confide in you.'

Jane took her hand. There were tears in her eyes. 'I had no idea. That is not the story Ambrose told us.'

'He's a very good liar, Jane.'

'But Roger ... '

'Roger will do whatever Ambrose wants and you are no match for either of them.'

'I don't understand what has happened to Roger. These last months, he's changed.' Jane looked away, and Thamsine thought she could see the glint of tears in her sister's eyes.

'He wants no scandal to touch his prospects.' Thamsine held her tongue on the true reason for Roger's uncharacteristic behaviour. Jane did not need to know that her husband was an adulterer. She changed the subject. 'Let's talk of other matters. How are the children? Are they here?'

Jane shook her head. 'No, they have been staying with Roger's mother. They are happy there.'

'Are they well?'

Jane's face lightened. Her world revolved around her daughters, who bore the biblical names of Rachel and Rebecca. 'Oh, they're fine, Thamsine. I wish you could see them. Rebecca is a good, dutiful daughter but Rachel ... ' Jane's face softened at the mention of her youngest daughter. 'Rachel is so like you. She's always in trouble over some innocent misdemeanour or another, from climbing trees in the orchard to failing to learn her Bible verses.'

'I would love to see them, Jane.'

'Oh, I am sure you shall. Perhaps I could bring them to Hartley when ... ' Jane's face tightened and Thamsine answered for her.

'When I am married?'

Jane picked up the Bible. She frowned as she looked at the book, its spine broken when Thamsine had hurled it against the wall. 'The Bible is not to blame for your woes, Thamsine,' she said, rising to her feet.

She set the book down on the table, her hand resting on it momentarily.

'A short passage for you to consider, Thamsine. Ephesians 4, Chapters 25 to 31.'

When she was gone, Thamsine picked up the book and turned to the passage. It was a lovely piece that spoke of forgiveness.

... Let all bitterness, wrath, anger, clamour, and evil speaking be put away from you, with all malice. And be kind to one another, tender-hearted, forgiving one another, even as God in Christ forgave you ...

'Oh Jane,' she whispered. 'Do you think that will help?'

JANE RETURNED THE FOLLOWING MORNING. She smiled at Thamsine and held out her hands.

'Roger says you can help me this morning.'

Thamsine raised her head and looked at her sister's slight figure in the doorway. 'You mean I am allowed out?'

'Only to help me,' Jane said hastily. 'I am not to let you out of my sight.'

'That's very trusting of Roger. And how would you stop me if I made a bolt for freedom?'

Jane's lips tightened. 'I couldn't, but please, Thamsine, if you do try to escape, I will answer for it. Roger has made that quite clear.'

Thamsine stood up and shook out her crumpled skirts. It would be good to be free of the four walls of her prison. Roger did not need keys or shackles. He knew that this sort of emotional blackmail would keep her subdued for the time being. She had one more day before Morton returned to claim her and no plan to make good her escape.

'What do you need help with?' she asked, tying the apron Jane handed to her as they went down the stairs.

'The stillroom needs cleaning out in preparation for the summer herbs.'

Thamsine wandered around the little room, opening the pots and smelling the concoctions. At least it was an activity, and as much as Thamsine had always hated matters domestic, there was a certain pleasure in working with the sweet-smelling herbs. She opened a heavy earthenware crock and picked out a dried, slivered root. Mindful that she had paid scant attention to any lessons on the art of the stillroom, she held a piece up.

'What's this, Jane?'

Jane's eyes widened. 'Put that back at once. That is the root of monkshood.'

Thamsine dropped the root back into the crock as if it had bitten her. Even with her limited herbal knowledge, she knew that monkshood was a poison. 'Why do you keep it?'

'I make it up as a rat poison sometimes,' Jane replied. 'Now you had best wash your hands.'

Jane coughed and Thamsine looked at her sharply, watching as

Jane's thin chest rose in an effort to gain air. The dark shadows around her eyes seemed to grow deeper.

'Jane, are you all right?'

Jane waited until the spasm had ended and gave Thamsine a thin smile. 'I am fine. It is just the tail end of that winter ailment I can't seem to shake.'

Thamsine picked up a pot. 'Not even with the help of your own wonderful elixirs?'

For the first time, her sister laughed. 'All I need is some warm weather, Thamsine. Now, you have a good hand. Open that book and start transcribing these receipts.'

The two sisters worked in companionable silence for an hour before Thamsine straightened her back and stood up. 'I'm stiff. Can we walk in the garden? I need fresh air.'

Jane looked surprised but raised one thin shoulder. 'As long as you won't ... '

'I'm not going to scale the garden wall. I just need to walk.'

As they stepped out into Jane's peaceful garden, Thamsine tucked her arm into her sister's and took a deep breath of fresh air. 'I smell spring,' she said.

Jane nodded. 'Not long now.' She stopped and took her sister's hands, searching her face. 'Thamsine, who is Christopher Lovell?'

The mention of Kit's name caused Thamsine's heart to jolt against her ribs. 'What do you mean?'

'I heard Ambrose mention his name in connection with you ... and another person. I just wondered who he was.'

Thamsine smiled. 'Kit Lovell is ... a terrible scapegrace, Jane. A penniless gambler and worse. But ... ' She fought down the pain that gripped her chest. '... He was kind to me when I needed a friend. That's all.'

'Are you in love with him?'

Thamsine gave a bitter laugh. *In love with Kit Lovell?* The idea was absurd.

'Of course not!' she said. 'He has half the women in London lusting for him.'

Jane's face took on a pinched look. 'And does he have a mistress called Lucy Talbot?'

Thamsine looked at her sister. 'Jane, what do you know about Lucy Talbot?'

Jane's face was still. 'Roger was a friend of Martin Talbot. When he died, his widow relied on his help with the business and the estate.'

Thamsine suppressed the picture of the sort of help Lucy had required.

'Have you ever met her?' she asked, trying to keep her tone even.

Jane began to walk again. 'She has visited here.'

Thamsine frowned. 'Here?'

'Oh yes, several times before Talbot's death. She was very much younger than her husband, and I had never met anyone like her before. Such a pretty, vivacious little thing. Quite irresistible.'

'Lucy Talbot is a very easy person to like.' Thamsine did not attempt to hide the bitterness in her voice.

'I didn't say I liked her,' Jane said, frowning. 'I should have said, irresistible to men.'

Thamsine looked at her sister. Did she know that her own husband had fallen under the spell of Lucy Talbot's charm?

'She professed a great interest in my stillroom,' Jane went on. 'She asked me questions about herbs and roots; which ones had healing properties and which ones were poisonous.'

Thamsine stared at her sister. 'Poisonous?'

'It was autumn and I had been drying some herbs and roots. She seemed particularly interested in the monkshood.'

Thamsine thought of the dried slivers of root in the earthenware crock and felt goosebumps rising on her arm. 'What does it do?'

'It causes vomiting and prostration. The victim has difficulty breathing and dies in great pain.'

'What a horrible way to die. Your poor rats,' Thamsine commented, trying to keep her tone light.

'I wasn't talking about rats, Thamsine. It can kill a person very quickly. Of course, it was not many months later that Martin Talbot died.' Jane looked at her sister, her meaning clear.

'You think ... ?'

'I don't think anything,' Jane said hurriedly, 'but I do know that after she left that day, a couple of the roots of monkshood I had been drying were missing. Now, enough talk of Lucy Talbot. We have work to do.' Jane pushed open the door of the stillroom again. 'You see those empty jars? They must all be washed and scrubbed.'

The sisters were so engrossed in the task that they did not hear Roger until he coughed. As one they looked up to see him standing in the doorway.

He smiled, almost pleasantly. 'Well, I am pleased to see this sight.'

Thamsine straightened and curtsied.

'Jane? Has your sister behaved?'

'She has been exemplary, Roger.'

Thamsine swallowed. She knew the words she was about to say would gall her but for Jane's sake, if not her own, they needed saying. She lowered her head, clasping her hands, like a true penitent, in front of her.

'Roger, I have had much time in the past few days to consider my past actions, and I see that I have acted wrongly.'

Roger narrowed his eyes. 'I am pleased to see you have reconsidered your willful behaviour, Thamsine. Am I to understand that you will no longer resist marriage?'

Thamsine hesitated for a very long time. 'I seem to have no choice in the matter.'

Roger let out a heartfelt sigh. 'I am relieved that you have seen sense, Thamsine. Morton will be delighted when I tell him when he returns tomorrow. You have made the right decision.'

Thamsine lay awake that night staring at the small, square window, where a distant moon cast a sickly, silvery light over her. All the pieces of the puzzle began to fall into place, and the players in the drama took their rightful places on the stage.

Pretty, frivolous, empty-headed Lucy was not the person she professed to be, or that men thought her. She remembered Lucy's hard, implacable face on the day Ambrose had come for her. Nothing stood between Lucy and what – or who – she wanted. The question was, who did she want now – Ambrose Morton, Roger Knott, or Kit Lovell?

Surely Kit had nothing to offer her except whatever talents he had in bed. Roger? He was a married man with a sickly wife and unexciting prospects. Ambrose? If he married Thamsine he would be a wealthy man and more significantly, a wealthy widower.

Thamsine shivered. When she married Morton, would there be a deadly dose of monkshood waiting for her in the future?

Despair engulfed her. If she ran now, she left Jane at the mercy of Ambrose Morton. Anyway, where could she go? Not to Kit Lovell. He was as much in Lucy's thrall as Roger. He would no more believe his mistress was a scheming murderess than Roger would.

She was on her own again.

CHAPTER 20

*A*mbrose Morton returned to Turnham Green the next evening. Thamsine heard his voice in the parlour and crept to the head of the stairs. She could not make out the conversation, but Morton and Knott appeared to be arguing. Occasionally Jane's voice interceded, and after a little while, Jane came out of the parlour.

She stood at the bottom of the stairs looking upwards.

'Thamsine? Ambrose is here. You must come.'

Thamsine stared down at her. 'Jane, I can't.'

Roger appeared behind his wife. 'Thamsine, come down here at once.'

His voice compelled her to move. At every step, she felt nausea rising in her stomach. Roger took her by the shoulder and steered her into the parlour.

'Curtsey,' he hissed in her ear.

She complied, forcing her stiff, wooden legs to bend.

'Thamsine.' Ambrose smiled and took a step towards her. She recoiled.

'I have nothing to say to you, Ambrose.'

'Now, Thamsine, that is not what you told me,' Roger wheedled.

Ambrose took her hand, enclosing it firmly within his own. 'Thamsine, I wish for nothing more than we should be the friends we once were.'

She tried to withdraw her hand but he held it secure, his grip tightening.

'You betrayed any vestige of friendship a long time ago, Ambrose. Let go of my hand.'

He looked pained, almost sorrowful, and the grip tightened, causing her to wince. 'Thamsine, what happened between us was a terrible misunderstanding.'

'There's been no misunderstanding, Ambrose. You tried to force yourself on me. I have no illusions about you. You see only my fortune and you will stop at nothing to obtain it.' The words tumbled out, impervious to her resolutions to play along as the meek, penitential bride.

His eyes flashed for a moment and then, with what appeared to be masterly control, he smiled. 'Thamsine, how wrong you are. I have always loved you.'

'Loved me?' she spat. 'The only true feeling you have ever entertained for me is one of greed – for my body and my estate.'

He raised her hand to his lips, his eyes glittering. 'Please, Thamsine. I've changed. I want to settle with you by my side. We could be happy, you and I.'

She gave a strangled cry and wrested her hand from his grip, turning sharply on her heel to face her sister and brother-in-law.

'Roger, Jane. You are my witnesses. Please do not allow this travesty to happen,' she appealed helplessly.

Roger remained standing at the door and Jane, a helpless spectator, turned her eyes to her husband, willing him to act.

Ambrose's eyes narrowed. 'You have no choice. We will be married, and we can do it on terms of truce or we can do it as enemies. It is entirely in your hands.'

Thamsine leaned on the table as she sought to control her thoughts. For her own sake, she needed to make peace. It would be the only way she could survive. Perhaps once they were wed, the relationship could be renegotiated.

She swallowed. 'Ambrose, I'm tired.' She looked up at him. 'I can't go on fighting you. I don't have the strength.'

Ambrose smiled. 'Ah, Thamsine, I knew you would see reason. Roger is in agreement. We will be married as soon as it can be arranged.'

A wave of nausea engulfed her and she doubled over, fighting back the urge to vomit. Ambrose moved behind her and took her by the shoulders, forcing her down onto a chair. She felt his hands, hot and heavy through the cloth of her dress, the strong fingers tightening, grinding her bones. She gritted her teeth against the pain.

'There is one more thing you owe me, Thamsine Granville,' he hissed into her ear.

'I owe you nothing!'

'You tried to kill me. I want to hear you apologise.'

'I should have killed you,' she said.

His fingers tightened.

'This is wrong!' Jane stepped forward. 'No court in the land will force her to marry against her will. Roger – ' she turned to her husband '– stop this madness.'

'If you have any wisdom, wife, you will not interfere,' Knott replied

Ambrose released Thamsine and took a step toward Jane. Jane's eyes widened as he loomed over her slight figure.

'She is my sister,' Jane said. 'I can't allow this travesty to occur.'

Ambrose struck without warning, a cracking open-handed blow to Jane's face that sent the frail woman flying against the door. Roger uttered a cry and Thamsine rose to her feet. Ambrose pushed her down as Roger knelt beside his stunned wife, cradling her in his arms.

'You see, Thamsine, it's not just you,' Ambrose said. 'There are others involved. Your sister, those two pretty little nieces of yours … ' He left the sentence unfinished but his meaning was clear. Thamsine shuddered.

'And what of your sister?' she said. 'What has become of Annie? Did you punish her for handing me the pistol?'

'Annie has nothing to do with this. You know I would never hurt her.' The nerve in Ambrose's temple began to twitch, and she knew what she had always suspected. Annie, with her bright, innocent eyes, was his Achilles' heel.

'But you think nothing of hurting other women. That maid I found you with, my sister, who knows how many others … '

Ambrose turned away, waving his arm in a gesture of disgust. 'Enough of this talk, Thamsine. We will be married within the next few days, whether you consent or not.'

'And who will you find willing to marry us if I have to be dragged protesting to the altar?'

'There will be someone,' Ambrose said. 'There is always someone whose conscience can be eased with a few coins. You will marry me, Thamsine, or someone close to you is going to be hurt.' He looked meaningfully at Roger, who shrank away from his gaze, still holding Jane in his arms.

'Morton, I must protest,' Roger said, his voice lacking conviction. 'If you wait just a little longer … '

'I've had enough of waiting, Knott. You have had your chance to make her see reason and she shows no sign of repenting her past stubbornness. Our arrangement is at an end. I am taking her with me and I assure you I have far more effective ways of breaking this stiff-necked pride.'

'I will rot in Hell first!' Thamsine spat as she leapt to her feet.

'Indeed you will,' Ambrose hissed in her ear. 'Because Hell is precisely where you are going. You need some time to consider your future, Thamsine Granville, and after a few days I can guarantee you will be crawling to me on your knees.'

He made to grab at her but Thamsine ducked out of his reach. An absurd game of tag around the table ensued until Ambrose drew his sword. He pushed Roger aside and pulled Jane to her feet, holding the tip of the sword to her throat.

'Enough. Come here, Thamsine,' he said.

Thamsine gasped and Ambrose smiled as he drew the sword lightly across Jane's throat, leaving a thin, bloody line. She did not doubt that he would kill Jane if she did not obey.

As soon as she was within arm's reach, Ambrose thrust Jane at her husband and struck out at Thamsine, the same hard blow that had sent Jane to the ground.

Her head reeling, Thamsine fell back against the table and slid to the ground. Unable to move, the world fading from her consciousness, she heard Roger's shaky voice.

'Where are you taking her?'

'I told you. I'm taking her to Hell.'

Ambrose lifted Thamsine, throwing her across his shoulder like a bag of chaff. His shoulder dug into her abdomen. Unable to breathe, she lost consciousness.

CHAPTER 21

*K*it stared into his ale. The French did not know how to make good ale. He took a swig of the tasteless beverage and set the pot down, his fingers clenching and unclenching around the handle.

Henshaw, Fitzjames and Gerard appeared to be turning in ever-decreasing circles, meeting first with one party and then another. No decisions, no promises of help. The King remained obdurate. He would not countenance a move on Cromwell without the support of the Sealed Knot. The delay frustrated Kit beyond measure.

The Sealed Knot – the Sealed Knot seemed aptly named. The composition of this mysterious committee was one of the few well-kept secrets in the court. He had nothing to take back to Thurloe.

He hated every moment spent in Paris and realised that for the first time in his life he wanted a home and hearth and a good woman. A good woman, not the likes of Lucy Talbot.

He took a deep draught of his ale as he dismissed that thought.

Experience had taught him that women were nothing but trouble, a distraction he did not need.

So why, then, did thoughts of Thamsine Granville keep him awake at night? In the dark hours, he imagined the tilt of her chin, the warm, brown eyes, the humorous lift of her mouth. He missed her intelligent companionship and her high-handed disrespect for him.

'Deep in thought, Lovell?'

Kit looked up. He knew and disliked the man who sat down unbidden at his table. Colonel Bampfield was known to turn his coat with the frequency of his linen. Despite having executed a daring rescue of the young Duke of York from under Parliament's nose some eight years previously, he enjoyed a worse reputation than Henshaw for suspect loyalty.

'Colonel Bampfield. The air in here has suddenly grown rather pungent,' Kit snarled.

'My dear Captain Lovell, you are hardly one to start throwing stones, are you?'

'What do you mean?'

Bampfield leaned towards him and said in a low, conspiratorial voice, 'I mean that I know that you and I serve the same master.'

'I have no idea what you are talking about.' Kit set the empty pot down with a thump. 'If you are calling my loyalty to the King into question then I should call you out here and now.'

'You could do that, but I know you won't. I have some letters for delivery to London,' Bampfield continued in the same low voice. 'Call them love letters to someone I care for deeply. I could send them in the usual manner but I would rather they went in safe hands.'

'That is all you ask of me?'

'Of course. I am not asking you to confess your dirty little secrets to me. Merely act as my courier.'

Kit bridled. 'I have no dirty little secrets, Bampfield. However, if you insist, I will take your papers.'

Bampfield rose to his feet. 'You are a gentleman, sir.' He handed Kit a small packet of papers. 'To your safekeeping.'

Kit thrust the papers into his jacket. 'I hope our paths do not cross again, Bampfield.'

'I am sure we can avoid that.'

As Bampfield rose to leave, Fitzjames, Henshaw and the younger Gerard entered the inn. Bampfield stood still, forcing Kit to introductions. He wondered if any of them had seen the letters pass from Bampfield to himself. If they had, nothing in their faces betrayed any suspicion.

Kit looked up at Bampfield. 'It was a pleasure to make your acquaintance again, Colonel.'

Bampfield bowed. 'And yours. Be sure to give my regards to my friends in London. Gentlemen.'

It was evident that Fitz and Gerard had news. They sat down, their faces taut with expectation. Fitz waited until Bampfield had left the room before leaning forward, his face alive with the news he had to impart.

'We have reached an agreement, Lovell.'

'At last,' Kit said, with genuine relief in his voice.

'We have spoken with the Queen and Prince Rupert and we are agreed that we will continue with our plan,' Gerard said. 'You and Fitzjames are to leave now for London to start the arrangements.'

'And you?'

'We have some business still to do here but we will follow by week's end.'

'Rupert wants an army of ten thousand,' Henshaw said.

Kit looked at him in disbelief. 'In England? We've just been through this. We can't raise an army of ten!'

Jack Gerard's eyes burned. 'Scotland, Lovell. The Queen believes that if my uncle were to take the Duke of York and Rupert to Scotland, we will get the support.'

'We did that in '50, Gerard, and look what became of that venture!' He looked at Fitz. 'We were lucky to escape with our lives.'

'This time it will be different. If our plan goes well, Cromwell will be dead and the army in disarray. England will fall.'

Young Gerard's eyes burned with a passion Kit remembered only too well from his youth: the absolute certainty of the rightness of a cause. However, he kept his peace and forced himself to recall that it was not his place to argue against the plan but to go along with it.

He nodded. 'And the King?'

'To remain on the Continent until such time as his kingdom is secure,' Gerard concluded.

Kit looked at Fitz. 'So we leave now?'

'I suggest the morning. A hard ride to Calais to catch the evening tide,' Fitz said.

Kit nodded with relief. There was nothing he wanted more than to be back in England.

CHAPTER 22

it had faced death in many forms and had always managed to stare it down. Now he lay wrapped in his cloak on the rough bunk bed praying for a speedy demise. God had never intended him to be a sailor. He had puked until he had nothing more to puke and dry-retched into the noisome bucket by his bunk and now woke from a fitful sleep.

The lantern, illuminating the cabin in a sickly yellow light, tossed and swayed with the motion of the boat. He closed his eyes to avert the wave of nausea and realised that what had woken him was the sense of another person being in the room, of a shadow obscuring the light and a furtive shuffling.

He opened his eyes again and saw Fitzjames bent towards a lantern. He held Kit's jacket in one hand, and in the other were Bampfield's papers. The paper crackled as Fitz opened one of the letters.

Kit shifted his weight slightly to allow himself leverage from the bunk, and through half-closed eyes, he saw Fitz turn to him.

With his normally sharp reflexes dulled by seasickness, he had not anticipated the speed with which Fitz could move. Fitz turned on him, grabbed his shirt and pulled him into an upright position, his eyes burning with anger.

'You bloody traitor!'

'What?'

Fitz waved the paper in Kit's face. 'What the Hell is this about?'

'I have no idea. Bampfield asked me to deliver them in London. He told me they were love letters.'

'Love letters?' Fitz spat. 'They contain reports of all our meetings. Reports that leave me in no doubt that you are the one referred to as 'our friend'. How long have you been in Thurloe's pay, Lovell?' He stared at Kit as the realisation of the extent of Kit's duplicity crossed his face. 'Every move we've made, every discussion we've had has gone straight back to Thurloe, hasn't it? The Ship Inn, was that your work?'

'Let go of me, Fitz. You are talking nonsense.'

The anger began to die in Fitz's face and the grip on Kit's shirt slackened. 'I'd heard whispers after The Ship Inn but I couldn't believe them. Not of you, Lovell. I thought I knew you better.'

Kit removed Fitz's hand from his shirt. 'Fitz, as God is my witness, I had no idea what these letters contain. You know Bampfield's reputation.'

'And Henshaw and Wildman, but you, Lovell … ' Fitz shook his head.

'Bampfield told me they were for his mistress.'

'How can I believe you?'

'You can't, Fitz. You just have to trust me.'

Fitz thrust the paper he was holding into his pocket. 'I need fresh air.'

Kit looked at the pitching, swaying lantern. 'Fitz, it is blowing a gale up there.'

But his friend did not hear him. With heavy steps, he dragged himself to the ladder and up into the cold air of the Thames Estuary.

Kit sat on the edge of the bunk for a minute, his head in his hands. Slowly he pulled on his boots and jacket and climbed the narrow ladder. It still lacked a few hours to dawn. The night was dark and the sea a boiling, angry cauldron. Only a dark mass on the horizon gave any indication of their proximity to land.

Fitz leaned against the rail, his hair and cloak blowing in the gale. They were alone except for the helmsman who stood at the wheel, seemingly impervious to the pitching deck.

Kit grasped the rail beside Fitz.

'Why, Lovell?' Fitz did not even turn to look at him.

Kit sighed. *No more lies.* 'I have my reasons, Fitz.'

'Is that reason anything to do with Daniel?'

Kit was silent for a moment. 'Yes. It is everything to do with Daniel.'

'He's dead, Kit. You sold your soul for a vain hope.'

'No,' Kit said with emotion choking his voice. 'No, I won't believe he's dead until I dig his stinking corpse from the ground.'

'I thought I knew you,' Fitz said with dull resignation in his voice.

'Nobody can really know another person, Fitz.' Kit grimaced.

'Well, I must give you credit, you are very good at what you do. You had me completely fooled.' Fitz could not hide the bitterness in his voice.

Kit turned to look at his friend. 'What are you going to do, Fitz?'

'I have no choice. I have to advise the King and the others that you are not to be trusted. You're finished, Lovell. When word gets around you will probably be a dead man, and it will all have been for nothing.'

Kit felt a momentary panic. 'Give me time, Fitz. Let me fade into the background. I will go to the Colonies as I planned, as we discussed so often.'

'I can't, Lovell. You know that. You know too much and we don't have the time. I have no choice.'

Fitz turned to face him, the light from the helm flashing on his pistol. Kit didn't flinch. He lifted his hands away from the rail and turned to face his friend.

'I'm unarmed, Fitz. My sword's below. You can kill me now if you have to,' he said quietly, keeping his eyes firmly fixed on his friend's face.

Fitz hesitated, and in that fraction of a second, the boat pitched, throwing them both off balance. Fitz staggered backward, falling against the rail. The boat righted and Kit fell forward towards Fitz. He put out his hand to hold onto his friend but in the space of a heartbeat, Fitz had overbalanced, tipping over the rail of the boat.

Catching at the rail to stop himself from falling as well, Kit saw his friend's mouth open in a silent scream, his arms flailing as he dropped into the dark abyss. Kit's hands grasped frantically at thin air. He screamed Fitz's name, the wind carrying his voice away unanswered into the dark, foul night. He pulled himself up and leaned over the rail, but the dark, seething water had claimed the only man he had called his friend.

He looked up at the helmsman. 'There is a man overboard!'

The man shrugged. 'I saw. There is nothing I can do, m'sieur. He is gone.'

Kit stared at the man, torn between seizing the wheel and beating him to a pulp.

'Why do you care? He would have killed you,' the helmsman observed. 'It wasn't your fault he is dead.'

The boat pitched and Kit staggered against the rail, his hands clasping at the slimy wood. He cast the sea one last regretful glance and like a man in a daze, returned to his bunk in the cabin, where he was violently ill. This time it had nothing to do with seasickness. He curled up on the narrow bed and faced the damp wood and waited for the morning.

CHAPTER 23

*O*nce ashore, Kit found the nearest inn and drank himself into insensibility. Alcohol's amnesiac properties were only illusory. He awoke to find himself lying in a filthy alley, where he had been thrown from the last inn he had visited.

Heavy, dismal rain soaked him through to the bones and he pulled himself into a sitting position, laid his arms over his knees, lowered his head onto them and, as the memory of Fitz's death came back with cruel, clear clarity, he wept. Slowly he raised his head and considered the grey, unappealing sky.

He let the rain wash his face and rose to his feet. A quick check revealed his pockets had been turned out for the few coins they contained but the papers he carried, that Fitz had died for, were still safe.

He stumbled through the narrow streets, oblivious to the sidelong glances and looks of disgust that his filthy, disreputable state attracted. Outside the respectable house he sought, he stopped and looked up at the lighted windows. Although it still lacked an hour or so until nightfall, the dark and dreary afternoon had drawn in the gloaming.

Dragging his feet, he ascended the well-scrubbed steps and banged on the front door. A manservant opened the door, took one look at Kit and made to shut it again, but Kit had pushed past the man and stood in a respectable entrance hall that smelt of beeswax and wood smoke.

'Where's Thurloe?' he demanded.

'The master'll not see you. You must leave at once.' The man's nose wrinkled with distaste as he made a grab for Kit's jacket. 'Now get out before I call the watch.'

Kit shook him off. 'He'll see me.'

He paced the front hall.

'Thurloe!' he yelled, his voice echoing up the stairwell. 'Thurloe, come out and face me, you whoreson.'

A respectably dressed woman appeared at the top of the stairs, her face pinched with fright. 'Who are you? How dare you! Get out of my house.'

A door opened and Thurloe appeared in the hallway.

'John? Who is this frightful man?' The woman's voice quavered with apprehension.

'It's all right my dear, I'll deal with it,' Thurloe said calmly, adding in a hard voice, 'In here now, Lovell!'

Mustering what was left of his dignity, Kit marched past the supercilious manservant through the door that Thurloe held open. The door shut behind them both.

'What is the meaning of this intrusion?' Thurloe's voice was icy.

Kit reached into his jacket and slapped the packet of papers down on the table.

'These are for you.'

'They could be delivered in the usual manner.'

'No, they couldn't. These reports have been bought and paid for with a life, Thurloe. You will find one of them missing. If you care to drag the Thames Estuary you will find it on the body of my friend Fitzjames.'

'What do you mean?'

'I mean Fitzjames discovered Bampfield's little love letters.' He took a deep shuddering breath. 'He would have betrayed me.'

'You killed him?' Thurloe sank onto a chair.

Kit took a deep breath. 'No. It was an accident. A bloody, tragic accident.'

'I see.' Thurloe looked down at the papers. 'It was clever of you to put the papers on him. When we recover the body, the word will go about that Fitzjames was the spy. You did well, Lovell.'

Kit turned away, his face contorted in grief and disgust.

'Poor, bloody Fitz,' he said. 'He was as loyal a servant as Charles Stuart would ever find and you will paint him the traitor?'

Thurloe looked up at him. 'You're overwrought. Go home, Lovell. After you've cleaned up and had a good night's sleep, you will see that you had no other choice.'

Kit flung himself down on a chair and buried his face in his arms on the table. 'I'm heartsick of this, Thurloe. Haven't I done enough? I want to be left in peace.'

Thurloe's voice was icy. 'It's too late for you to be developing a conscience now, Lovell. Go home and tumble your mistress. Amazing what a few hours of female company can do for the soul.'

'I don't have a soul,' Kit mumbled into his arms. 'I sold it to you, remember?'

'And you can have it back when this job is done. You can give me your report on matters in Paris when you are in a fit state.'

Thurloe stood and crossed to the door. 'Oh, and by the way, your little friend has disappeared.'

'What friend?' Kit raised his face.

'Mistress Granville.'

Kit rose uncertainly to his feet and looked Thurloe in the eye. 'What do you mean, disappeared?'

'Failed to appear for her lessons with Mistress Skippon. She's been missing for over a week. I would like her found. She still owes the Commonwealth money.'

Thamsine? Kit's tired mind tried to grapple with the possible circumstances of Thamsine's disappearance but exhaustion was asserting itself. Thamsine was a problem he would face in the morning.

He passed through the door Thurloe held open for him without conscious thought. Outside it still rained, more heavily if that was possible, but it didn't matter. He wasn't going to get any wetter or colder or more miserable than he already was.

AT HOLBORN, Lucy's maid, Mag, opened the door.

'Well, well,' she said, with a sneer of distaste, 'look who's back.'

'It's a pleasure to see you too, Mag,' Kit replied coldly. 'Is your mistress at home?'

'No, she isn't,' Mag said.

'Good. I'd rather she didn't see me looking like this. Draw me a bath in the kitchen, Mag, and be quick about it.'

Mag opened her mouth to protest and muttering to herself, stomped off to the kitchen.

Kit followed her and downed a glass of Martin Talbot's best brandy while Mag and the kitchen maid drew the bath. Ignoring Mag and the kitchen scullion, who stared at him with large eyes, her hands wrapped in her grubby apron, he stripped off his filthy, reeking clothes and climbed into the small tub, his knees around his chin. With some of Lucy's favourite rose-scented soap, he scrubbed at his self-disgust.

Thurloe had been right about one thing: being clean did make a difference to his view of the world. Mag fetched him a clean set of clothes and he retired to the parlour with a plate of cheese and a hunk of fresh bread and waited for Lucy.

He did not have to wait long. Lucy, her hair damp from the rain, came through the parlour door, her eyes lighting up when she saw him.

'Kit. Oh, Kit, you're home!' She flung herself at him, covering his face with kisses that he returned with fulsome enthusiasm.

When they both paused for breath, Lucy exclaimed, 'You smell nice! Is that my soap?' She held his face in her hands and looked at him. 'You look terrible! Have you been ill?'

'I had a trying journey,' he mumbled, sitting down.

'Oh, you poor thing!' Lucy stroked his face with tender concern in her eyes. 'Was Norfolk that dreadful? How was your aunt?'

Kit shrugged. 'I'm very tired, Mouse.'

Lucy sat on his knee and laid his head against her shoulder, her hand slipping under his shirt to run her fingers through the hairs on his chest. She smelt divine, and despite his exhaustion, he could feel his ardour rising. Thurloe may have been right about that too. A few hours of sport with Lucy and he could forget everything.

'Did you bring me a present?' she teased.

'From Norfolk?' Kit said. 'What do you think I would find for you there? No, dearest, I am afraid all I bring you is myself.'

She made no protest as he began unlacing her bodice, and he gave an appreciative sigh, allowing oblivion to wash over him.

CHAPTER 24

it didn't stir from the house in High Holborn for two days. On the third morning he woke to a grey and gloomy day. He lay for a long time, staring at the dark fingers of rain beating at the casement. Beside him, Lucy stirred but did not wake. He slipped from the bed, wrapped a blanket around his shoulders and crossed to the window.

He stared up at the bleak sky, obscured by the high pitched roofs of the houses, and thought of his childhood home, Eveleigh Priory, what was left of it. He had tried not to think about his home in Cheshire for a long time but now he had a sudden, desperate urge to escape London and return to the soft, green countryside and bury himself in the obscurity of restoring the estates.

He sighed and stretched. He had spent the hours with Lucy trying to forget what had transpired on the Thames Estuary. He had convinced himself that nothing he could have done would have prevented Fitz's death, and he no longer felt it like a sharp pain, more a dull ache. A dull ache he could live with.

He needed to get back to work and he had to find out what had happened to Thamsine.

'Kit?' Lucy's sleepy voice made him turn around. She had turned over and was looking at him, her eyes half closed. 'What are you thinking?'

'I am thinking it is time I was dressed and abroad, Mouse. I have loitered too long.' He located his clothes and began to dress.

She patted the bed. 'It's early and pouring with rain. Come back to bed.'

He looked at her for a moment and shook his head. 'Sorry, Mouse, I have things to do.'

She pouted. 'What things are so important?'

He crossed to bed and bent down, kissing her on the forehead. 'Things that are no concern of yours.'

She frowned and flung her arms around his neck. 'Oh Kit, you're so tiresome. Since you've been home it feels as if you are not here at all.'

'What do you mean?' Kit extricated himself from her Medusa tendrils.

'You are no fun anymore!'

'I have things on my mind, Mouse.' He paused. 'When did you last see Mistress Granville?'

'Is that what's bothering you? You can forget your little music teacher. I told you I haven't seen her in over a week. If she's gone then good riddance.' Lucy's mouth took on a downward cast.

Kit frowned. There was something in the tone of Lucy's voice he disliked. He had asked her a couple of times about Thamsine, and both times she had dismissed his question with a wave of her hand and a comment about Thamsine failing to turn up at the appointed hour.

'I am afraid, Mouse, my principal concern at present is the earning of some coins,' he said coldly, ignoring her petulance.

Lucy rolled over again. 'I can give you money.'

Kit smiled. 'Thank you but no. I prefer to earn my own way, where and when I can.'

Lucy sighed. 'How long will you be gone?'

He shrugged. 'However long it takes.'

Lucy sat up in bed, the covers slipping away from her. For once Kit regarded her naked body and felt nothing.

'Be home tonight.' The sharp and querulous tone smacked of an order.

Kit raised an eyebrow. 'I will return when I am ready, Mouse.'

As he turned towards the door, a bolster hit him in the back. He straightened but did not turn to look at her. With deliberate care he closed the door behind him.

Domestic life had begun to pall.

As he walked the familiar streets to the Ship, he went through the matters in hand. He had a rebellion to organise. Lord Gerard was following close behind and would be back in London by now. The plot would be gathering momentum and he still did not have the names of the Sealed Knot.

Then there was the irritating matter of the missing Thamsine Granville. Damn the woman! He had enough to worry about without fretting about her whereabouts.

'Cap'n Lovell.' May wrapped herself around him as he stepped into the warm, familiar taproom.

Kit took off his coat and shook his wet hair. As soon as he sat down, May perched herself on his lap and ran her fingers through his hair while Nan fetched him a pot of ale.

Nan set the ale down. 'You look tired,' she commented.

'Travelling,' Kit took a welcome draught of the ale.

'So where have you been?' May asked.

'France.'

'Did you bring me back anything special?' May asked.

Kit shook his head. 'No! No presents for anyone. It was business.'

Nan pulled a face. 'Shame on you!'

Kit looked at both girls, his face serious. 'Does either of you know where Thamsine Granville is?'

The twins looked at each other, then at him. 'We thought you might know,' Nan said.

'What do you mean?'

'She went out last Friday and ain't been home since. Not a word, not to collect her things, nothing. We asked around but no one's seen neither hide nor hair of her.'

'Where did she go?'

Nan looked at her sister. 'That new person she started going to just before you went away.'

'Mistress Talbot?'

May shrugged. 'If that's her name.'

Jem wandered over. 'If you're talking about the Granville woman,' he said, with a voice that had a grumble in it, 'I needs to know if I hold on to her room, 'cos if not, I'll pack her things up and let it.'

'Come on, Jem, it's not as if you have customers beating a path to stay at this inn,' Kit commented.

'It's been over a week,' Jem said. 'These your friends?' He jerked his head towards the door, where Lord Gerard and Willys stood, shaking the rain from their hats.

Kit deposited May on the stool beside him and stood up, gesturing for the two men to join him in a quiet corner.

'Did you have a good crossing?' Kit asked Lord Gerard.

'Damned rough crossing,' Gerard replied. 'I heard about Fitz-james.' He poured a glass of wine from the jug as Kit dealt a round of cards.

'Did you know they found his body washed up on the shore? You were with him. What happened, Lovell?' Willys asked.

Kit's fingers tightened on the stem of his wineglass.

'You know what I'm like at sea, Willys. It was a damnably rough crossing. I stayed below. I can only assume he went up for air and fell overboard. I didn't even realise he was gone until we docked.'

Willys sighed. 'I'm sorry, Lovell. I know he was a friend of yours.'

Kit took a large draught of wine and hoped his shaking hand did not betray him.

'I know he was your friend, so what I have to say may come as a shock.' Willys' voice held a conspiratorial air as he carefully rearranged his cards. 'I have heard that Fitzjames was carrying letters to Thurloe.'

'What?' Gerard looked up at Willys.

'That's right. Found in his pocket. Fitzjames was one of Thurloe's agents.'

Kit stared at him. 'Fitzjames? I don't believe it.' He could feel the bile rising in his throat even as he spoke.

Willys shook his head. 'I know, I didn't believe it either, but my source was quite sure. You just can't tell who to trust, can you?'

'That explains Dutton's plot,' said Kit, hating himself.

'And other matters,' Gerard agreed. He threw down his cards in disgust. 'Lovell, you have the luck of the Devil.'

'Ah, Messieurs, I am too late to join you for cards, perhaps?'

They all looked up at the incongruous figure of the Baron de Baas. Unbidden, Baas sat down at the table, carefully removing his purple gloves.

''Fraid so,' Willys said. 'Lovell here has just cleaned our purses.'

De Baas' gaze flicked to Kit. 'I don't believe I 'ave 'ad the pleasure of Monsieur Lovell's acquaintance.'

Kit inclined his head. He knew De Baas by sight of course, but close-up he presented an even more ridiculous picture. He dressed in what Kit knew to be the latest French fashion, lace and bows and a casually knotted cravat rather than falling bands, a costume made all the more incongruous by the shabby setting.

'You seem particularly adept at cards, monsieur' De Baas remarked.

'Years of practice, my dear Baron.' Kit shuffled the deck in his hands. 'Will you play me?'

'But of course.' De Baas picked up the cards in his gloved hand.

They played in silence for a few minutes. To Kit's surprise De Baas won. 'I think I have met my match,' he said, ruefully pushing the coins across the table.

'Another hand? Perhaps your luck will change.'

'Thank you, but no. I don't feel luck is on my side at present, so I will keep my small purse intact.'

'I hear our friend Fitzjames is dead,' De Baas said.

'Drowned at sea,' Willys said shortly, 'but we have another to take his place.'

'And who may that be?' De Baas enquired.

'Peter Vowells. He's a schoolmaster from Islington.'

'A schoolmaster?' De Baas' lip curled in distaste. 'What can a schoolmaster do?'

'He has good contacts and can raise the London apprentices,' Willys said, his tone even.

De Baas raised an eyebrow. 'The London apprentices? That is a considerable talent.'

Gerard leaned forward. 'It is generally agreed that the plan will go forward. Baron, is your promise of a … friend still certain?'

De Baas nodded. 'I am returning to Paris in a couple of days, and I shall make the necessary arrangements. Only the very best, I assure you.'

Willys flinched. 'Baron, I'm not sure we can afford the very best.'

De Baas smiled, showing a row of even, white teeth. 'You may repay us when the deed is done.'

Gerard nodded. 'Well, gentlemen, we are agreed.'

'When do we plan to accomplish the task in hand?' Kit asked.

'I think we should aim for early in May. That gives us a month to finalise matters,' Gerard replied.

The conspirators stood, briefly clasped hands and dispersed. Kit remained at his table, his hand curled around the stem of his wineglass, considering what more he needed to do.

With a rustle of skirts the two girls sat down opposite him. He looked at them questioningly. Nan punched May on the arm.

'Go on,' Nan said. 'You tell him what she told us.'

'Ow!' May gave her sister a rueful look. 'It's about Thamsine,' she said. 'She made me promise not to tell and I'm a girl of me word.'

Nan gave a snort of disgust. 'Gawd, May, she could be lying dead in some ditch. You tell him.'

'She told us that she was running away from a man what wanted to marry her for her money,' May said in a rush.

Kit nodded. 'I know that much,' he said. 'Did she mention the man's name?'

May shook her head. 'No, but she said he were mean and vicious.' Her eyes widened. 'You don't suppose … ?'

'I don't suppose anything, May,' Kit said quickly, the same thought crossing his mind. He rose to his feet and took May's face in his hands, kissing her forehead. 'You did right to tell me.'

May looked relieved. 'So you'll find her?'

He smiled. 'Of course I will, and I'm sure she will be just fine.'

~

KIT STUMPED UP to the parlour of Lucy's house, tossed his hat in a corner, and sat down beside the parlour fire, toying with his pipe, which lacked the tobacco to smoke. Lucy was not at home and he felt an odd sense of relief. Since his return from Paris, he had found Lucy's company cloying and a little too demanding.

A timid knock on the door jolted him from his reverie. The kitchen scullion stood in the doorway, twisting her hands in her apron. He didn't even know her name. Something plain – Mary or Jane?

'Beg pardon, sir.'

'Yes?' he snapped.

She flinched, her eyes darting to the door. 'It's not my place,' she began. 'But I didn't think it were right.'

Kit looked at her in irritation. He didn't need some petty domestic matter to solve. 'What's not right ... um ... Mary?'

'Bess, sir.'

'Bess. What's not right?'

'I'm a good girl, sir. Bought up a proper God-fearing Christian, I am,' the girl gabbled.

'Bess ... ' Kit fought his impatience. If the girl was going to tell him something, he didn't want to scare her.

'There are things that happen in this house, sir. Men who come to call. When you're not here, of course,' she added.

'Bess, that is none of your concern,' he said sternly. He didn't need to be reminded by a kitchen scullion that his mistress was free with her favours.

'I don't mean you, sir. You're different. You're a gentleman. Always nice to me. But there are some ... ' She tailed off. 'That's why I thought you should know, seeing as how she's a friend of yours.'

'Who?'

'The music teacher.'

Kit's heart skipped a beat. 'Go on, Bess.'

'Well, there's been this man what's been calling while you've been away.'

That hardly surprised Kit. Lucy had the morals of an alley cat.

'Do you know his name?'

Bess shook her head. 'Really handsome. Taller than you, darker too. Wears his hair longer.'

Ambrose Morton? Kit felt a surge of annoyance with Lucy. While he accepted the fact that other men kept her bed warm in his absence, it irked him that she had chosen Ambrose Morton.

'I don't like him,' Bess continued. 'There's a way he looks at a person. Gives me the shivers.'

Kit wasn't a woman but he had to agree. There was something in those cold, grey eyes that made his flesh crawl, too.

'While you was away, the music teacher came to give Mistress Talbot her lesson. Halfway through the lesson he turns up. I were in the kitchen but I could hear them from down there. Terrible fight there was, furniture banging, and I heard her scream.'

'Mistress Talbot?'

'No, not her, the music teacher! I sneaked out of the kitchen and I saw him carrying her down the stairs. She's kicking and scratching but he's got his hand over her mouth.'

'What happened to her, Bess?' Kit felt the hairs on the back of his neck rise.

'He shoves her into a carriage and they takes off. I had to get back to the kitchen afore Mistress Mag saw I was gone.'

'Can you tell me anything about the carriage? Did you see a coat of arms, anything to distinguish it?'

Bess shook her head. 'It were just a plain carriage. Nothing special. There was another man following behind, but I didn't see who it was.' The girl looked at him anxiously. 'Did I do right to tell you, sir?'

He forced a smile. 'You did quite right, Bess. Here ... ' He tossed her a coin that she caught before smiling, curtseying, and turning back for the kitchen.

Kit stood and crossed to the window, looking out at the bleak, cold evening. What was Lucy's involvement? And what in God's name was Thamsine's relationship with Ambrose Morton?

Then it all fell into place. Morton himself had as good as told him. He had the stories from both sides, but he had never thought to connect them. Thamsine was Morton's runaway bride, the girl who had fled to London, supposedly with another man. Morton was the mean and vicious man who had wanted to marry Thamsine for her money.

Now he had found her and the consequences for Thamsine could only be dire. He slammed his fist on the windowsill in frustration. He didn't even know where to find Ambrose Morton, let alone Thamsine.

He trawled his memory for every conversation he had ever had with Morton. Turnham Green. Morton said he had lodged with a friend at Turnham Green. A lawyer at Turnham Green. For the life of him he could not remember the name, but it would not be too hard to find a lawyer living in Turnham Green.

Kit snatched up his hat and gloves and strode out of the house.

CHAPTER 25

Kit's hired horse had a mouth as hard as a rock and seemed in no hurry to reach the pretty village of Turnham Green, about an hour's ride on a good horse from London. If nothing else, the steady pace allowed Kit time to think and by the time he reached the village, he had remembered the name of the lawyer that Lucy said she had known. Knott. *An appropriate name*, he thought, for the tangle he found himself in.

The name of the village rang in his memory as the site of the first confrontation of the war when the King marching on London had been turned back at Turnham Green. Such a monumental day had left no echoes in the quiet streets, and after some judicious enquiry, he found the Knotts' neat house a little way out of the village, set well back from the London road.

A timid maid answered his knock on the door. She asked his name and showed him into a tidy parlour. The plain, unadorned furniture glowed with many polishings, and a bowl of early spring flowers sat squarely in the centre of the table. Kit touched the fragile blooms.

A man entered the room, shutting the door behind him. Kit's eyes flicked over his unprepossessing appearance. He stood barely middle height, his thin body concealed behind dark clothes and his straight, greying hair had been brushed over the top of his pate to conceal a receding hairline. His pale face bore a downcast expression, which to judge from the lines was habitual.

'Captain Lovell?' he enquired.

Kit bowed. 'Master Knott.'

'What business brings you to my house?'

'I am looking for a friend, a Mistress Thamsine Granville.'

The man's thin lips trembled slightly. 'I cannot help you, Captain Lovell.'

The door opened and a slight woman entered the room. Like her husband, she wore plain clothes, her greying hair covered by a neat, white cap.

'Captain Lovell,' she said, 'my name is Jane Knott, I am Thamsine Granville's sister.'

'Thamsine's sister? I had no idea ... Your servant, ma'am.' Kit bowed.

He scanned Jane Knott's face for some resemblance to her sister and found none. A purple bruise marred the right side of her face and he cast the husband a quick glance, wondering if this man was capable of such violence against a woman.

As if conscious of his thoughts, Jane's fingers touched the bruise and her eyes flickered. She turned to her husband.

'Roger, I believe Captain Lovell is a friend of Thamsine's. He is the only one who can help her.'

Her husband opened her mouth, but Jane put a hand on his arm.

'Please, Roger. Thamsine needs our help.' She turned to Kit. 'Please sit, Captain Lovell.'

Kit removed his gloves and took the proffered chair at the

table. The Knotts sat straight-backed on the hard chairs across from him as if he were interviewing them.

Kit held up a hand. 'Mistress Knott, you must understand I know little of Thamsine's history. I am trying to piece it together.'

Jane's eyes widened. 'But I thought you were friends?'

Thamsine had her reasons not to trust me, Kit thought bitterly.

'We have an unusual relationship,' he said. 'More of a working relationship that I care not to go into here.' Then, realising by the shocked looks on both the Knotts' faces, he hastily added; 'I assure you it was quite respectable.' *Whatever "respectable" meant.* 'Do you know where she is now?'

Jane's lip trembled. 'No.' Her hand closed over her husband's. 'He took her away. Even Roger doesn't know.'

She shot her husband a quick sideways glance and he nodded unhappily.

'He?' Kit prompted.

'Ambrose Morton. Do you know him?'

'I am acquainted with him,' Kit said through stiff lips. 'What business does he have with you?'

The couple shifted uncomfortably under his scrutiny. He decided that what he saw were two people overwhelmed by events and beset with guilt.

Kit turned to Jane Knott. 'Your face, Mistress Knott? Is that Morton's handiwork?'

Jane's fingers shook as they rose again to her bruised face and she nodded.

'My wife showed more courage than I did, Captain Lovell,' Knott said unhappily. 'I have been a fool in so many ways.'

He clasped his wife's hand and lifted it to his lips.

'It would help,' Kit said, 'if I were to know the full story.'

'I only know what Thamsine has told me,' Jane said. 'You must understand, the war separated us for too long.'

'Tell me what you know, then,' Kit said, with enormous patience.

Jane swallowed. 'I am somewhat older than Thamsine and her brother. My mother died when I was eight and my father remarried. Thamsine was born when I was eleven and Edward two years later,' Jane began. 'Shortly before the war I married Roger.' Jane looked at her husband and smiled. 'At much the same time, Thamsine became enamoured of our neighbour, Ambrose Morton. He was past twenty and she was but sixteen. He wooed her with considerable charm and ardour and she begged my father for a betrothal, which he granted.'

'What did Ambrose Morton want with Thamsine?'

'Her dowry was generous enough, but what she stood to inherit from her mother's estate was considerable,' Knott said. 'Her mother was the daughter of one of Elizabeth's merchant venturers. He amassed a fortune in his lifetime and, under the terms of his will, it passed to his daughter Elizabeth, Thamsine's mother, and then directly to her children. Edward and Thamsine were to share it. After Edward's death at Worcester, of course, it all passed to Thamsine.'

'The Morton family has been less fortunate,' Jane continued. 'They are a Catholic family. Ambrose's mother, Isabelle, was a spendthrift, and what little was left of their fortunes she squandered.'

Kit sighed as it all became clear. 'So, Thamsine's fortune, enhanced by her brother's death, was very attractive. But Mistress Knott, you said they were betrothed before the war? That is twelve years ago.'

'You must understand,' Jane said hurriedly, 'that the war divided us. Roger sided with Parliament ... ' She cast her husband a quick, sideways glance, '... my father for the King. I did not see Thamsine from early 1642 until late last year, when she came to us seeking help, which ... ' She paused, her eyes unhappy, ' ... we were not able to give.'

Kit narrowed his eyes but let the comment pass.

'So, what had happened between Thamsine and Morton?' he said.

'She told me she broke the betrothal in 1646 after coming across Morton in the act of ... ' Jane swallowed, ' ... congress with a maid. She did not believe it was consensual.'

Kit stared at her. He felt neither shock nor surprise. Morton enjoyed taking women by force. He had intimated as much in one of their conversations.

'And after that?' Kit moved on.

Jane shrugged. 'Morton went to the Continent. My father, stupid besotted fool, married Isabelle Morton, and Ambrose came home. After Edward's death, Ambrose and his mother persuaded my father that Thamsine was not capable of inheriting such a vast estate in her own right. My father changed his will, making Ambrose her guardian and at the same time executing a deed of betrothal between Thamsine and Morton. He bound her to that monster for life. After our father died early last year, Thamsine did what she could to delay the wedding but Morton grew impatient. One night he tried to force her ... ' Jane took a deep breath. 'She was only saved by Annie.'

'Annie?'

'Ambrose has an imbecile sister, of whom he is very fond.'

That surprised Kit. He could not imagine Morton being fond of anything or anyone.

'Annie gave Thamsine Ambrose's pistol and she shot him. She thought she had killed him so she ran to us here in London for sanctuary. Only, we failed her.'

Jane looked at her husband, who looked away. She continued, 'It transpired that Morton had only been grazed by the pistol ball.

He came here looking for her but Thamsine saw him and managed to escape.'

'We … he spent the last four months scouring the streets of London, looking for her,' Roger Knott concluded.

Kit looked from one to another. Knott looked away. There was more to this story. He addressed the man directly.

'I'm sorry, Master Knott, but I don't understand your role in this. Surely as Thamsine's closest relative, you should have protected her. What power of persuasion does Morton use on you?'

Knott's tongue circled his thin lips.

'Tell him.' Jane's voice was soft but beneath her gentle demeanour, Kit sensed an iron will. Jane Knott knew her husband well.

'Blackmail, Captain Lovell.' Knott turned to his wife and clasped her hands in his. 'I have told Jane all and she has forgiven me.'

Blackmail? What in God's name had this inoffensive little man done to warrant blackmail?

Knott continued, 'An indiscretion. Some letters, involving a lady of the town.'

'Her name?' Kit enquired.

Knott shook his head. 'It is no concern of yours.'

'Lucy Talbot,' Jane Knott said.

Kit had already known the answer before Jane spoke. *Lucy.* It all came back to Lucy.

Knott turned to look at Kit, his eyes wide with fear. 'Captain Lovell, you must understand my position. I hold a post with the government. If word were to get out – the scandal would ruin me.'

Kit looked at the man with distaste and tried to picture him with Lucy. It gave him no pleasure to know he had ploughed a furrow already seeded by this pathetic model of manhood.

'So, what has become of Thamsine?'

'Morton,' Knott said, 'with the connivance of Mistress Talbot, apprehended her and brought her here. I hoped to be able to persuade her to the sense of the marriage without recourse for further violence, but ...'

'You failed?'

'She continued to refuse him. Obstinate girl!' Knott said.

'He threatened my children.' Jane's eyes glinted with tears and Knott covered his face with his hands.

Kit leaned forward. 'Where is Thamsine now?'

Knott lowered his hands and he and his wife exchanged glances.

'I don't know,' Knott said. 'I really don't know. He came for her three days ago and took her away.'

Jane's face twisted. 'You may be too late, but please, Captain Lovell, you are her only hope.'

'Where has he taken her?'

Jane's face dissolved. 'He said he was taking her to Hell.'

Kit felt a cold hand claw at his guts.

'He said within a few days she would be begging him for marriage. I am so scared for her.' Jane swallowed and rose to her feet, her hands clasped in front of her. 'As you love her, Captain, you will find her. Find her and keep her safe.'

CHAPTER 26

*K*it put the spurs to the lazy horse and drove it hard back to the city, his mind reeling. Jane had said *As you love her.* Did he love her?

He had told a dozen, or more, women he loved them. They liked to hear it. The pretty words had pleased them and suited him, but what he had felt for those girls was nothing like the emotion that pulsed through his veins now.

If loving someone meant that life without them was unendurable, that thoughts of that person occupied every waking moment, then yes, he conceded, maybe he was in love with Thamsine Granville, and if that was the case he was the biggest fool in the country. How had he allowed himself to fall in love with a woman he knew nothing about?

Above all, he didn't need the distraction of foolish emotions such as love at this point in his life.

He returned the horse and took some refreshment at the Ship while he tried to gather his thoughts. Damn it, where was she? He was quite sure Morton had meant it when he said he would take her to Hell but where was Hell? Somewhere in the City of London or … where?

He dismissed the thought of tackling Ambrose Morton without at least a dozen armed men at his back. Even if he knew where Morton was, he was no match for a man of Morton's size, cunning, and formidable reputation as a swordsman. However, there was one other person who might know where Thamsine was being held, and who could be more easily managed. He risked overplaying his hand but the risk was worth it.

He borrowed a knife from Jem, slipping it into his sleeve, clapped his hat on his head, and strode to the house in Holborn Hill.

He found Lucy alone, working on embroidery by the window in the parlour. He paused at the door, watching her for a moment. The bitter, angry thoughts seething in his brain, provided a stark contrast to the scene of pleasant, domestic bliss that she presented.

For a moment he hesitated. What if he was mistaken and Lucy was innocent? She looked up, setting her work down in her lap.

'Where have you been?' she demanded in a petulant tone, destroying the illusion.

He laid his hat and gloves on the table. 'That is my concern, Lucy.'

'I waited up for you till late last night and all today. No word, not even a note.' She stood to face him.

'Well, that was foolish. You should know me well enough now to know not to expect such things of me.'

'You're here now. That's all that matters.' She insinuated her arms around his neck, pressing her body to his, her mouth seeking his …once more his sweet, playful Mouse.

He broke away from her, wiping his mouth with the back of his hand, revolted by her.

Her eyes narrowed, her brow creasing with distress as she said, 'Kit, dearest, is something wrong?' She placed her hands on his chest and smiled a cherubic, wheedling smile that two days ago would have reduced him to clay in her hands. 'Have I done something to upset you?'

Kit looked at her with disgust, seeing her for what she was: a pretty, spoiled, manipulative little woman who within a few years would lose her teeth and her looks and end up an embittered, ugly hag.

She looked up at him and her eyes widened when she recognised the grim purpose on his face. She played a desperate card, laying her head against his chest.

'Kit, dearest Kit, you must know I love you.'

He almost laughed. 'Don't be ridiculous. You mistake lust for love, Lucy. You wouldn't know what love is. I'll have my box sent around to my new lodgings. Our little bit of fun is over.'

'Kit, please ... ' She fell against him, clinging to him, crying soft tears. 'What have I done for you to treat me so cruelly?'

With a deft movement, he slipped the knife from his sleeve and, seizing her by the shoulder, twisted her away from him. He wrenched one arm up behind her back and held the knife to her throat. She gave a gurgling cry, her eyes bulging with fear.

'Where is Thamsine Granville?' he hissed in her ear.

'I don't know,' she spluttered.

'Yes, you do. Where is she?'

His grip tightened and she let out another cry.

'It's no concern of yours!'

'You're wrong. It is every concern of mine.'

'Why?' Lucy's tone was defiant through the tears of pain. 'She's nothing, a nobody.'

'I suspect you know that's not true. What has Morton told you?'

At Morton's name, Lucy stiffened in his arms. 'Morton?'

'I'm no fool, Lucy. I know he's the one who's been warming your bed in my absence. Now, where is Thamsine?'

'I can't tell you. He'll hurt me,' she whined.

Kit twisted her arm higher and she yelped.

'Like this? Lucy, I've no time for games. I am holding a very sharp knife and I am not the most patient of men. Like you, I have little aversion to removing annoying obstacles. The fact you are a woman makes no difference.'

Sweat beaded Lucy's pretty face. 'I c-can't tell you,' she stammered in one last display of bravado. 'Kill me, if that's what you intend!'

Kit sighed and shifted his grip on the knife, laying it against her nose. 'You're wrong, Lucy. I don't intend to kill you, but I can cause you a great deal of pain before I leave you hideously scarred. You will find it hard to woo bed-mates with the mark of the whore on your face. Now, are you going to deal with this sensibly?'

It went against everything he believed him to threaten a woman in this manner and he hated himself, but he hated himself more for throwing Thamsine in the path of Ambrose Morton.

Lucy swallowed. 'You don't know what he'll do to me if I tell you.'

'I couldn't care less what he does to you! It's the other women I care about, the ones he takes by force, uses and throws away. You know, you're very alike, you and Morton. When you see something, you take it.' He paused, realisation dawning on him. 'Tell me, Lucy, why you chose me. What do I have that you want so badly?'

'I know who you are!' she screamed. 'You are heir to Lord Midhurst. I could have been Lady Midhurst, if it wasn't for that milksop of a music teacher.'

The answer shouldn't have surprised him, but it did. It wouldn't have been hard for her to discover his true identity. There were a few who knew his antecedents, such as Fitzjames, who was not known for his discretion when in his cups. Morton could have extracted that information without much prompting.

'So you know who I am, or more correctly, who I will be? Well, that explains a great deal. You want a title? Did you think to snare me into marriage with you?' He twisted her arm a little harder, making her squeal. 'Well, I hate to disappoint you, but you're not the sort of woman men like me marry.'

He twisted her arm a little harder.

There were tears in her voice. 'Kit, please. You'll break my arm.'

'Good.'

'She's in Bedlam.' The words were so faint he had to strain his ears to hear them.

'What did you say?' Kit slackened his grip and she broke away from him, rubbing her arm, tears running down her flushed face, distress and fear now displaced with anger.

'She's in Bedlam,' she spat. 'Where she deserves to be!'

Morton had taken her to Hell. Hell on Earth had a name and that name was Bedlam. No need to ask why. A few days in Bedlam would make the sanest person beg to marry Ambrose Morton.

His fingers closed over Lucy's arm again. She shrank from him but he tightened his grip, forcing her to her knees, gasping from the new pain he was inflicting.

'Let us fetch your cloak and your purse, Mistress Talbot, we're going out.'

'Where are we going?'

'To Hell.'

CHAPTER 27

The stench of death and despair hung over the Bethlem Hospital like a pall. Kit looked up at the grim, grey walls of the building more commonly known as Bedlam and shuddered. Not even the truly mad deserved incarceration in such a place as this.

Ordering the carriage to wait, he thrust Lucy before him and hammered on the heavy oak door.

The porter who answered the door looked at them doubtfully.

'We've come to see one of the inmates,' Kit said.

'Well, I don't know,' the porter said doubtfully, ''tis very late for visitors.'

'Give him some money,' Kit hissed in Lucy's ear. Lucy complied, her fingers shaking. The porter handed Kit a lantern and unlocked the door.

'In yer go. Good luck.'

Keeping one hand on Lucy's arm and the other, concealed by the cloak, holding the knife pressed against her back, they entered the dark, noisome place. The stench caused him to cough and he swallowed down the bile that rose in his throat, pressing his arm to his face. Lucy recoiled against him, her hand going to her mouth and nose. The floors were mired with human filth and the inmates lay supine and oblivious on piles of filthy straw or gibbered about, pulling at Kit's coat and Lucy's skirts. Lucy squealed as one touched her face.

The women's ward was if anything could be, worse. Even as they entered, women sidled up to them, baring their breasts and spreading their legs. Kit propelled Lucy before him, scattering them in his path. Keeping his knife in Lucy's back he took the lantern, swinging it from side to side, trying to make out Thamsine among the shapeless forms on the straw-covered floor. They were considered no better than animals but even animals had better conditions than these poor souls, he thought.

'Who are you?' A slatternly wardress in a soiled gown and cap appeared out of the gloom. 'How dare you come in here upsetting the patients?'

'I am here to retrieve one of your patients,' Kit spat out the last word with contempt.

'Think you can find her here, do you?' the wardress sneered.

'I'll find her. In the meantime, do you have an empty room with a key to the door? Lucy, your purse.'

Lucy opened her mouth and closed it again as the knife pricked her flesh. She thrust the purse into his outstretched hand. Kit held up a gold coin. He saw the wardress' eyes open wide for a moment.

'Through here, sir,' she said, her manner now obliging.

She opened a heavy oak door on a room only a little bigger than a cupboard, with barely enough room to lie down in the same filthy, mouldy straw as the main room.

'We uses it for those patients who get a little upset,' the wardress said.

'Good. My friend here is somewhat overwrought and could do with a peaceful night,' Kit said.

'You're not going to leave me here,' Lucy wailed.

'That is exactly what I am going to do. It may teach you a little humility.'

Kit closed the door on her, pocketing the key. She threw herself against the solid door, shrieking curses that would have made the most hardened inmate of Bedlam blush.

'Oi, how d'yer think we're going to get her out?' the wardress protested.

Kit shrugged. 'Break the door down I expect, but it can wait till morning.' He tossed her a couple more coins. 'Now, I'm looking for a young woman brought in within the last couple of days. Chestnut hair, name is Thamsine Granville.'

'No one by that name here.' The woman frowned. 'Only one come in the last few days was a woman by the name of Morton, Annie Morton.'

The name of Ambrose Morton's sister. Kit closed his eyes in disgust.

'Take me to her,' he said in a low, uneven voice.

The wardress indicated a dark, dank corner. Hardly daring to hope, Kit touched the shoulder of the huddled woman who lay manacled to the wall. She recoiled beneath his touch, hunching herself smaller.

'Thamsine,' he said. 'It's me.'

At the sound of her name she uncoiled and turned towards him. The few days in Bedlam had wrought a frightening change. The Thamsine he knew had vanished within herself. Even in the faltering light of the lantern, he could see that beneath her filthy, matted hair, her face was pallid, her lips grey and her eyes sunken in great, dark holes.

Her manacled wrists came up in a defensive gesture. 'Don't hurt me,' she pleaded, looking into his face and not seeing him.

He knelt beside her and stroked her hair. 'Thamsine? It's Lovell.' He raised the lantern to his face.

She stared at him for a moment or two, her brow furrowed. Her breath came in short flurries. 'Lovell? It can't be. He's in Norfolk ... or France ... or ... '

She began to shake and he laid his hands on her shoulders to still her. She wore only her shift and the material beneath his hands was wet and cold to the touch.

Kit stood up and looked at the wardress. 'Why has she been treated this way?'

The wardress put her hands on her hips. 'Man what brought her in said she had a nasty, violent nature and suggested she be kept manacled.' She looked down at Thamsine. 'We find cold water normally quiets 'em down.'

Kit spared her a withering glance. 'I dare say it does! Undo those manacles.'

Taking her time, the wardress knelt and turned the key in the rusty locks. Kit took Thamsine in his arms. She clung to him, shivering and icy to the touch.

'Where are her clothes?' he demanded.

'Oh, they're long gone, ducky.'

'Well, fetch a dry blanket. She'll catch lung fever left like this.'

'Most of 'em do,' the wardress muttered as she ambled off.

Kit took off his cloak and wrapped it around Thamsine's slight figure. He held her to him, rocking her like a child. Another few days of this and she would have agreed to marry the Devil himself. Morton had a refined method of torture.

'It really is you, Lovell?' she whispered

'Yes.'

She screwed her eyes shut. 'No, it's a dream. I'm going to wake up and you will be gone.'

'I'm real enough.'

He stroked her face, fighting back the rage. When he next met Ambrose Morton he would kill the man.

The wardress threw down a ragged blanket. Kit looked up at her. 'Are you going to help me?' he asked with icy politeness.

Grumbling, the woman helped Kit wrap Thamsine in the blanket's grimy folds. Rising to his feet, Kit walked over to the cell where he had locked Lucy. Through the grate in the door, he could make her out huddled in a corner, her arms wrapped around herself.

'Are you comfortable, Mouse?' he said.

He jumped at the shriek of rage as she lunged for the door.

'Now, now, Mouse. If you behave like that they will throw cold water on you.'

'Let me out, Kit!' Her voice changed to a pathetic wheedling.

'I don't think so. By the time you've found a way out of there, Lucy dearest, I shall be gone from your life.'

'We'll find you, Lovell.'

'Not in London, you won't,' he lied.

He hoped Lucy would be fool enough to believe him. Dearly as he would like to take Thamsine and flee with her to France, he couldn't. Circumstances tied him to London. The little matter of Thurloe's business had to be completed first.

'Enjoy your stay, Lucy.'

In reply, she spat at the door as he turned away.

'Come, Thamsine,' he said, bending down and lifting her into his arms. She buried her face in his shoulder.

'Watcha doing? You can't just take her. What am I going to tell me superiors?' The wardress sounded agitated.

Kit looked around the grim chamber. 'Next woman that dies, tell them her name was Annie Morton. Perhaps this will help smooth the way.' He tossed the wardress the remains of Lucy's purse. 'Now see us out,' he ordered.

The other inmates howled and clawed at his legs as he marched through.

'You know, for a thin woman with no meat on your bones, Thamsine Granville, you certainly weigh enough,' he whispered.

He settled her in the corner of the hackney coach and gave the driver the order to take them to The Ship Inn. Morton probably knew that Thamsine lodged there, but for the time being there was nowhere else.

In the dark of the coach's interior, he took Thamsine in his arms again, holding her close.

'You don't smell very good,' he whispered in her ear.

A small vibration of laughter rewarded him. 'Neither do you. You smell of sweat and horses.'

'It's been a busy day.'

'How did you find me?'

'It wasn't easy. It would have helped if you had told me the whole story on the day we met. Then I would have known who Ambrose Morton was and what a threat he was to you.'

Her shoulders heaved as the sobs came in an unchecked flood.

He let her cry, soothing her in his inept, masculine way. It did not take long for Thamsine's slight body to become a dead weight, and he knew that shock had claimed her – that she had fallen asleep or slipped into the self-preservation of uncon-sciousness.

The coach drew up at The Ship Inn. Kit lifted Thamsine out and carried her through the back entrance to the inn.

Roused from their beds, and still in their nightclothes, the girls came clattering down the stairs. May gave a sharp cry. 'You found her! Oh Cap'n Lovell, what's happened to her? What'd he do to her?'

Kit marched past her and continued up the stairs to Tham-sine's chamber.

'She'll be all right. She just needs cleaning up and rest,' he said as he laid her on the bed.

May busied herself lighting a fire and he sat down on the bed beside Thamsine, chafing at her icy hand, trying to bring some life back to her.

'Talk to me, Thamsine,' he said.

Her eyes flickered open and she smiled.

'Kit,' she whispered, 'I'm so tired.' Her eyes closed again.

Nan brought a foul-smelling tallow candle closer. She shoved Kit aside with her hip. 'Get lost. I'll see to her.'

Kit crossed to the fire and stood staring into it, while behind him Nan and May stripped Thamsine of the damp shift.

'Where's she bin, to get into this state? She's cold as death,' Nan said.

'Bedlam.'

Both girls stared at him.

'Bedlam? Who put her there?' Nan expostulated.

'It's a long story,' Kit replied wearily.

'It was him, weren't it?' May scowled. 'The one that wanted to marry her.'

'Yes.'

'Who is this cove?' Nan's eyes narrowed malevolently.

'A man called Ambrose Morton. You may have seen him. Tall, dark-haired, handsome ... '

'Describing yourself, are we?' May said.

Kit gave an ironic laugh and turned to look at the girls. 'I'm only quoting someone else. He's taller than I am and if he does come here, he's not to find her. Is that understood?'

Nan shrugged. 'If you say so. There's plenty of hidey holes in this old place. We'll keep her safe.'

'Not much we can do about her hair except cut it!' May held up the filthy, matted mess. 'Pity. It's such lovely hair.'

The girls found a plain nightdress, and when they had cleaned Thamsine up to the best of their ability, they dressed her unresisting body in it and with Kit's help settled her into the bed.

'So why'd you bring her here and not to yer fancy mistress?' Nan asked.

'My "fancy mistress" is a duplicitous bitch,' Kit said savagely. 'She is responsible for handing Thamsine over to Morton.'

Both girls both looked around at him. 'So you've left her, 'ave you? Not before time. I always said she was no good,' Nan said.

'You never met her,' Kit said, bemused.

'I saw her with you and I formed me own opinions. You should've left her long afore this. This one,' May jerked her head at the bed 'now she's more than right for you. Well, I'm going back to me own bed. We'll leave her to you, my lovely.'

'She could do with a bit of warming up!' Nan gave him a wink.

Kit sat down beside the bed and picked up Thamsine's hand, noting for the first time the slender musician's fingers and the fine bones. Her eyes fluttered open and her fingers tightened on his. She had begun to shiver uncontrollably, her teeth chattering.

Kit pulled the blankets higher, but to no effect. It seemed he had little choice but to follow the twins' advice. He stripped down to his breeches and shirt and climbed into the bed beside her, folding her in his arms.

As the heat from his body began to permeate hers, the shivering lessened and she slept, curled within the circle of his arms as if she had always belonged there.

He'd never known this thing called "love" could be so painful. His heart ached for her but strangely, despite her proximity, he felt no carnal desire, just the pleasure of holding her, being near her, keeping her safe.

He held her tighter and kissed the top of her head, closed his own eyes, and let sleep wash over him.

CHAPTER 28

A bitter early morning wind blew up the river, bringing the small boat with the red sail in to dock at St. Katherine's. Kit hunched his shoulders into his cloak, stamped his feet and blew on his hands. They had been waiting hours and he was frozen to the bone.

A sailor flung a plank across the gap between the boat and the dock and De Baas, immediately recognisable from his hawk-like visage, pranced across it.

'*Mes cheres*,' he exclaimed, clasping Henshaw and Kit to his perfumed person. 'I 'ave brought him.'

A second man crossed the plank and stood beside De Baas – a slight figure, his face shadowed by the wide-brimmed hat. Despite himself, Kit shivered, feeling a dark malevolence in the very stillness of the man.

De Baas gestured at his companion. 'Monsieur Debigné, my English friends Henshaw and Lovell.'

The Frenchman bowed but did not speak.

The unseen eyes of the hired assassin seemed to bore into Kit's soul and his flesh crawled. He had killed men but it had always been in the heat of battle or self-defence, never in cold blood. He wondered what sort of person would undertake such a calling.

Henshaw cleared his throat. 'There is an inn nearby where our friends wait. I suggest we adjourn there and we can advise you of the plan.'

Gerard and the recruit, Vowells, had taken the private parlour. A luncheon of cold meat and cheese encircled a map.

'Cromwell is accustomed to visiting Hampton Court Palace every Saturday,' Henshaw said. 'We've been watching him. He takes the same route every time.' His finger traced the road from London to Hampton on the map. 'He travels by coach with a guard of twenty men. Wiseman and I have reconnoitred the route and we believe an ambush can be laid here.' His finger jabbed. 'It's heavily wooded and there is a bend in the road which will force the coach to slow.'

Kit translated for Debigné, then asked, 'How many men? To my mind, we will need at least forty. '

'We have three times that number,' Henshaw replied, speaking in French.

'Experienced?' Debigné spoke for the first time, in time, glancing at Kit to provide the translation.

Vowells shrugged. 'Some.'

'Forty men is a large number to secrete,' Debigné commented.

'It can be done,' Henshaw said. 'Our target is Cromwell. A select few will go in with the sole purpose of dragging Cromwell from the coach and Ireton if he is with him. Monsieur, you know your job. I do not need to tell you what must be done.'

Debigné nodded. 'It will have to be fast.'

'Once it is accomplished, we make haste for London. Vowells – you and Fox will have the 'prentices here and here,' Gerard pointed to places on the map within striking distance of Whitehall. 'There will be chaos when news of the Protector's death hits the streets. We must act fast. Ireton, Thurloe and the others – you have the names – must all be secured.'

'And what is your alternative plan?' Debigné asked mildly.

'Alternative?' Lord Gerard glanced at the Frenchman, then at Kit, to check that he had heard the word correctly.

'What if Cromwell does not choose to visit Hampton Court on this particular day?' Debigné asked.

'Why would he? He always does it.'

Debigné shrugged. 'Something may detain him.' He looked around the circle of faces. 'He may get wind of the plan.'

'Only those of us within this room know these plans,' Lord Gerard said firmly. 'Every man here is to be trusted.'

Debigné straightened. 'That is good,' he said. 'When next we meet we talk about an alternative plan. Now, gentlemen, I am weary from the voyage. Baron?'

'Where are you staying?' Kit asked.

Debigné's cold eyes met his. 'I make my own arrangements. You may leave a message with Baron De Baas and I will contact him.'

After Debigné and De Baas left, the conspirators turned to their usual occupation of wine and cards. Kit chafed with impatience. He would have liked to have followed the Frenchmen, but to have left immediately on their tail would have caused comment.

He forced himself to a few rounds before excusing himself. There were other things he needed to accomplish before the day was done, and the first required a ride to Turnham Green to tell Jane Knott that her sister was safe.

KIT CHOSE a horse with a better temperament than his last mount and made good time to the village. With the practice of years, he took up a position where he could watch the house in Turnham Green unobserved. He had no wish to see Roger Knott, so he dispatched a boy with a short, cryptic note that only Jane Knott would understand.

Wearing a cloak and hat and carrying a basket, Jane Knott left the house half an hour after the boy delivered his note. Kit slipped from his hiding place and followed her at a discreet distance.

She bought vegetables and some meat from the local stall-holders and, carrying her basket, walked down to the riverbank. When he was certain she was out of sight and earshot of the village he closed the distance between them and came upon Jane, sitting on the riverbank, her knees drawn up to her chest, like a child.

'Mistress Knott?'

She jumped like a startled rabbit and started to rise.

He held up his hand and sat down beside her. 'I'm sorry to startle you.'

'Your note was somewhat vague,' Jane said, 'but I hoped it was you.'

'I have just come to tell you that I found Thamsine.'

Jane looked up at him. 'Is she ... ?'

'She is alive and unhurt.' He paused, uncertain of how much to tell her. 'He had confined her to Bedlam.'

Jane put a hand to her throat. 'Oh, surely not that awful place?'

'She would have been dead or mad within weeks,' Kit stated. 'He used the name Annie Morton to secure her. His sister, I presume?'

Jane nodded. 'Yes, poor Annie. Is Thamsine all right? He didn't ... ?'

'Apart from a few bruises and shock she seems unharmed, and she is safe with friends for the moment.'

Jane closed her eyes. 'Thank God. Morton came to the house this morning in a fearful temper. He and Roger left for London two hours ago.'

'Morton needs your husband again.'

Jane lowered her eyes. 'I know. He and your friend Lucy Talbot hold him fast. He is so afraid of scandal. He would be ruined.'

'And what about you?' Kit frowned. 'Mistress Knott, your husband is a confessed adulterer of the worst sort. Have you never considered leaving him?'

She looked horrified. 'Those who God has joined together, let no man put asunder,' she said. 'And there are the children ... no, I could never leave him. Despite what he did, he does love me, Captain Lovell.'

Kit nodded. He was not sure he entirely understood but he respected her right to value security over honour.

'You may have found Thamsine and while she is safe for the moment, it will not end there, Captain Lovell.' Jane accepted his hand and allowed him to help her to her feet. 'It won't end until Ambrose Morton is dead or ... ' She looked at him.

'Or ... ?'

'Or Thamsine is wed to another.' She paused and looked up at him. 'My father's will does not name Ambrose Morton as a beneficiary. It states that the estate passes to Thamsine upon her marriage. Marriage will free her.' She grasped his hand. 'Captain Lovell, do you love her?'

She mistook his silence. Her voice faltered as she said, 'I suppose love doesn't matter. If you care for her at all, even if it is just as a friend, marry her.'

Kit spread his hands. 'Mistress Knott, I can't marry her! My life is ... complicated.'

Her eyes widened. 'Do you have a wife, Captain Lovell?'

He shook his head. 'No ... '

Tears shone in Jane Knott's eyes and her voice shook as she said, 'I am certain she loves you, Captain Lovell, and it would be the one sure way to free her from Ambrose Morton.' She smiled. 'Surely you must see that it would not be to your disadvantage either.'

Kit straightened his shoulders. 'I am not so far lost that I would marry her for her fortune, Mistress Knott. That would make me no better than Morton.'

'But you don't deny it would be helpful?'

'Of course it would be. An heiress for a wife would be the answer to my prayers.'

'Then marry her and be done with it, Captain Lovell,' Jane said. 'If you don't, and something happens to her, you will regret it for the rest of your days.'

He nodded. 'That is a hard choice you give me, Mistress Knott. My life ... '

She dropped her eyes. 'Is complicated. I'm sorry if I misunderstood the nature of your friendship with Thamsine.'

He took her hand and pressed it to his lips. 'I ... I want you to know that I do love Thamsine, but there are other forces at work here that are beyond my control. Rest easy, I will think on it. In the meantime, I will wish you a good day, Mistress Knott.'

He took his leave of her and rode slowly back to London. At every step, a single thought jolted through his mind.

Marry Thamsine.

CHAPTER 29

The lights of The Ship Inn pierced the gloom of the evening, and already the sound of raucous laughter spilled into the street. Kit stopped for a moment in the street outside and looked up at the flapping sign with its crudely painted image of a ship in full sail. It seemed a strange place to call home, but it was the closest place he had to a home on this earth and he was glad to be back.

Jem looked up as he entered and jerked his head in the direction of Kit's travelling chest that Jem had retrieved that morning.

'What news from Holborn?' Kit asked

'Place is in an uproar. The girl had your chest at the kitchen door. I could hear her mistress howling from the street,' Jem shuddered. 'My betting is he took none too kindly to finding his bird had flown.'

Kit tried to summon some sympathy for Lucy and failed. She and Morton deserved each other.

'And Thamsine?'

Jem nodded. 'She's right enough. You'll find her upstairs.'

Thamsine sat in a chair beside the small grate, her feet drawn up beneath her, squinting at a broadsheet. She looked up as he entered, pulling a badly made shawl closer around her shoulders. Her shortened hair fluffed around her head like a curling halo framing her pale face. A broken pot with some tatty flowers in it had been placed on a table next to her.

Her eyes followed his and she smiled. 'Jem brought me the flowers.'

Kit raised an eyebrow. His sergeant had never been one to reveal a sentimental side before. 'How are you feeling?' he asked.

'More like myself,' she said. Her hand went to the curls that framed her face, making her look years younger ... or more her own age. 'What happened to my hair?'

Kit looked at her. 'It was filthy and matted and the girls thought it easier to cut it.'

'I suppose it will grow back. The price of my freedom,' she said ruefully.

Kit resisted the urge to run his fingers through the riotous curls. 'I rather like it short,' he said.

Thamsine shuddered and drew her knees up to her chest, wrapping her arms around them and leaning her face on her knees. She closed her eyes and tears spilled from beneath her lashes, tracing a track down her cheek. Kit resisted an urge to wipe the tears from her face.

'I thought I was lost, Kit.' She raised her head and looked up at him. 'Kit, your Lucy is in league with Morton.'

'I know,' he said. 'I left her in your place in Bedlam.'

Thamsine stared at him and a smile twitched her lips. 'Good. I hope she rots there. She's as dangerous as he is. Jane thinks she may have murdered her husband.'

Kit stared at her. 'Murdered her husband?'

'She stole some monkshood from Jane.'

'It wouldn't surprise me.' Kit shook his head. 'I suppose I always knew she was shallow and manipulative, but after the last few days I've had a glimpse of what she is capable of and I wouldn't be surprised if she runs to murder.'

'What I can't understand was why she was so possessive of you,' Thamsine said. 'She said she knew something about you that made you valuable to her.'

He gave a wry smile. 'Not as valuable as she would have liked to believe.'

'What did she mean?'

Kit hesitated. 'It's not important,' he said.

'Kit.' She sought his eyes. 'Please, no more secrets.'

He sighed. 'She wanted me for a title. My grandfather is Viscount Midhurst, and on his death, I become Lord Midhurst. But that's all it is, Thamsine, a name, nothing more. The family estate is ruined. I find I prefer being just plain Kit Lovell.'

'To a woman like Lucy Talbot, that title would be worth fighting for ... worth killing for,' she said aloud.

'Lucy made the mistake of playing with an experienced gambler, Thamsine. She underestimated me.' He squatted down and poked at the fire.

'Where is your family estate?' she asked.

'Cheshire. The house was largely destroyed in the last siege, so my family lives in the few habitable rooms and I send them money when I can.'

'Your family?'

He looked up at her. 'My grandfather, my stepmother and her daughter, my sister Frances. So you see, little Lucy would have got a poor exchange for the title.'

'I wonder if that mattered.' Thamsine mused. 'And your business in Paris?'

Kit stiffened. 'An ordeal,' he said.

'Something happened there?'

He shook his head. 'No, not there. On the boat returning to England. Fitzjames is dead.'

At the mention of Fitz's name, he felt a stab of pain as sharp as a knife. He missed Fitz. He missed their long and easy camaraderie, and he bitterly regretted the betrayal that had led to his friend's death.

'I'm sorry,' Thamsine said. 'How did it happen?'

Kit jabbed at a log with the poker. 'He found some letters I was carrying.'

'Letters for Thurloe?'

Kit gave a barely perceptible nod of the head.

'You didn't kill him?' The horror in Thamsine's voice couldn't be disguised.

He turned to look at her. 'No, I didn't kill him, but he would have killed me had it not been for the pitching of the boat. He overbalanced and fell overboard. I couldn't save him.'

He rose to his feet and she slipped off the chair and stood before him. Laying her hands on his forearms she scanned his face. 'He was your friend, wasn't he?'

Kit's mouth quirked at the corner and he had to take a quick breath and look away. 'Perhaps the only one I had but, as Thurloe reminds me, I can't afford to have friends in this business.'

'What about me?'

He looked at her. 'Thurloe sent me to look for you. I found you. There is no more to it than that.'

'So I was just another job?'

He nodded. 'Just another job.'

Thamsine lowered her head and dropped her hands. 'I see. I thought ... '

Kit turned away from her, running his hand through his hair.

'You were wrong, Thamsine. I have enough concerns of my own without the encumbrance of friends of any sort.'

She sighed. 'If I had been honest with you when we first met, would things have been different?'

He grasped for words that seemed to have entirely escaped him, hating the lies coming from his mouth. 'Would I have betrayed you to Thurloe? I don't know, but I do know that I could have protected you from Morton.'

He turned back to her, holding her by the forearms and seeking out her eyes.

'Thamsine, I'm too used to lying. It comes naturally to me. A moment ago I told you that you were nothing more to me than just another task Thurloe had set me.' He took a step towards her and this time it was he who took her by the forearms, seeking out her eyes. 'I can't lie about that anymore. You are one of the very few people in this world I call my friend.' He took a deep breath. 'And I think I might have a solution to your problem if you are willing.'

'Go on,' she said slowly.

'Marry me, Thamsine.' The words rushed out.

She stared at him.

'If you marry me, then your problem with Morton will vanish.'

'If I marry you, I marry a whole set of new problems,' she replied. 'For instance, I don't know if you'll be alive next week.'

He shrugged. 'Then you will be a wealthy widow and free to choose whatever man you wish. Jane told me of the terms of your father's will. If you marry someone other than Morton, he loses his control over you. Even if I were to die next week, you will be free of him and have full control of your own estate.'

She smiled, a small, bitter smile. 'And what do you get from the arrangement? A solution to your financial woes?'

'I want to be clear about this, Thamsine. I don't want your

money. I confess it would be useful, but if you wish we can enter into an agreement by which I forgo my claim on your property. It will be a proper business arrangement.'

She clapped a hand over her mouth and for a moment he thought she was going to cry or throw up. Instead, she laughed.

'Kit, that has to be the most romantic proposal a woman would ever want to receive.'

Kit bridled. 'This isn't about romance, Thamsine. This is about practicalities. Think about it, if you wish.'

He turned his back on her and kicked at the fire before turning back to face her.

'Marriage to me wouldn't be so bad, surely? We ... seem to get on quite well, and ... ' He paused. 'I can't think of anyone else I would rather marry.'

She shook her head. 'No,' she said slowly, 'I don't think it would be so bad, Kit, and I don't need to think about it. It sounds like a perfectly sensible solution to my woes. When did you have in mind?'

'As soon as possible. Tomorrow?' he said. 'I have found a celebrant who does not ask too many questions. Jem and the girls can stand witness.'

'I see you have it all planned,' Thamsine remarked dryly. 'You assumed I'd say yes?'

He looked at her. 'I don't have time to spare,' he said. 'If you said no, it would have made no difference.'

She rose to her feet and crossed to him. She took his hands. 'Thank you, Kit. I know how difficult this must be for you.'

He caught her fingers in his and looked into her steady brown eyes. He longed to kiss her, wrap his arms around her, breathe in the scent of her and lose himself in her. He wanted to tell her he loved her, and that, far from a business arrangement, his heart rejoiced at the thought of marrying this woman.

Instead, he kissed her on the forehead.

'I am glad that is settled,' he said. 'Until tomorrow, Thamsine. Good night.' He released her hands and turned for the door.

'Kit ...'

He turned sharply. Thamsine smiled a slow, sad smile.

'Thank you,' she said.

CHAPTER 30

Thamsine tugged at the low bodice of the outmoded, much-darned amber satin gown the twins had produced for use as a suitable wedding dress. She picked up a wide collar and fastened it to her neck.

'Oh, don't wear that!' May protested. 'It looks nice without it, it does. That colour suits you. Now hold still while I try to do summat with this hair.'

May tugged a comb through Thamsine's shorn locks.

'Hated having to cut it. You've such pretty hair,' May mumbled more to herself than Thamsine.

'It will grow back,' Thamsine said.

'I know, but still.'

'Well,' began Nan, who sat on the edge of the bed threading flowers for a wreath. 'I always knew there was something with you and the Captain.'

'What do you mean?' Thamsine asked. 'How could you see something I didn't even suspect?'

'Go on with you.' Nan guffawed. 'I've seen the way he looks at you. What wouldn't I give for him to have looked at me that way. In't that right, May?'

'Potty about you, he is,' May agreed. 'Maybe we know him better than you do.'

Something about their familiarity when talking about Kit made Thamsine aware that, in their own way, these two probably did know Kit Lovell better than she did.

'I don't think you understand,' she said. 'He's not marrying me because he loves me.'

But the twins just laughed.

'You just wait till he gets you into bed. He's a gentleman, he is. Not like most.' Nan said.

'That's right,' May agreed. 'Likes to make sure a girl has a good time too, if you know what I mean.'

Thamsine felt the colour rising to her cheeks. 'No, I don't know what you mean.'

'Go on! How old are you?' Nan asked.

'Twenty-six.'

'And you've never 'ad a man?' May enquired.

Thamsine shook her head. 'No.'

May stared at her in disbelief. Thamsine felt the colour rise to the roots of her hair.

'Well, love, you've chosen well, then,' May continued. 'The Cap'n, he'll be as good a teacher as any, I reckons. Taught him a few tricks ourselves, haven't we, Nan?' May winked at her sister.

Thamsine looked from one to the other. Surely a bride did not normally hear such candid revelations about her future husband's skill as a lover, but then nothing about her relationship with Christopher Lovell had been the least conventional.

Nan arranged the circlet of flowers on her curls. 'There, you look lovely! Turn around.'

Thamsine obliged. 'Come on, they'll be waiting for us!' May said.

Kit had found an obliging priest, happy to fulfil the requirements of a speedy marriage. With banns and licenses outlawed, the only requirement was for a priest or Justice of the Peace to announce the impending nuptials in a public place. The letter of the law had been complied with, and Kit waited at the church of St. Sepulchre at the end of the Old Bailey for his bride to appear.

Thamsine walked slowly down the aisle and stood beside him, looking up at him with a small, shy smile. Not for the first time that morning, she wondered whether she had made the right decision. Had she merely jumped from the frying pan into a fire?

Kit smiled back at her. He found her hand and gripped her cold fingers. Hidden from general view within the folds of her skirt, he gave her hand a reassuring squeeze.

In the space of a short ceremony, Christopher Lovell of the parish of Eveleigh in Cheshire became tied in the eyes of God and the State to Thamsine Granville, spinster of the parish of Hartley in Hampshire.

CHAPTER 31

A welcoming fire burned in the grate of The Ship Inn's best bedchamber. The twins had lit the room with expensive wax candles and left a cold supper set on the table.

Kit closed the door behind him and turned the key in the lock. He paused just to watch Thamsine. In the light of the candles, he could not see the darns and frayed edges of the amber gown and it glowed like a jewel, shimmering as she walked towards the window. The low cut of the bodice exposed her back, the long line of the stays lending an elegant grace to her slender figure.

She stopped by the window, looking down into the street, her hand resting on the sill, her face half-turned away from him. His heart ached at her beauty and the sudden realisation that she was beautiful. Every woman he had ever known paled into insipid prettiness beside her.

That thought made her unattainable and untouchable. A few days ago he had slept with her in his arms; now he stood in his wedding chamber like a virgin youth, at a loss to know what to say or even what to do.

She turned to look at him. 'What are you thinking?'

He paused for a moment before replying, unable to concoct a suitable answer that did not sound hackneyed or ribald or just plain stupid, so he opted for the truth.

'I was thinking how beautiful you are,' he said.

A small smile lifted the corners of her mouth. 'No one has ever told me that before.'

'No one has ever seen you looking as you do now. That gown becomes you well.'

She looked down at the bodice. 'I thought it a little immodest,' she said, 'but then I have very little to be immodest about.'

Kit forced his wooden feet towards the table and poured a glass of wine from the jug. Jem had assured him it was the very best the inn had to offer. He took a sip and, satisfied that Jem was correct in his opinion that it was marginally better than the usual gut rot served in the taproom, he poured Thamsine a glass and walked over to where she still stood by the window.

'I was watching life go by,' she said. 'And thinking how fortunate the people in the street are to be just going about their business.'

'They probably have their share of problems,' Kit replied pragmatically. 'Life is hard for everyone, Thamsine.' He raised his glass. 'Shall we toast a new beginning?'

She gave a small, tight smile and raised her glass to his. 'A new beginning for both of us.' She sipped the wine and sighed. 'This feels strange.'

'In what way?'

'Well, here we are, man and wife, and yet we know so little of each other.'

'Would it make a difference?' Kit asked. 'I doubt one person ever really knows another. Anyway, we have a whole lifetime to make those discoveries.'

She frowned. 'A whole lifetime! We have to survive the next few weeks first, Kit.'

Kit set his glass down and took her hand. 'I refuse to let any thought of what lies outside this room intrude on us tonight, Thamsine. What little time we have is for us and us alone to start learning those little things about each other.'

She looked up at him and her eyes twinkled. 'The twins have already told me things about you that I am sure you would be flattered to hear.'

He pulled a face. 'I can only imagine what they have been saying.' His eyes sought out hers. 'Thamsine, I make no apologies for my life. I have never made a pretence of being a saint. I have made love to a number of women but I want you to know, I have never loved a woman as I do you.'

There – the words were out.

Her brown eyes seemed large and luminous in the dim light as she searched his face. 'Did you say you loved me, Kit?'

He reached out and touched her face. The softness of her skin beneath his rough fingers sent bolts of lightning through his body. She leaned into his hand, drawing it around to her mouth, her lips brushing the palm and the fingers. He closed his eyes for a moment.

His other hand released hers. He slid it around her waist, drawing her towards him. He bent his head, his lips skimming the soft, chestnut hair.

'Yes,' he whispered. 'Yes, I love you.'

Her arms slid up behind his neck and she drew his face down towards her. 'Well, that is probably a good thing,' she said, 'seeing as I have loved you for a very long time.'

'So,' he whispered, 'that makes this marriage even more convenient?'

'It does,' she replied.

He kissed her and her head arched back, allowing his lips to slide down her neck, finding the soft place at the base of her throat. She stiffened, pulling away from him.

'Kit, I have little experience ... after all the other women in your life ... '

He laid a finger on her lips.

'*Croyez moi* ... trust me in this, Thamsine.'

Her eyes held his for a moment. 'You're a liar, a cheat and a rogue, Kit Lovell, but I trust you with my life.'

He lowered his mouth to hers again, gently brushing her lips with his. Thamsine tightened her arms behind his neck, locking them together in a hungry embrace.

They fell back onto the enormous old bed, hung with dusty, moth-eaten, red woollen curtains, laughing.

Thamsine raised her hand and touched his face, tracing the line of the silvered scar over his right eye, the length of his nose and the curve of his lips. 'I will remember this moment for the rest of my life,' she whispered. 'I don't think it is possible to be so completely happy.'

Tears collected on her lashes, and Kit brushed them away. Was she ready for this? Should they wait?

'Thamsine, we don't have to ... '

She slid her arms behind his neck. 'You silly man, I'm crying because I'm happy. Now, kiss me again.'

His smiled. 'Kiss you? Again? You are a demanding wench. In good time. My turn.'

He propped himself up on one elbow and with a finger traced the outline of her face, the orbs of her eyes, the length of her nose, the circumference of her mouth. She tried to bite at the finger but he removed it. They played that game a few more times before he replaced his finger with his lips, tracing the same route, moving down her throat as he had before and lingering in the sensitive hollow of the base of her throat. Thamsine moaned and he propped himself up again and slowly began to unlace the stomacher of her gown.

She, in turn, reached up to the laces on his shirt and undid the cord. He slipped the shirt off and she ran her fingers through the soft hairs on his chest. At her touch, he closed his eyes, the fastenings on her bodice momentarily forgotten, before bending his head and kissing her again.

Beneath his questing hand, she stiffened.

Kit backed off, his hand on her face. 'Thamsine? Am I going too fast?'

She shook her head. 'No, it's wonderful. I love you, Kit Lovell, and I trust you completely.'

He smiled and stroked her hair. 'Then let us be rid of these damned clothes.'

No two people had ever divested themselves of their clothes so quickly. Thamsine curled up in the circle of his arm, suddenly shy. Kit uncurled her, looking down at her slender body.

'You're beautiful, Thamsine.' There was wonder in his voice.

'I thought you liked women with more meat on their bones.'

He shook his head. 'Don't know what gave you that idea. You're perfect.'

He silenced any further comments with his lips, allowing his mouth to trace the path of his finger, leaving a trail of gentle kisses down the length of her body and the world beyond the window faded away to become just the two of them.

THAMSINE AWOKE as the first light of dawn filtered through the close-built street and the grimy windows. Kit's head rested on

Thamsine's chest, his arms encircling her, his weight pressing on her but not crushing her.

He stirred and drew her tighter into the circle of his arms, kissing her hair, his hand gently stroking her cheek. She wriggled away from him, propping herself up on one elbow, studying the strong curve of his mouth and the line of his unshaven jaw

'What do you see?' he enquired.

'You are beautiful,' she said.

He laughed. 'No one has ever called me that before.'

She traced the lines of his scars with her finger; the puckered flesh on his left shoulder, the long silvered slash on his upper right arm, and an ugly scar that marred his right thigh, the legacy of Worcester that had almost succeeded in killing him.

'Will you tell me about these?'

He shook his head. 'Not now, Thamsine. Today is for us, not who we were and where we come from.' His eyes widened as her hand slid down the long length of his torso. 'And, my dear wife, if you keep doing that to me, we will probably forget ourselves completely.'

CHAPTER 32

it's fingers drummed the windowsill of John Thurloe's room in the Palace of Whitehall. Below him, soldiers drilled in the courtyard and dark-suited men came and went with purposeful steps, but his mind was elsewhere.

He had left Thamsine still sleeping, her hair tousled and her lips slightly parted. He had not quite come to grasp the extraordinary power of their relationship. No liaison he had known with a woman had ever had this effect on him. Thamsine was – Kit struggled for superlatives – wonderful, beyond comparison. He longed with all his being to be back with her, in the private world of their own making.

In the past few days, curled up on the big, old bed, they had talked of their childhoods, hopes, dreams. He'd told her of his father's death on the steps of Eveleigh Priory, but he still couldn't bring himself to talk about Worcester ... or Daniel.

And he still had to see to Thurloe's business. There had been meetings in smoky taverns for which he had no heart. He had done what needed to be done and hurried home to be with Thamsine, intent on not wasting a single moment of their time together.

'Lovell?' Thurloe's voice snapped. 'Pay attention!'

He turned back to look at Thurloe. 'Sorry. You were saying?'

'I was saying that I intend to do nothing.'

Kit's hand tightened. 'Thurloe. This Frenchman is dangerous.'

Thurloe pressed his fingertips together. 'If the Protector does not go to Hampton Court as is his custom, the finger of suspicion will point straight at you. However, if he were merely to change his mode of transport, it may look less suspicious. He will travel to Hampton Court by water, not road.'

Kit nodded. 'That is a sensible precaution.'

Thurloe leaned forward. 'I presume there is an alternative plan?'

It had been thrashed out at a long, fraught meeting the previous night.

'Sunday – when he is leaving chapel.'

'Audacious!' Thurloe's eyebrows rose.

'I agree. It stands a reasonable chance of success, particularly if Ireton is with him. They intend to take him too.'

Thurloe steepled his fingers, as he did when in thought.

'If I were thinking as your fellow conspirators, as a plan it probably stands a better chance of success than the original concept. It's a public place; His Highness would be quite unprotected.' Thurloe frowned. 'I'll let word get around that the Lord Protector travels to Hampton Court by water. In the meantime we must try and find the Frenchman. Do you know where he is?'

Kit shook his head. 'No. I've tried following him, but he keeps himself well hidden and changes his lodgings every few days. I doubt even De Baas knows where he is. If I were to start asking too many questions I might arouse suspicions.'

Thurloe nodded. 'So what is your role in all of this?'

'I have to organise the final meeting.'

'They'll all be there?'

Kit nodded.

'Good.' Thurloe narrowed his eyes. 'You make whatever arrangements need to be made. I'll let matters go ahead for the moment and step in when I judge the time is right.' Thurloe looked up at Kit. 'Make no mistake, Lovell, I'm quite serious. I want as many of these misguided malcontents as possible, and I want the evidence to deal with them appropriately. They must be made an example. I also want De Baas. All you need to do is tell me where and when this meeting is to take place.'

Kit's head went up. 'And you will move then?'

Thurloe nodded.

'And me?'

'In the confusion I'm confident you will make shift for yourself, Lovell.'

Kit made for the door and stopped at Thurloe's voice. 'And, Lovell … a little concentration, please. You seem distracted. Whoever she is, forget her!'

KIT STARED at the shuttered windows of The Ship Inn and his heart stopped. When he had left that morning, all had been as normal. The inn never closed unless something was wrong, very wrong. He knocked on the door and Jem opened it to him. The big man's face was uncharacteristically pale and strained.

'Thamsine?' Kit's voice caught in his throat as he pushed past Jem.

'I'm all right, Kit,' Thamsine rose from a stool by the fire.

'Morton's been here, looking for me. He bided his time, waited until you and Jem were gone, then he struck.'

Kit took her in his arms and kissed the top of her head. 'Thank the Lord he didn't find you.'

Thamsine broke from the embrace and placed her hands on his chest. 'I was well hidden but ... ' She looked up at Jem and then at Nan, who sat hunched on a stool by the fire, her face hidden by a curtain of hair, ' ... he took May.'

'He said ... ' Nan looked up, her eyes red-rimmed. 'He said he's to be found at the house in High Holborn. You are to bring Thamsine with you and then May will be released.'

'And if I don't?' Kit's arm tightened around Thamsine's shoulders.

'If you don't come by midnight, he said he'll kill her.' Nan's voice bordered on hysterical.

'He's bluffing,' Kit said without conviction.

Thamsine shook her head. 'No, he doesn't bluff.'

Three anxious faces turned on him, willing him to find a solution to the problem.

'Jem, what time is it?' he asked.

'Must be gone eight,' Jem said. 'We've not much time.'

'I'll go with you,' Nan said. 'He'll be looking out for a woman. With a cloak and mask, I can pass in the dark. I've some pattens half a foot high, that'll give me height.'

Thamsine shook her head. 'No. I must go. Perhaps he can be persuaded to see reason?'

'Didn't seem in the mood to be too reasonable this afternoon,' Jem commented. 'Do you have a plan, Captain?'

His former sergeant's eyes were fixed on Kit with the absolute certainty of a soldier who trusts his commander implicitly. In the absence of a dozen men, Jem would have to do.

Kit looked at the two women. 'Neither of you are going with me. I'm not negotiating with him.' He looked at the three taut and anxious faces. 'Just you, Jem. It's only Morton and Lucy. Between us we should manage.'

CHAPTER 33

*K*it and Jem stood outside the house in High Holborn, looking up at the shuttered windows and solid oak door.

'How're we going to get in?' Jem asked doubtfully. 'It's shut up well and proper.'

'Through the garden at the back. The kitchen won't be quite as impenetrable.'

A lane ran down the side of the house, and the men scaled the rough stone wall without too much difficulty. Keeping to the shadows, they crept up to the kitchen that stood out from the main part of the house to lessen the risk of fire.

The door stood open, and Kit could see Bess the scullion sitting on a stool beside the great open fireplace, her head in her hands, weeping. He scanned the room but could see no sign of the odious Mag. He crept up to the open door.

'Bess!' he hissed.

She looked up. Her eyes, wide and terrified, darted around the kitchen. Kit stepped into the light of the doorway so she could see him and, putting his finger to his lips, he beckoned to her. She came to the doorway.

'Cap'n Lovell,' she whispered. 'Oh, there's terrible doings upstairs. Mag won't let me out of the kitchen. Says I'm not safe.'

Mag went up in Kit's estimation.

'What terrible doings?'

'It's that Colonel Morton,' Bess said. 'He's been here the last few days, in a terrible temper. He and the mistress have been yelling at each other fit to burst. Then today he goes out and comes back with a girl.'

'Are they upstairs now?'

She nodded.

'Where's Mag?'

'Up there with them. She won't let the mistress alone with him.'

Kit beckoned for Jem, who stepped out of the shadows. Kit looked at the girl's pale, spotty face.

'Leave this house, Bess and don't ever come back.'

'Why?'

'Because Mag is right, you're not safe here. Do you have somewhere to go?' Kit asked.

'My sister in Blackfriars.'

'Go there and stay there. And if you need work, this here is Master Marsh, owner of The Ship Inn near the Old Bailey. He'll help you out.'

She opened her mouth to protest, but saw the grim determination on the men's faces and thought better of it, running from the kitchen.

'You know your way around?' Jem enquired as Kit stepped into the kitchen.

'I lived here, Jem.'

'Didn't think you'd got much beyond the bedroom,' Jem commented.

'That's enough insubordination from you,' Kit growled.

The stillness of the house was oppressive as if Morton's presence had descended on it like a black cloud. They crept through the house, traversing the space of the ground floor that had been Martin Talbot's place of business. Apart from a few remaining barrels it was now empty, dusty and unused. Kit led Jem up the back stairs to the first floor, where the parlour and a small room Talbot had used as a study served as the main rooms of the house. On the floor above there were two bedchambers.

A light shone from beneath the parlour door. The floorboard creaked under Jem's weight. It sounded like a shot in the gloom but no one stirred from the parlour, so they edged closer to the door, one on each side.

As they stood poised to kick it open, the door opened and Mag came through it.

She didn't see them until it was too late. Jem brought the pistol butt down on the back of her head and she fell sprawling to the floor. Stepping over Mag's large, prostrate form, the men burst through the door. Lucy and Morton sat at the table, evidently at their evening meal. Both jumped to their feet as the men entered the room. Lucy screamed and Ambrose Morton reached for a pistol that lay on the table.

'Don't move a muscle, Morton,' Kit said, closing the distance between them, his pistol pointed at Morton's head.

'Where's the girl?' he demanded

Morton straightened and smiled. Kit's blood ran cold.

'Well, well ... I underestimated you, Lovell.'

'Where's my sister?' Jem stormed across the room and seized Morton by the neck. Morton was a large man, but Jem overtopped him both in height and weight.

'Upstairs,' Morton spluttered.

Jem released him, pushing him down on the chair with a pistol at his head. Kit looked at Lucy for the first time. The pretty face looked strained, her eyes red from weeping or exhaustion.

'Well, Lucy, shall we go and fetch her?' Kit jerked his pistol towards the door. 'Jem, watch Morton.'

Lucy did not move.

Kit narrowed his eyes. 'You may recall, Lucy, I have a rather nasty side to my nature when I'm crossed. Did you enjoy your stay in Bedlam?'

Lucy shot him a glance of pure hatred and rose to her feet. Kit took her arm, keeping his pistol at her head.

As they reached the door he said, 'And I want the letters, too.'

She stopped and looked at him. 'What letters?'

'Roger Knott's letters.'

She drew her lips back, baring her teeth like a cornered rat.

'They're in my bedchamber,' she said.

He stood at the bedchamber door while she retrieved the letters from a locked cabinet. In the second chamber, he found May lying on the bed, bound hand and foot and gagged. She raised a tear-streaked face as they entered the room.

'Untie her,' Kit ordered and Lucy complied.

May tumbled off the bed and threw her arms around Kit's neck, sobbing hysterically. He disengaged her and, with one arm around the girl, he prodded Lucy with the pistol and they made their way back down the stairs.

As soon as May saw Morton, she cowered and the tears began anew. Kit cast her a sideways glance, taking in the dishevelled clothing and bruised and tear-stained face. It didn't take much to deduce how Morton had spent the afternoon.

'You whoreson.' Kit breathed the words, white-hot anger

flaring behind his eyes. He jerked his head at Lucy. 'This baggage too obliging, is she? You like it a bit rough?'

'The girl's a doxy,' Morton replied and shrugged. 'And I got bored,' he added.

Jem, a little slower on the uptake, looked from one man to the other, then to his sister. As realisation dawned, he bellowed with rage and struck a fist into Morton's face. Ambrose's nose exploded in a fountain of blood and a howl of pain.

Jem raised his arm again, but Kit stepped forward and put his hand on the man's shoulder.

'Leave him to the law,' he said. 'Let's get out of here. Lucy, the letters?'

Lucy tossed the letters onto the floor at Kit's feet, forcing him to stoop to retrieve them. That moment was all it took for Lucy to produce a small, neat pistol, which she held to May's head.

He cursed himself for a stupid lapse. She must have kept the weapon in her bedchamber and retrieved it when he sent her for the letters.

Lucy's lips curved in a tight-lipped smile. Morton, holding his nose, snorted something unintelligible and retrieved the pistol from the table.

Jem and Kit exchanged glances. Kit scanned the room trying to formulate a plan. Lucy obstructed their exit by the door and Morton stood between them and the window. A large sconce with half a dozen candles burned on the table in front of them.

'Drop your weapon, Kit, and you ... ' Lucy gestured to Jem.

Kit held Lucy's eyes and slowly moved towards the table, making to place the pistol on it. As he reached it, he swept the candlestick from the table. It fell clattering to the floor, the candles extinguishing, plunging the room into darkness. At that moment, Jem launched himself at Lucy with a roar. Lucy screamed and her pistol fired as Jem knocked her to the ground with one swipe of his massive arm.

Jem gathered his sister in his arms and looked at Kit.

'Get out of here,' Kit yelled.

Jem picked up his sister and flung her over his shoulder. He rushed for the door with Kit behind him. They vaulted Mag's still recumbent body and headed for the stairs. Jem took them first, his feet clattering on the wooden boards. A candle burned from a sconce at the head of the stairs, casting enough light to take them safely.

Jem scrabbled at the front door as Morton, diving over Mag, fired his pistol. Kit, poised at the top of the stairs, felt the pistol ball whistle past his ear, slamming into the wall behind him. He turned to face Morton, who came at him with his sword drawn.

Kit fired his pistol and heard Morton grunt as the pistol ball found its mark somewhere on his body, but the impetus of Morton's charge carried him forward. He fell on Kit, the weight causing him to lose his balance. Locked together, they tumbled down the steep stairs.

For a moment neither man moved as they caught their breath. Kit lay face down on the dusty floor of the old shop with Morton's weight on top of him. Just a few inches beyond his outstretched right hand, Morton's sword glinted in the faint light cast by the candle on the stairwell. Kit inched his fingers towards it.

A hand grasped his wrist, pinning it to the floor. Suddenly Morton was off him, and with a bellow of fury the man brought the heel of his boot down on Kit's hand. Before Kit had even registered what had been done, Morton repeated the act, grinding his heel into the bones. He followed this up with a boot to Kit's ribs.

With a howl of pain, Kit doubled up, clutching his hand to his chest as Morton, panting heavily, his face a mask of blood from his broken nose and his left hand dripping blood, most likely from Kit's pistol shot, retrieved his sword and stood over him.

With his right hand, he hauled Kit upright and flung him against the wall, pinning him by the throat.

'You don't want me dead,' Kit said, holding the man's crazed eyes with his own. Morton stood half a head taller than Kit, with a longer reach and a greater body weight.

'No, you're right, I don't want you dead. I want you to tell me where Thamsine Granville is,' Morton snarled, tightening his grip on Kit's throat.

For a moment Kit weighed the possible consequences of telling Morton that Thamsine had married him, but decided that if Morton knew the truth, then he would certainly be a dead man. Alive, he was of considerably more use both to Morton and to Thamsine.

Ambrose Morton's hand crashed against his face. Kit's head snapped back against the wall and a panoply of bright lights and stars flashed before his eyes.

Morton hauled Kit's head up by the hair. 'Now, are you going to tell me where she is?'

Kit spat blood from a cut lip into Morton's face. 'Safe from you.'

'I want my wife.'

'She's not your wife! She never will be.' He jerked his head towards the stairs where Lucy stood watching them. 'Marry this little bitch. She'll serve you just as well.'

Another backhander across the face knocked the remaining breath from his body. Morton let him go, and clutching his hand to his chest Kit sank to the floor. Morton pressed the point of his sword to Kit's throat. Kit felt the prick of the metal and the warmth of blood trickling down his neck. One wrong move and he was a dead man

'Marry this strumpet?' Morton said, panting heavily as he looked up at Lucy, 'Why would I do that? For her money? Well, my dear Lovell, she doesn't have any. What fortune her husband has left her is quite gone, isn't it, my dear? An expensive taste in clothes and a gambling habit. A little too fond of backgammon is our Mistress Talbot. Come here, my dear.'

Lucy complied, standing beside Morton as he stroked the fair curls with his good hand.

'It seems you didn't know her quite as well as you thought you did,' he said.

Kit raised his eyes to look Lucy in the face.

'I didn't know her at all,' he gasped and turned back to look up at Morton. 'So, are you going to kill me?'

'Eventually, when you've told me what I need to know. Where is she?'

'Go to hell,' Kit spat.

Morton sighed heavily. 'I see I need to cause you more pain before you see sense.'

He lowered the sword and leaned over Kit. Placing one boot on his chest to hold him in place, he wrenched Kit's injured hand away from his body. With an almost studied care, he bent the broken fingers backward. Kit arched back against the wall in agony, his feet scrabbling for purchase against the dusty floor as a scream tore from his throat.

'Ambrose, please.' Lucy's voice sounded strained.

'You enjoy this,' Kit panted.

'Yes, I do,' Ambrose snarled. 'Now, where is she?'

He bent the fingers again, and through the pain, Kit prayed for the blessed release of unconsciousness.

'Go on, kill me!' he said between gritted teeth. 'It will serve you naught. Thamsine is free of you.'

'What do you mean?' Morton's boot in his chest pressed harder.

Kit took a breath and forced himself to look up into Morton's eyes, holding them with his own.

'She's my wife, Morton. She married me. Even if I die, you have no hold over her.'

'You're lying!'

Morton bent his fingers back with such ferocity that this time Kit lost consciousness. From somewhere a long way away he heard a bellow of rage and the sound of a fist on bone.

Released from Morton's grasp, Kit slumped back against the wall. He fought for some control over the agonising pain in his hand, but it consumed him. Dimly he was aware that the shadows in the room leapt and danced without clear substance. He heard voices and scuffling and grunting and a woman screamed. There was more scuffling, and then silence.

A shadow bent over him and he flinched as a hand rested on his shoulder.

'He's made a pretty mess of you in a few short minutes, Lovell.'

'Jem!' Kit said, aware that he struggled on the edge of consciousness. It would so easy to let himself go, to sink into oblivion.

'Come on, let's get you home.'

Jem's strong arm circled his shoulders, pulling him upright into his strong grasp with surprising gentleness.

CHAPTER 34

Thamsine sat by May's girl's bedside and looked down at the tear-stained face of the sleeping girl. The physical bruises would heal but the memory of her encounter with Morton would stay with her forever. Who knew how many other women had been victims of Morton's sport?

She blamed herself. She had brought this man into May's life, and May had paid the price of Thamsine's freedom.

Nan appeared at the door, holding a candle.

'How is she?' she asked.

Thamsine looked up at her friend. All Nan's brashness seemed to have leeched from her. She looked tired and spent.

'Asleep at last,' Thamsine said.

'Jem's downstairs,' Nan said. 'He went back for Lovell.'

Thamsine gathered up her skirts and ran down the stairs to the taproom, where Jem stood by the fireplace staring into the dying embers of the day's fire.

'Where's Kit?' Thamsine asked.

Jem jerked his head at the large oak settle beside the fireplace, where Kit sprawled like a broken puppet. Her heart in her mouth, Thamsine knelt beside her husband and held the candle up. Even in the dim light of the fire, she could see blood on his face, one eye already closing and swollen, and a cut and bruised lip.

For a moment she thought he was unconscious, but his un-blackened eye opened and he managed a crooked smile.

'Your face, Tham! Do I look that bad?'

'What did he do to you?' Thamsine asked, her breath tight in her throat.

Kit's left hand moved to his face. 'This … this is just bruises. It's my hand,' he muttered faintly. 'My sword hand.'

For the first time, Thamsine noticed that his right hand was tucked inside the front of his jacket. With shaking fingers she undid the jacket and, holding his forearm, lifted out his hand. Kit gave a strangled groan and tensed back against the settle, his jaw locked as he fought the pain.

Thamsine's stomach churned when she saw the damage. Nan let a low whistle. 'Looks like it's been through a meat grinder,' she said. 'What'd he do?'

'He trod on my fingers,' Kit muttered between gritted teeth.

'Trod on them? Looks like he took a hammer to them,' Nan said.

Thamsine stood up. 'He needs a chirrurgeon.'

Jem looked at Nan and nodded.

'Rouse that lazy stable lad and send him for the chirrurgeon on the Strand.'

Nan nodded and kilting up her skirts ran from the room.

'What did you do to Morton and that bitch?' Kit looked up at Jem.

'Not as much as I would have liked to,' Jem said, grimly. 'I got halfway down High Holborn afore I realised you wasn't behind us, so May told me to go back to fetch you. Luckily for both of us, it looks like you'd put a pistol ball through Morton's left arm. He was bleeding like a stuck pig. Didn't put up much of a fight ... one blow and he went over like a rotten tree in a high wind. I flung him down the cellar stairs and sent the Talbot woman and that ugly maid of hers after him. I just hope he broke his neck.'

Kit's face creased in pain. 'You should've killed him.'

'After what he did to May, it was all I could do not to,' Jem agreed. 'But I didn't want to end up at the end of a rope for murder. You're all done in, Lovell.' He looked at Thamsine. 'Come on, lass. Let's get him upstairs to a bed while we wait for help.'

With difficulty, Thamsine and Jem manoeuvred the Kit up the narrow stairs to the large, airy bedchamber that Kit and Thamsine now occupied. He hung between them, barely conscious and a dead weight. As they laid him on the bed, Nan brought a bowl of water and a cloth and began to wash the blood from his face.

Jem rested Kit's damaged hand down across his chest and shook his head.

'That looks bad, Lovell.'

Thamsine forced herself to look down at her husband's battered face and then moved her gaze to his hand. His fingers, those wonderful, magical fingers, were bloodied and broken like splintered wood. Thamsine backed away. She felt the bile rising in her throat.

'I ... I think I'm going to faint.'

Jem put a hand on her arm and guided her to a stool. He forced her head down between her knees.

'Just what we need,' he muttered, 'a fainting female.'

As the grey dawn light began to creep in through the grimy windows, Thamsine raised her head. She had fallen asleep in the chair beside Kit's bed, her head resting on the covers. She stood up and stretched her cold, stiff limbs and looked down at Kit.

He had been unconscious or asleep for hours following a torrid session with the chirrurgeon and the bonesetter, both of whom seemed to think the only solution for Kit's broken fingers was to amputate his hand, a proposal Kit, with the last vestige of consciousness, had resisted vigorously. As a result his hand, splinted awkwardly and heavily bandaged, lay intact on the bed covers.

She touched his face, her fingers rasping against the rough stubble of his unshaven chin. She picked up his good hand and pressed the fingers to her lips. Kit groaned and moved and his face contorted with pain. His eyes opened and a string of voluble French curses accompanied his return to consciousness.

'Kit?'

He turned his head slightly to look at her. He opened his eye and looked up at her.

She gently stroked his forehead. 'Is the pain bad?'

'Stop beating me on the head, it hurts. Everything hurts,' Kit mumbled, shutting his eyes again.

Thamsine withdrew her hand.

Kit lifted his good hand to his face, probing the bruises. 'Am I going to live?'

'We think so. You have several cracked ribs, a black eye, your right knee is badly bruised and swollen and your hand...' Thamsine trailed off on the inventory of Kit's injuries. 'I just hope that Ambrose is in a similar sorry state.'

Memory flooded back into his face and she had a fleeting glimpse of the terror of the previous night.

'I thought he would kill me,' he said. 'Very slowly and very painfully. Thank God Jem came back for me.'

He turned his head to look down at his heavily bandaged right hand. Thamsine saw the muscles of his right arm flex experimentally as he tried to raise his hand. The effort produced another string of blasphemous oaths and he turned back to look at her, his face sheened with sweat. She answered the question in his eyes.

'The bonesetter has splinted it as well as he can. You have three broken fingers and broken bones in your hand. It will take months to heal and even then he is doubtful you will have the full use of it again. He wanted to amputate it.' She smiled. 'But you were adamant that you wouldn't let him.'

Kit's eyes widened. 'They wanted to take my leg after Worcester, but I survived quite well with it intact. I can do so again.'

'But your hand ... ' Thamsine demurred.

'I am better with a crippled hand than no hand at all,' Kit said. He closed his eyes and grimaced. 'As for Morton, it was his mistake not to kill me when he had a chance.'

Thamsine looked away. 'Oh Kit, I'm so sorry. It is all my fault that you and May were hurt.'

His left hand sought hers and he gave it a reassuring squeeze. 'Thamsine, don't blame yourself. Morton is a vicious swine. We couldn't leave you to his tender mercies.' He closed his eyes and took a breath. 'Oh God, that hurts!' After a moment he opened his eyes again. 'May? Is she all right?'

'As well as can be expected.'

'I know what he did to her,' Kit said. 'I'm sorry, Tham.'

'What have you to be sorry for? This is my doing!' Thamsine's voice choked as the tears she had been fighting back threatened to overwhelm her. 'Kit, both May and I owe you our lives.'

He flinched again as he tried to shift his weight and Thamsine bit her lip at her own helplessness. He glanced at the window where a fitful early morning light filtered through the grimy glass.

'What time is it, Tham?'

She looked at the window. 'About eight in the morning.'

'Eight? Oh, dear God. Where are my clothes?' With difficulty, he propped himself up on his left elbow.

'Downstairs, being cleaned. They were covered in blood. What are you doing? You're not going anywhere, Kit!'

He looked at her with desperation written on his face.

'I have to. Help me sit up.'

Thamsine rose to her feet. 'No! Kit, you're half dead. You've been unconscious for hours.'

He glared at her.

She crossed her arms and tightened her lips. 'All right then, go ahead. You try and get up and if you can take two steps without falling down then I will find some clothes for you to wear.'

He scowled at her and she watched on as he tried to raise himself into a sitting position using his good arm. The effort had him gasping for breath with the pain, and as soon as he tried to move his right hand, she knew he was defeated. He fell back and laid his left arm across his eyes.

'This couldn't have happened at a worse time.'

'If you insist on trying to fight it, you will be dead before week's end,' Thamsine said grimly. 'You've been hurt before, Kit, you know it's going to take time and rest.'

He grimaced. 'I know, Thamsine. You don't have to tell me.' He looked at her. 'You're going to have to do it for me.'

Her eyes widened. 'Do what?'

'You know the business I am involved in. God willing it will come to conclusion in the next day or so, but I need you to deliver a message to Thurloe.'

She paled. 'No, Kit. Not John Thurloe. I can't face that man again, particularly as I failed him so dismally.'

'You didn't fail him, Thamsine. You were forcibly removed. Thurloe knows that. I've told him everything. I even asked him to investigate Morton's treatment of you. He should know about

May, too. God knows I would like to see Morton hang.' He lifted his arm and his eyes were steely. 'You're still in Thurloe's debt. Help me now and he will clear your name. I promise.'

She looked at him for what seemed an eternity. 'I will do it on one condition.'

'No conditions, Thamsine.'

'I am only asking you to tell me what it is that John Thurloe holds over you.' She bent and kissed his bruised cheek. 'I am your wife, or had you forgotten? Your concerns are my concerns. You have to tell me everything, Kit. No more secrets.'

He managed a weak smile. 'I'm a pretty inadequate excuse for a husband right now. Very well, you have my word. I'll tell you everything, but only when this is over and we can go to France and leave this whole sorry mess behind us.'

She knelt beside the bed and lifted his uninjured hand to her lips.

'I love you, Kit.'

He gave her a crooked smile. 'I'm sorry, Thamsine. There will be a more appropriate time for such tender moments. We have to finish this business.' He ran his left hand over his eyes as if trying to pull together his scattered thoughts. 'Tell Thurloe that there is to be a meeting tonight to co-ordinate the simultaneous seizing of the Whitehall Guards and the Tower of London by the London apprentices and others. Can you remember that?'

Thamsine repeated it back to him and he nodded. 'Where is the meeting to be held?'

He frowned. 'The Swan, at eleven. After you've seen Thurloe you must send a message to a man called Peter Vowells. He's the schoolmaster in Islington. He is to come here.'

Thamsine rose to her feet. 'Here?'

'Well, I can hardly go to him, and there are some details we need to discuss that are too complex to send by message alone.'

He gave an unwise snort of laughter, wincing as his broken ribs caught. 'It won't do my cause any harm for him to see that I am physically incapable of participating any further. Perhaps that is one thing I should thank Ambrose Morton for.'

'And Thurloe will move on the meeting?'

Kit nodded. 'They'll all be there. He will snare the lot.'

'How do I get in to see Thurloe?'

'Tell them you have been sent from Master Green. Go now, Thamsine. There's very little time.'

CHAPTER 35

To her surprise, Thamsine encountered little opposition in her request to see Thurloe and she was shown through to his rooms with no questions.

Thurloe looked up from the paper he had been writing as she entered and ran the quill through his fingers as he looked her up and down.

'Well, well, Mistress Granville. What a pleasant surprise. You're sadly missed by Mistress Skippon.'

Thamsine swallowed. 'My disappearance was not my choice,' she said defensively.

'Lovell has told me. A domestic matter, I believe. All resolved now I trust?'

'Not entirely.'

Thurloe studied her for a moment before speaking.

'I was told you had a message for me. Is there some reason why Lovell couldn't come in person?'

'He had an encounter with some footpads last night,' she lied.

'And he didn't come off well?'

'No.'

'That's unusually careless of him. He is quite capable of taking much better care of himself.' Thurloe's eyes took on the hooded, predatory look she recognised from their previous encounters. 'Convenient for him though. What is the message?'

'Before I give it to you, I want your assurance that this work is a discharge of the debt I owe you.'

Thurloe's face betrayed nothing. 'Mistress Granville, what gives you the right to start making demands of me?'

'I know what Lovell has been doing for you. The message I bear is the key to the whole operation. He told me it was of sufficient gravity for you to consider my work in delivering it a discharge of that duty.'

'Indeed? How presumptuous of him.' Thurloe raised an eyebrow. 'Does it concern a meeting?'

'Yes.'

Thurloe nodded. 'Very well, consider your debt discharged, Mistress Granville. Now, the message, please.'

She repeated Kit's message and Thurloe, his fingertips pressed together, nodded approvingly.

'You've done well, Mistress Granville. You may give Captain Lovell a message from me. Firstly, you must tell him that the arrangements must go ahead as described. You may also tell him that if he is right and there is a satisfactory conclusion to this matter, then his debt to me will also be considered discharged.'

'What is your hold over him?' Thamsine asked.

'That is between Captain Lovell and myself, Mistress Granville. Now, good day to you.'

Thamsine hesitated at the door. 'Lovell,' she said, turning back to look at him. 'My name is Lovell. We were married a week ago.'

Thurloe's eyes widened with genuine surprise. 'Indeed? I had not thought of Lovell as the marrying kind. I must say, you seem ideally suited to each other. Good day to you … ' he paused and the corners of his mouth twitched. 'Mistress Lovell.'

THAMSINE STOOD at the window of Kit's bed chamber watching the tall, lanky figure of the schoolteacher, Vowells, striding away from the Ship Inn, his head lowered against the cold rain. He carried with him the details of a meeting that night. A meeting that would probably mean his death. She turned to her husband, her eyes flashing silent accusations.

'Don't look at me like that.' Kit turned his head away.

'You've sent him to his death. How do you live with yourself?' When he didn't reply, Thamsine sat down on the edge of the bed. 'We had a bargain. I want to hear the whole story.'

'My confession?'

'If that is how you wish to put it.'

Kit laid his good arm across his forehead. 'I'm Thurloe's agent because I am a coward, Thamsine. Well, partly because I am a coward. The second reason is probably more honourable.'

Thamsine leaned against the wall, her arms crossed. 'Go on.'

'After Worcester … ' He broke off and sighed. 'I was wounded at Worcester, badly wounded. I was lucky to survive. It was only because the wife of one of the sergeants took pity on me that I survived.'

'Was she pretty?' Thamsine smiled.

'No, she wasn't,' Kit snapped. 'She was as wide as she was tall and as strong as any man. I was in no position to argue with her. I survived and found myself in a hellhole. No other word for it, Thamsine. I had ample cause to regret that I had not died and I prayed for death because it seemed the only release. That's how

Thurloe found me. He promised me liberty and offered a means of persuasion that could not be resisted.'

'Did he torture you?'

Kit shook his head. 'He didn't need to, Tham. He knew I would acquiesce.'

'Why?'

'Because he held my brother. Did I mention I had a brother?'

Thamsine nodded.

Kit's lips tightened. 'Like you and your brother, Daniel and his sister, Frances, are the children of my father's second marriage. Daniel would be twenty-one now. Frances is two years younger.'

'They're both alive?'

'Frances lives with her mother and my grandfather at Eveleigh Priory. Eveleigh was one of the last sieges of the war. My father and I held it for two months before Parliament's troops took it by storm. The house was largely destroyed, my father killed, and I was taken prisoner. They released me in '47 and I went straight to France.'

He took a breath. 'My brother Daniel had been a boy when Eveleigh fell. When I returned in '51 he was eighteen, fearless and spoiling for a battle. Just as I had been ten years earlier.'

'Like Edward.'

'Indeed. I had regaled him with too many stories of the high times and glory. I didn't think ... didn't notice that he hung on every word. He saw this as his chance to regain the family fortunes and he begged to come with me. In the end, I agreed to take him. My stepmother was hysterical but she could no more have stopped him than I. He would have come anyway and it seemed far better to let him come with me, under my protection. I promised his mother I would look after him and keep him safe.' Kit gave a hollow laugh. 'You know how the battle went? God knows it was as hard a battle as ever I had fought. I kept Daniel at my side but the fighting separated us. He was beset on all sides and I tried to reach him but I was cut down and a musket stock –' He touched his head above the right ear '– took the last fight out of me. I woke up a prisoner in Worcester Cathedral. No one could tell me what became of Daniel and for months after the battle, I thought he was dead.'

'But he survived?'

Kit swallowed. 'Six months after Worcester, Thurloe came to Warwick Castle, where I was held, with his proposition. He had me dragged to a window. Below in the courtyard in the cold, the mud, and the rain were a group of Scottish prisoners who were to be transported to Barbados. Daniel was among them, shackled and beaten, with barely a rag on his back. However bad my lot had been, his had been infinitely worse. Thurloe told me that Daniel would be transported with the other prisoners and unless I co-operated he would be dead by year's end. Barbados.' Kit spat the word out. 'I don't know if you have heard of the conditions in Barbados, Thamsine?'

She shook her head.

'The men, black and white, are treated like animals, and those who don't die of the maltreatment die of disease. Thurloe gave me a choice. If I agreed to his proposal Daniel would be well treated. If I did not, then he worked the fields as one of the slaves. He was right. The boy would be dead within a year. What choice did I have?'

He looked away. Thamsine placed her hand over his and said nothing.

With his face still turned from her, he said, 'Daniel has spent two years on that pestilential island.'

Thamsine's mouth went dry and she swallowed. 'Do you know if he is still alive?'

'Thurloe says he is, and I would rather live with that hope than see England plunged into civil war again.' He looked at Thamsine, his face creased with a pain that was not physical. 'It was all Thurloe needed to secure my co-operation. It came to a simple choice between my brother's life or an indefinite life in prison. It was no choice, Thamsine. If I refused, both Daniel and I would be dead. My answer was a given. I took the coward's choice.'

Thamsine shook her head. 'Kit, any man would have done what you did. Why do you think it was a coward's choice?'

He looked at her. 'You're not a man, Thamsine. You don't understand the concept of honour. There is no honour in betraying my friends and comrades, no matter how good the personal cause may be. Thurloe offered me freedom, and at that nadir of my life that was all I craved, whatever the cost. Daniel was not given that choice.'

She stared at him for a long moment, trying to make sense of what he had just told her. This misguided concept of *honour* had killed her brother and changed her life forever.

'You're right, I don't understand "honour",' she said, fighting the bitterness in her voice. 'How would your death in prison have helped your brother?'

He gave what passed for a shrug and grimaced. 'It was a Devil's bargain, Thamsine. I've kept my word and mercifully now it is nearly done. Daniel will be freed and once he is safely returned to England, you and I shall leave this cursed island and go wherever our hearts take us.' He shifted uncomfortably, grimacing. 'I want to be free of England, Thamsine.'

'I have lands in Virginia.'

Kit's eyes gleamed. 'Virginia. That would be a new start for us both.'

He took her hand in his good one, his thumb circling the palm. 'Do you think, for a moment, we can let ourselves believe that there will be a future without John Thurloe or Ambrose Morton?'

'I think we have to believe that, Kit,' she replied. She laid a hand on his battered cheek. 'I only know that whatever that future is, it has to be together.'

His fingers tightened on hers and he lifted her hand to his lips. Beneath the bruising he looked pale and pinched, his eyes lost in dark circles. Thamsine kissed him gently and stood up.

'You're exhausted,' she said. 'I promised Nan I would help in the taproom tonight. May is … ' She left the sentence unfinished.

May had not left her bed. She lay under the covers, curled up like a child, too exhausted to cry and too traumatised to move.

'I'll bring you some supper and then you can sleep.'

THAMSINE HAD PROMISED to help Jem in the taproom, but there were few customers and as soon as she had a chance, she warmed some broth to take upstairs to Kit. She had not expected to find him standing in the middle of the room, a blanket inadequately draped around him. In her haste to get to him, she slopped soup onto the tray.

'What are you doing?' She reached him as his knees buckled and he sat back on the bed.

'I was looking for my clothes,' he said.

His hair, tangled and still matted with his blood, stood on end. His bruised face was taut and grey with pain and his eyes glittered with fever.

'Why do you want your clothes?'

'I have to warn them,' he said.

Thamsine knew he meant the conspirators, who even now were gathering at the Swan.

'Kit, you're too late. You know that.'

'Maybe not. If I hurry – '

'You couldn't hurry if the hounds of Hell were after you.' She sat down beside him on the bed and took his good hand in hers. 'It's too late for a conscience now, Kit,' she said.

He turned to look at her. 'They'll hang, Thamsine.'

'You knew that, Kit.' She stroked the hair away from his eyes, his beautiful green eyes, dulled by pain and anguish. Kit Lovell, always so confident and in control, stared into a vision of Hell that she could not understand.

'I'll go,' she said. 'I can warn them. I'll attract less attention than you.'

He stared into the far corner of the room, his shoulders rising and falling with every painful breath.

'All right,' he said at last.

She stood to go and he caught her hand.

'Thamsine, be careful.'

'I won't take unnecessary risks, I promise.'

She smiled and kissed him, drawing the tumbled bedclothes back around him. His cloak hung over the back of the chair. She snatched it up and ran out into the dark streets.

SHE ARRIVED TOO LATE.

The street outside the Swan Inn heaved with horses and soldiers and she melted into the shadows of a back alley to watch as Kit's former comrades were led out. Vowells, Gerard and other familiar faces. She shook her head and turned to go.

'Where d'ya think you're going?' A soldier stepped across her path.

'Just headin' home, love.' Thamsine dropped into a London accent. 'What's 'appening here?' She jerked her head at the scene in the street.

'Traitors,' the soldier said. 'You head off home, love. The night's no time for pleasant strolls.'

Thamsine returned to the Ship Inn with a heavy heart. As she pushed open the door to the bedchamber, Kit straightened, his eyes wide and expectant but as his gaze scanned her face, he turned away.

Thamsine shut the door behind her, leaning against it.

'There's nothing you could have done,' she said. 'It looked like Thurloe got them all. What did you hope to achieve by warning them?'

He laid an arm across his eyes. 'I could have redeemed myself, somehow.'

'You've done enough. You were always playing a dangerous game. You knew the price. It's done. You're free. Kit. We're both free.'

He lifted his arm away from his eyes. 'We're neither of us free until we are quit of England, Thamsine.' The fingers of his left hand crushed the bedclothes. 'Leave me. I need some time alone.'

Thamsine hesitated, torn between throwing her arms around him to assuage the terrible pain that went beyond his physical injuries and recognising that he had to come to terms with his betrayal. She closed the door behind her. He needed to be alone with his demons.

CHAPTER 36

*M*ay carefully tilted the pan of hot wax across the candle moulds.

'Hold it still, Thamsine,' she grumbled. 'You really aren't cut out for hard work, are you?'

Thamsine shook her head.

May set the pan down and sank onto the stool. Her natural good spirits were returning, but she had moments of terrible melancholy and Thamsine recognised now as one of them. The girl's brow creased and a tear ran down her cheek. Thamsine moved to take her in her arms but May held up a hand.

'I'll be all right in a minute.' She took a deep, quivering sigh. 'When do you suppose it stops hurting?'

Thamsine knew she meant the emotional pain, not the physical bruises, which after three days were already fading to a purple-green. May's bruises served as a reminder of her own violent encounters with Ambrose Morton. If it hadn't been for Kit Lovell, who had dulled the pain with his love, she may have been lost forever.

'I don't think it does, May, not really. It's always there.'

May looked at her and took her hand. 'I forget you've had your moments with the bastard. I've always liked a bit of a romp with a man,' she said. 'No harm done, a bit of fun and a shilling perhaps for later, but always my choice. Never done it against me will before. What he did ... '

Another tear started to course down her cheek.

'What he did was done to your body, May, not to your heart.' Thamsine put a hand on her friend's chest. 'He can't hurt what's inside you.'

May's lips twisted into a weak smile. 'Listen to me. What a misery. I'll be fine. Just see if I'm not!'

Thamsine reached out for the girl's hand and squeezed it.

'I'll see the brute dead. You both have my word on that.'

Both women looked up to see Kit sitting at the bottom of the kitchen stairs, roughly dressed in breeches and a shirt.

'How long have you been there?' Thamsine demanded.

'Not long. It took me a full five minutes just to get down the stairs. I'm surprised you didn't hear me.'

'Well, you shouldn't be up, and how did you get dressed?' Thamsine demanded.

'With difficulty,' Kit responded with a glimmer of his old humour, 'but I'm not going to lie in bed being fussed over any longer. Three days with you wittering women is enough for any man. Where is everyone?'

'Nan's gone to do some shopping. Jem's in the taproom,' Thamsine replied.

Kit pulled himself to his feet, wincing as he did so, and holding his ribs with his good hand, limped over to the chair where he subsided.

Thamsine poured him a cup of small ale.

'What are you doing?' he asked.

'May has been showing me how to make candles. My sister would tell me that work is good for the soul,' Thamsine said.

May smiled. 'Helps make things seem more normal.'

The door opened and Nan stepped in, shaking the water from her cloak.

'Pelting down, it is.' She glared at Kit. "Ere, what you doing out of bed?' She set the basket she carried on the table. 'Never mind. There's bin no sign of that devil Morton. Jem has a boy watching the house ... says he's laid up good and proper.'

'If he feels anything like me, he'll be keeping his head down for a few weeks yet,' Kit said with what Thamsine detected as a gleam of satisfaction in his eye.

'With any luck you killed him,' May responded.

Kit shook his head. 'I don't think so.'

'More's the pity,' Nan responded. 'I've a message for you.' She handed over a grubby, slightly damp piece of paper.

Kit took it and gave it to Thamsine. 'You read it. I recognise the seal and I don't want to know what's in it.'

Thamsine broke the seal and read the few scrawled lines. She swore in an unladylike fashion. Thurloe required Lovell attend him immediately. She handed it to him and he read it without emotion on his face.

'He calls, I must go,' he said with weary resignation.

'And how do you plan to get to Whitehall?' Thamsine asked.

Kit managed a watery smile. 'Very slowly.'

'I'm coming too,' Thamsine declared flatly. 'Whatever Thurloe has to say, he can say to both of us.'

THEY FOUND Thurloe in his office in Whitehall. He rose to his feet as they entered and looked them both up and down.

'Well, well, the Lovells. What a fine pair you make.'

'Excuse me, Thurloe. I am in no mood for your jesting.' Kit lowered himself painfully onto a chair and rubbed his right knee.

'You have looked better, Lovell,' Thurloe remarked. 'Footpads, your wife tells me?'

'That's right,' Kit said. 'Ten of them.'

Thurloe raised an eyebrow.

'Why do you want to see me?' Kit continued.

'I thought you might like to know that we got everyone, except Henshaw and you of course. Happily for you, Henshaw managed to get away in circumstances that might suggest to the casual observer that he could have been the agent.'

'Is he one of yours?' Kit enquired.

Thurloe shrugged. 'I don't care about Henshaw. However, I do care that we haven't found the Frenchman.'

'De Baas?' Kit asked.

Thurloe's lip curled. 'That popinjay is already on his way back to France with a flea in his ear. No, the other Frenchman, the assassin.'

'Debigné? He was not with De Baas?'

'No,' Thurloe replied sourly. 'And De Baas swears he has no idea where he is. Says Debigné operates alone. Is there any chance you know where he could be?'

Kit shook his head. 'No. I couldn't find him. He changes lodgings every day or two and I doubt even Henshaw or Gerard would know where to find him. They used to leave messages in a location I wasn't privy to if they wanted to meet him.'

Thurloe pressed his fingertips together. 'Do you think he'll carry out the plan even though the plot is discovered?'

Kit considered for a moment. 'He's a professional, Thurloe. He has been well paid to do a job. Yes, I think he would.'

'So when will he strike?'

'What day is it?'

'Saturday.'

'Tomorrow then, as Cromwell leaves the chapel. He'll be there,' Kit said with certainty.

Thurloe was silent. 'You're the only one who knows what he looks like.'

Kit raised his head. 'Thurloe, look at me! I am in no condition to stop a determined old woman, let alone an assassin.'

'I just need you to identify him, that's all.'

'Just stop Cromwell going to chapel tomorrow,' Thamsine put in.

Thurloe looked at her. 'If this man is a professional, do you think changing the Lord Protector's routine will make a difference? None of us will be able to sleep at night until Debigné is caught.'

Kit looked at his master. 'Are you scared, Thurloe?'

Thurloe returned the look. 'I'm not a soldier, Lovell, and I've no wish to spend my life looking over my shoulder on the off-chance a murderous French assassin may be on the lookout for me. I know I was on the list.'

Kit ran his good hand over his eyes.

'I don't have a choice, do I, Thurloe?'

'Lovell, you have my word that this will be the very last time I call on you.'

Kit looked up at Thamsine. 'Did you hear that, Thamsine? I have the Secretary's word that this is the last time.'

Thamsine took Kit's hand and looked at Thurloe. 'Then we are free?'

Thurloe nodded. He looked at Kit. 'When Debigné is caught, we will settle our final account, Lovell.'

CHAPTER 37

small crowd had gathered outside the little chapel in the Palace of Whitehall. They pushed against the barriers for a view of the Lord Protector, who would be leaving the building within the next few minutes.

Kit scanned the crowd looking for the narrow face of the Frenchman.

'Where do I look? There's any number of places he could be concealed,' Thamsine whispered

'That will depend on the accuracy of his weapon,' Kit murmured.

Jostled by the crowd, Kit winced as a large man brushed his hand.

'Are you all right?' Thamsine slid her arm around his waist as he caught his breath.

'I'm just fine! Stop fussing, Tham!'

'Well?' A quiet voice behind them made them both turn. Thurloe, soberly dressed in black with a hat pulled down well over his brow, surveyed the crowd with nervous eyes. 'Can you see him?'

'No,' Kit shook his head.

'He must be here somewhere.' Thurloe's lips tightened.

'And what do we do if I see him?' Kit said. 'Yell? Because I am damned if I can do anything else.'

Thurloe looked at him. 'I don't care what you do. I've men scattered through the crowd, so you're not alone.' He hunched his shoulders. 'His Highness will be leaving presently.'

Hearing the upstart Cromwell referred to as *His Highness*, always provoked anger in Kit. Oliver Cromwell was a farmer from the fens pretending to be king in all but name.

'Might it help if you told us what he looks like?' Thamsine asked, the impossibility of the task weighing on her.

Kit shook his head. 'Nondescript. Slight, dark hair, clean-shaven but he could have grown a beard since I last saw him.'

There were plenty of faces in the crowd that fitted that description, but none registered as familiar. The movement of the soldiers at the door to the chapel indicated that the service had ended. Cromwell would be leaving any moment.

Thamsine tensed in desperation. The crowd was not so large that Debigné could remain hidden much longer. Out of the corner of her eye, she saw a woman carrying a wrapped bundle detach herself from the crowd, taking up a position in the shadows.

'Kit.' She touched his arm. 'We've been looking for a man. Could that be him? There in that doorway, dressed as a woman.'

She was correct. There was no mistaking the narrow face beneath a goodwife's broad-brimmed hat. Debigné had picked his spot well. He had a clear view of the doors of the chapel, but he was at least fifty yards away from Kit and Thamsine with a crowd between them.

Kit looked around. 'Where's Thurloe?'

Thurloe had melted back into the crowd and Kit swore as the

chapel doors opened. As they watched Debigné, the assassin raised the cloth-covered weapon.

'It's a crossbow,' Kit said. It hadn't crossed his mind that the man would employ such an antique weapon but it was an ideal killing machine, deadly and silent.

Thamsine gathered up her skirts and pushed through the crowd. Kit swore and took off after her, every step sending shards of pain through his body. He caught her and grabbed her elbow.

'What do you think you're doing?'

'I'm going to stop him.'

'You'll get yourself killed,' he said.

He thrust her behind him, and moving with his injuries momentarily forgotten, he pushed through the crowd towards Debigné.

If the man had seen him coming he gave no sign. Cromwell stood for a moment, framed in the chapel door. Debigné raised the crossbow to his shoulder and fired. Someone pulled Cromwell back inside the chapel and the bolt missed its mark, crashing harmlessly into the door as it slammed shut.

'To me!' Kit yelled, hoping Thurloe's men were nearby.

For the space of a few breaths, no one moved, and then half a dozen men broke away from the crowd and crashed after Kit.

Debigné, cornered, scrabbled for a second bolt. In the time he took to reload, Kit had reached him. Debigné raised the butt of the crossbow and swung it at Kit. He ducked, but his bad leg betrayed him and the butt crashed into his injured hand. With a sharp cry he went down on his knees, his hand pressed to his chest. Debigné raised the weapon again but by this time Thurloe's men had him.

In the chaotic moments that followed, as Debigné was led away and the excited crowd buzzed and murmured, Thamsine reached him. Dimly, he sensed her kneeling beside him and she laid her arm across his back.

'Your hand …' she began.

Before he could respond, a shadow fell across them.

'Good work,' Thurloe said. 'I won't forget it. My coach is waiting. It will take you wherever you have to go.'

Kit raised his head and looked up at his tormentor.

'Is that it, Thurloe?' he gasped through the pain.

Thurloe nodded. 'That's it, Lovell. Lay low, recover your strength, and we will talk soon.'

CHAPTER 38

'It's no good,' Nan pronounced. 'You should never have gone gallivanting around London in your condition. You've done yourself no good at all and your hand ... ' she shook her head, ' ... those fingers will not mend straight now.'

Thamsine swallowed and forced herself to look down at the swollen, mangled mess that had been Kit's sword hand. Debigné had hit it hard and what little the bonesetter had accomplished had been completely undone.

'You heard the bonesetter,' Nan continued. 'There's naught he can do. Would be best if it came off afore it turns bad and kills you.'

'You're talking about my hand!' Kit said, his tone a mixture of anger and despair.

'There's one person who might be able to help,' Thamsine said. 'My sister.'

Kit gave a derisive snort. 'I don't think so, Tham. What can she do that the bonesetter can't?'

'I know no one else with her skill,' Thamsine said.

'We'll send Jem to her.' Nan turned to her brother, who lounged in the door of the bedchamber.

'I don't know if this is a good idea,' Jem said slowly.

'Neither do I,' Kit agreed. He shivered, hunched his shoulders and closed his eyes.

'I'm not going to stand by and watch you die!' Thamsine said.

'I'm not dying, Thamsine!' Kit protested irritably. 'I've a few broken bones, that's all.'

'You'll die if that hand is not treated properly! Jane can help. She can be trusted.'

Kit grimaced and waved his good hand. 'Go, Jem. We'll have no peace until she's had her way.'

THAMSINE MET her sister in the kitchen of the inn.

'I must have your word, Jane. Please don't tell Roger where I am.'

Jane put her hand on her sister's cheek. 'You have my word,' she said. 'Now, where is the patient?'

'Upstairs. I'll show you.'

Kit sat hunched at the table, a jug of wine to one side and a book laid out before him. He looked up as the women entered, and closed the book. Jane set her basket down and picked up the book.

'An interesting choice of reading, Captain Lovell,' she said.

Kit retrieved his battered and much-worn copy of Francis Bacon's *Essays* and set it back on the table, the fingers of his uninjured hand tracing the worn leather spine.

'Old Bacon here has been a long-time companion of mine. I would hate to lose him,' he said.

'Which is your favourite essay?' Jane asked.

'*Of Nature and Men,*' Kit replied. 'You read Bacon?'

Jane smiled. 'I have done. Now, I had a message you were dying,' she said.

'I'm bruised and battered but not quite at death's door,' Kit replied.

Jane placed a hand on Kit's forehead. 'No, I don't think you're dying.'

'You're so much better at this than your sister. Did you know she faints at the sight of blood?' Kit commented.

Jane glanced at her sister. 'Do you?'

Thamsine shrugged. 'Apparently.'

'So, this is Morton's work?' Jane gently raised the bandaged hand. 'What did he do?'

'He trod on my fingers,' Kit said.

'It all took a further battering the day before yesterday,' Thamsine put in. 'The bonesetter says his hand should be amputated but I thought maybe you ... ' She trailed off as Jane cast her a grave look.

'Thamsine, I'm a housewife. What do you think I can do that a bonesetter cannot?'

Thamsine felt her small hope beginning to fade.

Jane sighed. 'Well, I suppose I can at least see what harm has been done. Now,' she said, addressing Kit, 'I am going to look at your hand. This will hurt.'

She began to unwind the bandages, stopping when Kit tensed to let him catch his breath.

'If it's any small consolation, I hear Ambrose Morton is no better,' Jane said as she worked.

'Where is he?' Thamsine asked.

Jane's lips tightened. 'With that doxy, Lucy Talbot. A pistol ball in the shoulder and a broken ankle, I believe.'

'What about your husband?' Kit asked in a tight voice.

'Roger has gone to Kent on business. I don't expect him back for a couple of days, which is why I was able to come to you.' Jane drew a quick breath and shook her head. 'Oh dear, this is not good!'

Thamsine flinched as the bandages came away to reveal the blackened, swollen, mangled mess.

Jane looked up at her. 'What have you done for him?'

Thamsine outlined the rudimentary treatment suggested by Nan and the bonesetter.

Jane gently felt the broken bones. 'You're no fool, Captain Lovell. I am sure you can see for yourself that the bonesetter is right. If this is left, it will fester and you must know what that will mean.'

Kit closed his eyes and nodded.

'There must be something you can do?' Thamsine tried to hide the anxiety in her voice.

'I will do what I can to reset the broken bones. Thamsine, I need ...'

Thamsine stared at her sister. She could already hear the world beginning to roar in her ears, and the room had begun to pitch and tilt.

Distantly she heard her sister say, 'Thamsine, are you going to faint? Go and fetch that big man who brought me here and stay out of the way.'

Thamsine stumbled out of the room and passed out in the corridor.

AN HOUR LATER, she crept back into the room.

'Mercifully, he fainted too,' Jane said, indicating Kit's unconscious body on the bed. 'God willing he will sleep now, and that is probably the best cure.'

Jane picked up her cloak and tied it. She gestured at an array of bottles and flasks on the table.

'My own receipt, sister. Feverfew and chamomile.' She picked up the largest flask. 'It will help with the pain and any fever. I have reset the fingers and splinted them.' She held up a bottle. 'A poultice of this after twelve hours.'

'Will it work?'

Jane shrugged. 'It might, but if it worsens then the bonesetter is right. The hand will have to be amputated.'

Thamsine grimaced and her sister laid a hand on her arm.

'I don't want to give false hope. Even if it does heal, he will never have the full use of that hand again, but I think you both know that.' Her face softened. 'I'm sorry, Thamsine, but at least he will be alive and that is what matters, isn't it?'

She took her sister in her arms.

'I wish you didn't have to go,' Thamsine murmured.

Jane pulled apart, holding Thamsine at arm's length. 'You know I must. I have strapped his hand to his chest to stop him from moving it for the moment. Now, if you follow my instructions, you should be over the worst within the next twenty-four hours. Keep him cool, plenty of water, the feverfew, and this for the bruising.' She held up a pot. 'Don't forget.'

'I'm so useless,' Thamsine said with a rueful smile. 'I wish I were more like you.'

Jane touched her sister's cheek. 'No, dearest, you're not useless. Your talents are different, that's all. Now, remember to pray. That is always useful when all else fails.'

When Jane had left, Thamsine crept back up to the bedchamber. She stripped down to her shift and climbed into the bed beside her husband. He stirred but did not wake as she curled up against him and with her head resting against his shoulder she fell asleep.

CHAPTER 39

*I*gnoring Kit's complaints and curses, over the next few days Thamsine diligently followed her sister's instructions. As she opened the door to his bedchamber with his supper tray, she reflected that Jane had failed to warn her that convalescing males were not a pleasant species. However, for all his complaining, miraculously the hand had not worsened. Over the week Jane's poultices and unguents seemed to have had some effect. The swelling had begun to go down and the bones seemed to be knitting.

Kit slammed his book shut and looked up at the ceiling as Thamsine set down the tray.

'I'm so bored,' he grumbled. 'This is worse than jail. At least there I can play cards or talk to someone. Here, I'm stuck in the company of three over-solicitous women, and if that –' he pointed at a flask on the tray' – is any more of your sister's damned nostrums, forget it!'

'I thought you enjoyed the company of women?'

He glared at her and unexpectedly his face softened and his lips curved in a smile. 'Come here and sit down.'

He pushed the chair back from the table and patted his lap. Thamsine smiled and complied, perching herself primly on his knee. He picked up her hand in his good one and turned it over as if inspecting it. He laid it on the table and traced the lines on the palm.

'Do you see this, Tham?'

'See what? Since when have you been a palm reader?'

'A woman I knew a long time ago taught me a few things. This line is your lifeline. It tells me that you're going to live a long life.'

'That's reassuring.'

'Now this line is your love line.'

'And what does that tell you?'

'That you are going to meet an impossibly handsome, yet penniless rogue, who is not going to let you out of his sight for the rest of your life.'

'Oh dear,' Thamsine said. 'That sounds rather grim. I hope his name is not Ambrose Morton.'

'Ouch! I can't laugh.' Kit winced. 'Penniless aristocratic rogue, then!'

Thamsine smiled. 'Palm reading is a rather inexact science,' she said. 'What will happen to this penniless, aristocratic rogue?'

'He will fall in love with a beautiful, talented woman.'

Kit slipped his hand behind her neck, drawing her face towards his.

'Ah, but does the rogue truly love me?' Thamsine whispered.

'Oh yes, he truly does. The question is, do you love him enough to want to spend the rest of your life with him?'

Thamsine paused and frowned as if deep in thought. 'The rest of my life? You did say it would be a long life ... '

'I did.'

'Well, I suppose I could.'

'Good.' Their lips touched and the spark of desire leapt into flames.

'You must be feeling better,' Thamsine whispered.

His lips drifted to her ear. 'Much better,' he replied. 'Perhaps, if you promise to be gentle with me ... '

A knock on the door caused them both to start. Thamsine barely had time to jump to her feet before the door opened.

'Oh dear, am I interrupting?' Thurloe stood in the doorway, carefully removing his gloves.

Thamsine straightened her skirts. She gave Thurloe the benefit of a shaky curtsey.

He inclined his head. 'Mistress Lovell. Good evening.'

'Why are you here?'

'I've come to see your husband.' Thurloe looked Kit up and down. 'I trust you are on the road to recovery, Lovell?'

'I'm mending,' Kit replied.

Thurloe walked over to the window and stood looking out over the street, his hands behind his back.

'I have a problem,' he said. 'Or rather, you have a problem. I'm afraid your friends have been most forthcoming about your involvement in the plot. You've been named several times as one of the main conspirators, and I have troops scouring London with a warrant for your arrest. You'll be flattered to know that there's quite a reward for information leading to your detention.' He turned to face them. 'London is not a particularly healthy place for you to be right now, Lovell.'

'What are you going to do?' Kit inquired, lightly drumming the fingers of his left hand on the table.

'If they find you, there will be nothing I can do about it, but ... ' Thurloe reached into his jacket and produced a paper, which he flung down on the table, ' ... I'm mindful of our agreement.'

Kit picked it up and turned it over.

'It's an order to the Governor of Barbados to release one Daniel Lovell, with a full pardon for his youthful indiscretions,' Thurloe said.

Kit looked up at Thurloe.

'I have made enquiries after your brother and when last I heard, admittedly some months ago, your brother had been well treated and was in good health. He has the advantage of youth and education to set him apart from his fellow captives.' Thurloe answered the unspoken question.

Kit looked at the paper in his hand. 'I hope that's true, Thurloe.'

Thurloe shrugged. 'You can see for yourself. There's a boat sailing from Gravesend to Barbados tomorrow evening. Be on it, Lovell, or I can't help you anymore. You are looking rather pale. The sea voyage will do your health good.' He turned to Thamsine with a smile. 'And of course, your lovely wife will be accompanying you.' The smile faded. 'In short, I want the pair of you out of England. The sooner I am rid of the both of you, the sounder I will sleep in my bed.'

Kit looked up sharply. 'For how long?'

Thurloe shrugged. 'Until this business is over.'

'It will never be over, Thurloe. There will be other plots, and then there is the Sealed Knot ... ' Kit shook his head. 'What will become of the others, Thurloe?'

Thurloe's lips tightened. 'Without prejudicing an otherwise fair trial, I think I can confidently predict that there will be deaths. There has to be. An example must be set if we are to deter any more of these foolish idealists.'

'Who?' Thamsine asked.

'Lord Gerard, for one. Vowells. Maybe one or two others.'

Kit grimaced and looked away. 'Gerard was a friend of my father's,' he murmured.

Thurloe regarded him for a moment. 'Don't blame yourself, Lovell. If it hadn't been you, it would have been someone else. Lord Gerard was playing a fool's game. You will see in time that it was the right decision.' Thurloe shook his head. 'I get no pleasure from sending good men to the noose, Lovell. But to answer your question, I will not stop you from returning to England when the time is right. *But ...* ' His voice dropped and his eyes narrowed. ' ... it will be on the clear understanding that you renounce all ties with Charles Stuart, am I clear?'

Kit nodded. 'Quite clear. Before you go, Thurloe, what of Ambrose Morton?'

'Ah yes, Colonel Morton. I'm sorry, but there will be no action taken against Colonel Morton.'

Thamsine and Kit stared at him.

'Insofar as the charges you have levelled against him for the kidnap and assault on Mistress Granville, – my pardon,' Thurloe inclined his head in Thamsine's direction ' – Mistress Lovell, while I've no doubt there is truth to the story and Morton should be punished, it has been decided the scandal attaching to a trial, particularly as the chief witness will be out of the country,' – he gave Thamsine a meaningful look – 'would outweigh the benefit of our work of the last few months. As for the other allegation ... ' He shrugged his shoulders. 'The girl is a known doxy, and the charge will never stick.'

'So, Morton is free to roam the country at will?' Kit said.

'It would seem so, although I do hear that he has been rather unwell. Must be something contagious. Captain Lovell.' Thurloe picked up his hat and gloves. 'I am pleased we've had this talk. I wish you both a good voyage and a long and happy life together.'

The door closed behind him. For what seemed a long moment, Kit and Thamsine stared at each other.

'I'm sorry, Tham,' Kit said.

She shrugged. 'I expected it. He's not going to risk the scandal of a trial that involves you and me. It's in our interests to keep our anonymity, but it's May I feel for. How dare he call her a doxy!'

'That's what Morton called her too.' Kit shrugged unhappily. 'There's no justice for the poor.'

He picked up the paper Thurloe had left and turned it over, tracing the seal on the back of it.

'Barbados,' Thamsine said. 'It's the other side of the world. I thought France ... '

'France can wait, Thamsine. This is more important.'

She nodded, her fingers closing over his. 'Barbados, and then, maybe, Virginia?' she ventured. 'A new beginning?'

Kit nodded. 'A new beginning. Maybe we should try our hands at farming coffee? Come here, Mistress Lovell.'

She crossed to him and sat down beside him. He slid a hand around the back of her neck and their lips met, as they allowed time and their worries to slip away for a few short hours.

CHAPTER 40

'The boat sails at high tide,' Jem Marsh remarked. 'You better hurry.'

Kit rose to his feet, flinching as the bruises and cracked ribs caught in the unaccustomed movement. Thamsine secured his injured arm in a neat sling, tied his cloak, and picked up his hat.

'My sword?' Kit looked around the room.

She indicated his chest. 'Packed. You won't need it and you can't use it anyway.'

She slipped an arm around his waist but Kit shrugged her off.

'I can manage just fine, thank you,' he said, regretting his stiff-necked pride as he took a few uncertain steps towards the door. After the long inactivity, he felt stiff, sore, and as weak as a kitten.

Jem shouldered the box and followed Kit down the stairs. May and Nan waited at the bottom of the stairs. To his embarrassment, May was snuffling into her apron. She threw her arms around Kit, an action that caused him to recoil as every barely healed bone in his body jarred. Undeterred, she sobbed into his jacket. He patted her back and looked at Jem for help

'Come on, lass,' her brother said gruffly, ''nough of that. They're leaving and that's that.'

May let him go and sniffled, wiping her nose on her sleeve, before flinging herself at Thamsine, who kissed her on the cheek.

At the foot of the stairs, they stopped. Half a dozen heavily armed soldiers stood in the taproom.

'What will we do?' Thamsine clutched his arm.

'Well, I'm in no position to make a bolt for it,' Kit replied. 'We'll just have to brazen it out.'

Nan sauntered forward to address the officer in charge. 'What'll it be, Cap'n? A pot of ale for your men?'

The officer gave her a contemptuous glance and his gaze moved to Kit and Jem.

'We're seeking one Christopher Lovell,' he said. 'Last known to be lodging at this establishment.'

'Don't know who you mean, Captain. Now if you'll excuse us, this gentleman has a boat to catch.' Jem made to move but three of the soldiers now moved into his path, another three behind them.

The officer squared up to Kit. He stood half a head shorter, square and pugnacious next to Kit's lean form.

'A dark-haired man two yards high, injured arm.' He looked at the sling on Kit's right arm. 'Scar over the right eye. I think we've got the right man, lads. Christopher Lovell, I have a warrant for your arrest.'

'Indeed? On what charge?'

'Treason. Do you deny you're Christopher Lovell?'

Beside him, Thamsine gave a quick indrawn breath. He could neither run nor fight. He glanced at his wife. Surely she could see resistance was pointless?

He turned to the soldier. 'I'm in no position to deny anything. I am Captain Christopher Lovell, late of His Majesty's forces. Where do you intend to take me?'

'My orders are to convey you to the Tower.'

Kit closed his eyes to suppress the shudder that ran through him. He dreaded the Tower again, and this time he knew there would be little hope of reprieve. As the soldiers moved forward, Kit held up his good hand.

'I am unarmed and, as you can see, in no condition to resist arrest,' he said. 'I'll come peacefully. Just let me say farewell to my wife.'

He turned to face Thamsine, hating himself for the tears in her eyes. She had known the dangerous game they both played but he was responsible for everything that had befallen them and for that he would never forgive himself.

Taking her hand, he pressed it to his lips. 'I've no choice, Tham. This is a corner from which I have no escape.'

'This is Thurloe's doing!' she whispered in French, her voice tense with anger.

Kit shook his head and replied in kind. 'No. It's not his style. Whatever else he is, he's a man of his word. This could be any one of the others. They all knew where I lodged. I'm just surprised it has taken them so long to seek me here. Be strong, Thamsine,' he said and bent his head to kiss her.

Her lips quivered beneath his touch and she leaned her head against his chest. 'Kit ... '

He placed a finger on her mouth. 'Shhh ... '

He straightened, wincing as the cracked ribs caught. Nevertheless he managed a slight, dignified inclination of his head. 'I am at your disposal.'

As he walked out of the Ship Inn, Kit did not look back. He could not face the hurt in Thamsine's eyes again.

CHAPTER 41

'Mistress Lovell? An unexpected surprise.' Thurloe rose to his feet. 'Shouldn't you be on a boat to Barbados?'

Thamsine leaned both hands on the oak table. 'He's been arrested.'

John Thurloe's eyebrows lifted in a look of genuine surprise, but the unguarded moment was fleeting and the familiar guarded look returned just as quickly to the dark face.

'There is a warrant for his arrest. I did tell him that,' Thurloe said.

'But you know he was never intended to be arrested.'

He spread his hands. 'I can't control everything, Mistress Gran – Lovell. It's unfortunate that my diligent officers affected his arrest, but I assure you it is not of my doing.'

'Then undo it.'

Thurloe leaned back in his chair and shook his head. 'I regret it can't be undone.'

'But surely there is something you can do?'

His expression was bland. 'I warned him that there was nothing I could do if he was caught. I'm sorry, Mistress Lovell, but I'm afraid your husband is on his own and must face the consequences.' He paused. 'I'm sure I don't need to tell you what those could be.'

Thamsine felt the blood drain from her face. 'Are you saying that he could die?'

Thurloe's mouth was a grim line. 'Mistress Lovell, please understand, I can't save him without betraying everything I have worked for. If it comes to a choice between the life of one man and the good of the nation ... ' He spread his hand.

Thamsine sat down unbidden as the reality of Kit's fate sank in.

'Will there be a trial?' she asked.

'Of course.'

She looked at the man across the desk and felt her resolve begin to wane. 'But you said that there would be deaths.'

Thurloe looked away. 'Unavoidable but necessary. The message must be sent that these conspiracies will not be tolerated. Go home, Mistress Lovell, and pray. That is all you can do.'

Thamsine rose to her feet and placed both hands on the desk, leaning towards Thurloe, trying to hold his gaze. 'You can't let him die. Not after all he has done for you.'

Thurloe returned her gaze without blinking and said in an icy tone, 'He knew the risks.'

'But he was doing it for his brother, not for himself.'

'His motives are irrelevant.'

'You blackmailed him into it!'

Thurloe pushed back his chair. 'Mistress Lovell, don't be fooled into thinking your husband acted purely out of concern for his brother. He was paid and paid well for his work. His brother will be freed. As far as I am concerned, the books are closed.' He strode to the door and opened it. 'There is nothing further to be done. Now leave me.'

Thamsine felt her breath leave her body at the perfidy of this man who had used Kit for his ends and would now sit back and let him die. She turned on her heel and ran past the astonished secretaries in the outer room.

CHAPTER 42

*E*very morning for the next week Thamsine walked to the Tower of London, only to be turned away at the gate. After another abortive visit, she trudged back to The Ship Inn, which bustled with its usual dinnertime activity. May and Nan were back at work, skilfully avoiding the groping hands and ribald remarks.

Jem looked up from his position at the keg. 'Still won't let you see him?' he asked.

Thamsine shook her head.

'I'm sorry lass,' Jem shook his head. 'It's a grim lookout.'

Heartsick, Thamsine turned for the stairs.

'Hold on, lass. There's a man in the parlour waiting for you,' Jem said. 'I told him I'd not heard of you but he insisted on staying. Says he won't go till he sees you.'

Thamsine turned. 'Not … ?' Her heart skipped a beat.

Jem read her thoughts. 'Not Morton. I've not seen him before. Weedy specimen. Middle height, thin face, fair hair. Balding. He gave me this for you.' Jem held out a grubby note.

Thamsine took it and unfolded it.

Sister,
I know you will not wish to see me but I beg you hear me out. Jane has been taken ill and is asking for you. She has been ailing all winter and I fear she may not see out the summer. I have done many great wrongs by you and I beg this chance to be forgiven.
Yrs in penitence, Rgr Knott Esq.

Thamsine glanced at the parlour door. For a brief moment, she remembered that first night when she had sung for Kit Lovell. He had stood in that doorway, watching her, a tall, lean shadow with laughter in his eyes.

I saw a handsome proper youth
And he was wondrous fine
But when I understood the truth,
His case was worse than mine,
On wine and drabs, he did all spend
Which wrought his overthrow,
So fortune plac'd him in the end,
With beggars all a row.

She sang the words softly. So much had happened in those few short months since that day in February. She straightened her shoulders and opened the door.

"I'm right behind you, lass," Jem said. "If he tries anything, he'll have me to answer to."

Roger sat straight-backed in one of the oak chairs, his hat and gloves neatly placed on the table before him. He stood up as she entered, his eyes flicking to the sturdy figure of Jem Marsh looming behind her.

'She's dying, Thamsine,' were his opening words as he ran his fingers through his lank, thinning hair.

'She seemed in good enough health when I last saw her,' Thamsine replied coldly.

He shook his head. 'She's not been well for a long time. Her lungs, the doctor says. She wants to see you.'

Thamsine stood quite still. 'Did she tell you where I was to be found?'

Roger nodded.

Thamsine fixed him with her eyes. 'Did you betray Captain Lovell?'

Roger looked surprised. 'Captain Lovell? No. Why would I do that? What are you talking about?'

Thamsine searched his face but saw only confusion and worry.

'Wait here. I have something for you, Roger.'

She left him and returned with a packet of papers, which she threw down on the table before him.

'Your letters,' she spat. 'The letters you wrote to the Talbot doxy.'

Roger picked them up, counting them.

'They're all here,' he said and looked up at her in wonder. 'How ...?'

'Kit Lovell risked his life to get those, paid for them with his blood. Now I am buying your loyalty with them, Roger. I need your help.'

'What do you want of me?'

'I'm a married woman now, Roger.'

He paled. 'Not Morton?'

She shook her head. 'Not Morton. I married Kit Lovell. I am, like you, free of Morton.'

'You? You married Lovell?' Roger stared at her. 'Does Morton know?'

She shook her head. 'I don't know and I don't care, but I need your help to unwind his grasp from my estate. Can you do that?'

Roger nodded. 'Of course I can. I ... ' He tailed off, tears welling in his eyes. 'Words cannot express how appallingly I have failed you.'

She regarded him coldly. 'I am prepared to let the past be, for the moment. Now, what of Jane?'

'I have this for you.' Roger handed her a piece of paper. She unfolded it and a ring fell out. She caught it and held it in her fingers.

'My grandmother's ring,' she said, then turned to the note.

Dearest sister,

I am sending Roger to you on this errand in the hope that I can see you again before you leave. I dared not tell you about my illness for fear it would worry you and you seem to have enough worries. This may be the last time I will see you, so if it is possible, dearest, please come. Roger's contrition is genuine. He does not wish you any harm and you are free to leave at any time.

Yr. loving sister, Jane.

She looked at her brother-in-law, who seemed to shrink inside his collar.

'God is calling my wife. It's a punishment for my sins.'

Thamsine studied him with narrowed eyes. All the fierce pride and resistance had gone from him. He looked old, tired, and desperately unhappy. She sighed. There seemed little she could for Kit, Ambrose Morton was no threat for the moment, and there seemed nothing to be gained from ignoring his plea. Jane had come to her aid when she needed it and her skill had saved Kit's hand, if not his life.

'Very well, Roger, I will come with you, but it is on the understanding that I come and go of my own free will.'

The relief on Roger's face was pathetic. He rose to his feet and picked up his hat and gloves. 'We must leave now, Thamsine. There is not a moment to waste if we are to reach Turnham Green before dark.'

RIDING PILLION BEHIND ROGER, Thamsine began to regret her impulsive decision. What if it was another trap? What if Jane was hale and hearty and it was Ambrose waiting for her? Jem had argued with her about her decision to go, but then she remembered Jane's shadowed eyes and the cough and knew in her heart that all was not well with her sister.

The house in Turnham Green looked silent and grim in the gathering gloom as if death already waited by the door. She shivered as Roger helped her down off the back of his bay mare.

Thamsine followed Roger into the house and up the stairs to the main bedchamber. Roger had spoken the truth. Jane lay propped on the bolsters, her eyes sunken in her waxen face.

'She came, my dear.' Roger crossed to his wife, picking up her hand in a tender, intimate gesture that Thamsine had never seen before. 'I'll leave you with her.'

Thamsine stood by the bed and looked down at her sister.

'Why didn't you tell me how sick you were?'

Jane managed a wan smile. 'What concern was it of yours, dearest? I have known for a long time that it was the lung disease and it would kill me.'

'Do you cough blood?'

Jane nodded. 'I have for some months. Now, tell me, how is your Captain Lovell?'

Thamsine's face crumpled. 'He's in the Tower, Jane. They took him away a week ago and won't let me see him.'

'I'm sorry,' Jane said.

'I didn't tell you when we last met. Kit and I were married after he rescued me from Bedlam.'

She looked up and saw the sympathy and confusion in her sister's eyes.

'Why didn't you tell me that you were married?' Jane asked.

Thamsine shook her head. 'It didn't seem important. What mattered was his hand. We were to take a ship to Barbados when the soldiers came. There was no escape. An hour later and we would have been gone.'

Jane took Thamsine's hand in her frail grasp. 'What will become of him?'

'He ... ' Thamsine faltered, ' ... he may hang.'

'Your Captain is a good man, Thamsine. He pretends not to be, but in his heart he is a good man. I told him he should marry you and he did. You are free of Ambrose Morton now, and that is what matters ... '

Thamsine smiled. 'No, Jane, you don't understand. I didn't marry Kit for that reason. I married him because I love him. I have loved him from the day we met.'

Her sister studied her face. 'Then we must speak to Roger, get him the very best lawyer we can.'

She broke off, struggling for breath, her frail body wracked with coughing. Thamsine held her, holding a cloth to her lips, wiping away the bright blood. Gently, she laid her sister back on the bolsters.

'Thamsine, I'm very tired ... let me sleep a little. When I wake we can talk some more.' Jane's voice struggled with her breath.

Thamsine straightened the bolsters behind her sister's head. As Jane sank back into them and closed her eyes, Thamsine sat down beside the bed, taking Jane's hand in hers, overwhelmed by the depth of her emotions. Perhaps some of her strength would pass to Jane and she would recover.

Despite the years they had been apart, she could not imagine a life without her sister. How cruel to lose Jane just as she had found her again. Tears pricked her eyes and she choked them back, kissing her sister gently on the head.

The day slipped away and night had fallen before Jane woke. Thamsine stood at the window, her arms crossed in front of her body, staring out at the gloom. After the clear day, the stars burned brilliantly in the country air.

'Thamsine?' Jane's voice made her turn. 'Are you still here?'

Thamsine turned and gave her sister a weak smile. 'I'm not going anywhere, Jane. My place is by your side for the moment. There is little I can do for Kit. You, on the other hand, need me.'

Jane tried to pull herself up in the bed. Thamsine was by her side, straightening the bolsters and assisting her. The door opened and Roger stood in the doorway, in his shirtsleeves, a candle in his hand.

'How are you, my dear?'

'I have slept a little,' Jane replied. Her hand tightened on Thamsine's. 'Having Thamsine with me has eased the pain.'

'Mary is coming with a little supper for you, my dear,' Roger said. 'Thamsine, would you care to join me in the parlour?'

Thamsine nodded. She felt tired, desperately tired, as the events of the long day caught up with her. She bent and kissed her sister.

'I shall return after supper, Jane. Roger, I would like a cot made up in the closet so I can be near my sister should she need me at night.'

Roger nodded and stood aside as Thamsine passed him.

The table in the parlour had been set for two. Thamsine sank into a chair as Roger intoned a quick grace.

'Where are the children?' she asked.

'They are with my mother in Colchester.'

'Bring them home, Roger.'

'Do you think that is wise?'

'They should be with their mother. She needs them and they her.'

He nodded. 'I will send for them in the morning and you, Thamsine, will you return to London?'

She shook her head and looked down at the frayed cuff of her old gown. She had almost forgotten that she was a wealthy woman and the wife of the heir to Viscount Midhurst. She was not going to be afraid anymore.

'No, I shall stay here. I am tired of wearing rags and living my life in shadows, Roger. I am not going to run or hide anymore. Tomorrow you are to find the best lawyer my money can buy for my husband, and I shall find a tailor.'

CHAPTER 43

Kit woke to the sound of the key turning in the lock. He sat up too fast, his right hand striking the wall behind him and his barely healed ribs pulling painfully. He subsided with a curse against the wall as a lantern shone in his eyes.

'Is this him?' he heard the turnkey ask.

'This is him. Leave us.'

'Thurloe!' Kit recognised the voice. 'Pleased with your work?'

Thurloe set the lantern down on the table. 'For what it's worth, Lovell, this was not my doing. One of your comrades suggested you may be found at The Ship Inn, and an enterprising young officer decided to see if, by any chance, you were foolish enough still to be in residence. The first I knew of it was when your wife arrived at my door.'

'A few hours, Thurloe, and I would have been gone. Fate is a fickle mistress,' Kit said bitterly.

'It is,' Thurloe agreed.

'Have you come to get me out of here?' Kit asked, without hope.

'There is nothing I can do,' Thurloe replied. 'Justice must now take its course.'

'Justice?' Kit spat the word. 'You and I both know there's no justice here!'

'There will be a trial. We are constituting a special court to deal with the traitors.'

'Not so much a case of justice being done, but of being seen to be done?' Kit snarled. 'Just as it was for King Charles?'

'It's not as if any of you are innocent of the charges. I've seen the evidence. To a man, you are all quite guilty.'

Kit coughed and groaned, pressing his injured hand to his chest.

'Do you need a doctor? I will send my personal physician to see to you.' Thurloe's concern appeared genuine.

'Don't bother,' Kit snorted contemptuously. 'If I am seen to have your personal attention it will arouse greater suspicion, will it not?'

'Probably,' Thurloe conceded, 'but I want you to know that I wish there could have been some other way.'

'You have a conscience, Thurloe? How touching. So I am to be tried?'

'Yes. There is too much evidence against you. Your friends dig a deeper hole for you by the day.'

Kit looked away.

'You have, of course, yet to be interrogated,' Thurloe said.

'I can hardly wait.'

'It will go better for you if you admit your involvement.'

Kit looked up at Thurloe and gave a grim smile. 'Will it, Thurloe? How will it go better for me?'

'It may mean the difference between the noose, or ...'

'Transportation to some godforsaken place as a slave, like my brother? A lifetime of a thousand deaths? How is that better? All I want is my freedom, Thurloe. God help me, I earned it.'

Thurloe's cold eyes rested on his face. 'You're a card player, Lovell. There are no certainties in life except death.' Thurloe replaced his hat on his head and turned to go.

Kit looked at his back.

'Thurloe, if nothing else, will you see that my brother is released?'

'That is already in train. He will be returned to England as soon as my orders reach Barbados. On that, you have my word.'

'Thank you.'

Thurloe stopped in the doorway and, without looking around, said quietly. 'Admit your involvement, Lovell.'

'And?'

'I will not make any promises, but deny the charges and you will certainly hang.'

CHAPTER 44

The cold grey walls of the Tower of London loomed above the foetid moat. Trying hard to control her trembling hands, Thamsine raised her head and tightened her grip on the bundle she carried. This time she would be admitted, of that she was certain.

She demanded to see Barkstead. The guards looked her up and down and, as she had anticipated, she was admitted to his presence without argument. Barkstead rose to his feet and bowed. Beneath her black velvet mask, Thamsine smiled. His demeanour to a lady of rank bore a startling contrast to his treatment of Mistress Granville, the failed assassin of the Lord Protector.

'I'm here to see my husband.' She made it a demand, not a question.

'And you are?'

'Mistress Lovell. My husband is Captain Christopher Lovell.'

Barkstead's mouth opened and his eyes narrowed. 'Do I know you, Mistress Lovell?'

'I don't think so,' Thamsine replied.

'Your husband ... '

'My husband was brought here seven days ago. Is he being well treated?'

'I ... ' Barkstead shuffled some papers.

Thamsine laid a purse on the table. The clink made Barkstead's eyes widen. 'I want my husband placed in good accommodation with decent food,' she said. 'Treat him well and I will see you well rewarded.'

Barkstead blinked, ducking his head like a goose. 'Of course, Mistress Lovell. I will personally ensure his every need is catered to.'

'Good. Now I wish to see him.'

'What is in the bundle?' Barkstead indicated the bundle she carried. 'It's just I need to know ... ' he added, almost apologetically.

'Clean clothes,' she said, 'A few books, nothing more. See for yourself.'

Barkstead cast a cursory glance at the contents and summoned a turnkey.

'Mistress Lovell, it has been a pleasure. I shall make arrangements for your husband at once ... '

Thamsine bestowed a smile on him. 'Thank you, Colonel. I hope on my next visit I will find everything to my satisfaction.'

As she had expected, Kit had been cast into one of the gloomy cells similar to the one she had occupied. Not the worst accommodation in the Tower, but far from comfortable. The heavy door swung open and Thamsine stepped through it, blinking as she allowed her eyes to grow accustomed to the gloom.

'Thamsine?' Kit, who had been lying on his back on the cot, pulled himself up, staring at her. 'My God, Thamsine, I wouldn't have recognised you.'

Thamsine undid her cloak, removed her hat and mask and smiled.

'Neither did Barkstead,' she said. 'Amazing what a transformation a decent wardrobe can make.'

'Not just good clothes, Tham,' Kit said. 'You look different.'

'I've decided to take control of my life, Kit. I'm not leaving my future in the hands of stupid men like Roger Knott, nor will I allow myself to be terrorised by Ambrose Morton anymore. I am Thamsine Lovell, wife of the future Viscount Midhurst.'

Kit rose to his feet and took two steps towards her. He took her hand, looking her up and down.

'I think this new Thamsine will take some getting used to.'

'This new Thamsine is a creature of your invention, Kit.' She slid her arms around his neck, looking into his unshaven face. 'Now, are you going to kiss your wife?'

He bent his head and obliged. Thamsine laid her head on his shoulder and he kissed her hair.

'Oh Thamsine, I'm so sorry!' he murmured.

'For what?'

'For this mess, for marrying you, for … everything.'

'Don't be a fool, Kit.' Thamsine broke away from him. 'It's all arranged. I have a lawyer. Roger says he is the best … '

'Save your money, Tham.'

'Kit?'

'No lawyer in the world can save me. My colleagues have dug the grave for me.'

'No!' Thamsine protested. 'You're not just going to go to the gallows without a fight.'

Kit raised his good hand. 'Hear me out. I've seen Thurloe, and on his advice I've admitted my involvement in everything. I could hardly deny it. My comrades have betrayed me as surely as I did them.'

'What will Thurloe do?'

He shook his head. 'I don't know but I have to trust him, Thamsine. He's my only hope.'

'He's the spymaster, Lovell. You are expendable. Why should he help you?'

'Whatever else he is, he's a man of his word, Thamsine.'

'And what exactly has he promised you, Kit?'

Kit's silence gave her the answer she sought.

She turned away. 'Nothing? Kit, you've given away your hope on a slim promise?'

His face was still. 'I'm not scared of death, Thamsine. I faced my own mortality every time I rode into battle, every time I ever took a wound, but now ... now ... ' He cupped her face in his good hand, his thumb caressing the curve of her cheek. 'For the first time, I have a reason to live, and I am looking down a dark passage with no escape. They have selected four of us to try: Gerard, Vowells, Fox and me. The choice is deliberate – our fate is to act as a deterrent to those who seek to plot.'

'And how will Thurloe help you?'

He shook his head. 'He can save me from the noose.'

'For what? Imprisonment? Banishment?'

'For life, Thamsine but the late King said "While I have life I have hope".'

'And look what happened to him!' Thamsine could not disguise the bitterness in her voice.

'I will go to trial, admit my guilt, show contrition, remorse ... '

'And maybe, just maybe ... you will end up on a slave plantation in Barbados with your brother?'

He dropped his hand. The cell was not large enough for him to walk away but he took a step back.

'I have to believe that this is the right course of action, Thamsine.'

'I have a lawyer. He can advise you.' Thamsine could hear the note of desperation in her voice.

'For God's sake, a lawyer is not going to save me! They have my confession, they have the testimony of a dozen witnesses. A lawyer will just as surely send me to my grave.'

Thamsine picked up her cloak and mask and took a deep, steadying breath.

'If that is how you want it,' she said in a flat voice.

'That is how it has to be,' he said gently. 'Look at me, Tham.'

She raised her head and looked into his eyes. *Green eyes, nice eyes.*

'Trust Thurloe,' he said. 'Trust me.'

'I trusted you before and look where that got me.' She smiled without humour. 'It seems I have no choice.'

He smiled in return. 'That's better. Now, what's in that bundle?'

'Some clean linen.' She looked around the cell. 'Money buys favours. Barkstead will improve your accommodation. If he doesn't, he will have me to answer to.'

Kit smiled. 'I knew there was a good reason to marry a woman with money.'

'I will also have a tailor attend you,' she said. 'You will need to look well for your trial. Is there a date set?'

He shook his head. 'It will be a few weeks yet. They have to constitute a special court. They don't dare try us in open court before a jury. Too much public sympathy.'

'So much for justice.' Thamsine shuddered and changed the subject. 'How's your hand?'

He looked down at the filthy bandage. 'It took a couple of knocks on my way here, but it's healing. Every day I get a little more movement back, but ... ' His voice tailed off.

Thamsine unwound the bandage and touched the crooked,

still-splinted fingers. When she looked up, she saw the anguish in his eyes. He saw, as she did, that he would never use the hand again. Not for the things that mattered.

'I brought you Francis Bacon and a couple of your other books,' Thamsine said as she inexpertly rebound the hand with a fresh bandage, hiding the ruined fingers from sight.

She stood up and leaned her head against his shoulder and his good arm encircled her, drawing her close. His lips brushed her hair, and they stood wrapped in each other until the turnkey rapped on the door.

As they broke apart and stood looking at each other, hand in hand like children, Thamsine felt her self-control begin to crumble. She had never thought it possible to love anyone as much as she loved Kit Lovell. Their time together had been so short and yet so intense.

He lowered his head, his lips seeking out hers, his left hand meshing in her hair. They kissed as soulmates, drawing on each other's strengths, each willing the other to survive no matter what.

Thamsine took the few steps to the door of the cell and looked back. Kit did not move.

His lips moved with the words 'I love you.'

She smiled and nodded, mouthing 'And I you,' before the door closed behind her.

CHAPTER 45

'We have a fine day for it!' Lord Gerard looked surprisingly cheerful for a man who was about to go on trial for his life.

The cart carrying Gerard, Vowells, Fox and Kit to Westminster lurched, throwing Kit against Gerard. The four of them were manacled hand and foot. Kit raised his head to look at the bright blue cloudless sky. The warm July sun did little except exacerbate the stinking refuse in the street.

Gerard clapped him on the shoulder, with a clank of his chains. 'Come, Lovell. Don't lose hope. From what I hear tell you've been well looked after. You're fortunate to have a wife with the means to ameliorate your condition. Has she paid for the services of a good lawyer, too?'

Kit ignored Gerard's question. 'What do you intend to do, Gerard?' he asked.

'Vowells and I intend to dispute the jurisdiction of the court,' Lord Gerard answered.

Kit snorted. 'Really? Somewhat presumptuous of you.'

'It is a specially constituted court, Lovell. Cromwell knows if we go before a jury we will be acquitted.'

'And if the trial proceeds?'

Gerard's bearded chin jutted. 'I'll not admit involvement.'

'Gerard, you're a fool. The evidence is overwhelming.'

'You mean you intend to admit guilt?'

Kit shrugged. 'I am guilty.' He looked at his fellow conspirators. Vowells and Fox sat in silence, their grim faces failing to reflect Gerard's optimism. 'And as all of you have willingly borne testimony to that fact, how can I deny it?'

Gerard regarded him for a moment.

'You know there were whispers about your loyalty, Lovell. Some said you were Thurloe's man.'

'Did they?'

'I denied it, of course, and then once Fitzjames was unmasked, that silenced the doubters. I do not doubt that it was Henshaw who betrayed us. But come, Lovell, I've known you, man and boy, and it is not in your character to admit defeat. Why?'

Kit looked away and didn't answer. A few interested bystanders lined the streets but it would seem the fate of a small bunch of conspirators attracted little interest in the public. The cart lurched again and he winced as the barely knit bones of his hand jarred.

'Are you fit enough for trial?' Gerard asked, catching the pain on Kit's face.

'I've a few broken bones, not a broken mind,' Kit replied. 'Anyway, my trial will be brief. I told you, I will admit complicity.'

Gerard shook his head. 'I don't know, Lovell. Those footpads did more than break a few bones. Looks like they knocked the sense right out of you.'

WESTMINSTER HALL HAD SEEN the trial of a king. Now it would bear witness to the trial of those who would seek to kill a king.

Kit looked up at the vaulted roof and shivered. Despite the warmth of the day, the air in the hall felt chill. A guard pushed him forward and he shuffled towards the bench where the other three sat. The great room yawned cavernously behind them. When the King had been tried, stands had been constructed to hold the gallery of spectators. For this trial, there would be no witnesses.

He had known Thamsine would be waiting outside and looked for her in the crowd. Despite telling her to stay away, at the sight of her familiar figure, distinguished from the rest of the crowd by her height, her fine dress of dark blue with a matching mask, and the chestnut hair that curled from beneath her wide-brimmed hat, he felt comforted. In the six weeks since she had arranged an improvement to his conditions, she had visited him every day. They had been short, hurried meetings but they had made the days pass and given him something to look forward to, some reason to hope.

The four accused were seated on a backless bench, facing a raised platform where a table had been neatly set with feathered pens, ink and papers, ready for the judges. No spectators and no jury. In that respect Gerard was right. If they were tried before a jury they would undoubtedly be acquitted.

The four judges filed in and took their seats without even looking at the accused men. He didn't recognise any of them. Not that it mattered. The whole proceeding was a sham.

The charges were read and the men asked to plead. Gerard, as the senior in age and rank, rose to his feet.

'I refuse to submit to the jurisdiction of this court,' he declared, his beard jutting imperiously at the bench of judges.

'And I.' Vowells rose beside him. 'We are innocent of the

charges laid before you and we demand the right to a fair trial by a jury of our peers.'

The senior judge's eye moved to Fox and Kit. 'And you?'

Kit rose slowly to his feet. 'Sir, you have before you, no doubt, a full confession signed by me, admitting my complicity in a plot against the Lord Protector. I see no point in disputing the jurisdiction of this court when such evidence would secure a conviction before any court.'

There was a general nodding of heads and the eyes moved to Fox.

Fox, less sure of himself, rose to his feet. His hands shook as he nodded. 'I too have signed a confession,' he said. 'What Captain Lovell has said answers my case as well.'

'Be seated. Lord Gerard, let us hear your argument as to why this court is improperly constituted.'

Gerard argued long, loudly, and to no avail. At the end of the day his arguments were dismissed and the trials commenced.

Through the haze of self-despair, Kit heard his name. He looked up.

'I call as witness Captain Christopher Lovell,' the prosecutor said.

Kit rose to his feet. 'No. I will not give testimony against these men.'

'It's not a matter you have a choice about, Captain Lovell.'

'I refuse to answer any questions,' Kit said. 'You have my confession, you need no more.'

'You will answer the questions,' the senior judge glared at him, 'or it will be the worse for you.'

'How much worse can it be?'

'The difference between life and death.'

'I will not bear testimony against these men.' Kit looked across at Gerard and Vowells. 'I have done enough.'

He sat down and they called Fox. Unlike Kit, he proved happy to talk, digging deeper graves for his conspirators with every word. Kit lowered his head and closed his eyes, willing himself away from this place, in Thamsine's arms, in the world they had planned where they were safe and free of England.

The guilty verdict was delivered without consultation, and any deliberation on the severity of the sentence seemed to be arbitrary.

The senior judge cleared his throat and read from a paper before him.

'As to the accused Lord John Gerard, this court finds him guilty and sentences him to death by beheading. As to the accused Phillip Vowells, this court finds him guilty and sentences him to death by hanging. As to the accused Somerset Fox, the court finds him guilty, and in view of his admission of guilt and cooperation, sentences him to banishment to the island of Barbados. As to the accused, Christopher Lovell, the court finds him guilty and takes note of his admission of guilt, but given his close complicity in this heinous design, sentences him to death by hanging. These sentences are to be carried out as soon as is practicable.'

Kit hardly heard the words. Just for a moment, after the sentence on Fox was pronounced, he had hoped that some influence external to the court would prevail. He raised his head, scanning the room for John Thurloe, but he was not present.

He fought back the impotent rage that rose in his chest. He had trusted Thurloe, taken his advice, co-operated, and yet he would still die.

THAMSINE SET her mask and hat down on the table and pushed back the stray tendril of hair that clung to her damp forehead.

'Thurloe won't see me,' she said.

'I didn't think he would.' Kit set down his beloved copy of Francis Bacon and rose to his feet. In the two months of his incarceration, his beautiful Thamsine had changed. The fear had gone from her eyes and she carried herself with the confidence of her station in life. He took her in his arms and kissed her chestnut hair, smelling the faint scent of rosemary and chamomile.

Thamsine gave a faint half-smile. 'You must know every word in that book by heart.'

Kit picked it up again, flicking through the well-read pages. He held out the book to her.

'Take it, Thamsine.' His mouth curled in a rueful smile. 'It's all I have to give you.'

She took a step back. 'Don't talk like that.'

He closed his eyes. 'Thamsine, Thurloe won't see you because there is nothing he can or will do. I go to the scaffold in the morning.'

She straightened her shoulders, and he could see the strain in the line of her jaw and her throat as she swallowed. She would not make a scene or make parting any more difficult than it already was. That, in its way, was harder to bear than hysterics.

'Talk to me of ordinary things, Tham. Tell me some gossip.' He smiled and walked around the table, folding her in his arms.

She leaned her head against the soft linen of his shirt.

'May has a suitor,' she said.

'That is good news. Who is the man?'

'A carter. He's a good man, solid and reliable. Just right for her.'

'What about Nan?'

'She is honing her tongue. I swear it grows sharper by the day, but she is pleased for May, I think.'

'And Jem?'

'Henpecked by Nan. She all but runs the inn now..'

With closed eyes, he caressed the nape of her neck, curling his fingers in her soft hair and trying to impress on his memory her warm, living scent.

'And your sister?'

'She has her good days. Since the children have been with her, she has been better.'

Thamsine gulped and her shoulders stiffened as the tears she had been struggling to contain escaped.

He held her closer and they stood locked in an embrace. There seemed to be so much to say, and yet words were inadequate and unnecessary. All that needed to be said was in the tears that soaked his shirt and in the touch of his lips on her smooth forehead.

'I'm sorry, Tham. So sorry,' he whispered. 'It shouldn't have ended like this.'

'No,' she said, her voice muffled by his shirt.

In a sudden, swift movement he released her, his hands cupping her face, flushed with her distress, her tears spilling from her eyes. With savage ferocity, he kissed her as if he wished to draw the life force from her and hold it within himself. Thamsine's tears spilled unchecked down her cheeks and onto his hands.

He pushed her away and strode to the window, looking out but not seeing the busy courtyard, his back to her, his arms wrapped tightly around his body. He couldn't bring himself to look at her again. He couldn't trust himself to remain strong.

'Go, Thamsine,' he said in a voice tight with emotion.

'Kit ... ' Thamsine's voice wavered.

'Go ... ' he said softly. 'Please, for both our sakes.'

He heard the door open and shut. His left hand clenched the barely healed fingers of his right and he welcomed the pain. He needed the pain.

She appeared in the yard below him, moving stiffly as if a puppeteer controlled her limbs. Halfway across she stopped and turned to look up at his window, her face wet with tears. He swallowed, fighting back his tears as she turned and walked away with her head bowed as if it were she who walked to the scaffold.

CHAPTER 46

*I*n the dark, lonely hours before dawn, Kit sat at the table and wondered what he should be feeling. Death had always loomed at the edge of his consciousness, but always a sharp, brutal death on the battlefield, not a calculated, judicial determination of place, time, and means.

He had asked for and been granted paper and a pen, and he grasped the pen awkwardly in the fingers of his right hand. The fingers had knit as well as they could but they were stiff, the joints unyielding. He would never wield a sword again but then, he supposed, that was really of little importance now. He could at least try and write one last letter.

'*Dearest Thamsine,*' he began, and sat chewing the end of the pen. The awkward letters looked like the ill-educated scrawling of an eight-year-old child, not his usual immaculate hand.

He set the pen down and with a shuddering sigh closed his eyes, the memory of their farewell too painful. There had been so much left unsaid, so much he needed to say. Written words seemed so much easier than spoken words. Everything he had planned to say to her that afternoon had entirely escaped him when confronted with her love and her grief.

With renewed determination he picked up the pen and began:

By the time you read this, I will be dead. It is strange to know the exact hour of my death, a privilege not afforded many. I try not to think of the manner of my end and just pray that it will be swift. It is customary, I suppose, at times like this, to have regrets, but I find myself curiously thankful for my life. I have made many mistakes and done many things of which I am not proud but at no time could I ever say that my life was dull. One of the few good things I have done, and by far the best, was to pluck you from the crowd on that cold day in February. These few months that you have been a part of my life, you have brought me absolute joy and taught me for the first time what it is to love a person completely and unconditionally.

I have nothing of any value to leave you. A poor showing for my life, I know. Eveleigh and the empty title that goes with it will devolve to Daniel. I have to trust Thurloe's assurances that he will return safely. Pray for Daniel, Thamsine, as you pray for me.

Kit paused and shook his aching hand as he pondered how to conclude this farewell.

Finally, my dearest Thamsine, I can do nothing more than wish you a happy life. Free yourself of the past ties and enjoy what is now your fortune. If our marriage accomplished nothing but your liberation then I die happy in that knowledge. There is nothing more I can say, words are inadequate, but I will hold your face in my memory until the end. Remember me always.

Yr loving and affectionate husband, Kit Lovell.

Kit sanded the letter, shook off the sand and re-read the

scrawl. Carefully, he folded the paper and sealed it, addressing it to *Thamsine Lovell, care of The Ship Inn*, and set it aside. It still lacked a few hours to dawn, a few more hours to make his peace with the world. He sat by the window to watch and wait.

As the sky began to lighten through the window, he looked up at his last dawn and memories of other dawns flooded him – those he had spent around campfires before battles, in bed with pretty girls… No, he had no regrets, except that he would be parted forever from Thamsine.

He rose to his feet and dressed carefully in a new suit of good blue cloth, ordered by Thamsine. Unable to use his right hand, he hadn't shaved properly since his encounter with Morton, so he had ordered the services of a barber, who had attended to him the previous evening. He intended to go to the scaffold looking every inch the gentleman that he was.

The door opened and Barkstead loomed in the doorway. 'Ready to meet the Lord, Lovell?' he asked.

'You are optimistic about where I am headed,' Kit replied.

'I am a great believer in a forgiving God,' Barkstead said. 'The pastor is here if you wish to pray.'

'I've made my peace with God,' Kit replied. 'However, I have no objections to him saying a few words on my behalf.'

He picked up the letter to Thamsine. 'You will see this delivered?'

Barkstead nodded and stowed the letter in his jacket. Kit fastened his jacket, hoping Barkstead didn't notice that his fingers shook in the task. He straightened the collar and took a deep breath.

Barkstead gave an approving chuckle. 'Very nice, Captain Lovell. 'Tis a pity there will be no crowd to admire you.'

'No crowd?' Kit smiled. 'I hear Vowells had quite a send-off.'

'No, for you, 'tis a private affair, here in the Tower.' Barkstead shrugged. 'You must have a friend somewhere.'

Kit almost laughed. Was this the best Thurloe could do for him?

After the pastor had pronounced some solemn thoughts on the future of Kit's soul, Barkstead stood to one side.

'After you, Captain Lovell,' he said.

Kit took a deep breath, trying to calm the churning in his stomach. His limbs felt wooden and unresponsive. He closed his eyes and willed them to obey. He would not be dragged to the gibbet, hysterical and screaming, but would die with what little dignity he had.

He could, he supposed as he descended the narrow, winding stairs, have insisted on beheading. It was his right as a member of the aristocracy, but then few people knew who he was, and those who had known had forgotten or were dead. No, he would die, as he had lived, as a commoner and besides, from what the gossip had told him, Lord Gerard's despatch at the hands of a headsman had been unpleasant in the extreme. *Four goes to lop it off,* the turnkey had said.

A scaffold had been erected in the courtyard and the wood smelled crisp and fresh in the cool morning air. As he mounted the steps to the platform he forced himself to look up. The noose stirred slightly in the chill breeze off the river. His step faltered and for a moment he thought his nerve would fail him.

He looked away, seeing two men standing below the scaffold, well-wrapped in their cloaks, hats hiding their eyes. He barely glanced at them and wondered if they had their breakfast before or after the deed took place.

'Anything you wish to say?' Barkstead asked as one of his men secured Kit's arms behind his back.

In the hours before dawn, Kit had rehearsed several well-chosen words; now they escaped him completely. He shivered and looked at the banner of the Commonwealth flying high above the White Tower. He thought of Lord Gerard and his lengthy speech to the gathered crowd. For Kit Lovell, there was no crowd, and professions of innocence and declarations of loyalty to the King and his country seemed misplaced and hypocritical. He shook his head.

The hangman pulled him towards the stool and he stepped onto it.

He swallowed, took a last deep breath of air, tinged with the stench of a London summer, as the man hung the noose around his neck. The weight of the cord, pulled down by the heavy knot, hung slackly on his shoulders. A well-tied knot would see his neck snap. It would be quick.

He stood poised only for an instant before the stool jerked away from beneath him. The slack in the rope caught and tightened and in that split second Kit panicked. The knot had been badly tied and he realised he was doomed to die by slow strangulation. He wanted to protest but already the rope bit in, cutting off blood and air.

The instinct for survival was strong and he struggled for breath – for life – before a red mist closed over his eyes, blocking out the memory of the slender woman with chestnut hair standing in the yard of Westminster Palace. Her face was replaced by other images – Daniel's fear-filled face on a smoky battlefield, Fitzjames' eyes as he had gone over the side into the murky blackness of the Thames Estuary, other memories of his mother, his home — then nothing.

CHAPTER 47

$\mathcal{N}$an Marsh stood in the doorway of Thamsine's bed chamber at the house in Turnham Green, her eyes wet with tears and her mouth trembling as she held out a paper.

Thamsine did not move. She knew what news Nan brought.

'No,' she said, rising to her feet. 'I had hoped … a reprieve, surely.'

Nan shook her head.

'This morning,' she said. 'The man who brought this said it was this morning at dawn. Said he died like a gentleman. Jem said I was to bring it to you without delay.' Nan proffered the letter again. 'Take it, Mistress Thamsine. They said 'tis from him.'

Thamsine recoiled from the letter as if it were on fire.

'No, I can't … ' She wrapped her arms around herself, fearing that if she took the paper she would fall apart.

Nan swallowed, her mouth tightening. She crossed to Thamsine and took her by the arm.

'Take it,' she ordered.

Thamsine snatched at the paper and looked at her name

written in an awkward scrawl. She clutched it to her chest and from deep within her a howl of despair rose, an animal noise that had nothing to do with human reason but came from the very depth of primal despair. She sank to her knees on the floor, doubling over as the dry, retching sobs shook her.

Nan's arm circled her shoulders, her head resting on her back. She heard the girl's sobs but had no comfort for her.

Kit was dead. *Dead.* The word reverberated in her mind.

Everyone she had ever loved was dead. Even Jane would leave her before many more months were out.

'Mistress is asking what the trouble is.' Thamsine heard the maid's voice.

Nan rose to her feet. 'He's dead.'

'Who?'

'Her husband, you ninny,' Nan bridled, 'Here, she needs her sister, not us two useless lumps. Give us a hand.'

Thamsine allowed herself to be lifted upright, supported on either side and led, almost as a blind person, to the chamber where Jane sat in a well-cushioned chair before the window. At the sight of Jane's pale, anxious face looking up at her, full of concern and love, she ran to her sister. Like a child she fell at her feet, burying her face in Jane's skirts.

'Lovell?' she heard Jane ask.

Nan must have nodded. 'Oh dearest,' Jane whispered, stroking her hair.

At the touch of the loving hand, the tears began, an unstoppable flood of grief.

'There, you cry. 'Tis the best thing you can do.'

There was a pause and Jane's tone changed as she addressed Nan.

'When?'

'This morning,' Nan replied. 'They brought a letter for her.'

The letter Thamsine still held, crushed and unopened in her hand. 'Mistress, I cannot stay. I've got the loan of Jack's pony and he needs it back this afternoon.'

'Thank you ... ' Jane hesitated. ' ... Sorry, I can't remember your name.'

'Nan Marsh, ma'am. I'm a friend of Thamsine's and Captain Lovell's.' Nan's sharp voice cracked. 'Anything we can do, Jem, May, and I, anything. We loved him too.'

'Thank you, Nan,' Jane said. 'I'm sorry for your loss. Peggy, see that Mistress Marsh gets some refreshment before she returns to London.'

The door closed. Jane stooped and lifted Thamsine's face.

'Dearest, I'm so sorry.'

Thamsine rose to her feet and, shaking off her sister's hand, turned to look out at the garden, bright with summer flowers on a perfect, cloudless morning.

She looked down at the paper in her hand and laid it on the windowsill, smoothing out the creases, trying to get some sense of the man who had written her name. So much life, snuffed out like a candle, reduced to a cold corpse. Yet he had been alive when he had written this. Not even twenty-four hours had passed since she had last seen him.

She wondered where he was, what had they done with him. Had they buried him already? She frowned. Should she claim the body and return him to Eveleigh?

She ran down the stairs to the kitchen, where she found Nan just about to leave.

'Where is he, Nan?'

The girl looked at her. 'Jem asked where he were. Said you would want a proper burial for him but they said he were already ... ' The girl swallowed. ' ... Already buried. There in the Tower. Do you want ... ?'

Thamsine gasped and recoiled. Even the simple act of laying him to rest had been denied her?

She shook her head. 'No,' she said. 'Let him be for now.'

When she was stronger, when the shock had passed, then she would see Thurloe and claim him.

Nan sniffed. 'They brought his things. They're at the inn. I didn't think to bring 'em with me.'

Thamsine looked away as she struggled to regain her composure. She didn't have the strength to make any decisions.

'Keep them for me. I will send for them shortly.' She threw her arms around her friend. 'Thank you, Nan, thank you for everything.'

After Nan had left, Thamsine returned to Jane's room. She picked up the letter from the windowsill where she had left it and broke the seal.

'*Dearest Thamsine ...* ' she read aloud.

Her eyes filling with tears, she slid down to the floor and sat with her back against the wall, trying to decipher the terrible handwriting and make sense of Kit's last words to her. With her forefinger, she traced every letter.

When she had finished, she pressed the paper to her lips and inhaled deeply, trying to see if some scent of him remained. At least she had this. At least she knew he loved her. It was more than many women had. She thought of those women who had lost the men they loved in the long years of war. What comfort did they have?

'Thamsine?' Jane, who had kept her silence as Thamsie read the letter, held out her hand.

Thamsine rose slowly and slid to the floor at her sister's feet, laying her head against her knee. Jane stroked the hair away from her forehead as if she were a child again, just as she had done when Thamsine's mother had died.

'What will you do?' Jane asked.

With a slight shake of her head, Thamsine replied. 'I'll stay with you, Jane. You and the girls are all I have left.'

'Now is probably not the time to ask but I don't have much time and I would like to go home, Thamsine, back to Hartley, where we were both happy. I want to die at Hartley, not here where there are so many difficult memories.'

Hartley. Thamsine had not even thought about her family home, and now she felt it calling to her. Jane was right; London held too many difficult memories. At Hartley she could heal.

Thamsine nodded. 'I would like to do that for you,' she said. 'What about Roger?'

Jane's lips tightened. 'Roger's opinion is of no interest to me. Can we leave tomorrow?'

'Tomorrow,' Thamsine echoed. 'Why not? If a coach can be arranged.'

She leaned against her sister's knee, drained of life, incapable of moving, thinking, and making any more decisions. She just wanted to sleep, to sleep and forget that the man she loved was dead.

CHAPTER 48

*B*eyond a darkness so profound that it had a force of its own, a distant light seemed to grow stronger and brighter. Kit took a step towards it, wanting to reach it with a desperate longing. He reached out his hand and took another step, but long fingers held him tight, dragging him back into the darkness. He tried to cry out but could not make a sound. The light faded and a red-and-black mist of pain enveloped him.

Distantly, he became aware of voices, and of searing pain as his lungs struggled to regain air and his head pounded. He had never experienced a headache like this before. It felt as if his temples would burst; his throat hurt unbearably and every breath seared in his lungs.

Heaven or hell? Surely hell. Heaven brought peace, not this torment of pain and bright colours that flashed before his eyes.

'Praise the Lord, he's coming around,' a man said. 'It seems he'll live. Another couple of seconds and you would have been too late.'

Live?

'Can you see?'

He forced his eyes open and a bright light waved in front of his face. He put up a hand to shield his eyes from its intensity and closed his eyes again.

Kit tried to speak, but nothing came out but a strangled croak. He put a hand to his throat and swallowed with difficulty, arching his back against the pain of the effort.

A hand rested on his chest. 'Lie quiet. There will be pain. That's to be expected. And don't try to talk. It will be some time before you'll talk again. There's a great deal of bruising.'

How had he not died? The memory of the rope closing on his throat came back with cruel, stark clarity. He tried to swallow again but even that simple movement made him cough.

Kit ran his hands up his face and across his eyes, seeking the assurance he was still flesh and bone. Kit threw off the hand that held him down and tried to sit up but the effort was too much. He subsided, coughing. His back arched in the agony that the effort cost him and his limbs shook uncontrollably. Someone held a cup to his lips and he gagged as a sweet liquid dribbled down his tortured throat. Gradually the pain faded and he drifted into a place of nightmares.

When he opened his eyes again, the light in the room seemed to have changed. He blinked, trying very hard to focus as he looked around the small room, but everything remained blurred. Pinpricks of light indicated the location of a brace of candles. A shadow moved into his line of sight. He squinted and could make out the outline of a man wearing the robes and tight-fitting cap of a physician. The man leaned over him, scanning his face. He nodded and straightened

'He's awake,' the physician said, and Kit recognised him as being the man with the soothing, authoritative voice who had brought him back from the dead.

Another shadow moved across his field of vision. A man in dark clothes stood back a little way, his arms crossed, one hand raised with his finger against his lips. Kit recognised the gesture, even if the face remained blurred.

'Thurloe!'

Nothing but a croak emanated from Kit's throat. The effort caused a wracking coughing fit that made him contract in pain.

'Welcome back, Captain Lovell. You had me worried. I thought for a moment I was too late,' Thurloe said.

'Why?' This time something that vaguely resembled a word forced its way out of Kit's lips.

'It was the only way, Lovell,' Thurloe replied. 'We cut you down before any serious damage could be done. Although, as the physician said, probably just in time. You will hurt for a while but Dr Munn here assures me that you should make a full recovery.'

Kit narrowed his eyes and stared at Thurloe, wishing his face would come into focus so he could look into his eyes and try to understand how this man could let him go to the gallows, just to snatch him back from the jaws of death.

'I couldn't save you from the gallows without it appearing suspicious.' Thurloe read his mind again. 'A last-minute reprieve was not possible without awkward questions. This way, Christopher Lovell is dead. You are free to start a new life. All debts repaid.'

Kit shook his head. A mistake; the world roared in his ears and he pressed his hands to his head to try and ease the pain.

The doctor raised his head and held a cup to his lips. Kit drank gratefully, the cool, unidentifiable liquid soothing the pain of his tortured throat.

'Get him up,' Thurloe said. 'My coach is waiting.'

'He needs rest,' the doctor protested.

'He can have plenty of rest, but I want him out of here. I want him off my hands.'

Kit groaned as the doctor hauled him upright. It took both the doctor and Thurloe's bulky coachman, who had to be summoned to assist, to half-carry, half-drag him downstairs and out through a sally port to where a coach stood waiting in the shadows.

Kit subsided against the expensive leather seats and closed his eyes. Thurloe gave a sharp order and the coach moved off. He did not speak until it stopped again.

'Ah, we're here. Back to the warm and welcoming arms of your friends. All shuttered up, I see. There must have been a death in the family. Well, this is it, Lovell. This is farewell.'

Thurloe's voice came from the pale, disembodied circle of his face. He continued, 'You will come to thank me, Lovell. You have your life and a chance to start again. However, I think it prudent you avoid your previous haunts for some time. Your Lazarine resurrection from the dead may excite comment among your former comrades. In a few years, maybe they will have forgotten about you.'

The door of the coach opened.

'Goodbye, Lovell,' Thurloe said as his coachman hauled Kit bodily out of the coach and deposited him on the doorstep of The Ship Inn.

The coachman banged on the door and left Kit slumped against the doorjamb. By the time Kit heard footsteps on the flags of the taproom, Thurloe's coach had gone.

'We're closed.' Jem's voice boomed gruffly from behind the door.

Kit rested his face against the door and raised his hand to the wood, his feeble efforts making no more impression than the scratching of a mouse. He heard the bolt being drawn back and the door flung open. Kit got a brief impression of Jem's surprised face before falling forward into his arms.

There were voices in the dark, this time familiar voices.

Nan Marsh's said, 'What sort of 'orrible joke is this?'

''Tis no joke,' her brother replied. ''Tis Kit Lovell all right, and I can tell you this, girls, he ain't dead. Fetch me some of the brandy.'

Slowly, Kit opened his eyes and coughed. He heard a squeak of alarm and turned his throbbing head to find himself looking into the anxious face of May Marsh.

She touched his face. Just the gentlest touch, but every nerve in his body cried out in pain.

'You're really alive! I can't believe it.'

Her face looked red and blotchy from crying. He reached out a hand to touch her face and she grasped his fingers, pressing his hand to her wet cheek.

'Don't cry, May,' he said, or at least he thought the words came out, but she didn't seem to hear.

Jem Marsh's less appealing visage hove into view.

'Don't even try and talk, Lovell. I've seen this afore and it will be a while until you've a voice of your own.' Jem's arm slipped beneath his head and a cup of brandy was put to his lips. Kit let a little of the burning liquid slide down his throat. He gagged and coughed but life began to creep back into his fingers and toes.

May gave a choking sob and tightened her grip on his fingers. 'They told us you was dead and buried. They even brought a letter for Mistress Thamsine ... '

A strangled groan emanated from Kit's throat. He had written her a letter. Thamsine would think he was dead.

He propped himself up on an elbow and scanned the faces in the room: Jem, May and Nan. No Thamsine.

'She's not here. She's with her sister at Turnham Green.' Jem answered the question in Kit's eyes. 'I'll send May's Tom in the morning to fetch her.'

'Proper cut up she was when I told her ... ' Nan put in.

Thamsine wasn't here. She thought he was dead. Kit fell back and closed his eyes against this new pain. He wanted to hold her, to reassure himself that he had survived and they could be together.

Jem brought the candle lower and turned Kit's head, inspecting his neck.

'Another minute on the gallows and you'd've been done for,' he said.

Kit managed a nod of affirmation. Had this been the only way Thurloe could find to save his life or another of his cruel tricks?

The memory of what he had thought to be his last moments on Earth forced their way into his aching mind with absolute clarity and he put a shaking hand to his eyes. Thurloe's legacy would be a nightmare that would probably haunt him for the rest of his days.

Jem put an arm around his shoulders and raised him to his feet.

'Come on, lad. Let's get you into a bed. We'll hear the story when you're able to tell it.'

CHAPTER 49

hamsine leaned out of the coach window as they rounded the bend in the driveway that gave the first view of Hartley Court. It seemed a lifetime since she had fled its solid red brick walls, leaving Ambrose Morton lying in a pool of blood on the parlour floor.

She sighed and glanced at her sister's ashen face. She sat beside her husband, her fingers entwined in his. Roger had said little. He seemed to have gone into shock, unable to grasp the enormity of what now faced him. Ten-year-old Rachel slept with her head on her mother's lap. The older girl, Rebecca, sat beside Thamsine reading a book of sermons. The journey had been a trial, but the dying woman had been insistent. Jane wanted to end her days at Hartley.

Thamsine's gloved hand tightened on the sash of the coach door. Soon there would be another death to mourn. In the days since Kit's death, the living had commanded her attention and she had lavished her care on Jane. She dared not think about Kit. He was dead and beyond her love but Jane needed her. She knew the high tide of her suffering was yet to come. With Jane's death, would it all be unleashed?

She swallowed, forcing herself to think of the more pressing issue of her stepmother Isabelle, Ambrose Morton's mother, who would be at Hartley Court to meet her. She could already picture Isabelle's mean, pinched face, the thin lips dragging down at the corners. If Isabelle had disliked her before, her hatred would know no bounds when the woman who had tried to murder her son returned, the widow of another man.

She had sent word ahead that they were to be expected but to her surprise, it was not Isabelle who stood on the doorstep but her steward, Stebbings. He stepped forward and opened the door to the coach.

'Welcome home, Mistress Thamsine,' he said with a broad smile. Then he flushed. 'My apologies, Mistress Lovell.'

'Thank you, Stebbings. Is everything prepared for my sister?'

'It is. Mistress White has set aside the best bedchamber. Allow me ... Mistress Knott ... ' He turned to Jane, assisting her from the coach and then, supporting her, assisted her inside the cool house.

Thamsine let her servants and Roger settle Jane into the bedchamber. She wandered through the rooms, savouring the familiar smell of beeswax and lavender. Everything had been kept well in her absence. She supposed she should be grateful to Isabelle.

Where *was* Isabelle? She frowned and sent for Stebbings.

'Where is Mistress Granville?'

Stebbings' eyes widened. 'You hadn't heard?'

'Heard what?'

'Mistress Granville has been dead these three months past.'

One should not speak ill of the dead, Thamsine thought, and bit her tongue against the cry of jubilation that rose in her throat.

'What happened?'

Stebbings' lips tightened. 'She was, as you know, rather partial to a little Canary wine in the evening ... '

And the morning, and at lunchtime, Thamsine thought.

'She took it into her head to walk to Beverstock to see her daughter, Mistress Anne. She went without a hat or cloak and was caught in a heavy rainstorm. We reckon she must have slipped and fallen into a ditch. We didn't find her until morning and she died within the week.'

'Where is she buried?' Thamsine bit back the exultation in her voice.

Stebbings coughed discreetly. 'As there was no one to make a decision, we had her interred in the family plot at Beverstock.'

Thamsine nodded. Stebbings and her staff had no great love for Isabelle. She would have died unmourned by anyone except possibly her son and daughter. She wondered if Ambrose even knew of his mother's death. Isabelle had exerted a strong influence over her son. He would feel her loss.

A commotion could be heard on the stairs. Thamsine flung open the door and a wild figure broke free of the housekeeper and threw herself on the ground at Thamsine's feet, wrapping her arms around her ankles as if she intended never to let go. Thamsine looked down at the head of tangled black hair as the housekeeper and the steward both ran forward.

'It's all right,' Thamsine said.

She bent down to touch Annie Morton's shoulder, afraid if she tried to move she would topple over.

'Annie, please let go of me. I'm going to fall.'

Annie just tightened her grip.

'No one is going to hurt you. Give me your hand.'

Annie looked up. Slowly she extended a thin, dirty hand, releasing her vice-like grip on Thamsine's ankle. Thamsine pulled her upright and the girl snuggled against her, her stick-like arms wrapped around her waist.

'I'll have her sent back.' The steward stepped forward and took Annie's arm. Annie cowered closer to Thamsine, shaking off his hand.

'Where's she been living?'

Stebbings looked embarrassed. 'Well, ever since … ' He coughed. 'After Colonel Morton's unfortunate accident, he had her sent back to Beverstock. She's been there ever since.'

'Well, she's supposed to have been there but she's been coming around, looking for you,' the housekeeper put in. 'We keep sending her back. They promise to keep her under lock and key but she keeps escaping.'

'Look at the state she's in,' Thamsine said.

She tilted Annie's face towards the light, showing up scabs and sores, the pitiful thinness and the dirt. No one had cared for the girl, least of all her mother.

'She looks like a ragamuffin from the poorest streets of London, not a gentleman's daughter. Stebbings,' she addressed the steward, 'send someone to Beverstock to let them know she is here.'

Stebbings nodded.

'Annie, you can only stay here a little while,' Thamsine said. 'Then you must go home.'

Annie shook her head. 'No,' she moaned. 'Not there … '

'Go with Mistress White.' Thamsine pointed out the housekeeper. 'And you are to have a bath. Mistress White will give you some clean clothes.'

'Poor girl,' Mistress White said with a sniff of disapproval as she took Annie's arm. ''Tis shameful the way you've been treated. Come with me and I am sure Cook will find some dainties for you.'

But Annie wasn't listening. She reached out and fingered the black stuff of Thamsine's gown. 'Tham, are you sad … ?' she said.

Thamsine drew the girl to her and stroked the dark head. How could it be possible to feel so much affection for this girl and yet hate her brother so very much?

'Yes, I am sad,' she said, disengaging Annie. 'Someone I loved very much has died.'

'Is 'Brose dead too?' Annie's large, grey eyes filled with tears.

Thamsine felt a cold prickle at the back of her neck. Did Annie think Ambrose had died that night she shot him?

'No, Annie. Ambrose isn't dead.'

Tears trickled from Annie's eyes. 'Mama is dead. Are you sad because Mama is dead?'

Thamsine swallowed and lied, 'Yes, I am sad your mother is dead.'

Annie had loved her mother and her brother. She had to respect that.

'Now, Annie, go with Mistress White.'

Mistress White straightened and held out a hand. 'Come on, then. Don't waste Mistress Lovell's time. I'll make a lady of you yet!'

As the evening drew on, Thamsine stood beside Roger Knott at the wide bay window looking out onto the terrace, where Roger's daughters and Annie were locked in rapt concentration in a game involving dolls. Two young girls and one grown, but with the mental age of a three-year-old. She thought she had never seen Annie looking so happy.

'She's Morton's sister,' Roger said as if reading Thamsine's thoughts. 'She can't stay here. If he has word that she's with you, there'll be nothing more guaranteed to bring him running than his sister.'

Thamsine shook her head. 'What can I do, Roger? Stebbings

says Beverstock is deserted. There is no one to care for her. In the name of Christian compassion I have to keep her.'

'She's addled,' Roger said. 'Perhaps an institution where she will be cared for?'

Thamsine looked at him with loathing.

'You forget, Roger. I spent three days in Bedlam. She's not mad, or bad, just different. She didn't ask to be dropped by her nursemaid. If God was merciful she should be a beautiful young woman, maybe married with a family of her own. I'll not turn her away. She's welcome to stay.'

'She'll bring you trouble, Thamsine,' Roger said.

'Well, that is my concern, not yours, Roger,' she said and turned away.

CHAPTER 50

'*Y*ou can't catch me, Kit!'

In the well-kept gardens of Eveleigh Priory, Kit played hide-and-seek with his young brother Daniel and his sister, Frances. Always fearless, Daniel often had to be retrieved from the tallest oak tree by a hot and impatient brother.

'I'm over here.'

Kit heard Daniel's challenge and turned to see the boy's fair head disappearing behind a hedge. He set off after him, running hard, his booted feet sinking in the soft lawn.

Every so often Daniel's head would appear from behind a tree or a hedge, with a cheeky grin that split his freckled face from ear to ear.

'Catch me!'

Kit ran on. The well-kept grass gave way to tussocks and mud. He stumbled and looked down to see he had tripped over the body of a man, his dead eyes staring sightlessly into a grey sky. Around him were the bodies of other men and horses. A heavy pall of powder smoke hung over the battlefield.

He scoured the field around him, looking for his brother. He called his brother's name.

'Kit!'

Daniel was just ahead of him, running for his life as two burly foot soldiers bore down on him, their muskets raised like clubs.

Kit tried to run, but his legs would not move and his feet had become pinned to the ground. He screamed the boy's name again but the soldiers had caught up with Daniel, an up-swung musket carrying him to the ground with a dull thud.

Moving as if his feet had become anvils, Kit reached his brother, who lay face down in the crushed grass, his fair hair lifting in a slight breeze. With shaking hands he turned him over, to find himself looking into the face of a rotting corpse.

Kit woke with a shudder, his heart pounding, his breathing ragged. He sat up in the bed and tried to steady his racing pulse. He put his hand to his face and it came away wet. Kit ran the sleeve of his nightshirt over his face, fell back on the bolster, and stared up at the faded, red bed hangings.

His head felt clear and no longer hurt to move. He put a hand to his throat, touching the bruising, remembering. It hadn't been a dream. He really was alive.

'So, ye're back with us?'

He turned his head to see Nan standing in the doorway.

She set down the tray she was carrying and stood over him, her hands on her hips.

'Nan,' he croaked.

Nan shook her head. 'You've given us a scare, Lovell. We thought we was going to lose you all over again.'

Kit coughed and tried to speak again. He frowned and beck-oned for Nan to come closer. Nan leaned forward to hear, affording him a good view of her ample bosom.

'How long?'

'Five days, lover,' she said.

Five days?

'Thamsine?'

Nan straightened and considered him a moment, biting her lip.

'It's like this, lover. We sent May's Tom to Turnham Green but when he got there, the house was all closed up. He asked around and someone told him the whole family had gone but they didn't know where. The maid thought it was somewhere in Hampshire they was going. Anyways, by the time Tom came back,' she grimaced, 'it didn't look too good for you and we thought it would be cruel to tell Thamsine you was alive just to have you die again, so we thought we'd wait until we was sure you were going to live before we went looking some more.'

Kit ran a shaking hand over his eyes, trying to remember the name of Thamsine's home in Hampshire. *Hartley?* Where was that? Hampshire was a large county. He had no idea where to look for her.

Should he send Jem with a note? No, that would not be right. Breaking the news to his wife that he lived was something better done in person. For the moment he needed time to recover his strength. He doubted he could stay on a horse as far as Ludgate, let alone Hampshire.

Nan held out a cup. 'Here, drink this. 'Pothecary said it would help.'

Kit lifted his right hand to take the cup. When he saw his fingers, misshapen and useless, a red mist of anger flared. The twisted fingers represented everything that he had endured in the last year, events over which he had no control, that had left him broken and crippled.

Exhausted in mind and body, he had passed beyond the point

of endurance. With an animal cry of rage and frustration, he struck the cup from Nan's hand. It flew against the wall, shattering and spraying its contents across the floor. He had a brief impression of surprise on Nan's face before turning away from her, hunching down in the bed with his back to her.

CHAPTER 51

*J*em slapped a jug of wine down on the table so hard the ruby contents slopped over the edges.

'That's it!' he declared. 'That's the last you'll have of me.'

Kit raised his head and without responding refilled his cup. 'You don't mean that, Jem.'

'I do, Lovell, and make no mistake. I've had two weeks of watching you drinking yourself into oblivion. Two weeks of your foul tempers are all the gratitude we get. It's time you pulled yourself together and went looking for your wife.'

'She's better off without me.' Kit downed the cup of wine in one swill. 'I'm no good to her.'

'What do you mean by that?'

'Oh Christ, Jem.' Kit's mouth twisted. What did the truth matter now? 'Why do you think Thurloe had me cut down from the gallows?'

Jem shrugged.

'Because I've been in his pay for the last two years. Because I was the one who sent the rest of them to their deaths.'

Jem stared at him. 'You were the turncoat?'

Kit picked up the wine jug. His hand shook as he tried to pour the wine, slopping some on the table. When his cup was full, he looked up at his old friend, meeting Jem's incredulous eyes.

'I was the turncoat. I turned them all in.'

He could almost see Jem's thought processes as he digested the information. The man he had followed into battle, had respected and maybe even loved, had just confessed to being a traitor?

It didn't matter. Jem could not hate him any more than he hated himself.

'You turned her in, too?' Jem said at last.

Kit nodded.

Jem's massive fist swung at him without warning. It caught him on the jaw and knocked him off the stool. When he opened his eyes, Jem stood over him, his fist poised to deliver another blow. Kit flinched, bracing himself for the blow or a well-deserved boot to his still-aching ribs.

'You're a bastard, Lovell,' Jem said but there was no anger in his voice.

Kit opened one eye and Jem reached out his hand to pull him up. He returned to his stool, ruefully rubbing his jaw, and Jem sat down with a heavy sigh.

'I've known you these ten years past,' he said. 'You don't do anything without a good reason. Are you going to tell me what it is?'

'My brother, Daniel ... ' Kit swallowed. After all these years of lies, the truth came with difficulty. 'I was promised his release.'

'Lovell.' Jem shook his head and leaned forward. 'You told me that the boy is dead.'

Kit shook his head. 'No. They sent him to Barbados but under Thurloe's protection. He's still alive and, God willing, on a ship back to England.'

But even as he said the words, the nightmare that haunted him came back. What if Daniel was dead and it had all been for nothing?

'Does Thamsine know?'

Kit nodded. 'She knows everything about me. The very darkest corners of my soul.' He reached for the jug, pouring himself another cup. 'It was only a marriage of convenience, Jem. Let her think I'm dead and find someone better.'

'Someone better? Someone like that Morton, perhaps!'

Kit snorted.

'He's back in London.'

Kit looked up. 'Back from where?'

'I hear he's been on the Continent these last few weeks. Come back to find his lady love up to her ears in creditors, he has.'

'So?' Kit feigned disinterest.

'It hasn't occurred to your wooden head that as far as the world is concerned, your Thamsine is now a widow?'

Kit shrugged.

'A wealthy widow,' Jem added.

'He can't force her to marry him. Any agreement with her father is nullified. She's safe enough from him.'

Jem reached across the table and grabbed the front of Kit's shirt, hauling him up until they were nose to nose.

'And you think that matters to him? Remember Bedlam? What he did to our May? He can force her to do anything he damn well wants, and you're just going to sit there and let it happen?'

Kit stared into Jem's one bloodshot eye.

'Let go of me, Marsh,' he commanded in a voice Jem knew well.

The big man's mouth tightened but he let Kit go and he subsided back on the stool and picked up his cup.

'How do you know what Morton is up to?' Kit asked

'I've been keeping an eye on him, these last months,' Jem said, tapping his one good eye. 'Don't want him paying any unexpected calls on me and mine again.'

Kit raised the cup to his lips and set it down without taking a drink. 'Do you think he'll go after Thamsine?'

Jem shrugged. 'What choice does he have? The Talbot woman's no good for him now, and he's not a man to survive long without money.'

Kit ran a hand through his greasy and knotted hair. He hadn't dared to look in a mirror since the day he had "died" and dreaded he would see the face of a hanged man. Little wonder he had tried to expunge his nightmares with alcohol.

He swept the cup from the table, rose unsteadily to his feet and went in search of a looking glass.

Peering into the mottled depths of Nan's pride and joy, for a brief moment, he didn't recognise himself. The eyes of a madman stared back at him, the whites obscured by the red of broken capillaries. Nearly three weeks' growth shadowed his chin and his hair, as he had suspected, hung in greasy, knotted, unkempt strands. Both his beard and hair had streaks of grey where none had been before.

He tugged at the cloth he had tied loosely around his neck to reveal the livid shadow of the noose still marring his skin. He shuddered as his fingers traced the line of the rope, the very twists of the hemp still discernible.

He set the mirror down and leaned his head against the wall. He couldn't go on pretending to himself that Thamsine was better off without him. The truth was that he was no good without her. He needed her as a starving man needs food.

Jem had been right. The time had come to find her — if she would have him back.

CHAPTER 52

hamsine drew her knees up to her chin and stared out
of the window at the well-ordered gardens and
familiar view of her childhood.

'What are you thinking, Aunt?' Her niece's voice made her
jump, and she turned to look at Rebecca.

Rebecca's serious face studied her from beneath an immaculate white cap. She looked older and wiser than her fourteen
years. Thamsine patted the window ledge and the girl sat down
beside her, her back rigidly straight.

'I was thinking about my childhood,' she said. 'My brother and
I used to climb the trees in the apple orchard and ride our ponies
in the home paddock.'

Rebecca's eyes widened. 'You used to climb trees?'

Thamsine nodded.

'I would never … ' Rebecca looked down at the prayer book in
her hand. 'Aunt … '

'Rebecca?'

'Is mother dying?'

Thamsine sighed. Nothing would be gained from lies. 'Yes, dearest. I doubt she will see the week out.'

'What will become of us?'

'What do you mean?'

'Father says that we must leave Hartley and return to the house in Turnham Green.'

'Don't you want to go home to London?'

Rebecca shook her head.

Thamsine put a hand over the small, fine-boned hand clasping the prayer book. 'You will always be welcome to visit me here.'

Rebecca's face brightened. 'Promise?'

Thamsine nodded. 'I promise.'

'Will you come back to London?'

'No,' Thamsine said with absolute certainty. London held too many painful memories. Nothing would induce her to return to London.

'Will you marry again?'

Thamsine smoothed the folds of her black skirt and shook her head. 'No. I shall never marry again.'

'What was he like?'

'Who?'

'Your husband.'

Thamsine swallowed and looked away. 'I can't talk about him, dearest.'

'I would have liked to meet him. Mother says he was a rogue but in a nice way,' Rebecca continued.

'Yes, he was a rogue in a nice way.' Thamsine smiled. 'A terrible rogue, but you would have liked him.'

'There you are, Bec!' Rachel, her fair curls escaping from beneath her cap, bounded into the room. 'We've been looking for you everywhere! What are you talking about?'

Thamsine looked at Rachel and smiled. She had just turned ten and promised to be everything her sister was not. Where Rebecca was the picture of the obedient, Godly child, Rachel was rowdy, untidy and lacked a scholarly bone in her body.

'We were talking about Thamsine's husband,' Rebecca said.

'Was he very handsome?' Rachel asked.

Thamsine smiled, 'Yes.'

Rachel sighed. 'You must be sad he's dead.'

Thamsine drew a heavy breath. 'Let's not talk about him anymore. Rachel, come here, your hair is a mess.'

She made a fuss of Rachel's hair, trying to pin it back under the cap. If Rachel had been her daughter she would have given up the unequal struggle, but for Jane's sake, she persisted.

'Now,' she addressed both girls, 'shall we go and sit with Mama? I promised I would play her some music.'

Rebecca held up the book of prayers. 'And I said I would read to her.'

Taking Rachel by the hand, Thamsine straightened her back and led the girls into Jane's bedchamber. Despite the airy atmosphere and the bright vases of roses picked from the gardens, the bedchamber carried the atmosphere of imminent death which Thamsine remembered from her childhood, as her father had forced her to sit for long hours in her mother's sick chamber.

Jane's life ebbed away as each day passed in a battle to breathe. Even propped up on the pillows her thin face was ashen, the lips blue. Thamsine stooped to kiss her sister's brow. Jane's eyes flickered open and a faint smile lifted the ravaged countenance. Thamsine no longer asked how she felt.

Rachel bounced onto the bed beside her mother and curled up against Jane with her head on her shoulder.

'What have you been doing?' Jane asked her daughters.

'I've been down in the stable. Brown's dog has just had a litter of puppies. He said I could have one if Papa will let me,' she said.

Rebecca sat on the chair beside her mother's bed. 'I've brought some prayers to read with you, Mama, and Aunt Thamsine said she will play for you.'

Thamsine picked up the lute from where she had left it on the seat by the window.

'That will be lovely,' Jane whispered.

The sun streamed through the long casement windows, the stained glass scattered in the panes casting jewelled shadows on the floor and across the bed.

'Will you open the window?' Jane asked.

Rebecca looked at Thamsine, who nodded, and the girl threw open the casements. The smell of newly mown hay drifted in with soft sunlight.

Rebecca returned to her mother's side and began to read as Thamsine picked out a quiet, contemplative piece. Rachel lay snuggled in her mother's arm, listening to the words and the music, her eyes half closed.

'Mama?' Rachel cried out.

Thamsine glanced across at the bed. Jane's eyes were open, staring at the open window. The breath rattled in her throat, then there was silence.

'Mama!' Rebecca jumped up from her chair, her face stricken, the prayer book dropping to the floor.

Thamsine laid down the lute and crossed to her sister's bed. She leaned over and kissed her sister's forehead, feeling the last warmth of life just beneath the skin. Her hand passed over her sister's eyes, closing them forever.

Rachel rolled off the bed and threw herself at Thamsine, the tears flowing. Rebecca stood rigid staring at the bed. Thamsine moved to put an arm around the girl but Rebecca moved away.

'Go to your father,' Thamsine said, 'and bring him here.'

Rebecca turned and left the room, her face immobile. Thamsine sat down on the chair Rebecca had been occupying and pulled the weeping youngster onto her lap, holding her until the tears subsided into deep, gulping sobs.

CHAPTER 53

*J*ane's death left her husband broken. Roger Knott had not stirred from his chamber since the funeral two days previously and now Thamsine found him on his knees at the window, his hands clasped in prayer. Thamsine looked down at the man's bowed head. She had little sympathy for the pathetic specimen of manhood.

'Roger?' When he didn't move, she said, without warmth. 'Prayer will not bring her back.'

She had shed no tears for Jane. It was as if her grief went so deep it would never be expressed. In less than a year she had lost her father, almost murdered a man, become a beggar on the streets, and lost her sister and the man she loved so much that she could not even bring herself to think of him without a shard of pain so physical it made her ill.

'I pray for my soul, not hers. Jane has gone to our Lord with a soul unblemished and spotless, whereas I feel the fires of Hell already licking at my feet,' he said.

'Rightly so,' Thamsine responded. 'You're an adulterer. You

betrayed your marriage vows and allowed yourself to become a party to a despicable plot that nearly ended in my death.'

Roger's thin lips moved but no sound came out.

'I always loved Jane,' he said at last.

'Not enough, Roger. Now, I wish to speak with you about the future.'

He rose to face her, his shoulders bowed. He cringed from her like a whipped dog.

'What do you mean... the future?'

'If it were my choice,' she said, 'I would pray to God I never saw you again. However, you are the father of my sister's children and I must consider them. My dearest wish is that they will never have to suffer what I have endured. I have therefore decided that I shall settle upon them a comfortable amount to allow them to live independently should they so choose.'

'A dowry?'

'Not a dowry. It shall be a condition of my gift that it shall remain the property of the girls and not devolve upon any future husbands they might have.'

Roger looked up, life sparking into his dead eyes. 'But that is unheard of.'

'It is the condition of my gift,' she said and named the amount.

Roger looked down at his hands again. 'They don't deserve such generosity.'

'They are my only blood kin, Roger. When are you planning to return to London?'

'Do you want me to go?'

'Yes,' she said.

'Of course. You owe me nothing, yet I have one last thing to ask of you. Can I leave the girls here?'

Thamsine stared at him. What was he asking her? He was the children's father and they should be with him.

'Their place is with you,' she said.

Roger drew a deep breath. 'I have been a poor husband and a worse father. I do not deserve them. This will be my punishment.'

'Let me think about it,' Thamsine said and left the room.

In her own bedchamber, Thamsine stood by the window contemplating the peaceful countryside that had remained relatively untouched by the recent wars. Her father had been clever in his support of the King, never allowing his loyalty to his monarch to undermine his loyalty to his family.

She wrapped her arms around herself. She would never remarry and would have no family of her own. When Kit had first been taken from her, she had prayed that she was with child but it was not to be, and she had cried when her body betrayed her. Having the girls with her would be some comfort and ease the loneliness of a life of long widowhood.

She had nothing left of Kit except a battered copy of Francis Bacon that she kept under her pillow and the contents of an old chest, still at The Ship Inn. Her lips tightened. The time had come to collect up the remnants of Kit's life.

And what of Kit's family still alive at Eveleigh Priory; his grandfather, his stepmother, and his sister? Did they know of his death? She thought she would like to meet them and learn a little more of his life before she had known him and the boy he had sold his soul to try and save. Hopefully, even now, Daniel Lovell was on a ship returning from exile to the people who loved him.

That would have to wait. She didn't have the strength to face his family just yet, but she would retrieve his belongings from London.

She crossed to the desk and penned a short note to Jem Marsh.

CHAPTER 54

it balanced the sword in his left hand, studying his opponent's eyes as they circled each other. His opponent thrust and he parried, throwing his opponent off balance. As he moved in for the kill, Jem dropped his sword and backed up against the wall of the inn courtyard, his large face florid and sweating. He pushed the point of Kit's sword away from his throat.

'That's it, Lovell. No more. Seems to me it don't make much difference if it isn't your sword hand, you're still damned good with a sword.'

'You're getting old and slow, Jem.' Kit sheathed the sword and thumped the man's substantial belly. 'And fat.'

He doubled over coughing. The cough seemed to be a legacy of being hanged. His voice had returned but in a different form, lower and with a crackling edge to it. It would take a little getting used to.

A new voice, a new persona. Thurloe had been right in a number of ways. Kit Lovell, adventurer, gambler and spy, had died at the end of the noose. However, he still had no clear idea who had emerged from the shadows of the gallows.

Nan Marsh appeared at the door and stood there, her hands on her hips.

'If you two have finished playing sword games,' she said, 'I've something that might be of interest to you.'

She held out a piece of paper. Jem took it, squinted at the writing on it and handed it to Kit.

'You know I don't read. You read it.'

Kit took the paper and frowned. The writing seemed familiar. He opened the seal and read:

Dear Jem,

I trust this note finds you and the girls well. My sister died a week ago and I grieve for her as I still grieve for my husband. I would be much obliged if you could arrange the conveyance of his belongings to me. I am to be found at Hartley Court, beyond the village of Milston. I hope you may come in person.

Yr friend, Thamsine Lovell.

Seeing Thamsine's writing, Kit's hand shook as he struggled to control his emotions.

Jem clapped his large hand over Kit's. 'What does it say?'

Kit read the note aloud.

'No more excuses, Lovell,' Jem said. 'You know where she is and I reckon a personal delivery is called for.'

Kit pocketed the note and fought to control his shaking hands as he looked up at his old friend.

'What do I do? How do I ...?'

Jem thumped him on the back. 'You've a sizeable ride to figure on it, Lovell. I'll get you a horse in the morning.'

'Another day or two ...' Kit began.

Jem fixed him with a glare. 'Ye're a coward, Lovell.'

Kit looked up at his friend.

'I just can't appear, Jem.'

'Then write her a note!' Jem's voice betrayed a degree of impatience.

''Ere, Jem!' A ragged boy appeared at the gate to the courtyard.

'That's Master Marsh to you, Harry!' Jem growled. 'What news?'

The boy gave a cheeky grin. 'You asked me to tell you ... '

'Go on,' Jem interrupted.

'They left this morning first thing. Hired a coach and I followed for a while but after they crossed the river I couldn't keep up.'

'Headed south?'

The boy nodded.

Kit glanced from the boy to Jem's livid face.

'Morton?'

Jem nodded. 'Harry here's been watching the house in Holborn Hill these weeks past.'

Kit felt in his purse for a coin and tossed it to the boy.

'Thanks, Harry, you've done well.' The boy touched his forehead and vanished into the busy street.

Kit looked at Jem. 'If they've gone south, they could be heading for Portsmouth ... '

'Or Dover or Southampton or ... ' Jem's mouth tightened.

'Or Hampshire.' Kit finished the sentence.

If they were leaving England, it seemed likely Ambrose might choose to visit his old family home and see his sister cared for in his absence, or he could simply be after Thamsine again. His blood ran cold.

'Seems like you've no choice, Lovell,' Jem said.

Kit nodded. 'I'll need you.'

'What? You just want me to up and leave the Inn?'

'Nan will manage quite well without you. I'm not up to facing Morton by myself, you know that.'

He held up his right hand with the bent and twisted fingers.

Jem shrugged. 'Two 'orses it is, then.'

'Two good horses, Jem, and we leave now. Hang the cost.'

Jem gave a splutter. 'Hang the cost? Ye've not a farthing to yer name. I wouldn't mind betting that was your last coin you gave the boy.'

Kit smiled. 'I'll repay you, Jem. You know I'm good for my debts.'

'Oh yes?' Jem clapped him on the shoulder. 'Pack your things, Lovell. I'll be back shortly.'

CHAPTER 55

*I*n the cosy parlour, an early fire burned bright in the hearth while outside rain lashed the glass and the wind bent the trees, crushing the heads of the unharvested crops and bringing the day to an early end. Roger Knott sat by the unseasonable fire, reading his bible. Rebecca and Rachel sat on a settle opposite him, their heads also bent over bibles. The Sabbath had always been dutifully observed in the Knott household.

Annie sat by herself in a corner, absorbed in the dolls, an activity forbidden the other girls. Thamsine smiled as she caught Rachel casting Annie envious glances. She sat at the table working on some music. Music had been her solace in the days since Jane's death and this anthem to honour her sister had become an obsession.

Somewhere in the house, a door crashed. Everyone looked up.

'Just the wind,' Thamsine said.

From the corridor beyond the door, she heard heavy footsteps and the door opened. Thamsine looked, ready to berate Stebbings for not knocking.

'What a pleasant family scene.'

The blood froze in her veins at the sight of Ambrose Morton standing in the doorway in the act of removing his gloves.

Roger's book fell to the ground, and the two girls looked up with curiosity on their faces as they turned to look at the stranger.

"Brose!' Annie gave a cry of delight and hurled herself at her brother.

'Hello, Annie,' Ambrose kissed his sister before disengaging her arms. He took a few paces into the room. 'Thamsine, my dear. Black is not your colour.'

'If you came for Annie – ' Thamsine began but was interrupted by Roger's hysterical voice as the man rose to his feet.

'I told you! I warned you!' Roger pointed a finger at Morton.

Morton glanced at the man, who stood wringing his hands. 'Sit down, Knott.' He turned back to Thamsine. 'I've not come for my sister. Just a neighbourly call to see how you are faring in your sad widowhood.'

Roger subsided onto his seat and Ambrose wandered over to the girls. Rachel slipped her hand into her sister's as he smiled at them and patted Rachel on the head.

'These must be your daughters, Knott.'

Roger gave a strangled response and Ambrose turned his attention to Thamsine.

Thamsine raised her chin and looked him squarely in the eye.

'I let Annie stay because she was plainly being neglected at Beverstock,' she said. 'I would have thought as she is your only responsibility ... '

'Don't presume to lecture me on my responsibilities, Mistress Lovell.' The name spat from his mouth while his eyes blazed with hatred. 'News must travel slowly in this part of the country. The creditors have taken Beverstock. Annie has no home.' Morton shrugged and his face softened as he looked at his sister. 'But I suppose I should thank you for the care of her. She is looking well.'

'Annie is not responsible for your actions, Ambrose.'

Annie looked from one to the other, aware she was being discussed.

'I haven't forgotten she helped you escape. That was wrong, Annie.'

He glared at his sister and Annie shrank from his fierce, angry eyes, sensing but not understanding her brother's displeasure with her.

Thamsine swallowed, fighting to keep control of her voice. She could not let him see how her heart hammered beneath her bodice and her knees felt as if they had turned to water.

'If you've not come for Annie, then why are you here, Ambrose?'

Ambrose reached out and curled a lock of Thamsine's hair in his finger.

'That is an excellent question.'

'He's here to claim what is rightfully his.'

A woman's voice came from the doorway and Lucy stepped into the room. Kit's Mistress Mouse looked pale, travel-stained and weary, a far cry from the bright-eyed creature who had sold Thamsine into the hands of this man.

Ambrose glanced at his mistress. 'London has become a little ... uncomfortable, hasn't it, dearest?'

'What do you mean?' Thamsine demanded.

Ambrose sighed, 'Too many debts, too many memories. Time for a new start, in a new place.'

'What do you want, Morton?' Roger rose to his feet again, his voice strong.

'Oh, it's quite simple. I need money to finance my life in

France. In short, Thamsine my dear, I want anything of value in this house.'

Thamsine straightened, almost faint with relief. If all he wanted was money, he could take the pictures from the wall.

'You're surprised? Did you think I still wanted you?' He stroked her face. 'No, you're soiled goods now. Why would I want you after Lovell has swived you? Pity he's dead. I would have taken great pleasure in killing him myself. But you make a desirable widow, Thamsine. Mourning becomes you.'

He stepped away from her and removed two pistols from his belt. These he laid on the table before turning back and looking around the room with a genial smile on his face. He sat down on a chair and crossed his legs.

'I think some refreshments are in order before we discuss the contents of your strongbox. It has been a long, tedious journey, made more so by my companion's delicate condition.' Thamsine stared across his head at Lucy, who averted her eyes.

'You're with child?' Thamsine's barely aspirated words hung in the air. 'You told me you could not conceive.'

'Apparently the doctors were wrong. I have conceived.' She threw aside her cloak, revealing a high-waisted gown below which the swell of her stomach was visible. 'I am told the child will be born about Christmas,' she said, lowering herself into a chair with a sigh.

Thamsine did a quick mental calculation. The child must have been conceived in late February or early March when Kit was still with Lucy Talbot.

Oh, Kit, she thought, is there no justice in the world? *How could you leave this woman with child and not me?*

Ambrose appeared to ignore the tension between the two women as he looked around the pleasant room.

'And to think this was so nearly mine,' he said.

His eyes came to rest on Thamsine as Annie crept up next to him and put her hand on his knee.

"Brose?' she said.

With his eyes still fixed on Thamsine, he raised his right hand and hit out at Annie, a brutal blow that flung her several feet.

The two girls shrieked and Rebecca ran to Annie's side.

'You hurt her!' she cried.

'She may be my sister but she betrayed me in the worst way possible. Stop your snivelling, Annie, or I will hit you again.'

In one swift movement, he rose to his feet and grabbed Rebecca's arm, pulling her away from the sobbing woman-child.

Roger Knott stood up and took a step towards him. 'Let her go!'

Morton ignored him. He took Rebecca's chin in his fingers and forced her face upwards.

'How old are you, child?'

'Fourteen ... ' Rebecca's voice faltered.

Thamsine's blood ran cold. She recognised the hooded, wolfish look in Morton's eyes. She had seen it before. Roger gave a strangled cry and took a step towards Ambrose, but without even looking at him, Morton picked up one of the pistols and put it to Rachel's head. 'Sit down, Knott,' he snarled.

'Let her go, Ambrose.' Lucy sounded bored. 'She's far too young.'

'I like them young,' Morton said, but he released the frightened girl, who ran to her father, burying her head in his jacket.

Roger put a protective arm around both his girls, drawing them close.

'What have you done with the servants?' Thamsine asked.

'I've locked them up.'

Ambrose toyed with the pistol he held with one hand, while with the other he produced two keys. He placed them on the table beside the other pistol and looked at his mistress. Lucy struggled to her feet.

'Thamsine, go with Lucy and fetch the contents of your strongbox.'

Thamsine stood her ground. 'I'll not leave this room until I have your word that you will not harm anyone in it.'

Ambrose waved the pistol and gave her a pained look. 'I told you, I've no intention of harming anyone. I just want your money.'

He handed Lucy the second pistol. 'Here, dearest take this.'

'Do you even know how to use it?' Thamsine asked as Lucy stood aside to let her out of the room.

The pistol looked ridiculously large in Lucy's hands, and it took her both hands to hold it steady. The muzzle wavered and Thamsine considered herself at far more risk of an accidental discharge than a deliberate act.

'The coin,' Lucy said.

Thamsine led her into the study and lifted the strongbox out from its hiding place beneath the bricks of the fireplace, opening it with the key she carried at her waist. The month's rent money and the money from the harvest, maybe eighty pounds in all, were worth the price of her freedom. Lucy took the bags and weighed them in her hand.

'Is this all?' Her eyes glittered greedily.

'Yes, that's everything.'

'What about jewellery, silver?'

'There's no silver. It all went to the King's cause, as did the jewellery,' Thamsine said. 'I am not as rich as Ambrose supposes.'

Lucy regarded her with cold, narrowed eyes. 'Why do you suppose Kit Lovell married you? Don't delude yourself it was for love. He sought wealth.'

Thamsine smiled. 'The reasons Kit married me are long and

complicated, Lucy, and I have no intention of sharing them with you.'

Lucy's lower lip trembled. 'You know he would have been a Viscount. I would have had his title.'

'Instead, you have ended up penniless and pregnant and beholden to a man who I know is a monster. There is a just God after all.'

The pistol shook. 'You don't understand, Thamsine. Ambrose and I ... '

' ... are birds of a feather, Lucy. Kit would never have married you and you know it.'

Tears welled in Lucy's eyes and she took one hand off the pistol to dash them away. It occurred to Thamsine at that moment that Lucy may actually have loved Kit, but she could find no pity in her heart for this woman who had betrayed her to Ambrose Morton and stood by while he had beaten and crippled Kit. No, Lucy had got the reward she so richly deserved.

'Just take the coin and go,' Thamsine said. 'I want you both gone from my house.'

Lucy yawned. 'I'm tired, Thamsine. Pregnancy does that, but then I suppose you wouldn't know.'

The smugness in her tone and the way her hand rested on the swell of her stomach made Thamsine turn away. The thought of this woman giving birth to Kit's child sickened her.

Lucy jerked the heavy pistol. 'Pick up the coin.'

Thamsine complied and they returned to the parlour. No one appeared to have moved. Roger sat with his arms around his two terrified children. Annie huddled at his feet, her thin arms wrapped around her knees, rocking herself and mumbling. Ambrose sprawled in his chair, the pistol in his hand.

Thamsine set the money bags down beside him. 'That's all I have. Take it and get out.'

Ambrose glanced at the windows, where a heavy squall lashed against the glass.

'You seem anxious to be rid of us, Thamsine. As it is, you may have noticed the weather outside is vile. I have no intention of going anywhere tonight. The coach horses will take us no further and you are forgetting your skills as a hostess. I want food. Lucy?'

Ambrose tossed Lucy one of the keys. 'Go and find the cook and get him to make some food.'

Lucy glanced at a chair. 'Ambrose, I'm exhausted. I want to rest … '

'You'll get rest, I promise,' he said. 'Food first.'

With the sigh of a pregnant woman, Lucy lifted the heavy pistol again and left the room. Ambrose turned the pistol he held on Thamsine.

'Play for me, Thamsine, like you used to.'

'I hardly think … ' Thamsine began but saw his fingers tighten on the pistol. 'Very well. Anything in particular?'

'Something cheerful, I think,' he replied. 'And you … ' The pistol turned on Rebecca. ' … you can dance for me.'

'No.' Roger's arm tightened on his daughter.

'I don't know how to dance.' Rebecca said in a small voice.

'Oh yes, of course. Puritans. Annie will show you, won't you, Annie?'

Annie looked up, hope shining in her eyes. ''Brose?'

'Dance for me, Annie. You remember how you used to dance?'

She nodded and stood up, straightening her skirts. Thamsine began to play a little country jig and Annie responded, moving in her own unintelligible way to the music.

'Dance with your friend, Annie.' Morton indicated Rebecca and Annie took the girl's hands, leading her in a hopping dance that took them around the room.

Morton laughed. It sounded almost an avuncular, jovial laugh as if he genuinely enjoyed watching his sister.

The dancing continued until Lucy, labouring under a tray loaded with dishes, entered through the door. She set the tray down on the table and placed a bowl of soup and a plate of cold mutton before Morton.

'Annie, sit down there, where I can see you.' Morton gestured at a chair.

Annie obeyed and Rebecca returned to her father's side. Thamsine stopped playing.

'Oh, you can keep playing, Thamsine. Something sad and wistful, I think. Let us remember poor Lovell, dancing at the end of a rope. I wonder how long he took to die?' Morton laughed and picked up the soup bowl.

Morton ate as Thamsine played, trying to think of anything except Kit dying at the end of a rope but the tears fell unbidden onto her hands.

As Lucy picked at the food. The woman seemed so far removed from the bright creature who had captivated Kit. She wondered if she had come willingly with Morton, or had circumstance forced her hand?

Ambrose pushed the dishes to one side and belched. 'Come, Lucy, eat up.'

'I'm not hungry, Ambrose,' she said. 'I just want to rest.'

'Well, don't let me stop you,' he said. 'There are ample beds upstairs, or you can lay on that settle.' He indicated a large oak settle that stood against the wall. Lucy pushed aside her chair, gathered some cushions, and lay down on the settle.

Rachel had fallen asleep, her head on her father's lap. Roger's eyes were closed, his lips moving in prayer. Rebecca and Annie sat hand in hand, watching Morton as Thamsine did, waiting for his next move, his next words.

Morton picked up the jug that Lucy had brought with the tray of food and thrust it at Annie. 'Annie, go to the kitchen and find me more ale.'

Annie didn't move.

His voice rose. 'Annie!' She jumped to her feet and took the jug from him. 'More ale!'

Her lips moved and her unhappy eyes darted from Ambrose to Thamsine.

Thamsine stopped playing and tried to give the girl an encouraging smile. 'Do what he says, Annie.'

Annie's mouth twisted in a trusting smile. 'Ale,' she said. 'I'll get ale.' Repeating the word to herself, she left the room.

'Keep playing,' Morton ordered.

Thamsine looked up at him. 'My fingers are tired, Ambrose.'

He shrugged. 'Then rest them. You ... ' He indicated Rebecca. 'Come here.'

Roger's eyes flashed open and he put an arm around his daughter. Rebecca didn't move.

Morton's tongue flicked at the corners of his lips.

'Come here, girl.' The pistol pointed at the girl.

Rebecca rose to her feet and walked slowly towards him. She stood just out of his reach, her eyes large and fearful.

'Take that ridiculous cap off,' Ambrose said.

Thamsine rose to her feet.

'What are you doing, Ambrose?'

Ambrose ignored her. 'Take that cap off!'

The girl complied.

'Now the pins.'

With shaking hands, Rebecca loosed her hair, letting it fall in a shining wave nearly to her waist.

'That's better,' Ambrose said. 'Now the collar.'

'Father ... ' Rebecca turned to her father.

'Morton. That's enough. Let her go.' Roger had risen to his feet, his face ashen.

Morton laughed and raised the pistol to point at Rebecca's head. His meaning was clear; if Roger moved, Rebecca died. Roger stared at his daughter with large, stricken eyes.

'Father?' Rebecca's voice trembled and her eyes filled with tears.

'You unspeakable animal,' Thamsine said. 'Let her go, she's only a child.'

Morton glanced at Thamsine. 'Jealous, my dear? Don't worry, your turn will come later. We have all night—now, if either of you lifts a finger, the girl dies. Which do you prefer? The collar.'

With shaking fingers, Rebecca started to undo the knot on her collar.

'Hurry up!' Ambrose jerked the pistol at the girl.

''Brose! No!'

The jug of ale Annie had carried from the kitchen crashed to the floor in the doorway. She cried out like a wild animal in pain and hurled herself at her brother. Ambrose jumped to his feet and turned to face her. The pistol discharged, its sound muffled by Annie's body as she fell on him.

CHAPTER 56

*K*it dismounted and walked his horse up the long drive to the house. The rain had soaked him to the skin, and he longed for a warm fire and a hot meal. He was too soon out of his sickbed to endure this sort of a soaking.

Jem's horse had lost a shoe and Kit, anxious to keep moving, had left him behind in Alton, a decision he now regretted. If Morton had gone to Hartley, it meant that he risked facing him alone again, and he had no confidence in his ability to survive another encounter with Ambrose Morton.

Kit's soldier's instincts prickled as the house came into view. Through the rain, the fine Elizabethan house seemed quiet. He crossed the front of the house, seeking out the stables where he could leave his horse. He found them with no difficulty and his heart skipped a beat at the sight of the rain-soaked, mud-spattered carriage that stood in the stable yard, no horses in the traces.

He led his horse across to the dark stables. Cursing, he groped around and found a lantern and tinder and struck a light. The carriage horses had been brought in but still wore their harness. They looked up and whinnied at him. He patted a soft nose.

'Where's your coachman?' he asked.

Kit filled a bucket it with oats and another with water for his horse and the two coach horses. The horses' ears twitched and their heads turned at the sound of a muffled noise emanating from behind a door at the end of the stables.

Kit crept down the length of the stables and leaned against the door.

'Who's there?' he called.

A barrage of voices met him.

'One at a time.'

'Unlock this door!'

Kit looked at the massive padlock. 'It's padlocked and there's no key.'

A stable yard expletive returned from the other side of the door.

'Tell me, what's happened here?'

A voice with a London accent spoke. 'I was hired to bring a lady and gentleman here from London. As soon as I get here, he puts a pistol to me head and orders me into the stables ... '

A local voice broke in. 'He then orders us all in here and bolts the door.'

'How long have you been there?'

There was a momentary silence. 'A couple of hours.'

'And the man's name?' Kit asked, although he already knew the answer.

'Morton.' The Londoner spat the name out. 'Are my horses all right?'

'They've been brought in. I've fed them but they need to be rubbed down.'

This time, the expletive came from the gutters of London.

'Listen, Mister, is there naught you can do with the lock?' The local man spoke.

He looked at the lock again. He could try shooting it out, but he didn't want to risk the shot being heard. They would just have to wait.

'Not at the moment. You'll just have to sit on your hands for a while longer. I'll be back.'

'Don't be too long.'

'I'll be as long as it takes,' Kit replied.

He wasted a couple of minutes removing the harnesses from the two coach horses and gave all three horses a quick rubdown, while he considered his next move. Morton and Lucy were in the house, and he had no doubt Thamsine and her family were in the gravest peril. The thought of being on the wrong end of Morton's sword with only the use of his left hand made him break out in a cold sweat. Kit had never thought of himself as a coward but he had to admit he was terrified.

Gathering his courage, he left the stables and slipped around the house in the direction of the kitchens. A light shone from a window and he could see a woman moving around. A pretty girl with dark hair. Her clothes indicated she was not a servant. She carried a jug, which she set down on the table. As he watched she wandered aimlessly around as if looking for something. He saw no sign of any of the house servants.

Kit looked at the kitchen door. While he had the benefit of surprise, he didn't know the layout of the house and he didn't want to ruin it by blundering through. He decided it would be better to scout around the outside of the house and try and determine which room they were in.

Every nerve strained to breaking point, he pulled the pistol from his belt and balanced it in his left hand, hoping that he wouldn't have to use it. The powder was damp and he had less confidence in his ability to fire a pistol left-handed than he did in his left-handed swordsmanship.

He crossed the kitchen garden and passed through a gate in the wall, onto a well-groomed bowling green. The contrast with the ravaged gardens of his own home jarred. Even in the dark and the rain, he could see the front of the house faced down a pretty valley; the gardens well laid out and tended. Between the house and the garden was a wide paved terrace stopped only by a low wall that afforded him some cover from prying eyes.

Only one window burned with light. A ground-floor room with a bay window. The gravelled terrace would ordinarily have made it difficult to get close but the rain muffled his footsteps. Kit followed the low wall to the darkened end of the house and swiftly crossed the terrace. With his back to the house, he crept along the wall until he reached the window. The bay afforded him a reasonable chance to look in without being seen.

His blood turned cold. Thamsine sat at the virginals, her hands still, her body poised and watchful. Roger Knott stood beside the fireplace, his face twisted in anguish. The centre of everyone's attention appeared to be a young girl who stood before Ambrose Morton.

Morton sprawled in a chair, a pistol balanced in his hand and aimed at the child. Even though the girl had her back to him, Kit could see the child's shoulders shaking with fear or tears or both.

He did not need to see anymore and he knew he could not afford to wait for Jem. As he turned away to find an entry to the house, he heard a crash of falling crockery.

He spun on his heel in time to see the dark-haired woman from the kitchen throw herself at Ambrose. He flinched at the sound of the pistol shot but did not wait to see more. He turned and ran back towards the kitchen door, flinging it open. A child's hysterical screams provided all the directions he needed.

Outside the door to the parlour, he paused, peering through the crack formed by the open door long enough to take stock of what was happening within the room.

He could see the girl who had been standing before Morton. She held a younger girl cradled her in her arms, hiding her face from the sight before them.

Morton had dropped to his knees beside the dark-haired woman, his face ashen. With surprising gentleness he turned her over, resting her head in his lap.

'Annie, oh God, Annie! I didn't mean … ' His voice broke and he looked up at Thamsine who stood behind him. 'She's still alive. Help her!'

Kit swallowed as he recognised the name. The woman Morton had shot had been his own sister.

Thamsine knelt on the other side of Annie Morton, her hands fluttering helplessly over the growing crimson stain on the girl's bodice. Kit could see blood-stained bubbles flecking Annie's lips.

'You fool! Now you add murder to the crimes already to your account?'

Kit started and took a step back into the gloom of the corridor as he recognised Lucy's voice. She must have been out of his line of sight.

Ambrose said, 'Not murder. Not Annie. I never … '

Kit took a deep breath and drew his sword. Throwing back the door he stepped into the room.

Morton looked up and his eyes widened, the colour draining from his face. Lucy followed his gaze and screamed.

Morton laid his sister down on the floor and rose to his feet, taking a step backward.

Kit kept his eyes on Morton, only sparing Thamsine a quick glance to reassure himself that she was unharmed. She stared at him open-mouthed. Mercifully, the child stopped screaming.

Absolute silence descended on the room.

'You're dead!' Morton's voice held a note of hysteria.

Kit's eyes met Morton's. He saw genuine fear in the handsome face and knew he had the advantage.

'Dead?' Kit shrugged and took another step into the room. 'I may be just an apparition ... or I may not be. Are you willing to find out?'

Kit balanced the pistol lightly in his hand, trying to give an impression of confidence he did not feel. 'I assure you, the ball in this pistol is real enough,' he said.

'As is the ball in this one,' a cool voice to his left said.

Kit grimaced. He had forgotten Lucy. He glanced at the large, heavy pistol she held pointed at him.

'Shoot, Lucy,' Morton said.

Kit's eyes met Lucy's and he knew in that instant that she wouldn't fire.

'This is between you and him,' she said, lowering the pistol.

Morton gave a strangled cry and Kit turned back to face him. Kit tightened his grip on the pistol butt and raised it, his finger resting on the trigger. He pulled the hammer back and fired. Nothing happened. The powder was damp. He threw the useless pistol to one side and reached for his sword.

Morton seized the advantage.

'You really do have a death wish, don't you, Lovell?'

Ambrose's own weapon hissed from the scabbard. He balanced it lightly in his hand.

'This will be interesting. You were a good swordsman, Lovell, so I hear. But I'm better and left-handed you'll be no match for me.'

Kit hardly heard his words, only saw the red flashes of anger before his eyes. He did not need reminding of the reason he now fought with his left hand. He forced his breathing to slow. *Never,*

never fight in rage, his sword master had told him. The same sword master who had taught him to fight with his left hand.

Kit stepped forward. The two swords engaged with the barest ring of metal. Kit, calm now, met his opponent's eyes and they circled, gaining each other's measure. Morton gave first with a lightning attack. Kit countered with a stop thrust, his blade grazing the sleeve of Morton's jacket.

Morton stepped out of reach and regarded Kit with a new wariness in his eyes. He had underestimated his opponent and Kit took advantage of Morton's uncertainty, striking on the pass. This time his blade seared through Ambrose's sleeve, drawing blood. Ambrose hissed and responded with a furious forward attack, forcing Kit back against the table. Kit parried and riposted, thrusting Ambrose away from him and allowing him to slide out from underneath his opponent's sword.

Ambrose moved in again, forcing Kit onto his back foot. Backward and forward they moved across the room, their swords making sparks in the dim light. Ironically, the fact Kit fought left-handed was to his advantage. A right-hander faced with a left-handed opponent would take time to get the measure of his opponent and Kit could see the beads of perspiration on Morton's brow.

They knew each other's physical weaknesses. Kit had a bad leg, had been weakened by illness and hampered by having to use his left hand. Morton had the advantage of height, reach and fitness but the injury to his left ankle, the legacy of his encounter with Jem, obviously troubled him, so Kit did what he could to force Morton onto that foot.

Back and forth they moved across the room. Sheer determination and a burning desire to kill this man pushed Kit on against an opponent who seemed to be tiring. Sweat sheened Morton's forehead and his lips parted as he tried to draw in breath. Morton drew back before renewing his attack, his mouth set in a line of cruel determination. He feinted, drawing Kit's sword out of line and then closed in with a *redoublement*. Kit realised he had been trapped and stepped out of reach but, with a wall to his back, he had nowhere to go.

With a flick of his sword, Morton twisted Kit's sword from his hand, the point of his sword resting neatly at the base of Kit's throat.

'You surprise me, Lovell,' he said. 'You're a far better swordsman than I gave you credit for.'

As Kit's exhausted mind tried to formulate a plan to extricate himself, Morton's sword wavered and his face contorted in pain.

Kit seized the moment and slipped out from beneath the blade. He scrambled for his sword. As he straightened, prepared to meet Morton again, the other man staggered backward, his sword falling to the floor with a clatter. With a cry, he fell to the floor, doubled over and vomiting.

The youngest girl started to scream again. Lucy stepped forward and stood beside Kit. She looked down into Morton's pain-wracked eyes.

'It's a horrible death,' she said.

Kit stared at the woman. He had never seen such utter calm before.

'What have you done?'

Lucy smiled down at Morton. 'Monkshood. I keep a small supply with me, just waiting for the right occasion. I simply added it to the soup. I don't advise anyone else to drink it.'

The realisation that Lucy had poisoned him flickered across Morton's face.

'Bitch! Why?' He spat saliva and vomit as he spoke.

'You don't deserve to live,' Lucy said. 'You're a monster.' She laid a hand on her belly and looked down at where Thamsine still knelt with Annie Morton's head in her lap. 'This is his child, but no child deserves a father like Ambrose Morton.' She looked at Thamsine. 'Did you think that Lovell was the father? Kit was long gone before this one was conceived. It was fun watching your face though when you thought it was his.'

Kit couldn't bring himself to look at Thamsine ... not yet.

Morton turned desperate eyes to Kit.

'Kill me,' he said. 'Better to die at the end of your sword than this ... ' He doubled up, screaming in agony again.

Lucy placed a hand on Kit's sword arm.

'Don't kill him, Kit. I want to stand here and watch him suffer for every act of depravation, degradation and murder he has committed.'

Kit glanced at Roger.

'Take the children out of here.'

Roger nodded. Carrying his youngest daughter, and with an arm around the older girl's shoulders, he left the room.

Kit shook off Lucy's hand and stepped forward. He stood for a moment looking down at his adversary. Whatever his feelings for Ambrose Morton, it gave him no pleasure to watch this man writhing on the floor in vomit and faeces. He raised his sword and drove it down into Ambrose's throat. The blood spurted high into the air. Ambrose gurgled and lay still.

Overcoming rising nausea, Kit crouched down and closed the desperate, agonised eyes.

He looked up at the sound of boots in the hallway and Jem burst into the room, a pistol brandished in each hand.

Jem looked down at Morton's body and swore. 'There'll be none to mourn him, I wager, just that baggage – ' He waved a pistol in Lucy's direction.

Kit rose wearily to his feet. 'I have a job for you, Jem. Take that baggage to the nearest port and see she boards a boat.'

'Now?' Jem asked uncertainly.

'Now! I want her out of this house.'

Lucy smiled. She walked over to Kit and laid a hand on his cheek.

'Goodbye, Lovell. We had some fun, which I will always remember fondly.'

'The coin, Lucy,' Kit said.

Her eyes flashed momentarily but she saw no quarter in Kit's face. She turned and dropped the coin bags on the table and swept from the room like a queen.

'Kit?'

At the sound of Thamsine's voice, Kit turned, at last, to look at her. For a moment a hundred unvoiced questions and answers flowed between them. There would be time for that later. He walked over to her and looked down at the girl.

'This is his sister?'

Thamsine nodded. 'There's no hope, is there?' she asked.

Kit looked at Annie's grey face and blood-flecked lips. He watched the shallow rise and fall of her chest and shook his head.

'It's only a matter of time. All we can do is make her comfortable.'

He stooped down and picked Annie up. She moaned. 'It's all right, Annie,' he whispered. 'There will be no more pain soon.'

Thamsine rose to her feet, wiping her blood-stained hands on the black skirt. 'What about Ambrose?'

Kit gave the body a cursory glance. 'The living are more important than the dead,' he replied.

CHAPTER 57

*K*it laid Annie on the bed with the tenderness of a father for his child. He stroked the dark hair away from the girl's forehead and looked down at Morton's sister. Annie was unconscious at last, her face peaceful.

He looked up at Thamsine. 'He loved her, didn't he?'

She nodded. 'She was the only person who loved him completely and unconditionally. His mother saw him only as a means to her ends. She was a hateful woman.' Thamsine shuddered at the memory of Isabelle Morton's sharp, dissatisfied face.

'Aunt, can I come in?' Rebecca appeared at the door.

Thamsine turned to look at her niece. 'Rebecca, you should be in bed.'

'Rachel's asleep but I couldn't … ' Rebecca crossed to the bed and picked up Annie's hand. 'She's dying, isn't she?'

Thamsine nodded.

'She saved my life. I want to stay with her.'

Thamsine drew the girl to her side and slipped an arm around her shoulder.

'If you wish, dearest,' she said.

Kit straightened. 'I think I should find Knott and see to freeing the servants, and ... ' A shadow crossed his face. ' ... deal with other matters.'

Thamsine nodded. After fetching a cloth and a bowl of water, she sat down beside Annie to watch and wait for death to claim her.

It would not be much longer. The girl's breath rattled in her throat. Thamsine hoped she no longer felt pain. On the other side of the bed, Rebecca sat with her fingers locked around Annie's hand, her face twisted in grief. The two of them sat into the dark, wet night, unspeaking, keeping the vigil of death.

At some point, a shadow crossed the doorway and Thamsine looked up. Kit leaned against the door frame watching them. He did not enter the room or speak. In the dark, Thamsine could not see his face but she felt his energy as a palpable force, his love reaching across the dark void.

'Do you want me to stay?' he asked.

She shook her head. 'No. You must be exhausted. You will find my bedchamber at the end of this corridor.'

She listened to his boots echoing on the floorboards, heard the sound of a door shutting and shivered as silence descended on the room again.

Annie gurgled and a river of bright blood ran from the corner of her mouth. Rebecca's hand tightened as Annie's eyes opened and she gave one last, gulping breath and lay still. Thamsine wiped the blood away and stood up, closing Annie's eyes.

Rebecca laid her head on the bedcovers and began to sob. Thamsine walked around the bed and put her arms around the child's shoulders.

'She died loved, Rebecca. Come, dearest, there is nothing more we can do here and I think we both need our beds.'

She raised Rebecca to her feet and walked her to the bedchamber she shared with her sister. Rachel was already asleep, her face still stained with tears but peaceful. Thamsine helped Rebecca undress and tucked her into the bed.

'Aunt Thamsine,' Rebecca said, 'I am scared. Will that woman come back?'

Thamsine shook her head. 'No, she's gone. We're quite safe now.' She bent and kissed the girl. 'Try to sleep.'

Rebecca nodded and curled up next to her sister.

The overwhelming silence of the house sat heavily on her shoulders as Thamsine trudged wearily to her bedchamber. Her door stood ajar, a candle burning low on the table. A trail of clothing marked Kit's progress from the door to the bed, where he lay sprawled across the covers, still half-dressed and sound asleep.

Thamsine poured water into the washbowl and scrubbed at the blood and the memory of the night's terror. She stripped to her shift and looked down at the sleeping man.

'Kit?' She shook his shoulder.

He opened one eye and gave a sleepy smile. Despite her exhaustion, she felt a warm glow in the pit of her stomach.

'You can sleep in the bed or on the floor,' she said, 'but not on top of the bed.'

'In the bed sounds good.'

He pulled himself up and divested himself of the remainder of his clothes before sliding under the covers next to Thamsine.

The rain continued to lash at the windows as Thamsine curled up against her husband. She ran a hand through the soft hairs on his chest still not quite believing that he lived.

'You keep doing that and I'll forget how tired I am,' he murmured sleepily.

'You can't even begin to imagine what I ... how...?'

He laid a finger across her lips. 'Please, Tham, there will be time enough for questions in the morning. Now, stop talking and either go to sleep or kiss me.'

She wrapped her arms tightly around his neck, locking him to her. As their lips touched, the weeks of unspent grief and loneliness poured out of her. He held her close, kissing her hair, letting the tears subside before he turned her face towards him and they kissed again. Kit drew her toward him, and she fell asleep with her head in the curve of his shoulder.

CHAPTER 58

*R*ain still splattered against the windows in the light of a grey dawn. Thamsine woke with a start from a blood-stained nightmare and lay disoriented, trying to still her racing heart and remember the identity of the person in the bed beside her.

As memory returned she turned to look down at her sleeping husband. His unshaven face lay turned towards her on the bolsters. Even in the murky light, she could make out every feature. He seemed thinner, his eyes sunken. And if she had any doubts about what he had endured, the dark stain that still marred his neck told its own story. It had been true. They had hanged him. For a moment she thought she would be sick at the thought of the terror he must have faced.

With shaking fingers she touched the marks, letting her fingers brush the curve of his jaw. One eye opened and a slow smile twitched the corners of his mouth.

'What are you doing?' he asked.

'Just seeing that you were real and not some avenging spirit ...' she said.

For a moment he didn't move, just looked at her as she stroked his cheek and traced the curve of his mouth and the length of his nose.

'I assure you I am quite real,' he said, clasping her wrist and rolling himself onto his back, pulling her with him.

She kissed his nose, her lips travelling down his unshaven face, the bruised neck, down his hard, lean body.

'Tham ... ' he murmured, but she silenced him with a kiss.

There was no urgency in the passion of the morning. No grief, regrets or pain to expunge. Just a love rediscovered and renewed.

As the house began to stir behind the closed door, Thamsine lay curled in his arms.

'What are you thinking?' she asked.

'I was thinking that it was probably time we got up. Some matters need urgent attention this morning.'

Such as two corpses to give proper burials, Thamsine thought. She raised her eyes and touched the bruising on his neck.

'Are you going to tell me what happened?'

He swallowed.

'Thurloe kept his word but not until he had me on the gallows,' he said. 'They tell me if he had left it another minute I would have been dead.' He took a shuddering breath and she held him closer. 'It's over now, Tham. As far as the Commonwealth of England is concerned, Christopher Lovell is dead.'

She looked away, fighting back the tears. 'Too cruel,' she said. 'It's been four weeks. Why didn't you send me word?'

He stroked her hair. 'You don't die at the end of a noose and then expect everything to be as it was. I needed time to recover, and by the time I could function again, I had convinced myself that you were better off without me.'

She pushed him away and sat bolt upright, her eyes blazing.

'How could you think that? If you knew for a moment what I have endured these last weeks, thinking you were dead!'

'I'm sorry, Thamsine.'

'Sorry?' Her voice cracked. 'Sorry?'

Anger and grief spilled out of her. She beat her fists against his chest, the tears spilling down her cheeks. He grasped her forearms, stilling her and bringing her down to rest on his chest with his arms around her. All the sorrow she had borne over his death and her sister's death poured out of her as he let her weep. Spent by emotion, she drifted into an exhausted sleep.

When she awoke, she was by herself in the bed. Kit stood half-dressed beside the window, looking out over the garden.

'Kit?'

He sat down on the side of the bed and touched her face with the crooked fingers of his right hand.

'That day, that last day ... ' he began, ' ... I watched you walking away, knowing I would never see you again.' He pulled her towards him, folding her tightly in his arms. 'Thamsine, I'm never going to let you walk away again.'

She lightly kissed the broken fingers, studying his face, noting the grey shadows under his eyes, the lines of strain at the corner of his mouth, and the red flecks that stained the whites of his eyes.

'Oh, Kit. What did they do to you? Your eyes!'

He pulled a face. 'I'm sorry. I know I'm not a pretty sight.'

She put her hands on either side of his face, drinking in the love in his eyes like a shipwrecked sailor who has found land.

'The last six months have been hard. But you're alive. That is all that matters.' She let her hands drop. 'What do we do now? If Kit Lovell is dead, who are you?'

He shook his head. 'I don't know. I suppose I need to find a new name and try to untangle this knot that is my life.' Kit sighed and drew her towards him. 'When I was in the Tower, I dreamed of a peaceful life together, Thamsine.'

'There is plenty of time for a peaceful life," Thamsine said. 'I don't think you and I would settle well to such a life. Not yet awhile.'

He tilted her face upwards and smiled at her.

'Ah, Mistress Granville. There's a spirit in you that I loved from the first moment I saw you. You will have my undivided attention soon, I promise.'

She smiled. 'Don't make promises you can't keep, Kit Lovell.'

CHAPTER 59

*I*n the warmth of an autumn sun, Kit lay with his head in Thamsine's lap in the shade of one of the oaks in the park. She ran her fingers through the thick dark hair, now liberally peppered with grey that had not been there three months previously.

It had taken time for the physical evidence of Kit's brush with death to fade, but the dreadful invalid's pallor had gone, his eyes had returned to their normal colour, and only the faintest shadow of bruising still circled his neck. This he hid beneath a high neckcloth. The only physical legacy of the gallows seemed to be a change to the timbre in his voice. It now held a slight crackling edge to it. While the physical wounds had healed, she doubted anything could heal the terrible nightmares that caused him to wake in the night.

In the days following the final encounter with Ambrose Morton, they had seen that Morton and his sister laid to rest with their mother in the graveyard at Beverstock. Roger Knott had returned to London, leaving his daughters at Hartley, and something approaching a semblance of family life had settled over the house. In moments like this, it seemed almost possible to forget the dark days of their previous existence.

They had talked about what they should do, how they could exist in an England that no longer wanted them. The decision, when it came to be made, had seemed so simple. After a lifetime of adventuring, Kit no longer felt the lure of France or the Colonies. The lovely Elizabethan house, tucked away in the peaceful Hampshire countryside, offered them both the solace and healing they needed, so they had decided they would stay where they were, sufficiently distant from London to cause Thurloe no heartache.

Thamsine's nieces had settled into life with their unusual aunt and uncle, and Thamsine had engaged a proper tutor for them. When he thought she wasn't watching, Kit delighted in teaching them card games and tricks. Thamsine had asked Kit about his family in Cheshire but he refused to discuss them, saying he was not ready to face his stepmother, not yet, not until he had news of Daniel.

Thamsine bent over and kissed Kit's forehead. His eyes flickered open.

'What are you thinking?' he murmured.

'I was thinking that this is how it should always be,' she said, and straightened at the sound of raised voices coming from the direction of the house. 'Although I suspect we are about to be disturbed.'

'Come back, sir!'

At the sound of Stebbings' voice, Kit stretched and sat up.

Stebbings, who never hurried about anything, hastened across the lawn towards him in pursuit of a large, burly figure; a familiar figure with a badly tied scarf over his right eye.

'Master Lovell, I'm sorry. I couldn't stop him!' Stebbings panted to a halt behind Jem Marsh.

'Jem!' Kit jumped to his feet to face his old friend, seizing him by the hand.

Jem looked him up and down and nodded. 'Country life seems to suit you.'

Thamsine rose to her feet, shaking out her skirts. 'It is good to see you, Jem. How are the girls?'

'May's gone and married that carter,' Jem said. 'We miss her in the taproom.'

'I must send her a gift,' Thamsine said. 'And Nan?'

In answer, Jem rolled his eyes.

'What brings you here?' Kit asked.

'I've a letter for ye.' Jem fished in his jacket, produced a crumpled paper and handed it to Kit.

Kit turned the paper over and his lips tightened.

'Thurloe,' he said in a low voice.

'Perhaps it is news of Daniel's arrival,' she said, hopefully, but a premonition of dread ran down Thamsine's spine. Thurloe would not write unless he had very good reason.

'You must be tired after your journey, Jem. Stebbings, make sure Master Marsh has some food and drink and is shown to the guest bedchamber. We will come up to the house shortly.'

Jem nodded, his eyes resting on Kit's bent head.

'A strong ale won't go astray,' Jem said and set off back towards the house with Stebbings panting after him.

Kit handed Thamsine the letter. 'I can't open it,' he said.

She took the letter and broke the seal. Another packet fell out onto the ground. Thamsine retrieved it and turned the paper she held in her hand over. Thurloe himself had written nothing, so whatever news he wished to convey would be contained in the enclosure.

She took a deep breath and unfolded the missive, scanning the unfamiliar handwriting. A cry escaped her lips and she looked up at her husband, unable to contain the tears that started in her eyes.

'Daniel?' he asked through tight lips.

She nodded and handed him the paper.

He read the short missive aloud.

My Lord Thurloe,

Further to your enquiry regarding the prisoner Daniel Lovell, sent here as a traitor to the Commonwealth of England, I am reliably informed that he was indentured to one Jeremiah Pritchard of King's County. It is my sad duty to advise that the said prisoner died of the fever common to these parts in February of this year of our Lord. If I can be of any further service, Yr obedient servant Willoughby

Daniel took a step back, doubling up as if someone had hit him in the stomach, all the colour draining from his face.

'Kit ... ' Thamsine took a step towards him but he shook his head, sinking down with his back to the tree. The paper fell unregarded to the ground.

'No! I don't believe it,' he said. 'No, no, no ... it can't be true.'

Thamsine picked up the fallen paper.

'Kit, the Governor of Barbados himself says he is dead. He could just as easily have died of a fever safe in his own bed in England.'

'No!' Kit muffled the animal howl of pain in his hands. 'He can't be dead. It can't all have been for nothing.' He looked up at her. 'Every despicable act of betrayal I justified to myself with the thought it brought an innocent boy closer to his freedom. Now, all those deaths, those ghosts ... they haunt me, Tham. They will haunt me until the day I die and now, Daniel ... ' His face crumpled in despair. 'God help me, I should have died on that scaffold.'

Thamsine dropped to the ground in front of him and clasped

his hands between hers.

'I would be dead if it were not for you, Kit Lovell. You saved my life. Don't ever forget that. Your life was spared for a reason, and you have the rest of your time on this Earth to make amends for the events of the past years, but for now, you have to let yourself grieve for Daniel. He chose to take up a sword and he was not a boy. He made the decision as an adult. He was not your responsibility. You didn't fail him on that day or any of the days that followed.'

Kit shook off her hands and rose to his feet. He paced the ground beneath the tree, his face working with a thousand conflicting emotions as he ran his fingers again and again through his hair.

'No,' he said stopping his frantic pacing. 'No. I won't believe it.' He glanced down at Thamsine. 'Not until I stand by his grave.'

Thamsine rose to her feet.

'You are not suggesting that you go to Barbados?'

'Thamsine, I have to satisfy myself, know how he passed these last years. You have to let me go.'

She took a step towards him, grasping his shirt by the laces. She shook her head. 'I am not letting you walk away from me again.'

'Thamsine, please.'

'If you go, I go too.'

'Don't be ridiculous.'

'I will not let you go alone. Kit, I have lost you once. Don't make me lose you again.'

She glared at him and he returned her angry stare with a slow inclination of his head. 'Very well. We will go together, but first there is something else I have to do.'

'What is that?'

Kit's lips tightened. 'I have to face his mother.'

CHAPTER 60

othing remained of Eveleigh Priory but the east wing. Nature had reclaimed the blackened ruins of the once-great house, built in the later years of Great Henry's reign on the ruins of one of his ransacked monasteries. Ivy trailed through the empty window recesses like worms through the eyes of a skull, and the dried early autumnal leaves rustled together in eddies and gathered at his horse's hooves.

Riding pillion behind him, Thamsine's fingers tightened in Kit's belt and he turned to look at her.

'I warned you,' he said.

'I'd not imagined that it would be quite so bad,' she replied.

Kit put his heels to the horse, urging it forward. An old woman paused in sweeping the front steps leading up to the door. Her eyes widened as she recognised him. Before he could greet Old Alice, she dropped the broom and ran inside.

'M'lady, m'lady!' Kit heard her voice echoing through the house. 'He's back! Back from the grave.'

As Kit dismounted, a woman in a rusty black dress appeared at the door, wiping her hands on an apron. She pushed back a tendril of greying hair that strayed from beneath her cap and squinted short-sightedly at the visitors.

Kit lifted Thamsine down from the pillion saddle and turned to face his stepmother. He swept his hat from his head and gave her a low bow.

'Madam,' he said.

Disappointment flooded her face.

'You! I thought ... ' she began.

He knew what she had thought. She had been expecting Daniel. He walked towards her and stood at the bottom of the steps looking up at her.

'Margaret ... ' he started to say but got no further.

She picked up the abandoned broom and began to hit him. Kit put up his hands to protect his head from the frenzied blows Margaret Lovell rained down on him.

'I told you never to darken my doorstep again!'

She pursued him down the stairs and forced him back against the wall of the house.

'Margaret, please ... let me explain.'

One of the blows hit the fingers of his right hand, jangling the nerves of the barely healed fingers. Kit swore volubly and slid down the wall, pressing his hand to his chest while trying to shield himself with his left hand.

'Mother!'

A young woman appeared in the doorway.

'Mother, stop! It's Kit.'

'I know who it is,' Margaret said but she ceased her attack, throwing the broom down on the steps.

Frances Lovell cast her mother a warning glance and ran down the steps. She knelt beside her brother.

'Are you all right?'

'Fine,' muttered Kit through tight lips.

Frances took his hand and gasped.

'Kit! Your hand, what happened?'

'Another time,' Kit said, pulling his hand back.

With what dignity he could muster, he rose to his feet, retrieved his hat from the mud, took a steadying breath and turned to face his sister and stepmother. Frances took a step towards him, a broad smile on her face.

'I can't believe it's you!' she said. 'We thought you were dead. It was in the broadsheets ... '

He smiled at her. 'It's a very long story, Fran.'

Kit looked up at his stepmother, who had retreated to the top of the stairs, her arms crossed, glaring down at him. Margaret Lovell had only been seventeen, a pretty, vivacious girl with an abundance of brown curls when she had married Kit's father. The eight-year-old Kit, newly brought back from France and thrust into a house of strangers speaking a strange language, had worshipped her.

Now, the years of war and the loss of her son had dealt ill with her. What he could see of her hair seemed to be almost entirely grey, her face thin and lined. Looking at her, the weight of responsibility for her troubles settled back on his shoulders where they rightly belonged.

'Margaret, I don't know where to begin,' he said.

'I want my son back,' she responded, but all the anger had gone from her voice.

'Oh, Mother,' Frances sounded impatient, 'I'm so tired of this. You cannot hold Kit responsible forever.'

'I can and I do.'

'Well, I'm tired of blaming Kit for this family's ills!' Frances continued. 'He's my brother as much as Daniel, and I, for one, am glad to see him.' She fell into his arms. 'I truly am glad to see you,

Kit.'

He held her close, marvelling at how the enchanting child could have grown into such a sensible young woman. A discreet cough reminded him that Thamsine stood watching this touching family reunion. He turned to her, noting the gleam of amusement in her eye. He held out his hand and she took it.

'My wife, Thamsine,' he said. 'Thamsine, my stepmother, Margaret Lovell, and my sister, Frances.'

Both women stared at Thamsine and then back at Kit.

'You're married?' Frances exclaimed.

'Yes,' Kit said slowly. 'I did say she was my wife.'

Margaret sniffed and looked Thamsine up and down, taking in the elegant green gown and curling chestnut locks.

'I suppose you know that my stepson is a disgrace to this family,' she said.

Thamsine smiled. 'I know all there is to know of your stepson, Mistress Lovell. Between us, I suspect he only married me for my money.'

She winked at her husband, who responded with a grin. Margaret stood to one side of the doorway and gestured for them to enter.

'Seeing as you're here, you may as well come in.'

Frances tucked her arm into Kit's.

'Take no notice of her, Kit! I, for one, am happy to see you.'

'How's Grandfather?' he asked.

She stopped and looked up at him.

'You don't know?'

A chill of premonition settled on Kit's shoulders. 'Know what?'

'He's dead. You're Lord Midhurst now.'

Kit took a deep, steadying breath.

'When?'

'Last winter,' she said. 'Lung fever.'

The old man was dead? So he had been Lord Midhurst for months and he'd never known. He wondered what Lucy would have thought if she'd known he was already a Viscount. An empty title if ever there was one. How could another dead man inherit a title?

In the old room that served as a parlour, Margaret turned to face him.

'I am sorry about Grandfather,' Kit said. 'And more sorry that I did not know. How have you managed all these months by yourselves?'

Margaret drew herself up. 'We've managed because we've had to. Frances and I have been abandoned. First, they send Daniel to some Godforsaken corner of the world and then your grandfather … and then the news you were dead.' She drew her daughter to her side. 'We knew nobody would be coming to our aid.'

Kit laid his hat down on the table. 'I'm sorry, Margaret.'

'Sorry?' Margaret glared at him. 'Don't think we weren't grateful for the money you sent, but we needed you, Kit.'

Her words lashed him and he flinched at the pain that they caused. He had deluded himself into believing that the few coins he sent were enough. But there was nothing he could have done, even if he had known of their situation.

'So why are you here now?' Margaret's steely gaze moved from Kit to Thamsine.

'First and foremost, to make my peace with you.'

Margaret gave a hollow laugh. 'You're a little late for that, Kit Lovell.'

Frances broke away from her mother's side and went to stand beside Kit, clutching his arm. 'No, he's not! Mother, I don't blame Kit for what happened to Daniel. Daniel went of his own free will and nothing you could have said or done would have stopped him. The good Lord knows how much I miss

Daniel but,' she glanced up at her brother, 'I have missed Kit too.'

Margaret shot her daughter a quelling glance and looked back at Kit. 'And?'

'And?' Kit looked at Thamsine and she nodded. 'Thamsine and I have come to offer you a home.'

Margaret straightened, her chin coming up in a familiar gesture of defiance. 'This is my home.'

Kit ran a hand through his hair. Margaret had always been a stubborn, infuriating woman, but he loved her as much as he had his own mother.

'Fine,' he said. 'You can stay here, Margaret, living in four rooms in a broken ruin, if that's what you want. Frances?'

Frances looked up at him.

'You have a home? Where?'

'In Hampshire,' Thamsine said. 'There's only Kit and me and my two nieces. There is a comfortable dower house and ample room.'

'You really did marry her for her money.' Frances shot a mischievous glance at her brother.

'Absolutely,' Kit agreed.

'You're not going, Frances,' her mother said. 'We're not going to live on this woman's charity.'

Kit drew a breath and laid a hand on the table with deliberate care, though he would have dearly loved to smash his hand onto the table in frustration.

'Margaret,' he said slowly. 'God knows, I want to call a truce, but you are making it very difficult. I am now the head of this family and I am not offering you charity. You are my responsibility and I am offering you a home, nothing more. If Frances wishes to come to Hartley, she may. In fact, I insist she does. You, however, are quite free to stay here. I will make suitable arrangements to ensure you live in a modicum of comfort. Will that suit you?'

Margaret looked from one to the other and her shoulders slumped. 'I can't stay here alone,' she said, in a voice that lost its defiance.

'That is your choice,' Kit said. 'Think on it. Now, there is a third reason I have come. I have news of Daniel.'

Margaret stiffened. 'Daniel?'

Kit took two crumpled and stained letters from his jacket.

'This letter,' he said, holding up the first sheet, 'is an order for Daniel's release and a pardon.'

Margaret sank into a chair and looked up at him. 'How ... ?' she began, but Kit raised his finger to silence her.

'It doesn't matter how,' he said. 'I had secured this paper, and we were about to take ship for Barbados to bring him home when circumstances intervened.'

He glanced at Thamsine, reliving, as he still did in his nightmares, those black days. She nodded encouragingly and he took a breath and continued.

'You said you'd seen reports of my death. Well, they're true. To England, Kit Lovell is dead. Thamsine and I would have left months ago, but ... ' He paused. 'My health meant a delay to our voyage.'

'What has your health to do with Daniel?' Margaret demanded.

Thamsine glared at the woman. 'You have no idea, do you?' she said. 'Kit bought Daniel's freedom with his life. Show them, Kit.'

Frances and Margaret watched as Kit unwound the carelessly, and, he had hoped, fashionably knotted neckcloth, revealing the faint but still visible marks of the rope.

Frances put her hands to her mouth.

'They really hanged you?' she said in a small, tight voice.

'Yes,' Kit answered, retying the cloth around his neck.

Margaret frowned. 'Why?'

Thamsine answered. 'Kit had an agreement with the government that if he did certain work for them, Daniel would be freed. He met his side of the bargain, which is how he secured the pardon.'

'But why did they want to hang you?' Frances had paled.

'That's a long story,' Kit said. 'We can save it for another time. I had an assurance Daniel would be placed on the first ship back to England. '

'Why didn't you tell me?' Margaret demanded.

'I wanted to be sure he was safe.'

Margaret's gaze flicked from Kit to Thamsine. Kit took a deep breath and handed his stepmother the letter from Governor Willoughby.

Margaret held it at arm's length as if it would burn her. 'Who is Thurloe?' she asked.

'The Secretary of State. The letter is from the Governor of Barbados.'

Margaret read the missive aloud. Frances gave a strangled cry and sank into the nearest chair, her face buried in her hands, her shoulders wracked with sobs.

Margaret let the letter drop to the floor and looked at Kit, her mouth working. Kit lowered his head, unable to meet her accusing eyes. He had given her hope only to snatch it away. Daniel would never be coming home.

Kit shook his head and turned away. 'Everything I did... was for nothing.'

Thamsine laid a hand on his arm. There had been some dark days after the letter had arrived from Thurloe. Days when he had considered finished the job the hangman had begun. Only Thamsine's unwavering devotion and patience had brought him back from that brink.

He took a deep breath, regaining his composure, and turned to face his stepmother.

She slumped in the chair, all her defiance leeched from her, and she looked old and frail. Her son had died not once but twice, and he could not even begin to imagine what that meant.

'I have thought hard on this, Margaret,' he continued. 'I've been through too much to believe it was all for naught. I refuse to accept he is dead until I hold some evidence in my hand or stand beside his grave.'

Margaret looked up and Kit took her hand, meeting no resistance.

'Margaret, I couldn't have stopped Daniel from coming with me that day. If I had locked him in his room he would have found some way to follow. If I'd not been wounded ... ' He trailed off and went down on one knee before her. 'Please believe me when I say not a day goes by when I don't think of him. I will make you this promise here and now. I am going to Barbados and I will find out what happened to him.'

His stepmother nodded. 'I need to know, Kit,' she said.

'So do I,' he replied.

CHAPTER 61

HOLETOWN, BARBADOS JANUARY 1655

Kit Lovell, now calling himself the Comte d'Anvers paused in the doorway looking, he hoped, like all aristocratic Frenchman when faced with an Englishman; slightly contemptuous and vaguely disapproving.

The Governor of Barbados, Lord Willoughby, mopped his face with a large kerchief and rose to his feet to meet his visitor, acknowledging Kit's florid bow with an inclination of his head before gesturing to a chair.

Kit took the proffered seat as Willoughby seated himself behind his large table and considered his visitor from over his steepled fingers.

'And what is it that I can do for you, Monsieur?' he enquired.

Kit settled the ruffles of his shirt sleeves and began, 'I come on behalf of friends in England who seek news of a member of their family.' He spoke with an exaggerated French accent. 'The boy was taken prisoner after that foolishness some years ago at …,' Kit paused. '… Worcester, was it not?'

'Ah, yes!' Willoughby agreed. 'Most unfortunate. We had a great many prisoners sent here at that time.'

Kit produced the letter from Thurloe with the order for Daniel's release. 'I have here with me an order for the boy's release, but word has reached the family that the boy is now dead. I have been sent to verify the truth of this claim.'

The Governor picked up the papers that Kit pushed across the table at him. The man's gaze lingered momentarily on the twisted fingers of his right hand. Politeness forbade comment and Willoughby sat back to read the letter. 'Lovell? Oh, yes. Daniel Lovell. I remember.' He pushed the papers back again. 'Well, my dear sir, I can add nothing to what is written here. As I wrote to my Lord Thurloe after I received a missive from him directly, the man died of fever at the Pritchard Plantation last year. You have had a wasted trip. My condolences to the family.'

Kit struggled to control the veneer of the Comte D'Anvers' poise as he collected the papers and carefully refolded them.

'I see,' he said. 'I … they … the family hoped that there had been some error, but before I report back to my friends, I shall satisfy myself by paying a visit to this … Pritchard Plantation.'

Willoughby spread his hands. 'Of course. It's a good day's ride to the south, but I must warn you that you will find little to shed any light on the boy's death. John Pritchard was smitten by palsy and the estate has gone to wrack and ruin. Pity,' the Governor added, 'he was a good man and, if it is of any assurance to your friends, I can say with certainty that he looked after the boy well. I remember young Daniel. He could read and write, so Pritchard used him as the plantation clerk. We often saw him here in Holetown.'

Kit rose to his feet. 'Thank you, *monsieur*,' he said. 'You have been most helpful.'

The Governor rose. 'Is there anything else I can assist you with? Are you staying in Barbados for long? Perhaps you and the, errr, Comtesse may like to dine one night.'

'Thank you, but I am anxious to resolve this business with the Pritchard Plantation. Perhaps when we have returned. Good day to you, Lord Willoughby.'

With one last florid bow, Kit left the room. He returned to the comparative cool of the finest hostelry in Holetown. Taking the stairs two at a time he threw open the door to his bed-chamber.

Thamsine, reclined on the bed, dressed in nothing but her shift and fanning herself with a copy of the town broadsheet.

She sat up, putting the broadsheet to one side. 'Well?'

'Much as I expected,' he said. 'He confirmed what he wrote.'

He divested himself of his coat and flung it over the back of a chair, pulled at the suffocating folds of the linen kerchief he wore around his neck, and with a sigh, sank onto the bed next to his wife. He pulled her into his arms and kissed the top of her head.

Thamsine slid an arm around his shoulders and laid her head against his arm. 'I'm sorry, Kit,' she said.

Kit could find no words to express his feelings at that moment.

'My dear Monsieur le Comte,' Thamsine continued in French, 'you have done all you can. We have satisfied ourselves that Daniel is dead. Let's go home.'

Kit shook his head. 'I am going out to the plantation.'

'Hmm,' Thamsine closed her eyes, and the head against his arm became heavy. 'The plantation?' she added drowsily.

'Yes. I want to speak to this man, Pritchard, although Willoughby says he was struck by the palsy. Hopefully there may be someone there who can tell us more.' Kit nuzzled her hair. 'You smell nice,' he whispered.

She pushed him away. 'It's too hot!' she said but even as she said it, the nuzzling became a gentle nibbling and they collapsed backward onto the bed.

CHAPTER 62

'Barbados is quite beautiful,' Thamsine remarked as they rounded a bend in the road to find the thick jungle opened out onto a vista of azure sea dotted with round, green islands.

Her husband responded with a grunt. On the long horse ride from Holetown, he had been absorbed in his own thoughts, and she knew Kit well enough to know that they weren't happy thoughts. He blamed himself for Daniel's fate, and although she hoped he took some comfort in the knowledge that Daniel's lot had not been as dire as he had imagined, she doubted that it did.

It seemed incontrovertible that Daniel Lovell had died here in Barbados and, unless some new facts could be discovered at the Pritchard Plantation, that would be the news Kit had to carry back to his stepmother. Little wonder he stared morosely at the dusty, rutted road ahead of him.

The jungle gave way to fields of sugarcane, the wild, undisciplined rows rising to a height well above their heads, indicating that they were ready for harvest. A raised voice issuing orders accompanied the thud and thump and rustle of the cane being harvested. Among the cane men worked, naked black backs bowed to the hot tropical sun, crisscrossed with evidence of the lash. Black backs mostly but among them, browned and hardened by years of exposure, were white men. An overseer with a whip in his hand pushed his hat to the back of his head and watched as Kit and Thamsine rode past.

Kit glanced at Thamsine as a double-storied wooden house came into view. Perched on rising ground, it probably commanded a panoramic view from the higher floor. Behind it were the stables and a compound of small huts. A few scrawny chickens pecked around the driveway and a tethered goat bleated a plaintive welcome. What had once been a pretty garden had already begun to be reclaimed by the jungle and the whole property had an air of neglect and misery. A small black boy wearing nothing but ragged breeches ran out to take the horses.

The house appeared deserted. No sound came from within it, and it took several sturdy knocks on the door before it opened a crack. A young black woman with large, frightened eyes peered at them.

'Who is it, girl?' A man's voice, heavy with a Yorkshire accent, bellowed from the rear of the house.

The girl opened the door a little wider. 'Yes?' she asked.

'The Comte d'Anvers and his wife,' Kit announced.

The large eyes widened and a man dressed only in his breeches and shirt came up behind her. He put a large hand on the girl's shoulder and pushed her to one side. He stood in the doorway, hands on hips, his bulk blocking any entrance to the house.

'What did you say yer name was?' he demanded.

Kit met the man's bloodshot eyes. Even from where he stood, he could smell the stale stench of drink and sweat, and the man's dishevelled clothes and unshaven chin confirmed the impression of a drunken sot. If this was the overseer in charge of the estate, little wonder it looked neglected. He shuddered to think of the treatment being meted out to the labourers.

'What did ya say yer name was?' the man demanded.

'The Comte d'Anvers.' Kit drew himself up to his full height, but the other man matched him for height with the added advantage of breadth.

'The Compte d'what?' The Yorkshireman leered contemptuously before executing a bow with a sarcastic flourish. 'Yer grace, what is it we can do for you?'

'Who are you?' Kit demanded with an aristocratic curl of his lip, marking his disapproval.

'Outhwaite's the name. I run this 'ere plantation.'

'I thought to meet with a Monsieur Pritchard?'

The man ran a hand through his tousled hair. 'Well, Pritchard ain't up to visitors. I'm in charge. Compte or no, state your business and be gone.'

'Is this the best of island 'ospitality?' Kit became more French by the minute.

'Ye'll get no hospitality here. We don't like visitors,' Outhwaite said and leered at the girl, cowering at the foot of the stairs. 'Do we, Clara? They upsets the old man.'

A prickle of fear ran down Thamsine's spine and she glanced at Clara. The girl gave a barely perceptible jerk of her head in the direction of the stairs. Thamsine caught the look and understood. She swayed and grasped at her husband.

'Mon cher,' she said in French. *Je me sens faible. Aide moi.*

'What did she say?' Outhwaite said.

She glanced at Outhwaite but he did not seem to have understood what she said. *Good.* It meant they could converse in French.

'Cherie?' Kit caught her as her knees buckled as if she would fall into a dead faint at any moment. 'My wife is overcome by the heat, *monsieur*. At least allow us a few minutes respite from the 'eat.'

'I'll be all right if I can just lie down for a little while,' Thamsine said in English, adding in French. '*Quelque chose est très mal ici.*'

Something was very wrong.

Kit nodded. 'It is,' he agreed in a low voice. 'She says she needs to lie down,' Kit said.

Outhwaite frowned and jerked a head at the maid. 'Take her upstairs to the spare room.'

The girl came forward and slid her arm around Thamsine's waist. She barely came to Thamsine's shoulder.

'Does the girl speak French?' Kit enquired of Outhwaite.

'Barely speaks English!' Outhwaite scoffed. 'Jabbers away in that godforsaken tongue of hers.'

'*Dommage,*' Kit said.

The maid left Thamsine in a small chamber at the top of the stairs. The bedding on the narrow cot smelled musty and damp and as soon as the maid returned, with water and a cloth, Thamsine sat bolt upright.

The girl's eyes widened at Thamsine's instant recovery.

'You better?' she asked.

Thamsine put a finger to her lips. 'My name is Thamsine Lovell.'

The girl cried out, clapping her hand over her mouth. 'Lovell? Daniel?'

Thamsine nodded. 'My husband is Daniel's brother, Kit.'

The girl sank onto the bed beside Thamsine and turned tear-filled eyes on her. 'He was a good man, Massa Daniel.'

'Is it true he is dead?'

The tears spilled over and she nodded.

Thamsine felt her heart sink.

Clara glanced at the door. 'Tha's what Outhwaite told Master.'

Thamsine caught her breath. 'What do you mean?'

Clara shook her head. She had begun to shake.

'He a bad man, that Outhwaite.'

Catching the girl's hands, Thamsine sought her eyes and said, 'Is Daniel dead or not?'

As the girl hesitated, Thamsine clasped the little hands tighter. 'Please, Clara. We don't have much time. Tell me what happened.'

Clara took a shuddering breath. 'Outhwaite.' She screwed her face. 'He wanted to marry Miss Jane but Miss Jane, she love Dan'l and the Massa, he thinks Dan'l a good man for Miss Jane.'

A picture began to form in Thamsine's mind. Daniel, young, educated, intelligent and, if he resembled his brother in any way, handsome and capable of great charm, could quite easily have won the heart of Pritchard's daughter.

Clara's lip trembled. 'Just after Christmas, Miss Jane, she took sick and died. The Massa's heartbreak to bury his girl and Massa Dan'l, he loved Miss Jane. Massa took sick and Massa Dan'l tried to run the plantation.' She looked up. 'He a good man, but Outhwaite hate him, and one day he and Massa Dan'l have a terrible fight. Outhwaite tell him that he is not taking orders from a slave and he was in charge. He had Massa Dan'l flogged and put in the Hole.'

Thamsine bit back the question that sprang to her lips. Whatever the Hole was, it could not be pleasant.

'He ... ' Clara broke off at the sound of heavy feet on the stairs. She just had time to recline back on the bed Outhwaite flung open the door.

'How is she?' He addressed the slave.

Thamsine's eyes fluttered open. '*Ou est mon mari?*'

'*Ici, Cherie*,' Kit pushed past Outhwaite and held out a hand for Thamsine. 'What did you discover?' he continued in French.

'He did not die of fever,' Thamsine responded. 'The girl knows more.'

'Speak English,' Outhwaite said.

'My wife is still feeling unwell,' Kit said. 'And it is growing late. As a good Christian, please may we beg a bed of you for the night?'

Outhwaite scowled and opened his mouth to speak when someone downstairs bellowed his name. He stomped to the head of the stairs.

'What is it?'

'Trouble in one of the fields,' an English voice responded. 'It's that bloody Scot again, McPherson. You're needed.'

At the mention of the name, Kit stiffened.

'You know this man?' Thamsine whispered.

'I knew someone of that name ... at Worcester.'

Outhwaite swore. 'McPherson? Have him taken to the Hole.'

He turned back to the bedchamber.

'What is the 'ole?' Kit enquired. Thamsine wondered how he managed to make the question sound so ingenuous.

A twisted sneer crossed Outhwaite's face. 'Little invention of me own. The old man was too soft on these bastards. I had a hole dug in the middle of the slave quarters. Not long enough to lie in and not tall enough to stand, with nothing but a grate over the top. I find a floggin' and a few days in there brings 'em to heel pretty quick.'

The bile rose in Thamsine's throat and her hand tightened on Kit's sleeve.

'That sounds a little extreme,' Kit remarked in a mild tone of voice, while beneath Thamsine's hand the muscles of his arm had tensed.

'Vermin, that's what they are. Vermin, and deserve no better. I'd better see to the troublemaker. You can sleep here but don't expect to be entertained. Clara, you've got work. Get to it.'

He turned and stomped out of the room. The little maid turned one last despairing glance at Kit and Thamsine before scuttling after him.

Kit shut the door behind them. Thamsine sat up and recounted what Clara had told her. Kit's mouth tightened, and the fingers of his left hand clenched and unclenched.

'If Pritchard's an invalid, he'll be in one of the other rooms. Let's go and see if we can get any sense out of him.'

THEY WAITED until the house had gone quiet. Through the slats that covered the window, Kit could hear Outhwaite yelling. He shuddered to think what fate he intended for poor McPherson.

He glanced at Thamsine and nodded. 'Let's go.'

Four doors faced onto the landing. All were closed. They opened the first one, revealing a squalid rat's nest of empty bottles and worse. Filthy sheets covered the bed. Thamsine recoiled with her hand to her nose.

'Outhwaite's room,' she said.

The second room contained nothing except a broken pallet bed and a three-legged stool. The door to the fourth room appeared to be locked, but the key had been left hanging on a nail beside the door frame. Kit turned the key and opened the door. Even he gagged. The stench of illness, and worse, pervaded the dark, airless room.

As his eyes became accustomed to the gloom he could see a skeletal figure reclining under a sheet on the bed. He crossed to the bed and looked down into the waxen face. The left side of the man's unshaven face looked as if it had melted, the features dragged down and distorted. Only the eyes that scanned his face, showed the intelligence that still burned brightly within.

'I'm Daniel Lovell's brother,' he said without preamble.

The man's eyes moistened and he raised his right hand, gesturing Kit closer. The skeletal fingers closed on his wrist and he opened his mouth, a dribble of spittle sliding from the corner.

"An'l?'

'Aye. My name's Kit Lovell. Daniel was my brother. I came to take him home.'

The old man shook his head. 'Too late. Good boy, 'an'l. Tried ... ' The man's face twisted with the effort of speaking. 'My Janey ... ' he shook his head. 'Would've ... wed.'

'What happened to him?' Kit asked.

For answer, the man looked away. He raised his hand and waved at a dark corner of the room. "ible,' he croaked.

Thamsine followed the direction he indicated and produced a dusty box from a chest. She set it down on the end of the bed and opened it, lifting out a hefty Bible.

Pritchard burbled unintelligibly, gesturing at the book.

Thamsine turned the book upside down and shook it. A single sheet of paper wafted to the floor. She picked it up and handed it to Kit. From outside they could hear Outhwaite in a heated conversation with another man. Their voices were coming closer.

Kit folded the paper and stowed it in his jacket.

'Put the box back, Tham,' he said.

He looked down at Pritchard. 'Thank you. We will make this right.'

They barely made it back to the guest bedchamber before the front door slammed and Outhwaite came stumping up the stairs.

'I 'spose you want feeding,' he said. 'The girl'll have food on't table in an hour.'

'You are too kind,' Kit said.

He waited until he heard Outhwaite go back outside and unfolded the paper.

'It's Daniel's handwriting,' he said.

Thamsine clutched his arm. 'Read it.'

Kit took a breath and began,

This is the testament of Daniel Lovell of Eveleigh Priory, Cheshire. I am the grandson of the second Lord Midhurst and a prisoner of the Commonwealth for no more crime than loyalty to my King. I write this in the hope that the finder will bring justice, not just for me, because it is certain I will be dead before the week is out, but for the good man John Pritchard, who lies ill and untended on his bed, and the poor souls who labour in the fields under the lash of one Ebenezer Outhwaite. Since the death of his daughter Jane, John Pritchard has been taken with a palsy, and at his desire the management of the plantation has fallen to me, but Ebenezer Outhwaite covets the land, even as he coveted Pritchard's daughter. His manifest cruelties are listed below. These I have seen with my own eyes.

The death of the Scottish prisoner Brodie was dealt by Outhwaite's own hand. Every day another prisoner is selected by Outhwaite as an example for flogging or consignment to the hole he has had dug in the compound of the slave quarters. Rations have been cut and there is much illness among the labourers.

As for John Pritchard, no one attends him but the slave girl, Clara, who is inadequate to the care of such a sick man. I have resolved that tonight I will take flight and try to reach Holetown in the hope that I can bring my testimony of the dire deeds at the Pritchard Plantation to the attention of the Governor. I fear, however, that I will not make it. Outhwaite does not trust me and is waiting on an opportunity to move against me. I leave this testimony concealed in the hope that aid will come ere long.

Signed, Daniel Lovell, the twelfth day of February in the year of our Lord 1654.

A list had been attached detailing the barbarous treatment of the slaves and labourers on the Pritchard Plantation since Pritchard's illness. Floggings, deaths and rape.

Thamsine drew in a deep breath. 'What are we going to do?'

Kit stared at his brother's testament, a red mist of rage obscuring the words.

'We end this now,' he said.

KIT FOUND Outhwaite drinking in what would have once been the parlour of the plantation house. Like the bedchamber, Outhwaite had turned it into a pigsty.

'It's you,' the man said. 'If you want a drink, help yourself.'

Kit kicked aside an empty bottle and flicked the ruffles of his shirt sleeves. 'Actually, *monsieur*, I am most interested in your methods. I am considering investing in a plantation myself, and it is my understanding that these slaves need the strictest controls.'

Outhwaite drew his lips up in a sneer. 'Vermin. Tha's what they are, vermin.'

'Can you perhaps, show me this 'ole?'

'Your lady still indisposed?'

'She is,' Kit demurred.

Outhwaite set his bottle down and heaved himself to his feet. 'Don't see why not, seeing as you're interested.'

As they left the house, Outhwaite started on a monologue about the foolishness of treating slaves with too much leniency.

'They're not human like you and me,' he said as they approached the gate to the compound. Kit took a deep breath.

The stench of human waste hung like a miasma in the air. The slaves and indentured labourers were making their way down the road towards them. They walked like men on their way to the gallows, feet dragging, heads bowed. Outhwaite stood aside to let them into the compound. Kit did a quick calculation. There were thirty prisoners and three overseers. All but five prisoners wore chains. The unchained men, he assumed, were trusted by the overseers.

He scanned the faces but saw none he recognised among the Scottish prisoners. He just prayed that the man in the Hole, McPherson, was the man he knew.

'Line 'em up,' Outhwaite ordered. 'Bring out McPherson. I want him flogged and I want ye all to see what happens when you disobey an order.'

Six feet in front of Kit a grate had been set into the ground, a heavy padlock securing it. Kit's blood ran cold. The grating afforded no protection from sun or rain. Thamsine had told him that Outhwaite had confined Daniel in this instrument of torture, for there was no other word for it. For that reason alone, he would see Outhwaite hang.

One of the overseers, a man as filthy and disreputable as Outhwaite, stepped forward and unlocked the padlock. The man beneath them roared a Gaelic curse as Outhwaite gestured for two of the unshackled prisoners to step forward. Obviously familiar with the routine, the two men leaned into the Hole and dragged the man from it.

Kit's heart skipped a beat as the shaggy head emerged from within. Thinner and diminished by imprisonment, but definitely the McPherson of his acquaintance. He slid his hand into his jacket and withdrew the loaded pistol he had brought with him. With years of practice, he pressed the muzzle of the pistol against Outhwaite's head, just behind his ear.

'Don't move, Outhwaite,' Kit said.

The man let a squawk of surprise and the overseers moved forward. Two of them drew pistols from their belts.

'Not an inch,' Kit said, all trace of a French accent gone. 'The first man who moves, Outhwaite here dies.'

The overseers exchanged glances and it occurred to Kit that they may not particularly care if Outhwaite lived or died but it was also doubtful they would risk their own lives for him.

'And the second man who moves also dies,' said Thamsine from behind him. 'Lay your weapons down, gentlemen.'

She raised the second pistol Kit had brought with him. On the ship, Kit had taught her to load and fire the weapons and he had every confidence in her ability to bring a man down. The men glanced uneasily at each other and, to Kit's relief, complied.

'Capn' Lovell, as I live and breathe,' McPherson grinned, shaking off the hands of his captors.

'Lovell?' Outhwaite gasped.

'Aye, that's right. I'm Daniel Lovell's brother. McPherson, collect those weapons and lock those men up.' He indicated the overseers and the trusted prisoners.

The ranks of the other prisoners stirred and they glanced at each other, seeing for the first time some little hope for the amelioration of their misery. As one they started to rattle their chains.

'And you,' he shoved the musket harder against Outhwaite's head. 'In the Hole.'

'Please,' the man said, and the sour stench of urine rose to Kit's nostrils. Like most bullies, Outhwaite was a coward.

With one shove he pushed the man into the Hole and dropped the grate with a clang, turning the key in the padlock.

'What about us?' One of the Scots among the ranks of the chained prisoners called out.

If he turned them free he would have a riot on his hands and, he had no doubt, Outhwaite and his men would be dead before morning. He had no choice.

'McPherson, choose four men you trust. The rest have to be confined.'

A roar of disapproval met that statement, but faced with the weapons ranged against them held by Kit, Thamsine and McPherson, none were quite brave enough to chance their luck.

McPherson understood the situation, and with the help of four of his former comrades in arms, they had the angry labour force padlocked into their cabins.

'Make sure they get double rations,' Kit ordered.

'What about the others?'

'Nothing.'

'What now?' Thamsine asked.

Kit sat down on the edge of one of the large cauldrons used for boiling the sugarcane. 'We send word to Willoughby.'

CHAPTER 63

*A*s night descended on the plantation, Kit and Thamsine sat with McPherson on the broad terrace that faced out to sea. A soft, warm breeze brought with it the scent of jungle and sea. Behind the house, angry men demanded to be set free. Kit had set McPherson's men to guard the compound. It was a risk giving them weapons but he had no choice.

Thamsine had organised Clara and the other maids she had found cowering in the kitchens to clean John Pritchard's room. The condition of the man shocked her. He had been lying in his own filth for days, if not weeks. It took a strong stomach to bathe him and treat the dreadful, suppurating sores.

One of the younger Scots had been dispatched to Holetown bearing a letter from Kit along with a copy of Daniel's testimony. Nothing more could be done until Willoughby arrived, and now he had just one question to be answered. Where was his brother?

McPherson drew on a pipe he had liberated from Outhwaite's room and expelled a satisfied grunt.

'I've missed the tobacco,' he said. 'Now, I suppose you want to know what became of your brother?'

The stem of the clay pipe Kit held between his fingers snapped.

'Is it true? Is he dead?'

McPherson removed the long stem of his pipe from his mouth and considered the question.

'I dinna know,' he said at last. 'Daniel was in a bad position. He was still a prisoner, no better than I, so Outhwaite could do as he liked with him. While Pritchard was still in charge, Outhwaite couldn't touch him, but when Pritchard was taken ill, it left Outhwaite in charge. For a while there he let Daniel alone. He needed the lad. I doubt Outhwaite can read or write, but when Daniel started to object to Outhwaite's methods and the treatment of the labourers, Outhwaite became a wee bit nervous. There'd been a boy, Brodie. Outhwaite beat the boy to death. We all witnessed it, but Dan'l must have decided to go for help because Outhwaite moved on him. He had the lad flogged and locked in the Hole.'

Kit cleared his throat. 'How long?' he asked.

McPherson shook his head. 'Best you dinna know. It were long enough that they took the boy for dead when they pulled him out.'

Thamsine grasped Kit's hand.

Kit swallowed. 'What did they do with him?'

'Normal practice was to bury the dead in a burying ground behind the cabin, but there'd been a few too many deaths of late, so Outhwaite ordered his men to take the body into the jungle and dump it.'

Kit swore.

'He said as it were a lesson that we were no better than animals and should be treated as such. Big on his lessons, Outhwaite.'

'And was he dead?' Thamsine asked the question that Kit could not find the words for.

McPherson sighed. 'One of Outhwaite's men took me out into the forest a few days later. Said we were going huntin', but he wanted to see the lad covered decent and say a few words of prayer. He didn't think it right leaving a Christian out there without even a prayer being said over him. When we got to the place he'd been left, the body had gone.'

Kit's breath caught. 'Did he go back to the right place?'

McPherson shrugged. 'Aye. There were signs to tell me that someone had been there. Blood on't grass, broken ferns.'

Kit jumped to his feet. 'Which man? I must speak to him.'

McPherson shook his head. 'Died of the fever two months ago. Dinna get your hopes up, lady. Animals could've moved the body. Who knows? Even if he'd still been alive, he was sore hurt and his chance of surviving in the mountains … ' McPherson broke off. 'The man told Outhwaite and he sent out search parties. Not a trace of the lad was found. So, to answer your question, Lovell, I canna say for certain whether the lad lived or not.'

CHAPTER 64

*K*it and Thamsine stood together at the rail of the ship, watching as the brilliant green of the island of Barbados disappeared over the horizon. Above them, the sails cracked in the stiff wind and the ropes creaked against the timbers. A fair wind to carry them back home to England.

Willoughby had not wasted time answering Kit's summons and the situation at the Pritchard Plantation had been resolved as best it could. At least John Pritchard would now see out his days in Holetown being cared for in a convent. The black labour force had been distributed among the other plantations, where they faced a life little better than the one they had endured under Outhwaite. However, Kit had managed to persuade Willoughby to release McPherson and the remaining Scots and they were free now to work their passage back to England if that's what they wished to do.

Faced with Daniel's testimony and supported by the evidence of others who had witnessed or borne the brunt of Outhwaite's cruelty, Willoughby had put the man on trial, and Kit had the grim satisfaction of knowing Outhwaite would die for the murder of Brodie, if not for the death of his brother.

'I swore I would not believe in Daniel's death until I stood at his graveside,' Kit said at last.

Thamsine put her hand over his. She had no words left to comfort this man. He had come to Barbados seeking closure and now he only had more questions.

'What do I tell Margaret?' he said, glancing at her.

'The truth as you know it. You tell her that as far as you know he died in the cause of protecting those who could not protect themselves,' Thamsine said.

Kit's fingers tightened on the rail. 'Only a few more months, Tham, and he would have been free.'

Thamsine tightened her grip on the crooked fingers of his right hand. He had paid a terrible price to win his brother's liberty, and solecisms were easily spoken but no comfort to a man who had given his life to free his brother. Thamsine considered herself a good Christian. Kit had every reason to believe God had forsaken him, but she still had the power of prayer and now, that was all she could offer.

If, by some miracle – and it would require a miracle – Daniel had survived the treatment meted out to him by Outhwaite, he had his own reasons for disappearing into the forests of Barbados. He would no longer be the youth who had followed on his brother's heels, dreaming of honour and glory. He had been tempered in a fierce furnace, and perhaps one day their paths would cross, but it would be at a time of Daniel Lovell's choosing.

In the meantime, they could not regret what might have been. She and Kit had to find their own peace and make a life for themselves built on their shattered pasts. That would have to do for now.

EPILOGUE

BARBADOS

'*E*st-il mort?'

Is he dead?

Daniel Lovell groaned, his fingers digging into the sand beneath him. A shadow fell across him and someone seized a handful of his hair, jerking his head up from the warm beach.

'What's your name, boy?' This time the interrogative was made in heavily accented English.

Daniel struggled and failed to bring the bearded face into focus. He licked his cracked lips, tasting the metallic tang of blood. He could not even produce the spittle he felt the questioner deserved.

He considered his options. Beg for his life? Plead not to be returned to the plantation? Or he could muster what little strength and pride he had left and keep silent. He would die anyway, and here and now seemed as good a time as any.

'*Qu'il soit!*' The second voice held the tone of authority.

The first interrogator, obedient to the command to let him be, released his grip on Daniel's hair and let his head fall back onto the sand.

Daniel turned his face to the ocean where the gentle sea lapped on the shore. A ship's longboat had been pulled up on the golden sand and beyond it, nestled into this hidden bay, a frigate, its sails furled, bobbed serenely on the azure water.

Such a beautiful place to die, he thought. God in his wisdom had sent angels to release him; strange angels, definitely from the rougher end of Heaven.

'He's more dead than alive,' the first man said in French. 'Reckon he's a runaway?'

'Look at the state he's in. Bound to be,' the second man responded and squatted down beside Daniel. He wore only a shirt and breeches and a pair of well-worn and unpolished bucket top boots. A short sword and a pistol had been shoved through his belt.

He pushed a shapeless, broad-brimmed hat to the back of his head and scratched his bearded chin.

'Someone hated you, boy,' he said in English.

'Kill me if you must,' Daniel murmured, 'but if you've a Christian heart, don't send me back.'

'Ah, there we have a dilemma, my young friend,' the Frenchman replied. 'No man in my crew has a Christian heart, and a reward, if there is such a thing for your mangled hide, is tempting. However, it is fortunate for you that I'm not willing to risk putting my crew in the way of temptation for the sake of whatever paltry amount you would fetch when there is a reward of one hundred English pounds on my own head.'

Daniel's gaze drifted to the pistol in the man's belt. He wondered if he had the strength to seize it. One shot to his temple would be all it would take and he would be free.

The man let out a heavy sigh.

'Seems to me the choice is yours, boy. I can leave you here to die or, if you're unlucky, the search parties will find you first. Or ... ' he paused, ' ... I can take you with me, as an insurance, you understand, against such a time as I may need to have something of value to trade with the English.'

Daniel closed his eyes. 'Whoever you are, sir, my fate is in your hands.'

The man chuckled. 'My name is Broussard and I am the captain of *L'Archange*, a ship in the service of His Most Gracious Majesty Louis of France.'

He'd heard of *L'Archange*. Visitors to Pritchard's plantation had lamented its attacks on their ships. His angel in unpolished boots had turned out to be a French privateer. A small spark of hope flared in his chest.

'Take me with you,' Daniel murmured.

The Frenchman rose to his feet.

'*Allez!*' he ordered, and then added, almost as an afterthought, 'and bring him with us.'

AUTHOR'S NOTES

'In February 1654, a Miss Granville hurled a brickbat at the Lord Protector's Coach.' So writes historian Antonia Fraser in *Cromwell, Our Chief of Men* (Panther Books Ltd, 1975, page 494). Ms Fraser never goes on to explain who Miss Granville was or why she threw the brickbat, but the throwaway line caught my attention and provided the basis for this story.

While Thamsine Granville, Kit, and their close friends and relatives are fictional, the rest of the cast of characters, including The Ship Inn itself, were very much real ,as were the plots they were involved in. Even Bordeaux and his English mistress, Mary Skippon, have their parts in the history books. The Ship Inn Plot and Gerard's Plot both failed in much the manner described, with fatal consequences for the people involved. Bampfield, Henshaw and Wiseman were almost certainly double agents and Kit's friend, Fitzjames, who was closely involved in Gerard's plot, drowned on a crossing from France. His body was found washed up with incriminating letters in his pocket.

Mazarin's agent, Baron de Baas, was the brother of a certain

D'Artagnan of musketeer fame, on whom Dumas based his story. His disdain for the English court, expressed in the story, is based on his own observations.

John Thurloe ran a highly effective spy ring for most of the Protectorate and foiled not just these plots but the far more serious plotting of the Sealed Knot, which resulted in a small uprising the following year. Richard Cromwell famously described him as having "the key to wicked men's hearts". Whether he used the techniques I have attributed to him to secure their co-operation is based on my own supposition.

And who comprised the Sealed Knot? Well, Kit never did find out their names! Perhaps another time.

Finally, a disclaimer. The views expressed about slaves and slavery in the final chapter to this story do not in any way reflect the views of the author. However, sadly, they are based on contemporary writings of the period. The fate of the mostly Scottish prisoners of war sent to colonies such as Barbados was little better than that of the black slaves, whose importation from Africa had begun by the middle of the seventeenth century.

THANK YOU

Thank you for reading THE KING'S MAN.
If you enjoyed this story, I would love you to leave a review or a
rating on your favourite review site or bookstore.

AND YOU ARE INVITED TO SIGN UP TO ALISON'S
NEWSLETTER
for FREE READS and VIP Exclusives, including contests,
giveaways and advance notice of pre-orders.
www.alisonstuart.com

THANK YOU

www.alisonstuart.com

EXILE'S RETURN

Concluding THE GUARDIANS OF THE CROWN series with Daniel's story ... EXILE'S RETURN

England, 1659: Following the death of Cromwell, a new king is poised to ascend the throne of England. One by one, those once loyal to the crown begin to return ...

Agnes Fletcher's lover is dead, and when his two orphaned children are torn from her care by their scheming guardian, she finds herself alone and devastated by the loss. Unwilling to give up, Agnes desperately seeks anyone willing to accompany her on a perilous journey to save the children and return them to her care. After enduring imprisonment, exile and torture, the fugitive Daniel Lovell has returned to England, determined to find his brother and kill the man who murdered his father. But the King has one last mission for him and there is the small matter of a desperate woman who needs his help.

Agnes finds her protector in Daniel Lovell and thrown together with separate quests – and competing obligations – Daniel and Agnes make their way from London to the English countryside, danger at every turn.

When they are finally given the opportunity to seize everything they ever hoped for, will they find the peace they crave, or will their fledgling love be a final casualty of war?

~

EXILE'S RETURN
CHAPTER 1
London, 27 October, 1659

Agnes Fletcher gripped the windowsill as a distant clock struck twelve, marking the fall of the executioner's axe.

James Ashby, the third earl of Elmhurst, was dead.

She closed her eyes and prayed that death had been swift.

Taking a deep breath, Agnes turned to face the room. The cold draught that rose between the ill-fitting floorboards of the inn lifted her skirts as she walked across to where the two children were playing a noisy game of knucklebones.

'You cheated!' seven-year-old Elizabeth, the eldest of the two, exclaimed.

Four-year-old Henry hurled himself at his sister, issuing a loud and high-pitched disclaimer that rang in Agnes's ears, jarring her nerves.

'Stop it!'

Something in her tone made the two children fall silent.

They looked up at her, their eyes wide and mouths open in surprise. Agnes rarely raised her voice.

'Why are you crying?' Henry asked.

Agnes dashed at her cheek, where the betraying tears streamed from her eyes. She dropped to her knees and gathered the two now-silent children into her arms.

Dear God, what is to become of us?

'Your father ... ' A sob caught in her throat.

Lizzie stood rigid in the circle of her arms.

'He's dead?' Lizzie's voice cracked.

All Agnes could do was nod in reply as the tears coursed unchecked down her cheeks. Henry began to wail and burrowed his golden head into Agnes's shoulder.

They had gone to visit James yesterday, the last visit permitted by the authorities. Perhaps, she had thought, as James went down on his knees to hold his children for the last time, it would have been easier on them all if they had stayed away. The memory of James's fair head bent over his children filled her eyes again.

He had risen to his feet and taken her hands in his. 'Agnes, dear Agnes,' he had said. 'Tomorrow I die, and you are all the children have left. You must fight for them. There is no one else.'

No one else except James's cousin, Tobias Ashby, but for once Tobias's malevolent shadow stayed away. Even he had the decency to allow father and children this last farewell.

There had been so much she wanted to say to James, but the words stuck in her throat. He smiled, a soft sad smile, and picked up a book from the table.

'Take this,' he said, pressing it into her hands. 'A memento of me, and our affection for each other.'

Our affection for each other.

He had kissed her, a soft kiss on her forehead, and she had gathered up the children and walked away from him. He would never know how she had longed for him to take her in his arms, and for the kiss to be that of the lover she had known, not a dear friend.

The tread of heavy boots on the gallery outside the room

brought her back to the present. Agnes jumped to her feet, wiping the last of the tears from her face and straightening the children's collars as she waited for the knock on the door.

Three burly soldiers entered, followed by someone she had come to know well in the past few years; Captain Septimus Turner, Tobias Ashby's ever-present second in command. Turner scanned the room before bringing his gaze to rest on the woman and the two children who cowered behind her skirts.

'Madam, it is my unhappy duty to inform you that the traitor James Ashby is dead,' Turner said, without a flicker of emotion on his face.

Agnes tightened her grip on the children's hands. Henry shrank back and Lizzie buried her face in the bunched skirts of Agnes's gown, muffling her sobs.

Taking a deep breath, Agnes gathered her courage to ask the question that had kept her wakeful for too many nights.

'What is to become of the children?'

Turner glanced at Henry and Elizabeth with cold, dispassionate eyes.

'You will be summoned to Whitehall when your petition has been considered by the Committee. In the meantime, you are to remain here. You are not to leave London.'

'I can only pray that will not be too long,' Agnes said, thinking of her empty purse. 'The children should be returned to their home as soon as possible.'

Ignoring her, Turner turned to his men. 'We have the traitor's possessions. Where do you want us to put them?'

Agnes's resolve buckled at the sight of the familiar metal-bound box that James had taken with him into the Tower. Only her need to stay calm for the children steadied her.

'Well?' Turner demanded.

She waved vaguely at a dark corner of the inn room. 'Over there. Tell me ... was it ... quick?"

The man considered her for a moment. 'I was not present, but the Colonel assures me he died bravely and in the love of God, madam.'

Of course, Tobias would have been there.

Agnes straightened and replied in an icy tone, 'That is of no comfort.'

Turner's gaze met hers and for a brief moment some emotion, anger or amusement, she could not tell, flashed in his eyes.

He inclined his head and half turned for the door. 'I reiterate, you are not to leave London, Mistress Fletcher.'

'Am I under arrest?' Agnes raised her chin, cursing her lack of inches.

The man shook his head. 'No, but we will know if you try to leave and it will do your cause no favours.'

Agnes straightened. She could not imagine any other outcome other than a safe return home to Charvaley. She took a deep, shuddering breath. 'And where would we go, Captain Turner? I have no money and no friends who would take us in.'

Not if they did not wish to incur the wrath of the children's only other living relative, Colonel Tobias Ashby. Tobias had been high in favour under Cromwell. Of course, since the Lord Protector's death, the world had shifted on its axis, and she considered the betrayal of his cousin may have been Tobias's attempt to keep in favour with the new regime.

'I will pray to God and put my trust in this Committee. I would remind you that I am the children's aunt and closer by blood than the Colonel,' she continued.

Turner regarded her without expression. He had no interest in hearing her plead her case; his loyalty lay entirely with Tobias.

He inclined his head. 'You will receive word when you are to appear before the Committee. Good day to you, madam.' He jerked his head at his soldiers. 'Come.'

The door slammed closed behind them and Agnes's resolve failed. She sank to her knees, burying her face in her hands as she wept. This time the arms of the two children circled her, as they added their tears to hers.

For more information and to purchase EXILE'S RETURN visit
https://www.alisonstuart.com/ecwfic.html